THE PENGUIN CLASSICS

FOUNDER EDITOR (1944–64): E. V. RIEU

Present editors: Betty Radice and Robert Baldick

The five writers represented in this volume span the classical age of German literature.

LESSING, the dramatist and critic who has been called the founder of modern German literature, was born at Kamenz, in Saxony, in 1729, and died at Brunswick in 1781.

GOETHE was born in Frankfurt-on-the-Main in 1749 and died in Weimar in 1832. More than in the case of any other European writer, his life and his works form an indivisible whole. His *Faust*, completed shortly before his death, is the dominating work of German literature.

SCHILLER, the most famous dramatist of German Classicism and also a poet, was born in Marbach, near Stuttgart, in 1759, and died in Weimar in 1805. His passionate concern with personal and political freedom dominates much of his work, including his last play, *Wilhelm Tell*.

KLEIST, born at Frankfurt-on-the-Oder in 1777, was a member of an old aristocratic and military Prussian family. His *Der Zerbrochene Krug* is perhaps the finest comedy in the German language. He committed suicide near Berlin in 1811.

GRILLPARZER, an Austrian, was born in Vienna in 1791 and died there in 1872. His posthumous *Ein Bruderzwist in Habsburg* is one of the few great political tragedies in German.

F. J. LAMPORT is a Fellow of Worcester College, Oxford, and University Lecturer in German. His main interests are in the literature of the eighteenth century.

FIVE
GERMAN TRAGEDIES

Translated with an introduction by
F. J. LAMPORT

EMILIA GALOTTI
Gotthold Ephraim Lessing

EGMONT
Johann Wolfgang Goethe

MARY STUART
Friedrich Schiller

PENTHESILEA
Heinrich von Kleist

MEDEA
Franz Grillparzer

PENGUIN BOOKS

Penguin Books Ltd, Harmondsworth, Middlesex, England
Penguin Books Inc., 7110 Ambassador Road, Baltimore, Md 21207, U.S.A.
Penguin Books Australia Ltd, Ringwood, Victoria, Australia

—

Published in Penguin Books 1969

—

Translation Copyright © F. J. Lamport, 1969

—

Made and printed in Great Britain
by Hazell Watson & Viney Ltd,
Aylesbury, Bucks
Set in Monotype Garamond

CONTENTS

INTRODUCTION

GERMAN CLASSICAL TRAGEDY

The five plays which make up this volume are all works which are still alive, still read and, what is most important, still performed on the German stage today. But they are also illustrative of a historical development, and representative of the three principal forms which tragic drama took during the classical age of German literature. In *Emilia Galotti* we have the domestic or middle-class tragedy ('bürgerliches Trauerspiel'), in *Egmont* and *Mary Stuart* the historical drama which proved to be the most important form for German writers, and in *Penthesilea* and *Medea* the tragedy on a theme taken from the myth and legend of classical antiquity – though this type never successfully maintained in Germany the eminence it achieved in seventeenth-century France.

Germany itself had in the seventeenth century, the so-called baroque age, produced a very distinctive German form of tragic drama, but in the eighteenth century the tradition had been lost. The chief literary pundit of the twenties and thirties, J. C. Gottsched (1700–66) attempted to bring about a refashioning of German literature along neo-classic lines, following the examples of the French and of the English Augustans: his own tragedy *The Death of Cato* (1731) is largely an adaptation of Addison's *Cato* of 1713. Gottsched himself and most of his disciples in the neo-classic manner were lacking in genuine dramatic talent, and, moreover, the grand heroic style of tragedy was on the whole not well suited to the temper of the age, whose optimism, critical spirit and social concerns meant that its natural bent was rather towards comedy and a realistic portrayal of the contemporary world. Yet still German playwrights and critics pursued tragedy as a kind of cultural status-symbol to mark their arrival on the European literary scene. What happened in these circumstances was that the dramatic genres moved closer together. Tragedy, which had hitherto concerned itself almost exclusively with the affairs of the great, came down the social scale and portrayed the lives and sufferings of middle-class citizens, thereby coming almost willy-nilly to treat themes of class conflict and social problems; while comedy, traditionally more of a bourgeois genre, became sentimental and serious, approaching tragedy in its emotional effect. England set the fashion for 'domestic tragedy' with such plays as George Lillo's *George Barnwell or the London Merchant* (1731), and the genre was introduced to Germany by Lessing (1729–81) with his *Miss Sara Sampson* (1755). The immediate success of this work showed that the domestic drama was what the German theatre-going public had been waiting for, and it set a fashion which continued for twenty years and more, *Emilia Galotti* (1772) and Schiller's *Intrigue and Love* (1783) being two of the best-known examples.

Meanwhile in the late seventeen-sixties there arose the movement known as 'Storm and Stress' ('Sturm und Drang'). The writers of this movement continued to use the domestic drama in new guises, often sharpening the edge of social criticism. We see this in *Emilia Galotti* and in *Intrigue and Love*, and particularly in the plays of J. M. R. Lenz, whose tragicomedy *The Private Tutor* was felt by Brecht to have sufficient relevance to the mid-twentieth century to merit adaptation for his own didactic purposes. But the 'Stürmer und Dränger' also exhibited a new feeling for the great, heroic individual which had been lacking in the earlier part of the century, when audiences had wished above all to identify themselves with the characters on the stage rather than look up to and admire them. They were inspired by an interest in history linked with an idealization of primitive, 'organic' societies; they longed to create truly national, Northern and Germanic forms of literary expression; and they were fired with a tremendous if often somewhat uncomprehending admiration for Shakespeare, whom they saw as the great Northern bard, chronicler of heroic men and heroic deeds, and as the genius who was a law unto himself, free of all the restraints and 'rules' of the classical theatre. All these influences and aspirations combined in the young Goethe (1749–1832) to produce *Götz von Berlichingen* (1772 – recently adapted into English by John Arden under the title *Ironhand*), the first of a long line of historical dramas in German, including *Egmont* and many of the plays of Schiller (1759–1805), Kleist (1777–1811), Grillparzer (1791–1872) and Hebbel (1813–63). As the genre develops, from the romantic historical colouring of *Götz* we proceed to a more philosophical, analytical approach to the processes of history itself and their effect on human character.

From the middle of the eighteenth century onwards, German writers became more and more intoxicated with the ideal of Greece. This intoxication took many forms. The originator of what has been called 'the tyranny of Greece over Germany', the art-historian J. J. Winckelmann (1717–68), had praised as the supreme characteristics of the Greek mind and of Greek art a 'noble simplicity and calm grandeur'. It was in this light that Goethe and Schiller imagined Greece, and such a vision produces not tragedy, but rather the poise and calm supremely represented by Goethe's *Iphigenia in Tauris* (1787), where humanitarian virtues – honesty, trust and love – are optimistically shown to be victorious over adversity, and to provide solutions for potentially tragic problems. Kleist and Grillparzer, however, both saw the ancient world in a different light. This is – to use the terms later coined by Nietzsche – not an 'Apolline' but a 'Dionysiac' vision of Greece, savage and menacing. Just as in *Iphigenia*, the antique setting is intended to show us the pure essence of humanity freed from any particular historical circumstances, but *Penthesilea* and the 'Greek' plays of Grillparzer have no optimistic, humanitarian message for us: human beings are shown to be all too capable of tearing each other to pieces – literally as well as metaphorically.

Gottsched and his school had regarded the Alexandrine verse, which the writers of the German baroque had taken over from the French, as the only possible medium for tragedy. For the neo-classic school, dignity of expression was of prime concern. The adoption of prose for the domestic drama was the natural corollary of the desire felt by the writers of the mid-eighteenth century for greater faithfulness to reality and truthful representation of everyday life. The dramatists of 'Storm and Stress' continued to use prose, sometimes achieving genuine colloquial realism, but more often tending to bombast. Despite the writers' desire to be 'natural', they found it impossible to prevent tragic personages from appearing larger than life and speaking accordingly. It must also be remembered that the translations of their hero, Shakespeare, which began to appear in the seventeen-sixties, were in prose, and poetry translated into prose may well take on an inappropriately artificial and rhetorical character. That prose is capable of a wide range of expression can be seen in *Egmont*, which also (again after the manner of Shakespeare) introduces songs in lyrical measures. But after the initial violence of 'Storm and Stress' had subsided, dramatists began once more to think of verse as the proper medium for the dignified, disciplined expression of exalted sentiment. The French Alexandrine remained discredited, however. One or two attempts were made to introduce English blank verse into German drama as early as the sixties, but it was not until the eighties that this metre was decisively established: after Schiller's *Don Carlos* (1786) blank verse became the standard vehicle for the German classical drama.

EMILIA GALOTTI

Lessing's first completed tragedy, *Miss Sara Sampson*, is a 'domestic' modernization of a classical myth. It is a version of the story of Medea, Jason, and King Creon and his daughter, transposed to what purports to be a contemporary English upper-middle-class milieu, characterized above all by a high 'sentimental' moral tone such as is found in English domestic tragedy and the novels of Richardson. This transposition has the curious effect that the centre of tragic gravity is also shifted, perhaps lost: the passive, pathetic Sara (=Creusa) is made the principal focus of sympathy, rather than the dynamic and at least potentially more truly tragic Marwood (=Medea). *Emilia Galotti* is also a modernization of a classical story, and again the transposition has created problems whose solution is not entirely satisfactory. Lessing took from Livy (by way of other dramatists) the story of the plebeian Virginius who killed his daughter rather than see her lose her virtue to the lustful decemvir, Appius Claudius. In January 1758 he wrote to his friend Friedrich Nicolai that he was starting work on a 'domestic Virginia' in which the political element (the factor of class conflict) was to be completely removed. The original plan seems to have undergone a number of changes, and by 1772, when the play was at last completed, social and political criticism in literature, and particularly in the drama, was coming much more into prominence; one of the most impressive features of *Emilia Galotti* is its powerful recreation of the atmosphere of a petty eighteenth-century court (even though Italian rather than German!), with its hedonistic prince obeying only his own whims and the promptings of his current favourite, who panders unscrupulously to his master's desires, seeking only to maintain his own position. But Lessing's principal intention remained unchanged: namely to create what would be first and foremost a psychological tragedy, in which the catastrophe would be brought about not so much by external factors such as the pressures of class conflict, but rather by the characters of the protagonists. It is doubtful whether this could ever have been done with complete success; but Lessing has taken great pains over his characters and their motivation, both conscious and unconscious. Emilia and her father are both headstrong, impulsive characters with a strong sense of morality, expressed in lofty phrases, which however finds it difficult – to the point of impossibility – to translate itself into resolute moral action. Odoardo in particular is incapable of finding a mean between hot-headed violence and helpless passivity, and Emilia is spiritually shattered by the discovery that her father, whom she has clearly regarded as a paragon of virtue and a tower of strength, is simply abandoning her to her captor without any attempt at resistance. In their inability to translate their principles into action they are like the Romantic artist exemplified by the painter Conti, who goes so far as to take a perverse pride in his incapacity to transform inspiration into paint on canvas. In the fates of Emilia and her father we see that in life, as in art, inspiration is nothing without the power of execution: it is indeed a long way from eye to hand, 'so much is lost on the way'.

The other characters are drawn with equal care. The Prince is not a wicked man, though he is an irresponsible one: certainly no iron-willed tyrant, but almost pathetically weak (some critics have even seen him as a tragic figure), incapable of concentration, easily thrown off balance one way or the other by the merest whim or the slightest unforeseen development. The despot's apparently unassailable strength and his weakness are two sides of the same coin: on the one hand, for example, the grandiose, arbitrary gesture in granting Emilia Bruneschi's petition in the opening scene, on the other the blundering, verbose foolishness with which he confronts the heroine in Act III. But however weak as a man, he is in a strong position: this is of course one of the mainsprings of the tragedy, and it is an element in the story which cannot be completely reduced to a psychological treatment. The strength of the Prince's position is the strength of Marinelli, and Marinelli is the one figure of major importance in the play without psychological complexity. His dramaturgic next of kin are the scheming servants of traditional comedy, surviving, for example, in Figaro in *The Barber of Seville*: always ready for every new situation, always there to take responsibility and to get their helpless masters out of the latest fix. Lessing's transparent treatment of Marinelli contrasts sharply with the portrayal of villains by, say, Shakespeare or Goethe, who often give these characters as much psychological depth as their heroes. Appiani is the diametrical opposite of this cynical schemer: a 'sensitive soul', as Marinelli calls him. Like Odoardo and Emilia he is full of lofty moral sentiment; his wordy utterances make him sound a prig to modern ears. Lessing's contemporaries would have found him less unsympathetic, but once again his attitudes do not translate easily into action, and Lessing has emphasized this by portraying him as almost morbidly melancholic. He too finds himself 'a different and a better man' only when provoked. Orsina is a strange character: an abandoned woman, and a hysterical one – to describe her as mad is indeed not one of Marinelli's most outrageous lies – and she is also an amateur philosopher. This dual character reflects her dual role in Act IV: firstly to confront Odoardo with the possibility of a violent solution to his problem, to set his thoughts running in that direction, and to provide him with the means of putting them into practice; and secondly to introduce the theme of Providence, which lies at the centre of Lessing's thought, emphasizing that what seems coincidence is in fact a trial and an opportunity sent by Providence for man to seize and prove himself by. This is yet another element in the play's analysis of man's inability to translate attitude into action. In Lessing's 'enlightened' view of the world, Providence is benevolent, but demands man's active cooperation: as Odoardo says, it 'will have my hand'. Unfortunately it is only the amoral opportunist, Marinelli, who shows the ability to turn (almost) every situation to his advantage.

Lessing originally wrote that he intended to use the free forms of the English theatre, but finally, although the neo-classical 'unity of place' is slightly relaxed, that of time is strictly maintained. This is not, however, a mere external, but a vital dimension of the action: it adds to the urgency of the situation and makes the characters' responses to it of necessity all the more precipitate. The plot contains several strands, of psychological motivation, of intrigue, and of coincidence, each playing an essential part and all drawn together with masterly precision to the final scene where father and daughter meet on stage for the first and only time. Objection has often been made to the conclusion with its reference to the original story of Virginius. I think Lessing wished to emphasize that he intended the tragic relationship of father and daughter to be the true centre of the play. Yet perhaps one may read into Emilia's allusion to Roman history a lingering doubt on

Lessing's part as to the ultimate viability of domestic tragedy:
a doubt as to whether perhaps after all 'real' tragedy was not
by definition classical and heroic. Whatever the force of these
doubts, *Emilia Galotti* has stood the test of time; and if the
basic requirements of tragedy are 'an imitation of action ...
arousing pity and fear', then taking the play as a whole, these
requirements are admirably fulfilled.

EGMONT

Goethe began work on *Egmont* in the early 1770s, in his
youthful 'Storm and Stress' period, but this play too has a
long history and it was not completed until September 1787,
when Goethe was in Italy and already entering his 'classical'
phase. It is thus a transitional work, but betrays its early
origins by its 'Shakespearian' freedom, its attempt to paint a
broad historical background in the crowd scenes (toned down
from the original drafts, which Goethe as early as 1782 had
come to think were too 'unbuttoned') and above all in its
peculiar structure (or, by conventional dramatic standards,
lack of it) as a series of scenes revolving about the character
of the protagonist. In his *Notes on the Theatre* (1774) J. M. R.
Lenz had boldly and provocatively stood on its head Aris-
totle's dictum that 'tragedy is an imitation of action and not
of persons': according to Lenz, modern tragedy – unlike
Greek – must be concerned with the portrayal of great
individuals. But a play like *Egmont* illustrates the risks in-
volved in trying to construct a tragedy about a single figure
instead of a firm line of action. It has really no plot, and the
part of it which caused Goethe the greatest trouble was
apparently Act IV – 'der fatale vierte Akt', as he called it –
which is the only one in which anything actually *happens*.
What we have here is the depiction of a personality: we see
Egmont mirrored successively in the thoughts and actions of
others and in his own encounters with them – and it is a
curious feature of the play that there is only one character
(Ferdinand) with whom the protagonist actually appears on

stage more than once, if we discount his final dream-vision of Clara. The first encounter of Egmont and Ferdinand, again, is very brief; and yet it does subtly anticipate the final revelation of Ferdinand's love for Egmont, in that the subject of their conversation is Egmont's horse. The horse is a symbol of a noble, free and self-assured mode of life, and as such accompanies Egmont in word and deed throughout the play, almost like a leitmotiv. The structure of the play might indeed be called musical rather than dramatic, with its anticipations, repetitions and echoes of this and other themes, and the ending with its 'salto mortale into the world of opera', as Schiller called it.

There is also the question of whether the play can legitimately be described as a tragedy at all, or whether the transformation of Egmont's death into a triumph is not another instance of what has been called Goethe's 'avoidance of tragedy'. Alone of Goethe's major plays *Egmont* and *Faust* bear the designation 'tragedy',* but in neither of them is the conclusion as unequivocally tragic as that of the earlier *Götz*, which is simply called 'a play' ('Schauspiel'). Leaving aside the peculiar problems of *Faust*, we may say that both *Götz* and *Egmont* portray the downfall of a great man who has lived for freedom, and is conquered by despotism and treachery. In passing it may be observed at this point that neither of them is a revolutionary, seeking to create a new social and political order, like the idealist Marquis Posa in Schiller's *Don Carlos*. They are conservatives rather, seeking to preserve old-established freedoms and resisting changes which threaten these. So the argument between Egmont and Alva in Act IV is not merely between libertarianism and despotism, but also and probably more significantly between a conservative tolerance and acceptance of anomaly and a 'progressive' desire for uniformity and efficiency. Götz is not permitted a final triumph like Egmont's, but dies recognizing that treachery and cunning will be victorious in the times to come. Egmont goes to

---

* *Egmont* is called 'Trauerspiel' and *Faust* 'Tragödie'. German critics are wont to attempt distinctions between these two terms, but in the eighteenth century at any rate they were used interchangeably.

his death as if to battle, knowing that the cause of freedom will prevail and the Provinces shake off the Spanish yoke; and the effect of this brilliance is strange after the night and prison gloom of the preceding scenes of Act V. Again the effect is one more familiar in music: when at the end of the *Egmont* overture Beethoven, faithful to the play, changes from stern F minor to dazzling F major, there is no such sense of inappropriateness, but in Goethe's play the conclusion does not fit what has gone before. It is not so much that Egmont seems to have changed his attitude to revolution and violent resistance; logical inconsistencies of this kind are not of primary importance in art, and a great artist can often persuade us to accept them. It is a more serious flaw that Egmont goes off as if there were no scaffold and no executioners awaiting him; since he does not regard his own death as real, it loses some of its power to move us. If this were not so, it might well have seemed more truly tragic than Götz's, and this must have been Goethe's intention originally. Götz is betrayed by his enemies; Egmont by his own character. The fearless self-confidence and freedom that makes others love and cling to him is what makes him go on unheeding of repeated warnings. He himself is aware of this, strangely enough, as we see above all in the scene between him and his secretary, culminating in the famous images of the sleepwalker and the charioteer. He is one of the first examples in Goethe's work of what Goethe later called 'the demonic' ('das Dämonische') – the element in a powerful character which is not under the control of the will, but by which the character is, as Egmont tells Ferdinand, 'dragged on inexorably to meet his destiny'. This element of the demonic represents Goethe's particular attempt in *Egmont* to solve one of the perennial problems of tragedy: the relation of character and fate.

Consideration of *Egmont* must also include some mention of the question of historical accuracy. The dramatist is inspired by certain historical events, or by a certain historical figure. This necessarily involves the acceptance of certain significant facts, but for dramatic purposes others may legitimately be suppressed and still others altered or invented.

Here the contrast drawn by Strada, Goethe's historical source, between the characters of Egmont – handsome and self-assured – and William ('the Silent') of Orange – sombre and cautious – served as the starting-point for a complete reconstruction of the historical personage. His independence is emphasized by the omission even of any mention of Count Hoorn, with whom the real Egmont was arrested and executed, and by making him a bachelor with a young mistress instead of a married man with a large family. Clara and her companion, the pathetic Brackenburg, are invented; here Goethe is exploring one of his characteristic personal themes – faithfulness and faithlessness in love – which he also untraditionally imported into *Faust*. Margaret, the Princess Regent, was in fact an enthusiastic Catholic and persecutor of heretics; but here Goethe has drawn her closer in sympathy to Egmont, taking a cue from history and transforming it completely in his own personal, poetic way. Margaret was of a mannish nature: her 'little moustache' is historically attested, and in Motley's words 'her accomplishments, save that of the art of horsemanship, were not remarkable'. But in Goethe's mind the horse was symbolically associated with Egmont; and so a bond between Egmont and Margaret was forged in his imagination. They come to represent a moderate political position between the intransigent extremes of Orange and Alva – but here, as so often, it is extremism which is victorious. The events of history seem to have been compressed, although the play has no precise time-scale. In fact, the great outburst of image-breaking took place in August 1566; Alva arrived in Brussels in August 1567; Egmont and Hoorn were arrested on 9th September 1567, and executed on 5th June 1568. The historical background is made sufficiently clear, except for a couple of possibly obscure allusions which I have explained in footnotes.

Egmont is certainly not a flawless work, but it is an original, in many ways effective and often moving one.

MARY STUART

Schiller, like Goethe, began his career as a dramatist with a 'Storm and Stress' play, the volcanic, nonsensical (but also magnificent!) *The Robbers* of 1780. This had in its original version a contemporary setting, but his second play *Fiesco and the Conspiracy at Genoa* (1782) already deals with historical subject-matter. *Don Carlos* is the first historical tragedy in the new, fully-fledged German classical manner. Schiller's treatment of historical fact was notoriously free, particularly in *The Maid of Orleans* (1801) where history is, as Shaw observed, 'drowned in a witch's caldron of raging romance'. Though this is less than fair to the play, one may admit that Schiller did here overstep the limits of legitimate distortion; but this is not so in *Mary Stuart*, where the picture that emerges is substantially less distorted than that of *Egmont*. Here again some salient feature of the historical account is seized upon, other facts suppressed and new incidents invented. Mary came to England seeking comfort and aid against her rebellious Scottish subjects; instead she was kept in custody, while numerous Catholic plots to rescue her were hatched and discovered, culminating in Babington's conspiracy of 1586. Elizabeth was extremely reluctant to accede to Parliament's earnest requests for Mary to be executed as a danger to the peace of the realm. She attempted to evade responsibility, and tried to persuade Paulet, Mary's gaoler, to take it upon himself to murder her; eventually she signed the death-warrant, but afterwards claimed that she had never given orders for the execution, wrote to Mary's son James that it was a 'miserable accident' and sent Secretary Davison to the Tower as a scapegoat. Mary on the other hand displayed resolution and constancy, deliberately played the part of a martyr and declared that she died in a good cause, satisfied that she had done her duty. This historical contrast is the core of Schiller's play, and his inventions are designed to point it up. In fact Mary *was* guilty of encouraging Babington; the two queens never met face to face, Elizabeth persistently refusing Mary's demand to see her; and when she died Mary was forty-four, and no longer beautiful – though she had enjoyed the reputation of a legendary beauty in her youth – and Elizabeth was fifty. Schiller's distortions in these respects do not matter. The important thing in the play is again the contrast of two characters: closely linked both personally and within their political situation, one of them accepts and the other denies ultimate responsibility for her own actions and thus for her own fate. Specific historical events are made the medium for an exploration of the true nature of human free will.

To say that man has free will would appear to mean that he can do what he wants, and direct the future; and this would seem to be true above all for the ruler, the man (or woman) in a position of power, at the centre of great events. But in fact this is not so. As Elizabeth bitterly observes, she is forced into action by public opinion, by political necessity, by the pressures of *reality*; so no man can be a free agent in this sense, the public personality least of all. Any attempt to demonstrate their free will inevitably involves Schiller's characters in a head-on collision with necessity, with reality, with the greater, impersonal powers of history, life and death. Schiller wrote in his essay *On the Sublime* that the only way man could conquer such forces, and deny their power over his free will, was by voluntarily submitting to them. This involves recognizing that free will cannot be exercised prospectively but, as it were, only retrospectively: man cannot determine what *will* happen (even if he successfully wills something to happen, it will have further necessary consequences beyond the scope of his will), but he can accept responsibility for what has happened and is happening. Thus Mary, although she continues to protest her specific innocence of complicity in Babington's plot, admits that she is a guilty woman: guilty of the murder of Darnley and therefore responsible for the whole chain of events that has finally led up to her execution – so that her death becomes the consequence of her original exercise of free will and thus itself is made a demonstration of that free will. Her reconciliation to her death is not achieved without a struggle: she has to fight and overcome the temptations represented by Mortimer and Leicester. In the great scene between the two queens in Act III, Mary yields to the temptation of humiliating Elizabeth, as a woman, before Leicester, and actually reaches her moral nadir; but there has to be conflict before there can be victory, and she has to fall before she can rise again. Moreover, it is the taunt of bastardy which finally provokes Elizabeth into signing the death-warrant. Unlike Mary, Elizabeth does not accept responsibility for what she does; she denies it, and with it her claim to free will – in Schiller's eyes her most precious possession as a human being: in the essay already mentioned, he wrote, 'All other things act of necessity; Man is the creature that wills.' This means that Elizabeth is not what he called a 'sublime' character, but it does not mean that she is not tragic. She too suffers, and is left to go on suffering. She suffers because she does not accept responsibility; Mary finds acceptance of responsibility in and through suffering. Both queens are tragic figures, and it is Elizabeth we see at the last; with this Schiller counters the tendency for the play to end on a note of triumphant martyrdom. This tendency is given its head in *The Maid of Orleans*, with the flagrantly unhistorical death of Joan of Arc on the battlefield, banner in hand, beneath a sky tinged with a rosy glow (parodied by Brecht in his *St Joan of the Stockyards*). *Mary Stuart* in this respect strikes a balance between the romantic 'sublimity' of the *Maid* and the harsher, realistic pessimism of the *Wallenstein* trilogy Schiller completed in 1800. To my mind the trilogy is Schiller's finest achievement, but its size makes it impracticable by modern standards, and it must be admitted that *Mary Stuart* is superior in dramatic technique.

It is in fact, despite its length, an extremely stage-worthy play, with some very fine theatrical effects. There is much imaginative use of space: of particular note are the tremendous 'opening out' into the park scene of Act III and the strange descent of Mary to execution beneath Leicester's feet. The reader must accept without prejudice the fact that Schiller had a strong taste for rhetoric and melodrama, but neither of these terms is pejorative in itself, and only in the figure of Mortimer is this taste perhaps over-indulged here. The blank verse is handled with considerable freedom and variation of pace, and rhyme is used, in the Shakespearian manner, at the end of scenes and elsewhere in 'set pieces' for particular effect. There is genuine action, both outer and inner, and the play exemplifies that combination of 'classical' concentration with elements of Shakespearian breadth characteristic of the German drama at its best.

PENTHESILEA

For sheer ferocity and bloodthirstiness, few tragedies can compare with *Penthesilea*: Goethe was repelled and declared that it was the product of a diseased imagination. Kleist was indeed of a morbid and unstable temperament, and ultimately died by his own hand. As well as for his plays he is famous for his stories, in which too there is a continual recurrence of scenes and motifs of savage violence, the ferocity of man even (as in *The Earthquake in Chile*) outdoing that of nature at its most hostile. Yet strangely enough he is also the author of the finest comedy in German, *The Broken Jug* (1805), and of his plays only the first, *The Schroffenstein Family* (1802) and *Penthesilea* end in unrelieved tragedy; ambiguity is his characteristic dramatic effect. Kleist was obsessed with the idea that we have no reliable criteria for distinguishing truth and falsehood; as Kant had declared, we can never know 'things in themselves', but only a world of *phenomena*, which Kleist interpreted as meaning appearances which are almost certain to be deceptive. We have to take the world on trust, and often it seems that the gods who rule it are at best indifferent to us, at worst malicious and sadistically cruel. Yet there is such a thing as genuine human love and trust, which offers release into a world of truth and happiness; but even this is fraught with fearful perils.

The plays (and the stories) are full of false identities, of involuntary error and deliberate deceit, of dream-visions truer than truth itself, Chinese puzzles of illusion and reality. In *Penthesilea* we have a well-meant deception (of Penthesilea by Achilles) which has the most disastrous consequences, and a final loss of identity: the queen when she destroys him is not her true self, but 'beside' (or, as German says 'outside') herself, which for Kleist is more than a mere figure of speech. The play is not simply morbid: it is fierce and grim, but it has a 'terrible beauty' as well. Kleist took the legend of Penthesilea and Achilles (in an unfamiliar variant: the more usual version is that Achilles killed Penthesilea, then fell in love with her dead body) as an illustration of a world so out of joint, so incomprehensibly distorted, that man and woman meet in love, yet not in peace, but on the battlefield; a world in which meanings are so inaccessible that love and hatred in their violent extremes cannot be distinguished. Penthesilea is pure woman, 'daughter of the nightingale', beautiful, made to love and be loved; but for woman to exist in isolation she must, as in the Amazon state, change her nature and cease to be herself. If we are to look for the often overstressed factor of 'tragic guilt', then Penthesilea is guilty of disobeying the law of Tanaïs, and is punished for her disobedience; but that law is itself unnatural, and even after her fearful punishment Penthesilea urges the Amazons to renounce it. This is an element in the play which remains characteristically unresolved; but it is less important, it seems to me, than the simple collision of male and female natures in the two protagonists. For if Penthesilea is pure woman, then what Kleist has superbly created in Achilles is a type of total masculinity and self-assurance. This is magnificently conveyed in the first scene in which we actually see him, where his nonchalance makes the other Greek princes look faintly ridiculous; there is a similar note of grimly comic menace in his later scene with the uncomprehending Diomedes and the 'sour-faced moralist' Odysseus. Achilles desires Penthesilea. But what is the true nature of his desire? It seems that he does not want her merely as he has wanted all the other girls in his life; he speaks of hoping that she will follow him back to Phthia and be his queen; but he has also spoken of doing to her what he did to Hector – of making manifest his triumph over her by destroying her and humiliating her. Is this love? Similarly Penthesilea feels herself drawn to Achilles, but like him she does not know the nature of her desire nor of its object. Man and woman cannot know each other; in an embattled world they can only meet in battle. The result is outrage and betrayal, ending in the most terrible destruction. Throughout the play, as the pendulum of battle swings back and forth, we find tenderness and savagery, beauty and horror, or as Kleist himself wrote in a letter, 'squalor and splendour' ('Schmutz und Glanz'), side by side in violent juxtaposition.

It will be noted that there are no act divisions in *Penthesilea*; and despite the adoption of the classical technique of reported action (either simultaneous or subsequent narration of events which take place offstage) one wonders how, or indeed whether, Kleist envisaged actual performance of the play, which strains the limits of stage technique. The structure of the work is again a musical one, with many anticipations and echoes: not merely obvious premonitions of the final catastrophe, but little recurrent details with no definable meaning in themselves, such as the fetching of water or references to crested helmets, all have their part to play. The central images of the play are those of a hunt (with all its attendant details) and of lightning striking a tree. Both these recur again and again, and the resonance of the latter is extended in a way which the translator cannot capture: by puns on the word *Keil*, which means not only 'thunderbolt' but also 'wedge' – as when the Greek generals speak of setting 'reason like a wedge' to split Achilles' 'madness of determination'. Along with the vitality of its two central figures it is the mastery of language which makes *Penthesilea* the extraordinary work it is. Much of it is written in an extremely distorted syntax, with often apparently arbitrary word-order, impossible to imitate in an uninflected language like English. Partly this seems to be a deliberate imitation of classical epic verse, and of Greek in particular with its frequent postponed epithets ('the bow, the golden'); but it is found in all Kleist's plays, and also recalls the bizarre syntax of his stories. It is in fact an attempt to carry through into the very language the shattering of perception and the agonized attempt to restore and reconstruct relationships and meanings which are the essential features of the Kleistian universe and of his characters' response to it. But beside this there is an enormous range, richness and variety of linguistic texture of which I hope the reader will, even in a translation, perceive some glimmerings.

MEDEA

Grillparzer was himself one of those shocked and repelled by the violence and savagery of Kleist's work, particularly the stories which he read in 1818. But in his trilogy, *The Golden Fleece*, which he was writing at this time (1817–21) he uses the antique setting in a not dissimilar way. This work in particular may well have actually been influenced by *Penthesilea*, but Grillparzer's other plays in Greek settings, treating the stories of Sappho (1817) and of Hero and Leander (*Des Meeres und der Liebe Wellen*, 1829), also have for their principal subject the perils of love and sexuality. His other tragedies treat historical and national subject-matter and so present their themes in the less personal context of public duties and objective situations: here we have the essential human conflict, distanced only by the antique costume. The form of the trilogy is derived from Schiller's *Wallenstein*, but Grillparzer's is more genuinely a trilogy, rather than one long play split up into three, in that it presents three quite distinct phases of a complex action, and the greater independence of the three plays may be offered as some justification for here presenting the third of them, *Medea*, by itself. It is true that, as Jason tells Creon, 'You only see the summit, not the climb': Grillparzer took the familiar tragic subject of Medea's revenge on the faithless Jason as his starting-point, but felt that her monstrous deed could only be motivated adequately by tracing their relationship back to its very beginning. He went still further, however: the trilogy as a whole is not about Jason (who does not appear until the second part), nor even about Medea, but, as the title says, about the Golden Fleece and all it stands for. Even in *Medea* taken by itself the central importance attached to the fleece is clear, and it is this which is the most original and characteristic feature of Grillparzer's treatment of the story.

In the first play, *The Guest*, the Greek Phryxus brings to Colchis the Golden Fleece which he has taken from its temple at Delphi, and is treacherously killed by Medea's father, Aietes, king of Colchis. In the second part, *The Argonauts*, Jason comes to Colchis to recover the Fleece and take it back with him to Greece. Medea cannot resist him; she helps him to conquer the dragon that guards the Fleece, and goes with him to be his wife. Her brother Absyrtus jumps into the sea and drowns rather than be taken prisoner by Jason, and Aietes is left alone, cursing Jason and Medea in his despair. What more happens before the action of *Medea* begins, we learn in the course of the play. The Fleece itself is present throughout. It symbolizes guilt, the loss of man's (and woman's) innocence; it symbolizes those divine prerogatives, 'victory and revenge' (as proclaimed by Phryxus in *The Guest*) which it is presumptuous of man to claim; it symbolizes ambition and will. Grillparzer was obsessed with the problem of will, and his pessimistic conclusions have features in common with those of his contemporary, Schopenhauer. Jason, particularly as he appears in *The Argonauts*, is the embodiment of will; as Medea tells Creusa, he is 'selfish, yet for no end, but for its own sake'. The German ('Voll Selbstheit, nicht des Nutzens, doch des Sinns') is difficult to render literally, but what is meant is that when Jason wants something, it is the wanting that is important to him, not the thing itself. He wants the Fleece; but once he *has* it, since for that very reason he cannot *want* it any more, it is only a burden to him. The same is true of Medea herself, whom he once loved and desired. But once a man has acted, he has to accept all the consequences of his actions; they cannot be unwilled. Innocence once lost can never be recovered, and what is done cannot be undone. In *Medea*, however, the two protagonists are seen each engaged in a last, desperate attempt to bury the past and make a fresh start. Medea literally buries the symbols of her past, but they are dug up again and given back to her by King Creon: her past is still real and she cannot simply will it away from her. From the moment when at her father's prompting she 'innocently' took Phryxus' sword from him, she has been committed to the Fleece, to 'victory and revenge'; separated from the Fleece she is no longer herself – just as Jason is no longer himself when he is no longer the pursuer. And she is also committed to Jason, but this she admits, while he is torn between reluctant recognition of his commitment to her and the longing to go back to the beginning, to wipe out the whole episode and start his life again with Creusa where he left off in his youth. This is all the more tempting since Creusa is still 'the selfsame that I was', still innocent – it had never occurred to her to think of the *meaning* of her song; nothing has happened to her, she hardly seems even to have aged, and so it might look as though with her a happier past could be reconstructed. Jason and Creon both know that this is not possible, and neither of them really wills it, but between them they stumble into the fatal attempt: it happens, and no one but themselves has done it. So, ultimately, will is a phantom, though none the less real for that: for will and action are seen to be synonymous. 'What I do, I will,' the still-innocent Medea proudly proclaims at the beginning of the trilogy, but at the end the pride is gone, and there is nothing to do but 'bear it, endure it, atone'.

Throughout the trilogy, Greeks and Colchians are contrasted. In *Medea* the nurse, Gora, is pure Colchian, and Creon and Creusa pure Greek; but Jason and Medea, having lost their old identities, are drawn into a kind of limbo in between. Associated with this contrast is another: that of the images of day and night, light and dark. Greece is the land of civilization and clarity, Colchis that of gloomy barbarism. In *Medea* this has become blurred: with a shock we hear Jason at his first appearance say 'I love the night, the daylight hurts my eyes.' And the two nations are also contrasted in speech: regular blank verse is associated principally with the Greeks, while the characteristic speech of the Colchians is a jagged, irregular metre with a tendency to a dactylic pattern (one stressed syllable followed by two unstressed).

Grillparzer was nurtured in the Viennese theatrical tradition (he is the only Austrian dramatist in this volume) with its elaborate conventions of stage movement and use of gesture and costume. In *Medea*, his most concentrated and 'classical' play, there are few of the elaborate, operatic effects which are prominent in his historical plays, with their large casts and rich movement; but even so he has, as always, given careful thought to how he wanted his play to look on the stage. We may note Medea's change of costume from Colchian to Greek and back again, and her final appearance wearing the Fleece. The progress of the day, with its increase and decrease of light, also reflects the course of the action. The sea, beside which the play opens, seems to have been an essential feature of Grillparzer's imagined Greek landscape: in the other 'Greek' plays, both Sappho and Leander die by drowning, as does Absyrtus in *The Argonauts*. And, as I have suggested, that landscape was particularly associated by Grillparzer with the perils of love.

The conclusion of *Medea* may be compared with that of *Penthesilea*. Here too man and woman in their essential natures destroy each other, although here both are left alive at the end; for here love turns slowly and bitterly into hatred, while in Kleist's play they seem to explode simultaneously. But, whereas in *Penthesilea* we feel a reaching-out towards an ideal love of such terrible, incandescent beauty that it cannot but scorch and destroy creatures of mere flesh and blood, no such ideal beauty rises from the ruins of Creon's palace. Tragedy deals in paradox: traditionally, it portrays suffering and death as the necessary price to be paid for some ultimate good: the restoration of divine order, the freedom of man in some sense or other, even the fulfilment of love. But in the pessimistic vision of *The Golden Fleece* there seems to be no such ultimate good for which the price would be worth paying. Grillparzer's characters long to live in an eternal present, with neither past nor future, neither guilt nor fears nor hopes. Childhood represents this ideal to them; but once innocence is lost, nothing more – neither love nor freedom nor responsibility – can recompense them for it.

THE TRANSLATION

Tragedy is the most artificial of literary genres: the imitation
(to use the Aristotelian term) of unpleasant things in order to
give pleasure. Realistic tragedy is probably a contradiction in
terms, despite the domestic drama and its later derivatives.
Yet to break away from the alexandrine and write tragedies in
prose itself indicated a considerable will to realism. For this
reason, when steering the translator's familiar but ever-
hazardous course between the Scylla of a slavish literalness
which is not English (and at its worst not even compre-
hensible), and the Charybdis of a fluent English speech which
does not exactly correspond in content to the original, I have
in the prose plays preferred the latter direction, and, though I
have aimed throughout at as faithful and accurate a translation as possible, given myself perhaps a little more latitude
than in the verse plays. There is, of course, a great deal of
difference between the prose of *Emilia Galotti* and that of
Egmont: Lessing's prose is formal and stylized and, though it
is by no means undifferentiated, admits much less variation
between the different characters than that of *Egmont*. Here we
range from colloquial realism to a much more stylized utterance, sometimes even (as in the final scene) what is almost
blank verse written out as prose. In a play in verse the mode of
speech is deliberately distorted from the norm represented by
prose, as part of the intended effect: the shape imposed by the
author on his characters' words is much more obviously an
integral part of what is being said. I have therefore attempted
here as close a rendering as possible, using the metres of the
original together with the variations and irregularities which,
intentional or not, are nevertheless part of the flavour of the
verse. The use of rhyme, and actual changes in metre, such as
Schiller's employment of quasi-lyrical stanza forms for Mary's
speeches in the opening scene of Act III, the broken utterances of Penthesilea's penultimate 'Not you! Go to Themiscyra . . .', or Grillparzer's 'Colchian' free rhythms, had
obviously to be imitated, but I have also tried to register the

other factors which affect the pace and movement of the verse, so as to reproduce as accurately as I could, not necessarily individual lines, but the over-all shape of whole speeches and exchanges.

In *Emilia Galotti*, *Mary Stuart* and *Penthesilea* the French method of scene division (a new scene number for each entry or exit) is used, while in *Egmont* and *Medea* the scenes are not numbered. In the historical plays I have used the accredited English forms for the names of well-known figures, changing Goethe's 'Alba' to 'Alva', and have used English forms for first names. But there seemed to be little point in altering 'Hannah Kennedy' to 'Elizabeth' or 'Margaret Curle' to 'Barbara' merely because those happened to be their names in historical fact. Still less should 'Henry' (Heinrich) in Egmont's death-warrant be 'corrected' to the historical 'Lamoral'. (It may be a trifle, but it is none the less a curious fact, that Goethe also gives his Faust the untraditional name of Heinrich instead of Johann.) The names and references to classical mythology in *Medea* will, I trust, be either familiar or self-explanatory; but since this may well not be so in the case of *Penthesilea*, I have supplied a separate note on the use of names in that work.

The necessity for translation is an unfortunate one; but I hope that the reader will be able to form some impression not only of what my five playwrights had to say, but also of how they said it.

F. J. L.

Oxford
January 1968

EMILIA GALOTTI

Gotthold Ephraim Lessing

A tragedy in five acts
1772

CHARACTERS

EMILIA GALOTTI
ODOARDO GALOTTI
CLAUDIA GALOTTI } her parents
HETTORE GONZAGA, Prince of Guastalla
MARINELLI, his chamberlain
CAMILLO ROTA, one of his councillors
CONTI, a painter
COUNT APPIANI
COUNTESS ORSINA
ANGELO
SERVANTS

ACT I

Scene: a room in the Prince's palace

SCENE I

[*The* PRINCE *sitting at a desk covered with letters and papers, some of which he is looking through.*]

PRINCE: Complaints, nothing but complaints! Petitions, nothing but petitions! These dreary affairs of state; and still men envy us! Yes, indeed; if we could do something for everybody, that might be an enviable position. – Emilia? [*Opening another of the petitions and looking at the signature.*] An Emilia? But her name is Emilia Bruneschi – not Galotti. Not Emilia Galotti! What does she want, this Emilia Bruneschi? [*Reads.*] She asks a great deal; a very great deal. But she is called Emilia! Granted! [*He signs and rings a bell. Enter a* SERVANT.] I suppose none of my councillors will be in the antechamber so soon?

SERVANT: No, sir.

PRINCE: I am up and about too early. It is such a fine morning; I will take a drive. Marquis Marinelli shall accompany me. Have him called. [*Exit* SERVANT.] No, I cannot work any longer. Here was I so calm, so I thought, so calm – and all of a sudden, this wretched Bruneschi girl has to be called Emilia: my peace of mind is gone, and everything!

SERVANT [*entering again*]: The Marquis has been sent for. And here, a letter from the Countess Orsina.

PRINCE: Orsina? Put it down.

SERVANT: Her messenger is waiting.

PRINCE: I will send the answer – if there is one. Where is she? In town, or at her villa?

SERVANT: She arrived in town yesterday.

PRINCE: So much the worse – the better, I mean. The less need for her messenger to wait. [*Exit* SERVANT.] My dear Countess! [*Bitterly, picking up her letter.*] As good as read!

[*Throwing it down again*] Why, yes, I thought I loved her. The things we will believe! Perhaps I really did love her, too. But – no, not now!

SERVANT [*entering again*]: Conti the painter requests the favour –

PRINCE: Conti? Of course; let him come in. [*Exit* SERVANT.] That will give me something else to think about. [*Stands up.*]

SCENE 2

[*Enter* CONTI.]

PRINCE: Good morning, Conti. How are you? And how is Art?

CONTI: Struggling for its bread, your highness.

PRINCE: That should not be; that shall not be; not in my modest dominions, at any rate. But an artist must be willing to work like anyone else.

CONTI: Work? That is a pleasure to him. But *having* to work, and having to do too much work, that can rob him of the name of artist.

PRINCE: It is not a matter of quantity, but quality: a little will do, if it is well done. I hope you have not come empty-handed, Conti?

CONTI: I have brought the portrait which you commissioned, sir. And I have brought another, which you did not commission; but it deserves to be seen, and so –

PRINCE: The one I commissioned? – I can hardly remember.

CONTI: The Countess Orsina.

PRINCE: Of course. Only the order was rather a long time ago.

CONTI: Our beauties are not there for the painting every day. In the last three months the Countess has condescended to give me exactly one sitting.

PRINCE: Where are the pictures?

CONTI: In the anteroom. I will fetch them. [*Exit.*]

Scene 3

PRINCE [*alone*]: Her portrait! – well, maybe. The portrait is not the lady herself. And perhaps I shall find in the portrait again what I no longer see in the person. – But I *will* not find it again. This tiresome painter! I do believe she has bribed him. – And what then! If that other portrait, painted with different colours upon a different ground, will make room for her in my heart again – why, truly, I think I should be glad. When that was the way my thoughts went, I was always so gay, so happy, so carefree. Now I am quite the opposite of all that. – But no; no, no! Freer or less free, I am still better off as I am.

Scene 4

[*Re-enter* CONTI *with the paintings. He leans the one with its face against a chair, and arranges the other for the* PRINCE *to see.*]

CONTI: I beg you, your highness, consider the limitations of our art. Much of what is most attractive in beauty lies quite beyond it. – If you will stand here –

PRINCE [*after looking briefly*]: Excellent, Conti; excellent. That goes for your art, for your skill with the brush. But flattering, Conti; infinitely flattering!

CONTI: The sitter seemed not to think so. And really it is no more flattering than art has to be. Art must paint just as the creative force of nature – if there is such a thing – conceived the picture; without the falling-off caused inevitably by recalcitrant matter; without the deterioration caused by the assaults of time.

PRINCE: The artist who can think such thoughts is doubly to be admired. But the sitter, you said, found in spite of that –

CONTI: Excuse me, your highness. The sitter is a person who commands my respect. I did not intend anything derogatory to her.

PRINCE: My dear Conti, do feel free to speak! What did the sitter say?

CONTI: I shall be satisfied, said the Countess, if I am no uglier than that.

PRINCE: No uglier? Oh yes, I can hear her say it!

CONTI: And she said it with an expression – of which I admit you will find no trace, not the suspicion, in her portrait.

PRINCE: But of course; that is exactly what I meant when I said it was infinitely flattering. Oh, I know it, that proud, scornful expression, that would spoil the features of Venus herself! – I do not deny that a beautiful mouth is often all the more beautiful for the suspicion of a mocking pout. But it must be no more than the suspicion; the pout must not become a grimace, as the countess's does. And there must be eyes to watch over its voluptuous mockery – eyes such as our dear Countess simply does not possess. Not even here, in her portrait.

CONTI: Sir, I am taken aback –

PRINCE: But why? All the good that Art can do for the Countess's great, protruding, stiff and staring Gorgon's eyes, you, Conti, have well and truly done. Well and truly, did I say? Less truly would have been more truthfully. For tell me now yourself, Conti, does this portrait really show us the person's character? But a portrait should! You have turned pride into dignity, scorn into a smile, and gloomy introspection into gentle melancholy.

CONTI [*somewhat irritated*]: Ah, your highness, we painters count on the finished picture's finding the lover still just as warm as when he ordered it. We paint with a lover's eye, and only a lover's eye ought to judge our work.

PRINCE: Well then, Conti, why did you not come with it a month ago? Put it away. What is the other picture?

CONTI [*fetching it and holding it still turned away from the* PRINCE]: Another female portrait.

PRINCE: Then I think – I would rather not see it. It will never measure up to the ideal I have here [*pointing to his forehead*], or rather here [*pointing to his heart*]. I should like to see a different kind of subject, Conti, to admire your art by.

CONTI: There are more admirable forms of art; but certainly no more admirable subject than this.

PRINCE: Then I will wager, Conti, that it is the artist's own mistress. [*The painter turns the picture round to face him*] What is this I see, Conti? Your work, or the work of my imagination? Emilia Galotti!

CONTI: What, your highness? You know her, this angel?

PRINCE [*trying to control his emotions, but without taking his eyes off the portrait*]: Slightly! – enough to recognize her. It was some weeks ago, I met her with her mother at a soirée – since then I have only seen her in church – where it wouldn't do to stare. I know her father too. He is no friend of mine. He was my most outspoken opponent when I laid claim to Sabionetta. An old soldier, and a rough diamond; an honest man, though!

CONTI: The father! But here we have the daughter.

PRINCE: By heavens, her speaking likeness! [*Still staring at the painting*] Oh, my dear Conti, you know – when the work so takes our eye that we forget to praise the artist – that is real praise!

CONTI: And yet this left me feeling most dissatisfied with myself. But then again, I am very well satisfied with my own dissatisfaction! – Ah, why cannot we paint directly with our eyes? It is so far from our eye down through our arm into our brush; so much is lost on the way! – But as I say: knowing how much has been lost, and why it has been lost, and why it was inevitable that it should be lost – that makes me as proud and prouder than everything I managed not to lose. For it is that knowledge, rather than any actual achievement, that tells me that I am indeed a great painter, although my hand may sometimes fail me. Or do you not think, your highness, that Raphael would have been the greatest genius in painting, even if he had had the misfortune to be born without hands? Do you not think so, your highness?

PRINCE [*taking his eyes off the painting for the first time*]: What did you say, Conti? What is it you want to know?

CONTI: Oh, nothing, nothing! Idle talk! I can see your whole soul was in your eyes. I love souls like that, and eyes like that.

PRINCE [*with forced coldness*]: So, Conti, in all seriousness, you count Emilia Galotti one of the finest beauties of our city?

CONTI: So? One? One of the finest? and the finest in our city? – Your highness, you are mocking me. Or all that time you were no more looking than you were listening.

PRINCE: My dear Conti [*looking at the portrait again*], how can a man like me believe his own eyes? Really it is only the painter who can be a judge of beauty.

CONTI: And every man's own feelings should wait for a painter to give his verdict? Into a monastery with any man who asks us to tell him what is beautiful! But, prince, as a painter I must tell you this: one of the greatest pleasures of my life was having Emilia Galotti to sit for me. This head, this face, this forehead, these eyes, this nose, this mouth, this chin, this throat, this bosom, this figure, this whole shape have been from that day on my one and only primer of female beauty. The actual painting she sat for is in her father's possession; he is not in town. But this copy –

PRINCE [*turning quickly to him*]: What of it, Conti? You have not promised it to anyone yet?

CONTI: It is yours, your highness, if you would like to have it.

PRINCE: Like! [*Smiling*] This primer of female beauty of yours, Conti: how could I be better employed than in making it my study too? – The other portrait there you can take away. – Order a frame for it.

CONTI: I shall!

PRINCE: As rich and beautiful as the carver can make it. It shall hang in the gallery. But this one shall stay here. There is no need to make so much out of a sketch, and one does not want to hang it up either; one would rather keep it close to hand. I thank you, Conti; I thank you with all my heart. And as I said: in my dominions art shall not have to struggle for its bread; not until I have none myself. Send for my treasurer, Conti, and have him pay you for both the portraits. Make out the bill yourself; name your own price. As much as you like, Conti!

CONTI: Your highness, I almost think it is not art that earns such a reward.

PRINCE: Oh, is the artist jealous? No, no! Do you hear, Conti: as much as you like! [*Exit* CONTI.]

Scene 5

PRINCE [*alone*]: As much as he likes! [*Turning to the painting*] At any price *you* would be cheap! Ah, lovely creation of art, can it be true that you are mine? – But if I could possess you too, lovelier masterpiece of nature! Whatever you like, honest mother! Whatever you like, old curmudgeon! Ask! Just ask, both of you! – Most of all I should like to buy you from yourself, enchantress! This eye full of charm and modesty! These lips! and when they part to speak! When they smile! These lips! – I hear someone coming. No, I shall keep you for myself! [*Turning the painting to the wall*] It will be Marinelli. Oh, I wish I had not sent for him! How I could have spent the morning!

Scene 6

[*Enter* MARINELLI.]

MARINELLI: Your highness will forgive me. I was not expecting to be summoned so early.

PRINCE: I thought that I would like to go out. It was such a fine morning. But now the best of it is gone; and I no longer feel I want to. [*After a short silence*] What news is there, Marinelli?

MARINELLI: Nothing important, as far as I know. Countess Orsina arrived in town yesterday.

PRINCE: Yes, here is her good-morning already [*pointing to the letter*], or whatever it may be. I have no desire to know. Have you seen her?

MARINELLI: Am I not, unhappily, in her confidence? But, your highness, if ever again I accept the confidences of a lady who takes it into her head to fall in love with you in all seriousness, then –

PRINCE: No perjuries, Marinelli!

MARINELLI: What? Really, your highness? Could it happen

after all? Why, then perhaps the Countess is not so far from the truth.

PRINCE: Very far, I am afraid! If I am shortly to be married to the Princess of Massa, then in the first place all connexions of that kind will have to be broken off.

MARINELLI: If that were all, then indeed Orsina could not but be reconciled to her fate – just as the Prince is reconciled to his.

PRINCE: Which beyond question is much harsher than hers. My heart is sacrificed to some wretched political interest. All she has to do is take hers back; not give it away against her will.

MARINELLI: But the Countess may ask why she should take it back at all, if this is no more than a political marriage. Love may play no part in the Prince's choice of a wife, but beside a wife of that kind there is always room for – another. No, it is not a wife of that kind she is afraid of being sacrificed to, but –

PRINCE: A new love? Indeed! And are you going to tell me that that would be a crime, Marinelli?

MARINELLI: I? Oh, do not confound me, prince, with the foolish woman whose cause I plead – plead out of pity for her. For yesterday, I swear to you, I was strangely moved by her. She did not want to speak of her affair with you at all. She wanted to appear quite cold and unperturbed. But in the middle of the most casual conversation she would let drop one phrase, one allusion after the other, that betrayed the tortures of her heart. With the gayest manner she said the most melancholy things; and then the most laughable trivialities with the saddest expression! She has fled to her books, and I fear they will prove the last straw.

PRINCE: Just as they struck the first blow at her poor brain. But that above all was what turned me away from her, Marinelli: you are not going to use that to try to lead me back to her? If she loses her wits for love, then sooner or later she would have lost them without its help. – And now, enough of her. Let us talk of something else. Is there nothing happening in town?

MARINELLI: As good as nothing. Count Appiani is being married today; but then, that is little more than nothing at all.

PRINCE: Count Appiani? Who is his bride? I was not even told that he was engaged.

MARINELLI: They have kept very quiet about it. And indeed it is not the occasion for much excitement. You will laugh, your highness. – But that is the way with these sensitive souls! Love always picks them to play its worst tricks on. A girl with no fortune and no rank manages to lure him into her net; with moderate looks, but with a great show of virtue and feeling and wit; and what then?

PRINCE: A man who can so completely surrender, without further thought, to the impression that innocence and beauty make on him – I should have thought, was to be envied rather than laughed at. And who is the fortunate girl? For Appiani, for all that – I know you cannot endure him, Marinelli; no more than he can you – for all that, he is a very fine young man, a handsome man, a rich man, a man of honour. I should have been most gratified if I could have won his allegiance; I shall give the matter further thought.

MARINELLI: If it is not too late. For according to my information, it is not his plan at all to make his fortune at court. He is going to take his lady to his valleys in Piedmont; hunt mountain goats, and shoot marmots. What else is there for him to do? The misalliance he is making will be the end of him here. The best houses and all their circle will be closed to him now.

PRINCE: You may talk of your best houses! Ruled by ceremony, constraint, boredom and as often as not dull-wittedness. – But will you not tell me who it is for whom he is sacrificing so much?

MARINELLI: It is a girl called Emilia Galotti.

PRINCE: What, Marinelli? a girl called –

MARINELLI: Emilia Galotti.

PRINCE: Emilia Galotti? Never!

MARINELLI: Most certainly, sir.

PRINCE: No, I say; you are wrong, it cannot be; you have mistaken the name. – The Galottis are a large family. – Perhaps it is a Galotti; but not Emilia Galotti, not Emilia!

MARINELLI: Emilia – Emilia Galotti!

PRINCE: Then there must be another of that name too. – What did you say? – a girl called Emilia Galotti! If it were *she*, only a fool could speak of her so.

MARINELLI: Your highness, you are beside yourself. Do you know her then, this Emilia?

PRINCE: It is my place to ask questions, Signor Marinelli, not yours. – Emilia Galotti? The daughter of Colonel Galotti of Sabionetta?

MARINELLI: The same.

PRINCE: That lives here in Guastalla with her mother?

MARINELLI: The same.

PRINCE: Not far from All Saints' Church?

MARINELLI: The same.

PRINCE: In a word – [*seizing the portrait and thrusting it into* MARINELLI's *hands*] There! This one? This Emilia Galotti? – Let me hear your damned parrot-phrase once more, and it will be like a dagger plunged into my heart!

MARINELLI: The same.

PRINCE: Devil! – The same? This Emilia Galotti, married today –

MARINELLI: To Count Appiani! [*The* PRINCE *tears the portrait out of* MARINELLI's *hands and throws it aside.*] In a quiet ceremony on her father's estate at Sabionetta. Mother and daughter, the Count and perhaps a few friends will be setting out at about midday.

PRINCE [*throwing himself despairingly into a chair*]: Then I am lost! – Then I do not want to live!

MARINELLI: But what is the matter, your highness?

PRINCE [*leaping to his feet again to face him*]: Traitor! What is the matter? Why, I love her; I adore her! Why should you not know? Why should you not have known all along, all you who would rather have seen me enslaved to that madwoman Orsina for ever? – But that you, Marinelli, you who have so often assured me of your loyalty and friend-

ship – Oh, a prince has no friends! can have no friends! –
that you, you could be so faithless and so malicious as to
withhold from me until this moment the news of the danger
that was threatening my love: if ever I forgive you for taking such a liberty, may none of my sins ever be forgiven me!

MARINELLI: I can scarcely find words, sir – if you will allow
me to speak, that is – to assure you of my utter astonishment. You love Emilia Galotti? – Then oath for oath: if I
had the slightest knowledge, the slightest inkling of any
such love, then may angels and saints never know that I
lived! – That was exactly what I swore to Orsina, by all I
knew. Her suspicions lay in quite a different direction.

PRINCE: Then forgive me, Marinelli, [*throwing himself into his
arms*] and pity me!

MARINELLI: You see now, your highness! There you see the
fruits of your own reticence! 'Princes have no friends! can
have no friends!' And the reason why that is so? Because
they do not want any. Today they honour us with their
confidences, open up their whole heart and soul to us; and
tomorrow we are complete strangers again, just as if not a
word had been spoken.

PRINCE: Ah, Marinelli! how could I confide to you what I
scarcely dared confess to myself?

MARINELLI: And still less, then, I suppose, have confessed
to the one that causes you such torment?

PRINCE: To her? – All my efforts to speak to her a second
time have been in vain.

MARINELLI: And the first time –

PRINCE: I spoke to her – Oh, I shall go out of my mind! And
am I to stay and tell you the whole story? – You see me
swept away by the tide; why do you ask and ask how it
came about? Save me first, if you can, and then ask your
questions.

MARINELLI: Save? What is there to be saved? What your
highness has not been able to admit to Emilia Galotti, you
may now admit to Countess Appiani. If you cannot buy
the goods first-hand, then buy them second-hand – as often
as not, you will find it much cheaper.

PRINCE: In earnest, Marinelli, in earnest, or –

MARINELLI: Somewhat soiled, maybe, but –

PRINCE: You begin to be impertinent!

MARINELLI: And the Count wants to take the goods out of the country, too. – Yes, in that case we must think of something else.

PRINCE: And what? – My dear, good Marinelli, think for me. What would you do if you were in my place?

MARINELLI: First and foremost, regard a trifle as a trifle – and tell myself that I should not be what I was for nothing.

PRINCE: Do not flatter me with my power, I can see no use for it here. – Today, you say? this very day?

MARINELLI: This very day, and not before, – it is due to happen. But only things past cannot be prevented. [*After pausing to think*] Will you give me a free hand, your highness? Will you make no objection to anything I may do?

PRINCE: Do anything, Marinelli, anything that can turn aside the blow.

MARINELLI: Then there is no time to lose. – But do not stay in town. Go out to your hunting-lodge at Dosalo. It is on the way to Sabionetta. If I do not succeed in getting the Count out of the way immediately, then I think I will – But of course; I think he is sure to fall into that trap. Your highness will of course wish to send an emissary to Massa in connexion with your betrothal? Let the Count be that emissary; with the stipulation that he must leave today. Do you understand?

PRINCE: Excellent! Bring him out to me. Go, hurry! I will send for my carriage straight away. [*Exit* MARINELLI.]

SCENE 7

PRINCE [*alone*]: Straight away! straight away! – Where did it fall? [*Looking round for the portrait*] On the floor? Oh, that was too cruel! [*Picking it up*] But shall I look? – For the moment I do not want to look at you any more. Why thrust the arrow deeper into the wound? [*Laying it aside*] I have pined and sighed for long enough; but done nothing!

And for all this amorous idleness, I was within a hair's breadth of losing everything! – And if everything should be lost after all? If Marinelli could achieve nothing? – And why should I rely entirely on him? It occurs to me – at this time, [*looking at the clock*] at this very hour every morning the pious creature goes to mass at the Dominican church. What if I went and tried to speak to her? – But today, today, her wedding-day – her heart will be too full of other things for the mass. Yet who knows? Nothing ventured – [*He rings the bell; as he hastily gathers up some of the papers on the desk, enter the* SERVANT.] My carriage! Have any of the councillors arrived yet?

SERVANT: Camillo Rota is here.

PRINCE: Send him in. [*Exit* SERVANT.] I only hope he does not want to delay me. Not today! Another day I will be all the more willing to spend time over his scruples. – There was a petition from one Emilia Bruneschi – [*Looking for it*] There it is. But, my good Bruneschi, when your advocate –

SCENE 8

[*Enter* CAMILLO ROTA *with papers.*]

PRINCE: Come in, Rota, come in. This is what I have opened this morning. Nothing much to excite us! You will see what there is to be done. Take them.

ROTA: Very good, sir.

PRINCE: And here is a petition from a woman called Emilia Galot – Bruneschi, I mean. I have approved it, in fact. But – after all, the matter is no trifle – you had better let it wait. – Or not; just as you like.

ROTA: Not as *I* like, sir.

PRINCE: What else? Anything for me to sign?

ROTA: There was a death-warrant to be signed.

PRINCE: Yes, with pleasure. Let me have it; be quick.

ROTA [*hesitating and staring at the* PRINCE]: A death-warrant, I said.

PRINCE: Yes, I heard you. I could have signed it by now. I am in a hurry.

ROTA [*looking through his papers*]: Why, I must have left it behind. Forgive me, your highness; it will have to wait until tomorrow.

PRINCE: Very well! Collect these things; I must go. I shall have more to say to you tomorrow, Rota! [*Exit.*]

ROTA [*shaking his head as he picks up the papers*]: With pleasure? a death-warrant, with pleasure? I would not have had him sign it at that moment, not if it had been for my own son's murderer. – What dreadful words: they burn into my soul! With pleasure! with pleasure! [*Exit.*]

ACT II

Scene: a hall in the Galottis' house

SCENE I

[*Enter from opposite sides* CLAUDIA GALOTTI *and* PIRRO.]

CLAUDIA: Who was that galloping into the courtyard?

PIRRO: The master, madam.

CLAUDIA: My husband? Is it possible?

PIRRO: He will be here any moment.

CLAUDIA: So unexpectedly? – [*Hurrying to meet him*] Ah, my dear husband!

SCENE 2

[*Enter* ODOARDO GALOTTI.]

ODOARDO: Good morning, my love! There, that was a surprise!

CLAUDIA: And of the very pleasantest kind! – If there is no more to it?

ODOARDO: Nothing more! Do not be afraid. The happiness of the day woke me so early, the morning was so fine, and it is such a little way; I thought how busy you would all be here – and it occurred to me how easily you might forget

46

something. In a word: I have just come to see, and I must be off again without delay. Where is Emilia? Busy decking herself out, I suppose?

CLAUDIA: Decking out her soul! She has gone to mass. Today more than any other day, she said, I should be praying for grace from above; and she left everything, and took her veil, and hurried off.

ODOARDO: All alone?

CLAUDIA: Those few steps –

ODOARDO: One is enough to put a foot wrong!

CLAUDIA: Do not be angry, dear husband; come in, and rest for a moment, and have something to refresh you, if you would like it.

ODOARDO: As you think best, Claudia. – But she should not have gone alone.

CLAUDIA: And you, Pirro, stay here in the hall. You are not to admit any callers today. [*Exeunt* CLAUDIA *and* ODOARDO.]

SCENE 3

PIRRO: They only come out of curiosity. The things I have been asked in the last hour! – And who might that be?

ANGELO [*appearing in the wings, in a short cloak which he has drawn up over his face, and with his hat pulled down over his eyes*]: Pirro! – Pirro!

PIRRO: Someone who knows me? [ANGELO *comes onto the stage and throws open his cloak*] Heavens! Angelo? You?

ANGELO: You see it is. I have been creeping round the house long enough hoping for a chance of talking to you. Just one word!

PIRRO: And you dare to show your face again? You were outlawed after that last murder; there is a price on your head –

ANGELO: Which I hope you are not out to earn?

PIRRO: What do you want? Please, you are not going to do anything to me?

ANGELO: What with – this? [*Showing him a purse of money*] Take it! It's yours!

PIRRO: Mine?

ANGELO: Have you forgotten? The German, your last master –

PIRRO: Don't talk about that!

ANGELO: You remember you led him into our trap on the road to Pisa –

PIRRO: Suppose someone heard us!

ANGELO: He was so kind as to leave us a valuable ring as well. Have you forgotten? That ring! It was too valuable for us to turn into money straight away without arousing suspicion. But I've done it at last. I got a hundred pistoles for it; and that's your share. Take it!

PIRRO: I don't want any of it. Keep it all!

ANGELO: Just as you like; if you don't mind risking your neck for nothing – [*Making as if to pocket it again*]

PIRRO: Give it to me, then! [*Takes it.*] And what now? You didn't come to see me just for that.

ANGELO: Why not? You scoundrel! What do you think we are? Do you think we could keep a man's just earnings from him? Perhaps that's the way of honest people, as they call themselves, but it's not ours. Good-bye. [*Turning as if to go, then turning back again*] But one thing you can tell me – Old Galotti came galloping into town there, all alone. What did he want?

PIRRO: Nothing; he just came for the ride. His daughter is marrying Count Appiani this evening, on his estate, where he came from. He can't wait to see it –

ANGELO: And will he be going back there soon?

PIRRO: So soon that he'll find you here if you stay much longer. But you're not planning anything against him? Take care. He's a man –

ANGELO: Don't I know him? Haven't I served under him? As if that meant I could get anything out of him! – When are the young couple going out there?

PIRRO: About midday.

ANGELO: Many with them?

PIRRO: Just one carriage: mother, daughter and the Count. There will be a few friends from Sabionetta as witnesses.

ANGELO: Servants?

PIRRO: Only two; apart from me, riding on ahead.

ANGELO: Good. – One thing more: whose carriage is it? Yours, or the Count's?

PIRRO: The Count's.

ANGELO: Bad! That means another outrider, as well as a hefty coachman. But still –!

PIRRO: I don't understand you! What are you after? The bride might have a few jewels, but they'll hardly be worth the trouble –

ANGELO: Then the bride herself will be!

PIRRO: What? And I'm to be your accomplice again? Not this time!

ANGELO: You are riding on ahead. Ride, then, ride! And stop for nothing!

PIRRO: Never!

ANGELO: What? I do believe you're pretending to have a conscience. – Look here, lad, I think you know me. If you talk! And if one single thing is not exactly as you have told me! –

PIRRO: But, Angelo, for God's sake!

ANGELO: Get out of it if you can! [*Exit.*]

PIRRO: Ah! Let the devil once take hold of you, by a single hair, and you are his for ever! What am I to do?

SCENE 4

[*Re-enter* ODOARDO *and* CLAUDIA.]

ODOARDO: She will be too late to see me –

CLAUDIA: Another moment, Odoardo! She will be so unhappy to have missed you like this.

ODOARDO: I still have to see the Count as well. I can hardly wait to call that fine young man my son. Everything about him delights me. And most of all his resolve to live his own life in the valleys where his fathers lived.

CLAUDIA: It breaks my heart to think of it. Are we to lose her so completely, our dear only daughter?

ODOARDO: What do you call losing her? Knowing that she is in the arms of true love? Do not mistake your own pleasure in her for her happiness. Or you will wake my old suspicion: that it was the noisy distractions of society, it was being near the court, rather than the need to give our daughter a decent education, that made you decide to stay here in the city with her, so far away from a husband and father who loves you so dearly.

CLAUDIA: How unjust, Odoardo! But let me say just one thing for this city, this being near the court, that your strictness finds so hateful. It was only here that love could join together two people who were made for each other: it was only here that the Count could find Emilia – and he found her.

ODOARDO: That I admit. But good Claudia, does that mean you were right, because it has turned out right? I am glad to see the end of this city upbringing. Let us not claim credit for wisdom where we have been no more than fortunate. I am glad it has turned out like this! Now they have found each other, these two who were destined for each other; now let them go wherever innocence and peace may call them. And what should the Count have done if he were to stay here? Bow and flatter and crawl, and try to beat the Marinellis at their own game? all to make himself a fortune he does not need? all to be rewarded with some honour that would be no honour to him? – Pirro!

PIRRO: Here I am.

ODOARDO: Go and lead my horse to the Count's house. I will follow, and mount again there. [*Exit* PIRRO.] Why should the Count be a servant here, when there he can be his own master? And you do not seem to realize, Claudia, that his marrying our daughter will completely ruin him in the Prince's eyes. The Prince hates me –

CLAUDIA: Perhaps less than you fear.

ODOARDO: Fear! That would be something for me to fear!

CLAUDIA: I do not think I told you – that the Prince has met our daughter?

ODOARDO: The Prince? And where was that?

CLAUDIA: At the last soirée at Chancellor Grimaldi's when he honoured us with his presence. He behaved to her so charmingly.

ODOARDO: So charmingly?

CLAUDIA: Talked with her for such a long time –

ODOARDO: Talked with her?

CLAUDIA: Seemed so enchanted by her gaiety and wit –

ODOARDO: So enchanted?

CLAUDIA: Spoke of her beauty with such praise –

ODOARDO: Praise? And all that you tell me in a tone of rapture? Oh, Claudia! vain and foolish mother!

CLAUDIA: What do you mean?

ODOARDO: Never mind, never mind! Now we have come to the end of all that, too. – Ha! when I think – That would be the very place to strike me a fatal blow! – A rake, admiring, lusting – Claudia! Claudia! the mere thought of it sends me flying into a rage. – You should have told me about it straight away. But I do not want to say unkind things to you today. And I should, [*as she takes him by the hand*] if I were to stay any longer. Let me go, then! God speed, Claudia! A safe journey! [*Exit.*]

SCENE 5

CLAUDIA [*alone*]: Such a man! – Oh, what unyielding virtue! – if indeed it deserves that name. Everything is suspect, anything may give offence! Or if that is what is meant by knowing human nature, who would wish to know it? – But I wonder where Emilia is? – He is her father's enemy: and so – and so, if he has an eye for the daughter, must it be just to bring some disgrace on him?

SCENE 6

[*Enter* EMILIA *in anxious confusion.*]

EMILIA: Oh, how good, how good to be back in safety! Or

could he have followed me? [*Throwing back her veil and seeing her mother*] Did he, mother, did he? – No, heaven be praised!

CLAUDIA: What is it, my daughter? What is the matter?

EMILIA: Nothing, nothing –

CLAUDIA: And you look about you so wildly? And you are trembling all over?

EMILIA: Oh, what things to have to listen to! And such a place to have to hear such things!

CLAUDIA: I thought you were in church.

EMILIA: Yes, there of all places! But what does wickedness care for church and altar? Ah, mother! [*Falling into her arms*]

CLAUDIA: Speak, my daughter! Put an end to my fears! What can have happened to you there, in a holy place, that could be so wicked?

EMILIA: Never should my devotions have been more humble and heartfelt than they were to have been today; but never were they so little what they should have been!

CLAUDIA: We are human, Emilia. The gift of prayer is not always in our power. But Heaven will take the will to pray for prayer.

EMILIA: And the will to sin for sin!

CLAUDIA: But that was not my Emilia's will!

EMILIA: No, no, mother; Heaven's grace did not let me fall so low. But another's vice can make us its accomplice, even against our will!

CLAUDIA: Be strong; collect your thoughts as best you can, and tell me what happened.

EMILIA: I had just knelt down – further from the altar than I usually do, for I was late. I was just beginning to offer up my heart to God. But then someone came and knelt down close – so close behind me! I could neither move forwards nor sideways; however much I wanted to, for I feared that another's devotions would disturb me in my own. Devotions! that was the worst I feared. – But it was not long before I heard, close to my ear, – a deep sigh, and then – not the name of any saint, but the name – do not be angry,

mother! – the name of your daughter! My own name! –
Oh, that loud thunderclaps had stopped me from hearing
any more! Whoever it was, he spoke of beauty, of love; –
complained that this day, that should make me happy –
if it should make me happy – would set the seal on his unhappiness for ever! He implored me – I had to listen to all
this. But I did not look round; I tried to pretend that I did
not hear. What else could I do? Beg my good angel to
strike me deaf; yes, even if it must be for ever! That I did
beg; it was the only prayer I could utter. – At last it was
time to stand up again. The service was over. I was terrified
to turn round. I was terrified of setting eyes on the man
who had permitted himself such wicked liberties. And
when I turned round, when I set eyes on him –

CLAUDIA: Who was it, my daughter?

EMILIA: Guess, mother, guess – I thought the ground would
swallow me up – there he was, he himself.

CLAUDIA: Who himself?

EMILIA: The Prince!

CLAUDIA: The Prince! – Oh, blessings on your father's
impatience! He was here, a moment ago, and would not
wait for you!

EMILIA: My father here? And would not wait for me?

CLAUDIA: What if in your confusion you had told him these
things too!

EMILIA: Why, mother? What could he have found in me to
blame?

CLAUDIA: Nothing; no more than in me. And yet, and yet –
Oh, you do not know your father! In his anger he would
have taken the innocent victim of the crime for the criminal.
In his rage he would have held me responsible for something
I could not have prevented, nor even foreseen. – But go on,
my daughter, go on! When you recognized the Prince –
I hope you will have had enough presence of mind to show
him in a single glance all the contempt he deserved.

EMILIA: No, I had not, mother! When I saw who it was I
had not the courage to look at him a second time. I fled –

CLAUDIA: And the Prince followed you –

EMILIA: I did not know that until I reached the porch. I felt someone seize my hand – it was he! For shame I had to stand my ground; if I had tried to struggle free, people would have noticed us. That was the only reflection I was capable of – or the only one I can remember. He spoke; and I answered him. But what he said, and what I answered – if it comes back to me, very well, mother, I will tell you. I cannot remember anything of it now. My senses had taken leave of me. – I cannot think how I escaped from him, and got out of the porch. The first thing I knew was that I was in the street again; then I heard him behind me, drawing nearer; heard him coming into the house with me, climbing the stairs with me –

CLAUDIA: Fear has a sixth sense of its own, my daughter! I shall not forget how you looked as you came rushing in. No, he would not dare to follow you as far as this. – Heavens! if your father knew of it! How furious it made him even to hear that the Prince had met you recently and had not been displeased! But now be calm, my daughter. Think that it was a dream you had. And it will have no more consequence than a dream. Today you will escape all such unwelcome attentions for ever.

EMILIA: But mother, surely the Count must know of it. I must tell him.

CLAUDIA: Not for all the world! Why, what for? Would you rob him of his peace of mind for nothing, yes, for nothing? And if it did not happen straight away – let me tell you, my child, that a poison that does not take effect at once is no less dangerous a poison for that. What makes no impression on the lover can make it on the husband. The lover might even be flattered, to have beaten such a powerful rival; but when once he is beaten – ah, my child, then the lover often becomes quite a different creature. May you have the good fortune never to make that discovery!

EMILIA: Mother, you know how gladly I bow to your better judgement. – But if someone else were to tell him that the Prince had spoken to me today? Would not my silence sooner or later make him more suspicious? I think that I should prefer to have no secrets from him.

CLAUDIA: Weakness! the weakness of love! No, by no means, my daughter. Do not say anything to him. Do not let him notice anything!

EMILIA: Very well, mother. I am sure you know what is best. – Ah! [*With a deep breath*] And I begin to feel quite at ease again. What a foolish, timid creature I am! Am I not, mother? I might well have behaved differently, but whatever had happened I should not have forgiven myself.

CLAUDIA: I did not want to say that to you, my daughter, before you had heard it from your own good sense. And I knew you would realize it as soon as you were yourself again. – The Prince is full of gallantries. You are not familiar enough with the meaningless language of gallantry. It turns a courtesy into a deep feeling; a flattery into a promise; a whim into a desire; a desire into a resolution. It can make nothing sound like the whole world; it can say the whole world, and mean nothing at all.

EMILIA: Oh, mother! You make my fears seem quite absurd. Now I promise you he shall hear nothing of it, my good Appiani! He might well think me more vain than I was virtuous. – But now I think he is here himself! That is his footstep.

SCENE 7

[*Enter* APPIANI, *pensive and with downcast eyes. He approaches without noticing them until* EMILIA *rushes to greet him.*]

APPIANI: Ah, my dearest! I did not expect to see you here in the hall.

EMILIA: I would have you cheerful, signor Count, even when you are not expecting to see me. So solemn? so serious? Is not this day worth a little joy and gaiety?

APPIANI: It is worth more than all the rest of my life. But pregnant with such happiness for me – perhaps it is this very happiness that makes me so serious, makes me so solemn, as you call it, my dear Emilia. [*Seeing her mother*] Ah, you too, madam! You whom soon I am to honour with a dearer name!

CLAUDIA: It will be my greatest pride! – How happy you must be, Emilia! Why would not your father stay and share our delight?

APPIANI: I have only this moment torn myself from his company; or rather he has torn himself from mine. My dearest Emilia, what a man your father is! The image of all manly virtues! What aspirations fill my soul in his presence! My resolve always to be noble and good is never stronger than when I see him, than when I think of him. And how other than with the fulfilment of that resolve can I make myself worthy of the honour of being called his son; of being yours, my Emilia!

EMILIA: And he would not wait for me!

APPIANI: I believe because his Emilia would have moved him more deeply, have taken possession of his soul more completely than would be right on such a fleeting visit.

CLAUDIA: He thought you would be busy with your wedding-dress; and heard –

APPIANI: What I have since heard from him with the most affectionate admiration. – It is right and proper, my Emilia! My wife will be truly pious, but not one to make a show of her piety.

CLAUDIA: But, children, are you forgetting? Time is flying; come along, Emilia!

APPIANI: What do you mean, madam?

CLAUDIA: But signor Count, you are not going to lead her to the altar like that, just as she is?

APPIANI: Indeed, I had not noticed until now! Who can set eyes on you, Emilia, and have a thought to spare for finery? – And why not just as she is?

EMILIA: No, my dear Count, not like this; not just like this. But not very much more in the way of finery; not very much. A moment, and I shall be ready! None of my jewels, no, none of them, those last presents of your extravagant generosity! And nothing, nothing at all, that could only be worn with jewels like that! – I could bear them a grudge, those jewels, if they had not come from you. For three times I have dreamt of them –

CLAUDIA: You did not say a word of this to me.

EMILIA: I dreamt I was wearing them, and suddenly all the stones, every one, turned into pearls. But pearls, mother, pearls mean tears.

CLAUDIA: Child! Your meaning is more of a dream than the dream itself. Did you not always like pearls more than precious stones?

EMILIA: Yes, mother, yes –

APPIANI [*thoughtfully and in a melancholy tone*]: Mean tears – mean tears!

EMILIA: What? Does it seem strange to you, too? You?

APPIANI: Why, yes; I ought to be ashamed. But when once our imagination is attuned to sad thoughts –

EMILIA: And why should it be? – But guess what I thought I would wear. What was I wearing, how did I look, when first you noticed me? Do you remember?

APPIANI: Do I remember? In my mind's eye I never see you otherwise; to me you are the same, even when I see you are not the same.

EMILIA: Then a dress of that same colour and that same cut: full and free –

APPIANI: Excellent!

EMILIA: And my hair –

APPIANI: In its own beautiful brown, in the curling locks that nature gave it –

EMILIA: Not forgetting the rose! Yes, yes! A moment's patience, and you shall see me like that before you! [*Exit.*]

SCENE 8

APPIANI [*with a gloomy air, following her with his eyes*]: Pearls mean tears! – A moment's patience! – Yes, if time would only leave us untouched! If it were not so, that a minute on the clock-face could stretch out to years within us!

CLAUDIA: Emilia's observation, signor Count, was as prompt as it was just. You are more serious than usual today. Only one step from the goal of your desires – do you regret, signor count, that you set yourself that goal?

APPIANI: Oh, mother, how can you entertain such suspicions of your son? Yet it is true; I do feel unusually sad and gloomy today. But you see, madam, – if one is still one step from one's goal – in the end it is no better than if one had never even set out. Everything I have seen, everything I have heard, everything I have dreamt, since yesterday and before, has proclaimed this truth to me. This one thought links itself to every other that I summon, or that forces itself upon me. What does it mean? I do not understand it.

CLAUDIA: Signor Count, you disturb me –

APPIANI: One thing after another! I am irritated; irritated by my friends, irritated by myself –

CLAUDIA: How?

APPIANI: My friends absolutely insist on my telling the Prince about my marriage before it takes place. They admit that I do not have to do so; but they say that respect for him demands no less. And I have been weak enough to promise them that I will. I was on the point of driving to see him now.

CLAUDIA [*taken aback*]: To see the Prince?

SCENE 9

[*Enter* PIRRO.]

PIRRO: Madam, Marquis Marinelli has stopped in front of the house and is asking for the Count.

APPIANI: For me?

PIRRO: Here he is. [*Exit, after opening the door for* MARINELLI.]

MARINELLI: I beg your pardon, madam. Count, I went to your house, and was told that I should find you here. I have urgent business with you. – Madam, again I beg your pardon; it will be over in a few minutes.

CLAUDIA: I will not make it last any longer. [*Exit, with a bow to him.*]

SCENE 10

APPIANI: Well, sir?

MARINELLI: I come from his highness the Prince.

APPIANI: I am at his service.

MARINELLI: I am proud to be the bearer of such an exceptional honour. – And if Count Appiani will not refuse to recognize in me one of his most devoted friends –

APPIANI: No more preliminaries, I beg you.

MARINELLI: Very well. In connexion with his forthcoming marriage to the Princess of Massa, the Prince has to send an ambassador immediately to negotiate with the Duke, her father. He was long undecided whom he should name for this office. At last, Count, his choice has fallen on you.

APPIANI: On me?

MARINELLI: And – if friendship may be permitted to boast – not without my intercession –

APPIANI: Indeed you embarrass me, if I am to thank you for it. I have long ceased to think that the Prince would ever find any use for my services.

MARINELLI: I am assured that it has simply been for lack of a suitable occasion. And if this should not seem adequate to the dignity of a man such as Count Appiani, then I must admit that my friendship has been over-hasty.

APPIANI: Friendship, friendship, can you not say three words without it? Who is it then that I am talking to? I would never have dreamt that Marquis Marinelli was any friend of mine.

MARINELLI: I acknowledge that I have wronged you, Count, wronged you unforgivably, in not asking your permission to be your friend. But leaving that aside: what does it matter? The Prince's favour, the honour offered to you, remain what they are, and I do not doubt that you will be delighted to accept.

APPIANI [*after pausing to consider*]: Yes, I accept.

MARINELLI: Come, then.

APPIANI: Where?

MARINELLI: To the Prince, at Dosalo. Everything is in readiness, and you must be on your way today.

APPIANI: What did you say? Today?

MARINELLI: And rather this very hour than the next. It is a matter of the greatest urgency.

APPIANI: Indeed? Then I am afraid that I must decline the honour which the Prince has in mind for me.

MARINELLI: What do you mean?

APPIANI: I cannot leave today; nor tomorrow; nor even the day after that.

MARINELLI: You are joking, Count.

APPIANI: With you?

MARINELLI: Incomparable! If the joke is at the Prince's expense, then it is all the more amusing. – You cannot?

APPIANI: No, sir, no. And I hope that the Prince himself will admit the validity of my excuse.

MARINELLI: I am very curious to hear it.

APPIANI: That is easily done. You see, today I am going to be married.

MARINELLI: Well? and what then?

APPIANI: What then? what then? Your question, sir, is confoundedly naïve.

MARINELLI: It has been known, Count, for weddings to be postponed. True, I do not believe it is always in the best interests of the bride or the bridegroom. It may well cause inconvenience. But yet, I should have thought, our master's command –

APPIANI: Our master's command? our master's? A master one chooses to serve is not a master in that sense. I admit that you owe unquestioning obedience to the Prince. But I do not. I came to his court of my own free will. I sought the honour of serving him; but I did not come to be his slave. I am the vassal of a greater master –

MARINELLI: Greater or lesser: a master is a master.

APPIANI: I do not wish to dispute the matter with you. Enough; tell the Prince what I have said: that I regret I am unable to accept this honour, since this very day I am about to seal a bond on which my whole future happiness depends.

MARINELLI: Will you not even tell him with whom?

APPIANI: With Emilia Galotti.

MARINELLI: The daughter of this house?

APPIANI: Of this house.

MARINELLI: Hm! hm!

APPIANI: What is it?

MARINELLI: I should have been of the opinion that in these circumstances there could be even less objection to postponing the ceremony until after your return.

APPIANI: The ceremony? And is it only the ceremony?

MARINELLI: Her good parents will not be so pernickety.

APPIANI: Her good parents?

MARINELLI: And Emilia will still be well and truly yours.

APPIANI: Well and truly? well and truly? Why, sir, you with your well and truly are – well and truly, a despicable dog!

MARINELLI: You say that to me, Count?

APPIANI: And why not?

MARINELLI: Heaven and hell! You shall hear more of this.

APPIANI: Pah! A spiteful cur, but –

MARINELLI: Death and damnation! Count, I demand satisfaction.

APPIANI: Certainly.

MARINELLI: And I would seek it this very moment; only I do not want to spoil the tender bridegroom's day for him.

APPIANI: How considerate! Oh, no, sir, no! [*Seizing him by the hand*] I am not going to have myself sent to Massa today, it is true; but I have plenty of time to take a walk with you. Come along, come along!

MARINELLI [*wrenching himself free*]: Patience, Count, patience! [*Exit.*]

SCENE 11

APPIANI [*alone*]: Go, you scoundrel! – Ha, that has done me good! It set my blood racing. I feel a different and a better man.

[*Enter* CLAUDIA, *anxious and in haste.*]

CLAUDIA: Heavens, signor Count, I heard sharp words being spoken. And your face is burning. What has happened?

APPIANI: Nothing, madam, nothing at all. Chamberlain

Marinelli did me a great service. He has made it unnecessary for me to go to the Prince.

CLAUDIA: Can it be true?

APPIANI: Now we can start so much the sooner. I will go and stir up my men; I shall be back in a moment. Emilia will be ready by then too.

CLAUDIA: And I need have no anxiety, Count?

APPIANI: None at all, madam. [*Exeunt: he goes out of the house,* CLAUDIA *withdraws.*]

ACT III

Scene: an entrance-hall in the Prince's hunting-lodge

SCENE I

[*The* PRINCE *and* MARINELLI *in conversation.*]

MARINELLI: It was useless: the honour that was offered to him he contemptuously rejected.

PRINCE: And that was that? So it will happen? So Emilia will be his today?

MARINELLI: It looks very much like it.

PRINCE: I thought nothing more would come of your ideas! And who knows what a ridiculous figure you have been cutting! Even if a fool sometimes gives good advice, it takes a clever man to carry it out. I ought to have remembered that.

MARINELLI: This is a fine reward for my pains!

PRINCE: For what pains?

MARINELLI: For my willingness to risk my life over this affair as well. When I saw that neither earnest nor mockery could make the Count put his honour before his love, I tried to provoke him. I said things to him which made him forget himself. He insulted me; I demanded satisfaction – and demanded it on the spot. I thought – it will be one or the other of us. If he is killed, the field is ours. If I am –

why then, he will have to flee, and the Prince will at least have gained time.

PRINCE: Would you have done that, Marinelli?

MARINELLI: Ah! one ought to know beforehand, if one is fool enough to be willing to sacrifice oneself for the great – one ought to know beforehand how much recognition to expect.

PRINCE: And the Count? He has the reputation of not easily standing for that sort of thing.

MARINELLI: That depends, no doubt. Who can blame him? He replied that he had more important things to do than break his neck with me. And so he put me off until a week after his wedding.

PRINCE: To Emilia Galotti! The thought of it drives me mad! – And so you agreed, and left him; and come back here and boast of how you have risked your life for me, sacrificed yourself for me –

MARINELLI: But sir, what more would you have had me do?

PRINCE: What more? – As if he had done anything at all!

MARINELLI: And tell me too, sir, what you have achieved in your own cause. You were fortunate enough to snatch a few words with her in church; what rendezvous have you made with her?

PRINCE [*scornfully*]: Curiosity in plenty! And all I have to do is satisfy it. – Oh, everything went as I had wished it. You need trouble yourself no further, my busy friend! She came more than half-way to meet my desires. I should simply have brought her away with me on the spot! [*Coldly and imperiously*] Now you know what you wanted to know, and you may go!

MARINELLI: And you may go! Yes, yes, that's the end of the song. And it would still be the same, even if I were to attempt the impossible. Did I say the impossible? Well, it might not be so impossible; daring, yes. – If we had the bride in our power: then I guarantee you that there would be no wedding.

PRINCE: Guarantee! whatever next? Now I suppose I need only give him a company of my bodyguard, and he will go and lie in ambush by the highway, and jump out himself and attack the carriage – with a mere fifty men to help him – and carry off the girl and bring her to me in triumph.

MARINELLI: A girl has been abducted by force before now without its having looked like a forcible abduction.

PRINCE: If you knew how to do it, you would not be standing here all this time gossiping about it.

MARINELLI: But one should not be asked to guarantee the outcome. There might be an accident –

PRINCE: And I am in the habit of holding people responsible for things that are not their fault!

MARINELLI: Then, sir – [*A shot is heard in the distance.*] Ha! what was that? Did I hear aright? – Did you not hear a shot, sir? – And another!

PRINCE: What is it? What is happening?

MARINELLI: What do you think? Suppose I had done more than you give me credit for?

PRINCE: More? Then tell me –

MARINELLI: In short: what I spoke of is happening.

PRINCE: Is it possible?

MARINELLI: But do not forget, your highness, what you just assured me. I have your repeated word –

PRINCE: But everything has been arranged –

MARINELLI: Down to the last detail! The execution of the plan is in the hands of men I can rely on. The road goes close by the fence that encircles the park. There some of them will have attacked the carriage as if to rob it. And the others, with one of my servants among them, will have rushed out of the park as if to help the victims of the attack. They will all make a show of fighting, and then my servant will seize Emilia, pretending to be rescuing her, and bring her through the park to the palace. That is what we have agreed. What do you say now, your highness?

PRINCE: This is a strange surprise! And I suddenly feel so nervous – [MARINELLI *goes to the window.*] What are you looking for?

MARINELLI: It must be in that direction. Yes! there is already a masked man galloping along by the fence; coming to report to me, without a doubt. Go into one of the other rooms, sir!

PRINCE: Ah, Marinelli –

MARINELLI: Well? Now I suppose I have done too much, and just now it was too little?

PRINCE: No, not that. But for all this I cannot see –

MARINELLI: See? Wait and see when it is done! Quickly, go into one of the other rooms; the man must not see you. [*Exit the* PRINCE.]

SCENE 2

MARINELLI [*going to the window again*]: There is the carriage, going slowly back to town. So slowly? And a servant at every window? Those are unwelcome signs: signs that the plan only half worked – that it is a wounded man they are carrying back so gently, not a dead one. – The rider is dismounting. It is Angelo himself. Foolhardy! But he knows the paths about here. He is waving to me. He must be sure of his errand. Aha, signor Count, you did not want to go to Massa, but now you have a longer journey to make! Who taught you what dogs were like? [*Going to the door*] They can be well and truly spiteful. [*Enter* ANGELO.] Well, Angelo?

ANGELO [*unmasking*]: Look out, my lord chamberlain! They will be here with her any minute now.

MARINELLI: And how did it go, apart from that?

ANGELO: Well, I think.

MARINELLI: What about the Count?

ANGELO: At your service! – But he must have got wind of it. He was readier for us than we expected.

MARINELLI: Quickly, tell me what you have to tell me! Is he dead?

ANGELO: My heart bleeds for the good gentleman.

MARINELLI: There then, for your tender heart! [*Gives him a purse of money.*]

ANGELO: And my brave Nicolo too! He had to sing for our supper.

MARINELLI: So there were losses on both sides?

ANGELO: I could weep for him, the honest lad! Although I get another quarter of that [*weighing the purse in his hand*] on account of his death. I am his heir, you see; because I avenged him. That's our rule; and as good a rule, I think, as ever was made for loyalty and friendship. This Nicolo, my lord chamberlain –

MARINELLI: Damn your Nicolo! The Count, the Count –

ANGELO: By thunder! the Count had let him have it. So I let the Count have it too! He dropped; and he may have got back into the carriage alive, but I promise you he'll not get out of it alive again.

MARINELLI: If only we can be sure of that, Angelo.

ANGELO: If it's not certain, then may I lose your custom! But was there anything else, sir? I have the longest way to go; we all want to be across the frontier before nightfall.

MARINELLI: On your way, then.

ANGELO: If there should be anything else, my lord chamberlain – then you know where to find me. Anything another man will take on, I shan't need witchcraft for either; and you'll find me cheaper than all the rest. [*Exit.*]

MARINELLI: Good! But no, not quite as good as it should be. For shame, Angelo! to be such a bungler! He would have been worth another shot. And perhaps he is now suffering agonies, the poor Count! For shame, Angelo! I call that doing the job with unnecessary cruelty; and making a botch of it. – But the Prince must not hear anything of that yet. Let him first find out for himself just how convenient this fatal accident is for him. – Fatal! what would I not give to be sure of it!

SCENE 3

[*Enter the* PRINCE.]

PRINCE: Here she comes, up the avenue, hurrying on ahead of the servant. Fear seems to give her feet wings. She cannot suspect anything yet. She thinks she is only escaping from highwaymen. But how long can it last?

MARINELLI: But for the moment, we have her.

PRINCE: And will not her mother come to look for her? Will not the Count be following her? And then shall we be any further forward? How can I keep her from them?

MARINELLI: For these questions I must admit I have as yet no answers. But we shall have to be patient, sir. The first step had to be taken.

PRINCE: What use was it if we have to take it back?

MARINELLI: Perhaps we shall not have to. There are a thousand things to be going on with. And have you forgotten the most important thing of all?

PRINCE: How can I have forgotten what I am sure I have not yet thought of? The most important? What is that?

MARINELLI: The art of pleasing, of persuading – the art a prince in love can never lack.

PRINCE: Can never lack? Except just when he needs it most urgently. I have already made one all too unsuccessful trial of that art today. With all my flatteries and protestations I could not draw a single word from her. She stood there silent and cowed and trembling, like a criminal hearing the death-sentence. Her terror infected me; I began to tremble too, and in the end I begged her to forgive me. I scarcely trust myself to speak to her again. At all events I dare not let her find me here when she arrives. You must receive her, Marinelli. I shall be here close at hand listening to what happens, and I will return when I have collected my wits a little more. [*Exit.*]

SCENE 4

MARINELLI [*alone*]: If she did not see it happen herself – And she cannot have done, coming away in such a hurry. Here she is. I do not want to be the first thing that meets her eye here, either. [*He retires into a corner.*]

[*Enter* BATTISTA *with* EMILIA.]

BATTISTA: Come in here, miss.

EMILIA [*breathlessly*]: Ah! ah! Thank you, my friend, thank you. But oh, heavens, where am I? And all alone? Where is my mother? And the Count? But they are following, of course? Following directly in my footsteps?

BATTISTA: I expect so, miss.

EMILIA: You expect so? You do not know? You did not see them? And did I not hear a shot behind us?

BATTISTA: A shot? No, surely not!

EMILIA: Yes, I am certain I did! And the Count will have been hit, or my mother.

BATTISTA: I will go and look for them straight away.

EMILIA: But not without me. I want to come with you, I must come with you; let us go, my friend!

MARINELLI [coming forward suddenly to join them, as if he had just entered]: Ah, my dear young lady! What misfortune, or rather what good fortune – what fortunate misfortune brings us the honour –

EMILIA [taken aback]: What? You here, my lord? Then this must be your house? Excuse me, my lord chamberlain. We were attacked by robbers not far from here. Then some good people came to our aid; and this honest fellow lifted me out of the carriage and brought me here. But it frightens me to see that I am the only one to be saved. My mother is still in danger. I even heard a shot behind us. Perhaps she has been killed; and I am still alive? – Forgive me. I must go – I must go back – where I should have stayed.

MARINELLI: Calm yourself, my dear young lady. There is no need to worry; they will soon be with you, your loved ones for whom you fear so tenderly. Meanwhile, Battista, go, hurry; they may very well not realize where the young lady is. They may very well be looking for her in one of the farm buildings. Bring them here without delay. [Exit BATTISTA.]

EMILIA: You are sure? They are all in safety? Has nothing happened to them? – Oh, what a fearful day this day has been for me! – But I ought not to be staying here; I ought to be hurrying to meet them –

MARINELLI: What for, my dear young lady? You are quite exhausted and out of breath as it is. Recover yourself, rather, and let me show you to a room where you will be more comfortable. I will wager that the Prince himself is already attending to your dear mother, and bringing the good lady to you.

EMILIA: Who, did you say?

MARINELLI: Our gracious Prince himself.

EMILIA [*with extreme alarm*]: The Prince?

MARINELLI: As soon as he heard the news he flew to your aid. He is furious that these fellows should have dared to commit such a crime so near to his presence – why, almost under his very nose. He has given orders for them to be hunted down, and when they are caught their punishment will be the severest imaginable.

EMILIA: The Prince! Where am I then?

MARINELLI: At Dosalo, the Prince's hunting-lodge.

EMILIA: What a strange coincidence! – And you think he might be here himself at any moment? But surely my mother will be with him?

MARINELLI: Here he is already.

SCENE 5

[*Enter the* PRINCE.]

PRINCE: Where is she? where? Dearest, loveliest young lady, we have been looking for you everywhere. You are well? Then all is well! The Count, your mother –

EMILIA: Oh, your highness, where are they? where is my mother?

PRINCE: Not far off; here, close at hand.

EMILIA: Oh, heavens, in what condition may I find them – the one or the other? Oh, surely! For you are keeping it from me, my lord, I can see you are keeping something from me –

PRINCE: No, no, dear young lady. Give me your arm and come with me, and do not be afraid.

EMILIA [*undecided*]: But if nothing has happened to them, if all my forebodings are groundless – then why are they not here yet? Why were they not with you, your highness?

PRINCE: Come quickly, and you will see all these terrors disappear at once.

EMILIA [*wringing her hands*]: What am I to do?

PRINCE: But dear young lady, I hope you do not suspect me in any way?

EMILIA [*falling on her knees before him*]: On my knees, your highness –

PRINCE [*lifting her up*]: You put me to shame. Yes, Emilia, I deserve your silent reproach. My behaviour this morning cannot be excused – at most forgiven. Pardon my weakness. I should never have sought to disturb you with confessions which can never bring me any advantage. And the shocked silence in which you listened to them, or rather did not listen to them, was sufficient punishment for me. And even if this coincidence, that once more, before all my hopes are dashed for ever – once more brings me the good fortune of seeing you and speaking to you – even if I could think that this coincidence was a hint of a kinder fate in store for me – think that my final condemnation had been miraculously postponed so that I might once again implore clemency; still, my dearest young lady – do not tremble! – still I should wait entirely upon your glance. Not a word, not a sigh will I utter that might offend you. Only do not slight me with mistrust. Only do not doubt for a moment that your power over me is absolute. Only do not ever believe that you need any other protection against me. And now come, my dear Emilia, come where joys await you which will meet with your better approval. – Follow us, Marinelli. [*He leads* EMILIA *off, despite her evident unwillingness.*]

MARINELLI: Follow us. – Which is as much as to say, do not follow us! And why indeed should I follow them? Let him see how far he can get with her alone. All I need do is see that no one disturbs them. The Count – I do not think is likely to. But her mother, her mother! I should be very surprised if she calmly went off and left her daughter to her fate.

SCENE 6

[*Enter* BATTISTA *in great haste.*]

MARINELLI: Well, Battista, what is it?

BATTISTA: The mother, my lord chamberlain –

MARINELLI: I thought as much! Where is she?

BATTISTA: If you don't stop her she will be here this very moment. I never intended to look for her – I knew you did not mean that order seriously; but then I heard her shrieking in the distance. She's on her daughter's track, and I only hope she's not on the track of the whole plot! She has collected all the people she can find in these lonely parts, and every one of them is all too willing to show her the way. Whether they have already told her that the Prince is here, that you are here, I don't know. What are you going to do?

MARINELLI: Let me see! [*Pondering*] Not let her in, when she knows that her daughter is here? That will not do. True, her eyes will pop when she sees the wolf already sniffing round the lamb. – Her eyes? I expect we can bear that much. But heaven be merciful to our ears! – Well, and what of that? The best lungs run out of breath; even a woman's! They all stop screaming when they cannot keep it up any longer. And, what is more, the mother is after all the very one we want to win over to our side. If I know mothers, most of them are flattered to find themselves a prince's mother-in-law – or something of the kind. Let her come, Battista, let her come!

BATTISTA: Listen! listen!

CLAUDIA [*offstage*]: Emilia! Emilia! My child! Where are you?

MARINELLI: Go, Battista, and just try to get rid of her inquisitive companions.

SCENE 7

[*As* BATTISTA *is about to leave, enter* CLAUDIA.]

CLAUDIA: Aha! This is the one that lifted her out of the carriage! This is the one that carried her off! Yes, I know you! Where is she? Speak, wretch!

BATTISTA: Is that all the thanks I get?

CLAUDIA: Why, if it is thanks you deserve [*in a gentler tone*] then forgive me, honest fellow! Where is she? Do not keep her from me any longer! Where is she?

BATTISTA: Oh, your ladyship, she could not be safer in the lap of the angels. My master here will take your ladyship to her. [*To a crowd of people who are trying to follow her in*] Back there, you! [*Exit.*]

SCENE 8

CLAUDIA: Your master? [*She sees* MARINELLI *and starts back*] Ha! Is that your master? You here, sir? And this is where my daughter is? And it is you, you who are to take me to her?

MARINELLI: With the greatest of pleasure, madam.

CLAUDIA: Stop! I remember – It was you, was it not? You that came to my house this morning to see the Count? that I left alone with him? that he had a quarrel with?

MARINELLI: Quarrel? Not that I am aware of; a few unimportant words over some business of the Prince's –

CLAUDIA: And your name is Marinelli?

MARINELLI: Marquis Marinelli.

CLAUDIA: Then I am right! Listen, signor Marquis. Marinelli – the name Marinelli, accompanied by a curse – No, I must not slander the noble man! There was no curse – the curse I am imagining; the name Marinelli was the last word the Count spoke before he died!

MARINELLI: Before he died? the Count? Count Appiani? You hear, madam, which of all your strange words I find the most remarkable. Before he died? the Count? What else it is you are trying to say I do not understand.

CLAUDIA [*slowly and bitterly*]: The name Marinelli was the last word the Count spoke before he died! Now do you understand? I did not understand it either at first; although the voice in which he said it – that voice! I can hear it now! Where were my senses that I did not understand it at once, that voice?

MARINELLI: Well, madam? I have always been a friend of the Count's; indeed his most intimate friend. Why then, if he named me with his dying breath –

CLAUDIA: In that voice? I cannot imitate it; I cannot describe it; but everything was in it! everything! What? Robbers, were they, that attacked us? Murderers they were, hired murderers! And Marinelli was the last word the Count spoke before he died – and in that voice!

MARINELLI: In that voice? I never heard of such a thing! To found on a tone of voice, heard in a moment of terror, an accusation against an honest man!

CLAUDIA: Oh, would that I could call it to witness, that voice! But what next! It is making me forget my daughter. Where is she? What? dead too? Was it my daughter's fault that Appiani was your enemy?

MARINELLI: I forgive a mother's anxiety. Come with me, madam; your daughter is here, in one of the nearby rooms, and I hope that she will soon have quite recovered from her shock. The Prince himself is waiting on her most attentively –

CLAUDIA: Who? Who himself?

MARINELLI: The Prince.

CLAUDIA: The Prince? Did I hear you say the Prince? our Prince?

MARINELLI: What other?

CLAUDIA: Why then – Oh, wretched mother that I am! And her father! her father! He will curse the day she was born. He will curse me.

MARINELLI: In heaven's name, madam! What are you saying?

CLAUDIA: It is plain to see! Is it not? Today, in church! before the eyes of the Most Pure, in the presence of the Almighty! there the villainy began, there it showed itself in its true colours! [*Confronting* MARINELLI] Ah, murderer, vile, cowardly murderer! Not brave enough to murder with your own hand; but despicable enough to murder – to hire a murderer – to satisfy another's lust! Scum of all murderers! No honest murderer would be seen in your company. You! You! For why should I not spit all my gall, all my venom into your face with a single word? You – you procurer!

MARINELLI: My good lady, these are wild imaginings. But at least moderate your screaming, and remember where you are.

CLAUDIA: Where I am? Remember where I am? Take the lioness's cubs away from her, and will she care whose forest it is she fills with her roaring?

EMILIA [*offstage*]: Ah, my mother! I can hear my mother!

CLAUDIA: Her voice? Yes, it is! She has heard me, she has heard me. And you would have me stop my screaming? Where are you, my child? I am coming, I am coming! [*She rushes into* EMILIA'*s room, with* MARINELLI *following her.*]

ACT IV

Scene: the same

SCENE I

[*Enter from* EMILIA'*s room the* PRINCE *and* MARINELLI.]

PRINCE: Come, Marinelli! I must recover my wits, and you must enlighten me.

MARINELLI: Oh, such maternal rage! Ha! ha! ha!

PRINCE: You laugh?

MARINELLI: Prince, if you had seen the mother's frenzied behaviour, here in the entrance-hall – you must have heard her screaming! – and then how tame she suddenly became the moment she caught sight of you – ha! ha! I know very well there is no mother who will scratch a prince's eyes out just for taking a liking to her daughter.

PRINCE: You are a poor observer. The daughter collapsed senseless in her mother's arms. That was what made the mother forget her rage, not her seeing me. It was for her daughter's sake, not mine, that she did not say louder and more clearly – something I would rather not have heard and do not want to understand.

MARINELLI: What was that, your highness?

PRINCE: Why the pretence? Out with it! Is it true, or is it not true?

MARINELLI: What if it were?

PRINCE: What if it were? Then it is? He is dead? dead? [*Threateningly*] Marinelli! Marinelli!

MARINELLI: Well?

PRINCE: By God! by Almighty God! I am innocent of this blood. If you had told me before that it would cost the Count his life – no, no! even if it had cost me my own!

MARINELLI: If I had told you before? As if his death had been any part of my plan! I had made it absolutely clear to Angelo that no harm should come to anyone. And it would all have gone off without any violence whatever, had not the Count been the first to employ it. He shot down one of my men, point-blank.

PRINCE: Indeed; he ought to have understood a joke!

MARINELLI: That Angelo then flew into a rage, and avenged his companion's death –

PRINCE: Was of course entirely natural!

MARINELLI: I have spoken to him about it.

PRINCE: Spoken to him? How kind of you! Warn him never to let me catch him in my dominions. I might speak somewhat less kindly to him.

MARINELLI: Very well! Myself, Angelo; intention, chance – it is all the same. I might point out that it was agreed upon beforehand, that it was promised beforehand, that I should not be held responsible for any accident that might happen in the course of the enterprise –

PRINCE: Might happen, did you say, or – would happen?

MARINELLI: Better than ever! But before your highness tells me in a word what you think of me, may I make one observation? The Count's death is anything but a matter of indifference to me. I had challenged him; he had still to give me satisfaction; he has left this world without so doing, and there remains a stain upon my honour. Granted that in any other circumstances your suspicions of my conduct might be justified – can they possibly be in this case? [*With a show of anger*] Any man who can think that of me –

PRINCE [*in a conciliatory manner*]: Very well, very well –

MARINELLI: I wish he were still alive! Oh, I wish that he were still alive! Anything, anything in the world I would give for that – [*bitterly*] even the favour of my prince, that inestimable favour, never lightly to be thrown away; even that I would give!

PRINCE: I understand. Very well, very well. His death was a chance, a mere coincidence. You assure me it was; and I, I believe you. But who else will? The mother? Emilia? The world?

MARINELLI [*coldly*]: Hardly.

PRINCE: And if no one will believe it, what will they believe? You shrug your shoulders? They will think your man Angelo was the instrument, and I the guilty one.

MARINELLI [*still more coldly*]: Very likely.

PRINCE: I! I myself! Or from this moment I must give up every design on Emilia –

MARINELLI [*with complete indifference*]: Which you would also have had to do if the Count were still alive.

PRINCE [*furiously, but immediately regaining his self-control*]: Marinelli! – But you shall not make me lose my temper. So be it, so it is! And what you are telling me is simply this: the Count's death is a piece of good luck for me – the best piece of luck I could have – the only piece of luck that could be of any service to my love. And since it is that, then – why worry how it may have come about? One count more or less in the world –! Is that how you would have me think? Very well, then! A bargain! I am not afraid of a little crime either. But, my friend, it must be a quiet little crime, a nice tidy little crime. And you see, that was just what ours has not been: neither quiet nor tidy. Yes, it has cleared the way, but it has barred it at the same time. Every-one will accuse us to our faces – and unfortunately it was not even we who did it! And all that, is it not, is because of your wise and wonderful plan?

MARINELLI: If it please your highness –

PRINCE: What else? Speak! I demand it!

MARINELLI: I find items being charged to my account that do not belong there.

PRINCE: Speak, I say!

MARINELLI: Very well then! What part of my plan was it that will cause such obvious suspicion to fall on the Prince in this matter? I will tell you: it was the master-stroke with which he himself was graciously pleased to interfere in my arrangements.

PRINCE: I?

MARINELLI: May I be permitted to tell you that the step you took this morning in the church – with whatever circumspection it was taken – however irresistibly you were driven to take it – that that step was nevertheless no part of this particular dance.

PRINCE: What difference did it make?

MARINELLI: Well, it may not have spoilt the whole dance; but it has for the moment put us on the wrong foot.

PRINCE: Hm! Do I understand you?

MARINELLI: Briefly and simply, then. Is it not a fact that when I undertook this affair, Emilia knew nothing of the Prince's love? And Emilia's mother even less. What if now I built upon that fact? and the Prince meanwhile was undermining the foundations of my building?

PRINCE [striking his forehead]: Damnation!

MARINELLI: If he himself betrayed what his intentions were?

PRINCE: Cursed folly!

MARINELLI: And if he had not betrayed them himself? Then indeed I should like to know how my plan could have in any way led mother or daughter to suspect him in the slightest?

PRINCE: Oh, you are right!

MARINELLI: Which of course puts me in the wrong. You will forgive me, sir –

SCENE 2

[*Enter* BATTISTA *in haste.*]

BATTISTA: The Countess has just arrived.

PRINCE: The Countess? What Countess?

BATTISTA: Orsina.

PRINCE: Orsina? – Marinelli! – Orsina? – Marinelli!

MARINELLI: I am no less astonished than you are yourself.

PRINCE: Go, Battista, hurry; do not let her get out of her carriage. I am not at home. I am not at home to her. She must return to town immediately. Go, quickly! [*Exit* BATTISTA.] What does she want, the foolish woman? What is this liberty she is taking? How does she know that we are here? Perhaps she has come to spy us out? Perhaps she has already heard some rumour? Marinelli! – speak, answer, will you! – Is he offended now, the man who claims to be my friend? Offended by nothing but a few wretched hasty words? Must I beg him to forgive me?

MARINELLI: Ah, prince, as soon as you are yourself again, then I am yours again, heart and soul! – Orsina's coming here is a riddle to me just as it is to you. But we shall scarcely be able to turn her away. What do you propose to do?

PRINCE: On no account speak to her; hide from her –

MARINELLI: Good! Do so, then, quickly. I will receive her –

PRINCE: But only to send her away again. Do not have any further dealings with her. We have other things to do.

MARINELLI: Come, come, your highness! Those other things are done already. Courage! What still has to come will come of its own accord, be sure of that. – But can I not hear her already? Hurry, your highness! In there [*pointing to a small side-chamber, into which the* PRINCE *retires*] if you wish, you will be able to hear us. – I am afraid, I am afraid, she could hardly have picked a worse hour for her call.

SCENE 3

[*Enter* ORSINA.]

ORSINA [*not at first noticing* MARINELLI]: What is this? No one comes to meet me, only an impertinent wretch who would rather have turned me away? But am I at Dosalo? The same Dosalo where in days gone by a whole army of eager servants would rush to meet me? where love and untold joy used always to await me? The same place it is; but – but! – Ah, there, Marinelli! I am glad the Prince has brought you with him. – No, I am not glad! What matters I had to discuss with him, I had to discuss with him alone. Where is he?

MARINELLI: The Prince, my dear Countess?

ORSINA: Whom else should I mean?

MARINELLI: You think that he is here? know that he is here? – He at all events is not expecting Countess Orsina.

ORSINA: Not expecting me? But did he not receive my letter this morning?

MARINELLI: Your letter? Why, yes; I remember he did mention a letter from you.

ORSINA: And did I not ask him in that letter to meet me here at Dosalo today? True, he did not deign to write me an answer. But I heard that he had left for Dosalo an hour later; I thought that was answer enough, and I have come.

MARINELLI: A remarkable coincidence!

ORSINA: Coincidence? But I tell you the appointment was made. As good as made. On my side, by letter; on his, by deed. – Why, signor Marquis, how you look! What a face! Is your little brain surprised? And at what, pray?

MARINELLI: Yesterday it sounded as though it would be a long time before the Prince ever saw you again.

ORSINA: I have thought better of it today. Where is he? where is he? Let me guess, then: in the room where I heard that shrieking and crying? I wanted to go in there, but the scoundrel of a servant barred my way.

MARINELLI: My own dear Countess –

ORSINA: It was women's shrieking – Am I right, Marinelli? Oh, tell me, I beg you tell me – if I am indeed your own dear Countess – Damnation on this court vermin! So many words, so many lies! What does it matter whether you tell me beforehand or not? I shall see for myself. [Going]

MARINELLI [holding her back]: Where are you going?

ORSINA: Where I should have been long ago. Ought I to be standing here in this anteroom allowing you to waste my time with your idle chatter, while there in that room the Prince is waiting for me?

MARINELLI: You are mistaken, my dear Countess. The Prince is not waiting for you. The Prince cannot speak to you here; he will not speak to you.

ORSINA: But he is here? And here on account of my letter?

MARINELLI: Not on account of your letter –

ORSINA: Which you said he had received –

MARINELLI: Received, but not read.

ORSINA [*vehemently*]: Not read? [*Quieter*] Not read? [*Sadly, and wiping a tear from her eye*] Not even read?

MARINELLI: Out of distraction, I am sure. Not out of scorn.

ORSINA [*proudly*]: Scorn? The very idea! And whom do you think you are talking to? Your consolations are impertinent, Marinelli! [*In a softer, almost melancholy tone*] I know he does not love me any more. That is certain. And something else has taken love's place in his soul. That is natural. But does it have to be scorn? It need be nothing worse than indifference – is that not so, Marinelli?

MARINELLI: True, true.

ORSINA [*contemptuously*]: True? – Such wisdom! He will repeat anything one cares to put into his mouth. Indifference! Indifference in the place of love? But that is to say nothing in the place of something. For let me tell you, little parroting court manikin, let me, a woman, tell you that indifference is an empty word, a mere sound, that means nothing, nothing at all. The soul can only be indifferent to a thing it does not think of; only to something that for it is nothing. And indifferent only to something that is nothing – that is as much as to say not indifferent at all. Is that far above your head, creature?

MARINELLI [*aside*]: Alas! what I feared is all too true!

ORSINA: What are you muttering there?

MARINELLI: Nothing but admiration! And who has not heard, my dear Countess, that you are something of a philosopher?

ORSINA: Is it not so? Yes, yes, I am. But do I show it now? Oh, shame on me, if I do show it; and if I have shown it before! Is it any wonder that the Prince scorns me? How can a man love a creature that insists, as if to spite him, on having her own thoughts? A woman who thinks is as distasteful as a man who paints himself. She should always be laughing, simply laughing, to keep the mighty lord of creation in a good humour. – Well then, Marinelli, what is there for me to laugh at here and now? Why, of course! Coincidence! I write and ask the Prince to come to Dosalo; he does not read my letter, and yet he happens to come to Dosalo! Ha! ha! ha! Truly a most remarkable coincidence! Most amusing, most farcical! And you are not laughing with me, Marinelli? Surely the mighty lord of creation can share our laughter, even if we poor creatures are not permitted to share his thinking. [*In a serious, commanding tone*] Laugh then!

MARINELLI: Immediately, my dear Countess, immediately!

ORSINA: Dullard! While you are waiting the moment will be gone. No, no, do not laugh. For you see, Marinelli [*gravely, almost pathetically*] what makes me laugh so heartily also has its serious side – and very serious it is. Just as it is with everything else in this world! Coincidence! Coincidence, that the Prince had no intention of seeing me here, and yet has to see me here? Coincidence? Believe me, Marinelli, the word coincidence is a blasphemy. There is no such thing under the sun as coincidence; and a thing like this! its intention so clear for all to see! – Almighty and all-gracious Providence, forgive me, talking here to this foolish sinner, for calling coincidence what so plainly is your work, surely indeed the work of your own hand! [*Turning quickly to* MARINELLI] Come now, tempt me once again to such wickedness!

MARINELLI [*aside*]: Soon she will go too far! – But, my dear Countess –

ORSINA: No buts! Buts cost more thought, and my head, my head! [*Holding her forehead with her hands*] Hurry, Marinelli, hurry; let me speak to him soon, the Prince, or I shall be quite incapable. You see that it is to be, we are to speak to each other. –

SCENE 4

[*Enter the* PRINCE.]

PRINCE [*aside*]: I must come to his aid –

ORSINA [*seeing him, but remaining undecided whether to approach him*]: Ah, there he is!

PRINCE [*goes straight past her across the hall to the other rooms, without stopping as he speaks*]: Why, see, our beautiful Countess! How much I regret, madam, that the honour of your visit can be of so little advantage to me today. I am occupied. I am not alone. Another time, dear Countess, another time! And now you must not wait any longer. No longer, I say! And you, Marinelli; I wish to speak to you. [*Exit.*]

SCENE 5

MARINELLI: Have you now, my dear Countess, heard from his own lips what you would not believe from me?

ORSINA [*stupefied*]: Have I? Can it be true?

MARINELLI: It is.

ORSINA [*with emotion*]: 'I am occupied. I am not alone.' Do I not deserve a better excuse than that? Those are words to turn away any importunate visitor, any beggar at the door. Do I not rate one single lie any more – not one single tiny lie any more, for me? Occupied? What with? Not alone? Who could be with him? Come, Marinelli; for pity's sake, dear Marinelli! A lie for me, on your own account! What will it cost you then, a lie? What is he doing? Who is with him? Tell me; tell me the first thing that comes to your lips, and I will go.

MARINELLI [*aside*]: On that condition I can even tell her the truth, or part of it.

ORSINA: Well? Quickly, Marinelli, and I will go. And the Prince – he did say 'Another time, my dear Countess' –

did he not? So that he shall keep his word, so that he shall have no excuse for not keeping his word: quickly, Marinelli, your lie, and I will go.

MARINELLI: The Prince, my dear Countess, is not alone, and that is the truth. There are persons with him from whom he cannot absent himself for a moment: persons but lately escaped from great danger. Count Appiani –

ORSINA: Is with him? I am afraid I have caught you out over that lie; be quick and think of another. For Count Appiani, if you have not heard, has just been shot dead by highwaymen. The carriage bringing his body back to town met me just as I left. Or is that not so? Perhaps I only dreamt it?

MARINELLI: No, unhappily, you did not dream it! But the others who were with the Count were fortunately able to take refuge in the palace: namely his bride and her mother, with whom he was on his way to Sabionetta for his marriage-ceremony.

ORSINA: They? They are with the Prince? the bride, and her mother? Is the bride beautiful?

MARINELLI: The Prince is exceptionally moved by her misfortune.

ORSINA: So I would hope, even if she were plain. For her fate is terrible. Poor, dear girl; at the very moment when he was to become yours for ever, to have him snatched away for ever from you! Who is she then, the bride? It may even be someone I know. I have been out of town for so long that I know nothing of what is happening.

MARINELLI: It is Emilia Galotti.

ORSINA: Who? Emilia Galotti? Emilia Galotti? – Marinelli! Do not let me mistake this lie for the truth!

MARINELLI: What do you mean?

ORSINA: Emilia Galotti?

MARINELLI: Whom I do not suppose you know –

ORSINA: Oh yes, oh yes! Even though it is only since this morning. In earnest, Marinelli? Emilia Galotti? Emilia Galotti, you say, is the unhappy bride whom the Prince is comforting?

MARINELLI [*aside*]: Have I already told her too much?

ORSINA: And Count Appiani was to have been this bride's bridegroom? Appiani who has just been shot dead?

MARINELLI: None other.

ORSINA: Bravo! Oh, bravo! [*Clapping her hands.*]

MARINELLI: Why do you say that?

ORSINA: Oh, I could kiss the devil that tempted him to do it!

MARINELLI: Tempted? Tempted whom? To do what?

ORSINA: Yes, I could kiss him, kiss him – and if you yourself were that devil, Marinelli!

MARINELLI: Countess!

ORSINA: Come here! Look at me! Straight into my eyes!

MARINELLI: What then?

ORSINA: Do you not know what I am thinking?

MARINELLI: How can I?

ORSINA: Did you have no part in it?

MARINELLI: In what?

ORSINA: Swear it! No, do not swear it. You might commit yet another sin. But why not? Yes, swear it. One sin more or less: what is that to one already damned! Did you have no part in it?

MARINELLI: Countess, you alarm me.

ORSINA: Indeed? Come now, Marinelli, does your kind heart suspect nothing?

MARINELLI: What? what about?

ORSINA: Very well, then I will tell you something in confidence: something that will make every hair on your head stand on end. But not here, so near the door; someone might hear us. Come over here! Now listen! [*Putting her finger to her lips*] Between us two! just between us two! [*She puts her lips to his ear as if to whisper, but then shouts very loudly*] The Prince is a murderer!

MARINELLI: Countess, countess! Are you quite out of your senses?

ORSINA: Out of my senses? Ha! ha! [*Laughing aloud*] Rarely if ever have I been so well satisfied with my wits as I am this moment. Be sure of it, Marinelli; but let it remain a secret between us – [*softly*] The Prince is a murderer! Count

Appiani's murderer! It was not highwaymen, it was the Prince's men, it was the Prince who killed him!

MARINELLI: How can you say such terrible things, even think of them?

ORSINA: How? Quite naturally. – It was this Emilia Galotti who is here with him – whose bridegroom has had to pack his bags and leave this world in such a hurry – it was this Emilia Galotti that the Prince was speaking to this very morning, in the porch of the Dominican church; and at some length. I know that: my informers saw it. They also heard what he said to her. Now, my dear sir? Am I out of my senses? I should have thought I could still put two and two together. Or is that a mere chance as well? Do you call that coincidence? Oh, Marinelli, if you do, then you know as little about human wickedness as you do about providence.

MARINELLI: Countess, you might be endangering your own neck –

ORSINA: If I spread that sort of thing around? All the better, all the better! Tomorrow I will go and shout it in the market-place. And if anyone denies it – if anyone denies it, he is the murderer's accomplice. Good-bye.

SCENE 6

[*As she is about to leave, enter* ODOARDO GALOTTI.]

ODOARDO: I beg your pardon, madam –

ORSINA: There is no need to beg my pardon, for it is not my place to be offended here. This gentleman will attend to you. [*Directing him to* MARINELLI]

MARINELLI [*seeing* ODOARDO, *aside*]: Now her father too! This is the last straw!

ODOARDO: Your pardon, sir, for a most anxious father, arriving unannounced in this way.

ORSINA: Father? [*Turning back*] Emilia's, without a doubt. Ah, welcome!

ODOARDO: A servant came galloping to meet me with the news that my family were in danger somewhere in this neighbourhood. I have come flying, and they tell me that Count Appiani has been wounded; that he has gone back to the city; that my wife and daughter have taken refuge in the palace. Where are they, sir, where are they?

MARINELLI: Set your mind at rest, colonel! Your good lady and your daughter have come to no harm; apart from the shock they have received. They are both well. The Prince is with them. I will go immediately and announce that you are here.

ODOARDO: Why bother to announce me?

MARINELLI: Because – of reasons – of reasons concerning the Prince. You know, colonel, how matters stand between yourself and the Prince. Not on the friendliest of footings. However graciously he may receive your wife and daughter – they are ladies; does that mean he will be pleased to see you so unexpectedly?

ODOARDO: You are right, you are right.

MARINELLI: But my dear Countess, may I first have the honour of accompanying you to your carriage?

ORSINA: No, no.

MARINELLI [*taking her not ungently by the hand*]: Allow me; it is my duty.

ORSINA: Just a moment, sir! I will excuse you. Why will you and your kind always make a duty of these formalities; and then treat your real duties as something by the way! To announce this gentleman, and the sooner the better – that is your duty.

MARINELLI: Have you forgotten what the Prince himself said to you?

ORSINA: Let him come and say it again. I shall wait for him.

MARINELLI [*quietly to* ODOARDO, *drawing him aside*]: Sir, I am obliged to leave you here with a lady who – whose – whose wits are – You will understand. I am telling you this so that you will know what importance to attach to the things she says – which are often very strange. It would be best not to let yourself be drawn into conversation with her.

ODOARDO: Very well. But hurry, sir. [*Exit* MARINELLI.]

SCENE 7

ORSINA [*after a pause, during which she looks at* ODOARDO *with a pitying gaze, he at her with fleeting curiosity*]: Whatever it was he said to you, wretched man –

ODOARDO [*half aside, half to her*]: Wretched?

ORSINA: It was certainly not the truth; least of all any of the truths that are awaiting you here.

ODOARDO: Awaiting me? – Do I not know enough already? Madam! – But go on, go on.

ORSINA: You know nothing.

ODOARDO: Nothing?

ORSINA: Dear, good father! What would I not give to have you for my father too! – Forgive me! those who are unhappy cling so gladly to each other. I would loyally share your grief and rage.

ODOARDO: Grief and rage? Madam! – But I am forgetting. Go on.

ORSINA: What if it were your only daughter – your only child even! But only child or not – the unhappy child is always the only one.

ODOARDO: The unhappy child? Madam! – What do I want with her? But in God's name, these are not the words of a madwoman!

ORSINA: Mad? So that was what he told you about me, in confidence? Let it be, let it be; it is not one of his most outrageous lies. I feel there might be some truth in it! And believe me, believe me: there are certain things that will rob anyone of his wits, unless he has none to be robbed of!

ODOARDO: What am I to think?

ORSINA: But at least you do not despise me! For you are not witless either, no, not you, good old man! I can see it in your face: I see determination, dignity. No, you are not witless either; but a single word from me, and you will be at your wits' end!

ODOARDO: Madam! madam! I shall have reached it already, before you tell me your single word, if you do not tell me soon! Tell me, tell me! Or it is not true; it is not true that you are one of those unfortunate good people, so worthy of our pity and our respect: you are not mad, you are only a common foolish woman. You have not lost your wits: you never had any.

ORSINA: Listen, then! What do you know, you who think you know enough already? You know that Appiani is wounded. – Only wounded? Appiani is dead!

ODOARDO: Dead? dead? Ah, madam, that is contrary to our agreement. You said you would rob me of my wits, but you break my heart instead.

ORSINA: Let that pass! There is more. The bridegroom is dead, and the bride – your daughter – worse than dead.

ODOARDO: Worse? Worse than dead? But tell me straight away, is she dead too? For I know only one thing worse –

ORSINA: No, she is not dead. No, good father, no! She is alive, alive! Her life is only just beginning! A life full of joy! The fairest, gayest, most carefree life – while it lasts!

ODOARDO: Your word, madam, your single word that will rob me of my wits! Out with it! Do you need a gallon of water to mix one drop of poison? Your single word! quickly!

ORSINA: Here it is then: spell it out for yourself! In the morning, the Prince speaks to your daughter at mass; in the afternoon, he has her at his – country pleasure-seat.

ODOARDO: Spoke to her at mass? The Prince, my daughter?

ORSINA: With such intimacy! with such ardour! It was no small matter they were arranging. And well and good, if it was arranged beforehand; well and good, if it was of her own accord your daughter sought refuge here! For you see, in that case it is not a forcible abduction, but nothing more than a little – assassination.

ODOARDO: Slander! damnable slander! I know my daughter. If there is to be any talk of assassination, then it was an abduction too! [*Looking about him wildly, stamping his foot and foaming*] Well, Claudia? Well, doting mother? What joy is ours! Oh, gracious prince! Oh, what exceptional honour!

ORSINA: Is it working, father, is it working?

ODOARDO: Here I stand before the robber's den – [*Opening his coat, and seeing that he has no weapon*] A wonder that I did not forget my hands as well, in my haste! [*Feeling in all his pockets, as if looking for something*] Nothing! Nothing at all, not anywhere!

ORSINA: Aha, I understand! I can help you there: I have brought one with me. [*Producing a dagger*] There, take it! Take it, quickly, before anyone sees us! Or if you prefer it, I have something else – poison. But poison is a woman's weapon: not for a man! Take it! [*Pressing the dagger upon him*] Take it!

ODOARDO: Thank you, thank you. My dear child, if any one ever calls you foolish again, he will have me to reckon with!

ORSINA: Put it away! away, quickly! I shall no longer have the opportunity to make use of it. But you will not lack that opportunity, and you will seize it, the first that comes to hand – if you are a man. I, I am only a woman; but my mind was made up when I came here! We, old father, we can trust each other completely. For we have both been wronged; wronged by the same seducer. Ah, if you knew – if you knew how monstrously, how unspeakably, how inconceivably I have been wronged and am still being wronged by him – you might even forget, you would forget your own wrong beside it. Do you know who I am? I am Orsina; betrayed, deserted Orsina. Deserted, true, it may be, only for your daughter. But can your daughter help it? Soon she too will be deserted. And then another, and then another! Ah! [*as if in ecstasy*] what a heavenly fantasy! If we one day – all of us, his victims – a whole army of deserted women – transformed into Bacchantes, into furies – if we could have him in our midst, tear him to pieces, dismember him, hunt through his entrails to find the heart that he promised to every one of us, the traitor, and gave to none! Ah! what a dance that would be!

Scene 8

[*Enter* CLAUDIA.]

CLAUDIA [*looking round, and rushing to her husband as soon as she sees him*]: I guessed as much! Ah, our protector, our saviour! Is it you, Odoardo, is it you? I thought from their whisperings and their looks that it must be. – What am I to say, if you have heard nothing yet? What am I to say, if you already know everything? But we are innocent. I am innocent, your daughter is innocent, innocent in every way!

ODOARDO [*trying to calm himself on seeing his wife*]: Good, good. Be calm, that is all, be calm and answer me. [*To* ORSINA] Not, madam, as though I had any doubts – Is the Count dead?

CLAUDIA: Dead.

ODOARDO: Is it true that the Prince spoke to Emilia this morning at mass?

CLAUDIA: True. But if you had seen how frightened she was, in what agitation she came home –

ORSINA: Now, have I lied to you?

ODOARDO: No, nor would I that you had! Not for the world!

ORSINA: Am I mad?

ODOARDO [*pacing furiously up and down*]: Oh no, nor am I – not yet.

CLAUDIA: You tell me to be calm, and I am calm. Dear husband, may I too – ask you –

ODOARDO: What do you mean? Am I not calm? Can a man be calmer than I am? [*Forcibly restraining himself*] Does Emilia know that Appiani is dead?

CLAUDIA: She cannot know. But I am afraid she suspects it, because he does not come.

ODOARDO: And she is weeping and whining –

CLAUDIA: No longer. That is over. You know what she is like. The most timid and yet the most determined of our sex. Her first impressions overwhelm her; but after the slightest reflection she is ready to face anything, to meet whatever comes. She is making the Prince keep his distance; she is speaking to him in such a tone – Only let us be quick, Odoardo, and come away from this place.

ODOARDO: I came on horseback. What can we do? – But madam, are you not driving back to town?

ORSINA: Indeed I am.

ODOARDO: Would you be so kind as to take my wife back with you?

ORSINA: But of course! I should be delighted.

ODOARDO: Claudia, [*introducing her*] Countess Orsina; a lady of great wisdom; my friend and benefactress. You are to go with her; then send the carriage out to us here immediately. Emilia must not return to Guastalla. She will be going with me.

CLAUDIA: But – if only – I do not like being parted from the child.

ODOARDO: Is not her father close at hand? They cannot refuse to let him see her. No more objections! Come, your ladyship. [*Softly to her*] You shall hear from me. Come, Claudia! [*Exeunt.*]

ACT V

Scene: the same

SCENE I

[MARINELLI *and the* PRINCE.]

MARINELLI: Here, your highness; you can see him from this window. He is walking up and down the colonnade. He has just turned towards the house; he is coming in. No, he is going away again. He has not yet quite made up his mind. But he is a good deal calmer – or seems it. It does not matter to us! – Of course! Whatever those two women have put into his head, will he dare utter a word of it? – Battista heard him tell his wife to send his carriage out here immediately. He came on horseback. – Wait and see now: when he appears in front of you he will most loyally thank your serene highness for the gracious care and protection you have granted his family here on the occasion of this unfortunate occurrence; will take leave of you on behalf of himself and his daughter, and will be beholden to your further gracious favour; will take her quietly back to town and await as your most humble servant what further interest it may please your highness to take in his poor, dear, unhappy daughter.

PRINCE: But what if he is not so meek? And I hardly, hardly think he will be. I know him too well. If at the best he stifles his suspicions and swallows his rage – but then takes Emilia with him, instead of back to town? Keeps her with him? Or even shuts her up in a convent, outside my dominions; what then?

MARINELLI: A lover's fears are long-sighted. Yes, indeed! But surely he will not –

PRINCE: But if he does! What then? What use will it be to us then that the business cost the unfortunate Count his life?

MARINELLI: Why these gloomy sidelong glances? Onward! says the victor, and let friend or foe fall beside him! – And even if! even if the old curmudgeon does intend to do as you fear, prince, [*thinking*] – that will do! I have it! He shall get no further than the intention. No, he shall not! But let us not lose sight of him. [*Going to the window again*] Why, he might almost have caught us! He is coming. Let us keep out of his way a little longer; until I have told you, your highness, how we can best prevent what we fear.

PRINCE [*threateningly*]: But, Marinelli! –

MARINELLI: The most harmless thing in all the world! [*Exeunt.*]

SCENE 2

[*Enter* ODOARDO.]

ODOARDO: No one here yet? Good. It is lucky for me: I need to be colder yet. Nothing more contemptible than a young hothead with grey hairs! That is what I have told myself so often. And yet I let myself be swept off my feet;

and by whom? By a jealous woman; by a woman driven out of her mind by jealousy. What has offended virtue to do with the revenge of vice? And it is virtue alone I have to save. And your cause – my son! my son! – I could never weep; and I will not learn it now! It is not I who will take up your cause. Enough for me that the murderer should not enjoy the fruits of his crime. May that torture him more than the crime itself! When he finds himself driven on, sated and disgusted, from one new lust to another, may the memory of this one lust that he was not allowed to satisfy sour his enjoyment of them all! Whenever he dreams, may the bridegroom still bleeding lead the bride to his bedside; and if still he stretches out his lustful arms towards her, may he wake with the mocking laughter of hell ringing in his ears!

SCENE 3

[*Enter* MARINELLI.]

MARINELLI: Where have you been, sir? Where have you been?

ODOARDO: Has my daughter been here?

MARINELLI: No, but the Prince has.

ODOARDO: I hope he will excuse me. I had to accompany the Countess.

MARINELLI: Well?

ODOARDO: Poor lady!

MARINELLI: And your wife?

ODOARDO: Has gone with the Countess, to send the carriage out to us here immediately. I hope the Prince will allow me to remain here with my daughter in the meanwhile.

MARINELLI: Why make such circumstance? Would not the Prince have been happy to take them both, mother and daughter, back to town himself?

ODOARDO: The daughter at least would have had to decline the honour.

MARINELLI: Why?

ODOARDO: She will not be going back to Guastalla.

MARINELLI: Not going back? Why not?

ODOARDO: The Count is dead.

MARINELLI: All the more –

ODOARDO: She is coming with me.

MARINELLI: With you?

ODOARDO: With me. I tell you the Count is dead, if you have not heard it yet. What business has she to remain in Guastalla? She is coming with me.

MARINELLI: Of course where the daughter is to spend her future days will depend entirely on her father's will. But for the moment –

ODOARDO: What, for the moment?

MARINELLI: I am afraid, colonel, that you will have to allow her to be taken to Guastalla.

ODOARDO: My daughter? taken to Guastalla? And why?

MARINELLI: Why? But consider –

ODOARDO [angrily]: Consider! consider! I consider that there is nothing to consider. She shall, she must come with me.

MARINELLI: But, sir, what need is there for us to become heated? It may be that I am mistaken; that what I think is necessary will not be necessary. The Prince will be the best judge of the matter. Let the Prince decide. I will go and fetch him. [Exit.]

SCENE 4

ODOARDO [alone]: What? Never! Dictate to me where she is to be taken? Keep her from me? Who will do such a thing? Who *can* do such a thing? – He that can do whatever he will here? Very well; then he shall see that he is not the only one who dares to overstep the mark! Tyrant, can you see no further than the end of your own nose? I will settle with you! He that obeys no law is as free as he that is subject to none. Did you not know that? Come then! come then! – But look: already, already my anger is running away with my wits again. What is it I want? First let it happen, before I fly into a rage about it. And these gossiping toadies, what will they not say? But if only I had let him go on gossiping!

94

If only I had let him tell me his pretext for sending her back to Guastalla! Then I could decide on my answer now. But what pretext can I lack an answer for? Yet if I should lack one, if I should – They are coming. Calm, old hothead, calm!

SCENE 5

[*Enter the* PRINCE *and* MARINELLI.]

PRINCE: Ah, my dear honest Galotti – and a thing like this has to happen before you will come to see me. You will come for nothing less. But no reproaches!

ODOARDO: Sir, I regard it as improper under any circumstances to foist oneself upon one's prince. If he knows us, he will summon us when he needs us. Even now I beg your pardon –

PRINCE: How many others I would wish shared this proud modesty! But to business. You will be anxious to see your daughter. She has been disturbed afresh by being suddenly parted from her mother. And why indeed did they have to be parted? I was only waiting for the fair Emilia to be completely herself again, and then I should have taken them both back to town in triumph. You have spoilt the triumph for me by half; but you shall not rob me of it entirely.

ODOARDO: You do us too much honour! Permit me, your highness, to spare my unhappy child all the sufferings of so many kinds which would await her in Guastalla at the hands of both friend and foe, of those who pity her and of those who take pleasure in another's distress.

PRINCE: To rob her of the sweet sufferings that pitying friends will inflict on her would be cruel. And as for those enemies who take pleasure in her distress: allow me, my dear Galotti, to make it my concern to shield her from them.

ODOARDO: Your highness, a father's love does not gladly share its concerns. I think I know what is the only fitting thing for my daughter in her present circumstances. To turn her back on the world; a convent, and as soon as possible.

PRINCE: A convent?

ODOARDO: And until then, let only her father's eyes see her weeping.

PRINCE: Such beauty to fade in a convent? Ought a single disappointment to turn us so irreconcilably against the world? But of course, her father's word must be final. Galotti, take your daughter where you will.

ODOARDO [to MARINELLI]: Well, sir?

MARINELLI: If I am to take that as a challenge –

ODOARDO: Not at all, not at all.

PRINCE: What is there between you two?

ODOARDO: Nothing, your highness, nothing. We are merely considering which of us was mistaken in you.

PRINCE: What do you mean? Speak, Marinelli!

MARINELLI: I do not like to stand in the way of my prince's generosity. But if friendship demands that I insist on the prior claims of justice –

PRINCE: What friendship?

MARINELLI: You know, sir, how I loved Count Appiani; how our two souls seemed joined together as one –

ODOARDO: Do you know that, prince? Then indeed you are the only man that does.

MARINELLI: Named by himself to avenge him –

ODOARDO: You?

MARINELLI: You need only ask your wife. Marinelli, the name Marinelli was the last word the Count spoke before he died; and in such a voice! in such a voice! May it never cease to ring in my ears, that fearful voice, if I do not seek by all the means in my power to bring his murderers to justice.

PRINCE: You may count upon my assistance in every way.

ODOARDO: And upon my keenest wishes! Good, good! But what then?

PRINCE: That I too should like to hear, Marinelli.

MARINELLI: It is suspected that it was not highwaymen who attacked the Count.

ODOARDO [*scornfully*]: No? indeed not?

MARINELLI: That a rival had him disposed of.

ODOARDO [*bitterly*]: For shame! A rival?

MARINELLI: None other.

ODOARDO: Why, then – God damn him, the murderous villain!

MARINELLI: A rival, and a favoured rival –

ODOARDO: What? Favoured? What are you saying?

MARINELLI: Nothing but what rumour is spreading.

ODOARDO: Favoured? by my daughter? favoured?

MARINELLI: That cannot possibly be true. I deny it absolutely, think what you will. But for all that, sir – for the best-founded presumption weighs nothing upon the scales of justice – for all that, it will not be possible to avoid questioning the dear, unfortunate young lady about the matter.

PRINCE: Yes, I am afraid we must.

MARINELLI: And where else? where else can that be done but in Guastalla?

PRINCE: Yes, you are right, Marinelli, you are right. Yes, that puts a different face on things, does it not, my dear Galotti? You see yourself –

ODOARDO: Oh, yes, I see. I see what I see. Oh God, God!

PRINCE: What is it? What is the matter?

ODOARDO: That I did not foresee what I see. That is what annoys me; nothing more. Why, yes; she must go back to Guastalla. I will take her back to her mother; and until she has been pronounced innocent by the most thorough investigation, I will not stir from Guastalla myself. For who knows, [*with a bitter laugh*] who knows whether justice will not find it necessary to question me as well.

MARINELLI: Quite possibly! In a case of this kind justice will not stint its efforts. And so I even fear –

PRINCE: What? What do you fear?

MARINELLI: That for the moment mother and daughter will not be allowed to speak to each other.

ODOARDO: Not speak to each other?

MARINELLI: It will be necessary to separate mother and daughter.

ODOARDO: To separate mother and daughter?

MARINELLI: Mother and daughter and father. The procedure of investigation absolutely demands this precaution. And I regret, your highness, that I find myself obliged to insist explicitly that Emilia at least be placed under particular surveillance.

ODOARDO: Particular surveillance? Prince! Prince! – But yes; of course, of course! Yes, indeed, under particular surveillance! Is that not right, prince, is that not right? Oh, what a delicate instrument is justice! Excellent! [*He reaches quickly for the pocket where he has the dagger.*]

PRINCE [*approaching him flatteringly*]: Calm yourself, my dear Galotti –

ODOARDO [*aside, taking out his hand again, without the dagger*]: It was his good angel that spoke!

PRINCE: You are wrong; you do not understand what he means. No doubt the word surveillance makes you think of prison and dungeons.

ODOARDO: Let me think that, and I shall be calm.

PRINCE: Let there be no mention of prison, Marinelli! In this case the strict observance of the law and the respect due to unspotted virtue are easily reconciled. If Emilia is to be put under particular surveillance, then I know the very place – the most proper place imaginable: my chancellor's house. No objections, Marinelli! I will take her there myself; I will entrust her there to the care of one of the worthiest of ladies. – You will be going too far, Marinelli, too far, in earnest, if you ask for more than that. – You know them, of course, Galotti, my chancellor Grimaldi and his wife?

ODOARDO: How should I not know them? I even know the charming daughters of that noble pair. Who does not know them? [*To* MARINELLI] No, sir, do not be satisfied with that. If Emilia is to be kept in custody, then you must insist she be kept in the deepest dungeon. Demand it, I beg you. – What a fool I am, with my begging! what an old buffoon! Yes, yes, she was right, the good sibyl: there are certain things that will rob anyone of his wits, unless he has none to be robbed of!

PRINCE: I do not understand you. My dear Galotti, what more can I do? Let us agree on it, I beg you. Yes, yes, my chancellor's house, that is where she must go; I will take her there myself; and if she is not received there with every possible attention, then my word is worth nothing. But do not be afraid. It is agreed! agreed! – You yourself, Galotti, are free to come and go entirely as you please. You can follow us to Guastalla; you can go back to Sabionetta; just as you wish. It would be absurd to dictate to you. And now, au revoir, my dear Galotti! Come, Marinelli, we shall be late.

ODOARDO [*who has been standing deep in thought*]: What? Then I am not to speak to her at all, my daughter? Not even here? – I agree to everything; I find all your arrangements quite excellent. Your chancellor's house is naturally a haven of virtue. Oh, your highness, do take my daughter there, there and nowhere else. – But I should dearly love to speak to her first. She does not even know yet that the Count is dead. She will not be able to conceive why she is being taken from her parents. To break the one to her, and calm her fears regarding the other – I must speak to her, your highness, I must speak to her.

PRINCE: Come then –

ODOARDO: Oh, surely the daughter may come to see her father. Here, just the two of us, and I shall soon have done. Just send her to me, your highness.

PRINCE: Very well! – Oh, Galotti, if you would be my friend, my guide, my father too! [*Exeunt* PRINCE *and* MARINELLI.]

SCENE 6

ODOARDO [*following them with his eyes; after a pause, alone*]: Why not? With all my heart – Ha! ha! ha! [*Looking round wildly*] Who was that laughing? God in Heaven, I do believe it was myself. – And what is wrong with that? Let us be merry, let us be merry! Soon it will be played out – one way or another. – But – [*Pause*] – if she were his accomplice? If it were nothing but the usual masquerade?

If she were not worth what I am going to do for her? [*Pause*] Going to do for her? What am I going to do for her, then? Dare I tell myself? I had a thought – Let it remain nothing but a thought! Terrible! Away, away! I will not wait to see her. No! [*To Heaven*] Let him who hurled her innocent into this abyss draw her out again! Why should he need my hand to help him? Away! [*As if to go, but then seeing* EMILIA *coming*] Too late! Ah! he will have my hand, he will have it!

SCENE 7

[*Enter* EMILIA.]

EMILIA: What, you here, father? And only you? And my mother not here? And the Count? Not here? And you are so disturbed, father?

ODOARDO: And you are so calm, daughter?

EMILIA: Why not, father? Either all is as it was, or all is lost. We can be calm, or we have to be calm – does it not come to the same?

ODOARDO: But which do you think it is?

EMILIA: That all is lost; and that we shall have to be calm, father.

ODOARDO: And so you are calm because you have to be calm? Who are you? A girl? and my daughter? Would you put a man to shame, and your own father? But let me hear what you call all being lost. That the Count is dead?

EMILIA: And the reason for his death! the reason! – Ah, then it is true, father? Then it is true, the whole terrible story that I read in my mother's wild and tear-filled eyes? Where is my mother? Where has she gone, father?

ODOARDO: On ahead; if we are to follow her, that is.

EMILIA: The sooner the better. For if the Count is dead; and if – *that* is the reason for his death; then why should we stay here? Let us go, and quickly, father!

ODOARDO: Go! – What need then? – Here you are, and here you must stay, in the robber's hands.

EMILIA: I, stay in his hands?

ODOARDO: And alone; without your mother, without me.

EMILIA: I, alone in his hands? Never, father. Or you are not my father. I, alone in his hands? Very well, then; leave me, leave me. I should like to see who will keep me here – who will force me – what man there is who can force another to do his bidding.

ODOARDO: I thought you were calm, my child.

EMILIA: And so I am. But what do you call being calm? Sitting with our hands in our laps? Suffering what we should not suffer? Enduring what we ought not to endure?

ODOARDO: Ah, if those are your thoughts – let me embrace you, my daughter! I always said that nature intended woman to be her masterpiece; but she took her clay too fine. That was her mistake; in every other way you are better than we are. Ah, if that is your calm, then I find my own in it again! Let me embrace you, my daughter! But listen: under the pretext of a judicial inquiry – oh, a pantomime fit for hell! – he will tear you from our arms and take you to Grimaldi's.

EMILIA: Tear me? take me? Will tear me, will take me? Will, will! As if we, we had no will of our own, father!

ODOARDO: Yes, in my anger I was on the point of taking this dagger [*bringing it out*] and piercing his heart – both their hearts!

EMILIA: In Heaven's name, no, father! This life is all the wicked have. No, father, give me, give me that dagger.

ODOARDO: Child, it is not a hairpin.

EMILIA: Then a hairpin will serve for a dagger! It does not matter.

ODOARDO: What? Is that what we have come to? No, no! Remember: for you too there is nothing more precious than life.

EMILIA: Not even innocence?

ODOARDO: That can resist any tyrant.

EMILIA: But not any seducer. Tyranny! tyranny! Who cannot stand up to tyranny? What men call tyranny is nothing; the seducer is the true tyrant. I have blood in my veins too, father, warm young blood like any other girl. My senses are senses too. I cannot promise anything; I cannot vouch for myself. I know the Grimaldis' house. It is a house where pleasure is all. An hour there, and in my mother's sight, and my soul was in such a tumult that weeks of prayer, and all our religion teaches us, could scarcely calm it! Religion! And what religion? It was to avoid nothing worse that thousands drowned themselves whom we call saints! Give it to me, father, give me that dagger.

ODOARDO: And if you knew what it was like, this dagger!

EMILIA: And even if I do not know! A friend unknown is still a friend. Give it to me, father, give it to me.

ODOARDO: What then if I give it to you – there! [*Gives it to her.*]

EMILIA: And there! [*She is about to stab herself, but her father snatches it from her hand again.*]

ODOARDO: See, how quick! No, that is not for your hand.

EMILIA: Then it is true, I must take a hairpin if I – [*She puts her hand to her hair to find one, and takes hold of the rose*] You, still here? Off with you! You do not belong in the hair of a – what my father wants me to become!

ODOARDO: Oh, my daughter!

EMILIA: Oh, my father, if I could only read what is in your mind! But no, it cannot be that either, or why did you hesitate? [*Bitterly, plucking off the rose's petals*] Long ago I believe there was a father who, to save his daughter from shame, took steel, the first that came to hand, and plunged it into her heart – gave her life a second time. But all such deeds are deeds of long ago! There is no such father in the world today!

ODOARDO: There is, my daughter, there is! [*Stabbing her*] Oh God, what have I done? [*He catches her in his arms as she falls.*]

EMILIA: Plucked a rose before the storm could bruise it. Let me kiss this hand, my father's hand.

SCENE 8

[*Enter the* PRINCE *and* MARINELLI.]

PRINCE: What is the matter? Is Emilia not well?

ODOARDO: Very well, very well!

PRINCE [*coming closer*]: But what do I see? Oh, horror!

MARINELLI: Ruined!

PRINCE: Cruel father, what is this you have done?

ODOARDO: Plucked a rose before the storm could bruise it. Is it not so, my daughter?

EMILIA: Not you, my father – I – I myself –

ODOARDO: Not you, my daughter, not you! Do not leave this world with an untruth on your lips! It was your father, your unhappy father!

EMILIA: Ah – my father! [*She dies, and he lays her tenderly down.*]

ODOARDO: Farewell! There, prince! Does she still please you? Does she still excite your desires? Still, as she is, with her blood crying out against you for revenge? [*After a pause*] But you are waiting to see how it will all end? Perhaps you are waiting for me to turn my dagger on myself, to finish off what I have done like a tawdry melodrama? You are wrong. Here! [*Throwing the dagger at the* PRINCE's *feet*] Here let it lie, the bloody evidence of my crime. I will go and give myself up. I will wait in prison for you to judge me. And then – I will wait for you there before Him who shall judge us all!

PRINCE [*after remaining silent for a while, staring at the body in horror and despair;* to MARINELLI]: Come here! pick it up! What then? You do not know – wretch? [*Snatching the dagger from his hand*] No, your blood shall not mingle with this. Go, and never let me see you again! Go, I say! Oh God, oh God! Is it not enough, and the misfortune of so many, that princes are but men; must there be devils too to pretend they are their friend?

EGMONT

Johann Wolfgang Goethe

A tragedy in five acts
1787

CHARACTERS

MARGARET OF PARMA, daughter of Charles V, Princess
  Regent of the Netherlands
COUNT EGMONT, Prince of Gavre
WILLIAM OF ORANGE
DUKE OF ALVA
FERDINAND, his bastard son
MACHIAVELLI, in the service of the Princess
  Regent
RICHARD, Egmont's private secretary
SILVA ⎰
GOMEZ ⎱ serving under Alva
CLARA, in love with Egmont
CLARA'S MOTHER
BRACKENBURG, son of a citizen of Brussels
SOEST, shopkeeper ⎰
JETTER, tailor ⎰
MASTER CARPENTER ⎰ citizens
SOAP-BOILER ⎰
BUYCK, a Hollander, soldier under Egmont
RUYSUM, a deaf Frisian veteran
VANSEN, a clerk
Crowd, servants, guards, etc.

Scene: Brussels

ACT I

A crossbow contest. Soldiers and citizens with crossbows.

[*Enter* JETTER *and* SOEST. JETTER *steps forward and draws his crossbow.*]

SOEST: Come then, shoot and let's be finished! You'll not beat me. Three bulls, you've never done that in your life. That makes me champion for this year.

JETTER: Champion and king; who'll grudge you that? You'll have to stand us twice as many drinks; you'll have to pay for your skill, it's only fair.

[*Enter* BUYCK.]

BUYCK: Jetter, I'll buy your turn; share the prize, treat these gentlemen; I've been here so long, and I've so many kindnesses to repay. If I miss, it can count as your shot.

SOEST: I ought not to agree, as I'll be the loser by it. But all right, Buyck, go on.

BUYCK: By your leave, master marker! One! Two! Three! Four!

SOEST: Four bulls? All right, then!

ALL: Hurrah! hurrah! Long live the King!

BUYCK: Thanks, gentlemen. As if champion weren't enough! Thanks for the honour.

JETTER: You can thank yourself for that.

[*Enter* RUYSUM.]

RUYSUM: I'll tell you what!

SOEST: What is it, old fellow?

RUYSUM: I'll tell you what! He shoots like his master, he shoots like Egmont.

BUYCK: Oh, I'm nothing at all compared to him. And give him a gun, now, and there's no one can touch him. And not just when he's in luck or in a good mood, mind; no, every time he takes aim, there it is, a clean bullseye. He taught me all I know about it. I'd like to see the man that served with him and didn't learn a thing or two! – Here, I'm forgetting! A king has to look after his subjects. Wine here, on the king's slate!

JETTER: The way we do it here is –

BUYCK: I'm a stranger here, and I'm the King, so I don't observe your laws and customs.

JETTER: You're worse than the Spaniard; after all, he's had to leave them alone so far.

RUYSUM: What?

SOEST [*loudly*]: He wants to treat us; he won't let us all put in and just pay double share as King.

RUYSUM: Let him! Only don't make a habit of it. That's like his master too, to lash out a bit when things are going well.

ALL: His Majesty's health! Hurrah!

JETTER [*to* BUYCK]: *Your* majesty's, that is!

BUYCK: Thank you, if that's how it is to be.

SOEST: Oh yes. We're not so keen on drinking his Spanish majesty's health here in the Netherlands.

RUYSUM: Whose?

SOEST [*loudly*]: His majesty King Philip the Second of Spain's.

RUYSUM: Our gracious king! God give him a long life.

SOEST: Wouldn't you rather have his father, Charles the Fifth?

RUYSUM: God be merciful to him! There was a king for you! He held the whole world in his hand, like the Almighty himself; and yet if he met you he'd greet you like a neighbour; and if you were afraid, he had a way of – you know what I mean; he went out, rode out, just as he fancied, didn't take a whole crowd with him. We all wept, you know, when he abdicated and we got his son here in his place – I mean, you know – he's not the same, there's more Your Majesty about him.

JETTER: He didn't show himself when he was here, except with all that pomp and circumstance. They say he doesn't talk much.

SOEST: He's not the sort of king for us here in the Netherlands. Our princes ought to be cheerful like us, and live and let live. We're not going to be pushed around or looked down on, even if we are a lot of easy-going fools.

JETTER: I reckon the King wouldn't be such a bad master if he had better people to advise him.

SOEST: No, no! He's got no feeling for the Netherlands, no heart for the people; he doesn't like us, how can we like him? Why does everyone think so much of Count Egmont? Why would we all do anything for him? Because you can see that he's one of us; because you can see it all in his face – cheerfulness, good will, a carefree life; because he's got nothing that he wouldn't share with anyone who needed it – or didn't, come to that. Long live Count Egmont! Buyck, it's your duty to give us the first toast. Let's drink to your master!

BUYCK: With all my heart then: here's to Count Egmont!

RUYSUM: The victor of St Quentin!

BUYCK: The hero of Gravelines!

ALL: Hurrah!

RUYSUM: St Quentin was my last battle. I could hardly move any longer, I could hardly carry my heavy gun any further. But I managed to let the French have one more round, and then I was hit in the right leg, and that was the end of me.

BUYCK: Gravelines! That was a battle, friends! That was our victory and no one else's. Why, the damned French had scorched and burned their way through the whole of Flanders; but we stopped them! Their veterans couldn't hold any longer, and we pushed on and fired and laid about us, and they made long faces and their lines began to give way. Then Egmont's horse was shot dead underneath him, and back and forth it went for a long time, man to man, horse to horse, troop to troop, there on the wide flat beach by the sea. Then all of a sudden, like a gift sent from heaven, up from the rivermouth, boom! bang! cannon-shot, straight into the thick of the French, again and again. That was the English, Admiral Malin's, who happened to be coming down from Dunkirk. They weren't all that much help; they could only bring their smallest ships in, and even they couldn't come close enough; they shot at us, too – But it was good they came! It broke the French and raised our spirits. Then up and at them we went! We killed them, we chased them into the water. Their fellows were drowning as soon as they tasted it; but we Hollanders were after them, and we're like frogs — we can live on the land too, but it's the water that really suits us best. We were at them there in the river, shot them up like ducks. And if any of them got away, the farmers' wives caught them and killed them with hoes and pitchforks. Then the King of France had to eat humble pie and make peace. And that peace you owe to us, to us and the great Egmont!

ALL: Hurrah! Here's to the great Egmont! and here's to him again! and again!

JETTER: If they'd only given us him instead of Margaret of Parma for Regent!

SOEST: No, no! Fair's fair. I'll have nothing said against her. Now it's my turn: long live our gracious lady!

ALL: Long live Margaret!

SOEST: Yes, that house breeds some fine women. Long live the Princess!

JETTER: She's a clever woman, and strikes a fair balance in everything she does; if only she weren't so thick with the priests. You can't deny she's partly to blame for these fourteen new bishops. What do we need them for? It's only so that they can put all these foreigners in the top places, instead of choosing local abbots as they used to. And we're supposed to believe it's for the good of religion. Yes, we know all about that. Three bishops was enough for us; everything went as it should. Now they'll all have to find themselves work to do, and there'll be trouble all the time. And the more you stir the pot, the thicker it will get. [*They drink.*]

SOEST: Well, it was the King's order; she can't do anything about it, one way or the other.

JETTER: And then we're not supposed to sing the new psalms. But they've made good verses of them, and given them fine tunes. Them we're not supposed to sing, though we can sing as many ale-house songs as we like. And why not? Because there are heresies in them, they say, and God knows what kind of things. Well, I've sung them, too, as one does, these days, and I couldn't see anything wrong in it.

BUYCK: What business is it of theirs? In our province we sing what we want. And that's because Count Egmont is our stadtholder; he doesn't worry about things like that. In Ghent, in Ypres, all over Flanders, anyone who wants can sing them. [*Loudly*] What could be more harmless than a hymn? Isn't that right, old fellow?

RUYSUM: Of course! It's a service in itself, it does your soul good, in its own way.

JETTER: But *they* say it's not the right way, it's not *their* way; and – well, it can be dangerous, so it's better not to. The Inquisition have their people everywhere, creeping about, watching, listening; there's many a good man has fallen foul of them already. They'll be trying to force our consciences next! Since they won't let me do what I want, they might at least let me think what I want, and sing what I want.

SOEST: The Inquisition won't make much headway here. We're not like Spaniards, letting them tell us what to believe. And our nobility will have to try and clip their wings one of these days.

JETTER: It's a bad business. Suppose they just get the idea of breaking into my house, and find me sitting there at my work, and I happen to be humming one of these French psalms, just because it comes into my head, not thinking anything about it at all; straight away I'm a heretic, and they'll lock me up. Or I'm on my way across country and I stop for a moment where there's a crowd of people listening to one of these new preachers, the ones from Germany; on the spot they'll call me a rebel, and I could lose my head for it. – Have you ever heard one of those fellows preach?

SOEST: They know their business. I heard one the other day, out in the open, there were thousands of people there. Not like ours, thumping away at the pulpit and giving you bits of Latin to choke on. No, that was a different kettle of fish: he gave it us straight from the shoulder, said they had made fools of us all along and kept us in ignorance, but we should come to see the light for ourselves – and all that, mind you, he proved, out of the Bible.

JETTER: There must be something in it. I've said so all along. I've thought a lot about it, you know, it's all been on my mind a long time.

BUYCK: All the people run to hear them, too.

SOEST: Of course; they know they'll hear something good, and new too.

JETTER: And what's wrong with it? Can't a man preach as he's a mind to?

BUYCK: Come there, gentlemen! With all this talk, you're forgetting the wine, and Orange.

JETTER: We mustn't forget him. There's a man for you, like a great rampart; think of him, and it's as if you could hide yourself behind him, and the devil himself couldn't get you out. Here's to William of Orange!

ALL: Here's to William of Orange!

SOEST: Now, old fellow, it's your turn. Give us a toast!

RUYSUM: Old soldiers! all soldiers! Here's to war!

BUYCK: Bravo, old fellow! Here's to war!

JETTER: War! war! Do you know what you're shouting there? It's all very fine for you, I suppose; but how we feel about it, I can hardly say. All the year long, drums, drums everywhere; and all you hear talked of is how one troop came up here and another there, how they climbed a hill and stopped by a mill, how many were killed here, how many there, how they press on and the one wins and the other loses, but all my life I shall never understand who's losing what and who's winning what. How they capture a town and kill the townspeople, and what happens to the poor women and the innocent children. It's a dreadful, terrible business, you hear about it all and you think to yourself, every minute, 'They're coming! Now it will happen to us too.'

SOEST: That's why a civilian has to know how to handle a weapon too.

JETTER: As if a wife and family weren't enough to worry about. Still, I'd rather hear about soldiers than see them.

BUYCK: What are you saying there?

JETTER: I don't mean you, you're one of our own people. But if we could be rid of the Spanish occupation we could breathe easier again.

SOEST: Ah, that was what lay heaviest on your mind?

JETTER: Mind your own business!

SOEST: That was quite a billetting, wasn't it?

JETTER: Hold your tongue!

SOEST: They drove him from his own kitchen, from his own cellar, from his own fireside, – from his own bed.

JETTER: You are a fool.

BUYCK: Peace, there! Is it the soldier who must cry peace now? Well, if you don't want to hear of us, let's hear your toast, your civilians' toast!

JETTER: That you shall! Peace and safety!

SOEST: Order and liberty!

BUYCK: Fine! That's good enough for us too.

[*They drink, and repeat the words cheerfully, everyone crying out a different word so that it becomes a kind of canon. The old man listens, and at last joins in too.*]

ALL: Safety and peace! Order and liberty!

Palace of the Princess Regent

[MARGARET OF PARMA *in hunting dress. Courtiers, pages, servants*]

MARGARET: Call off the hunt, I will not ride today. Send Machiavelli to me. [*She is left alone.*] I cannot stop thinking of these terrible things that are happening. It gives me no peace. Nothing can please me, nothing can distract me; all the time the same visions, the same worries plague my mind. Now the King will say this is all because I am too kind, too tolerant; and yet my conscience tells me I have always done what was most prudent, what was best. Should I have let loose a storm of anger to fan these flames and make them spread? I hoped to contain them, hoped they would choke of themselves. Yes, I tell myself these things;

I know they are true, they are my justification in my own eyes; but how will my brother look on it? For can it be denied that these foreign preachers have become bolder every day? They have blasphemed against all that we hold sacred, they have stirred up the dull brains of the mob and set a restless spirit loose among them. Impure spirits have been at work, and terrible things have happened, things which are fearful even to think of and which I now have to report to court, each one straight away as it comes, so that the vulgar rumour does not arrive first, so that the King shall not think there is still more that we are keeping from him. I see no way, be it harsh or mild, to keep this evil in check. Oh, what are we, we great ones, on the waves of mankind? We think we can command them, and they toss us up and down, they drive us to and fro.

[*Enter* MACHIAVELLI.]

MARGARET: Have you written the letters that are to go to the King?

MACHIAVELLI: They will be ready for your signature in an hour's time.

MARGARET: Have you made your report sufficiently detailed?

MACHIAVELLI: Detailed and circumstantial, after the King's heart. I tell him how it was around St Omer that the frenzy of the image-breakers first showed itself. How raving mobs came with staves, axes, hammers, ropes and ladders, only a few armed men with them, attacking churches, chapels and monasteries, driving out the faithful from their prayers, breaking open locked doors, wreaking all manner of havoc, tearing down the altars, smashing the images of the saints, defacing every painting; and wherever they found anything sacred and holy, wrecking it, tearing it to pieces, trampling it underfoot. How more and more join the mob as it goes on its way, and the citizens of Ypres open their gates to it. How in the twinkling of an eye they have wrecked the cathedral and burnt the bishop's library. How a great mob of people, fired with this same madness, spread out through Menin, Comines, Wervik and Lille, meeting no resistance anywhere; and how in a moment, in almost the whole of

Flanders, the monstrous conspiracy has proclaimed itself openly and set about its work.

MARGARET: Ah, my grief overwhelms me again to hear you recall these things to me! And with it there comes the fear that this evil cannot but grow and grow. Tell me what your thoughts are, Machiavelli.

MACHIAVELLI: I beg your highness's pardon, but my thoughts will seem mere whims; and although you have always expressed satisfaction with my services, it is rarely you have seen fit to follow my advice. Often you have laughed and said, 'You see too far, Machiavelli! You should take to writing histories: the man of action must take heed for the morrow.' And yet did I not foretell this whole history? Did I not foresee that this would happen?

MARGARET: I too foresee many things, but I cannot prevent them from happening.

MACHIAVELLI: Once and for all: you will not stop the new doctrines. Tolerate these people, keep them apart from the true believers, give them their rights but keep them in their place; and you will have the revolutionaries tamed in an instant. All other methods are useless. You will only bring devastation on the land.

MARGARET: Have you forgotten my brother's revulsion at the mere mention of toleration for these new doctrines? Have you forgotten how in every letter he insists on the maintenance of the true faith? insists that he will never have peace and unity restored at the expense of our religion? And is it not true that he has his spies here in the Provinces, who they may be we do not know, watching to see who favours the new opinions? Has he not told us to our amazement that such a one, and such a one, were guilty of heresy here under our very noses? Are not firmness and severity his orders? And you would have me be lenient? propose to him that he should show forebearance, toleration? Should I not lose all the trust and faith he has in me?

MACHIAVELLI: I know; the King gives you orders, he makes his intentions known to you. You are to restore peace and tranquillity by means that can only create more bitterness, means that will surely spread war over the whole country. Consider what you are doing! The leading merchants are affected, the nobility, the people, the soldiers. What use is it to stay fixed in one's mind, while all around us everything is changing? No, I wish some good spirit would whisper to Philip that it better befits a king to rule subjects of two different faiths than to set them at one another's throats.

MARGARET: Let me never hear you say these things again. I know that in affairs of state we can rarely keep faith, that our hearts learn to forget frankness, kindness and generosity. I fear in worldly matters that is all too true; but should we play God the tricks we play on one another? Should we be so indifferent to the fate of our established faith, for which so many have offered up their lives in sacrifice? Should we give it up for the sake of these upstart, uncertain and self-contradictory innovations?

MACHIAVELLI: I hope you will not think the worse of me for it.

MARGARET: I know you and know that you are loyal, and I know too that a man can be honest and wise even though he has missed the true, straight path to the salvation of his soul. There are other men, too, Machiavelli, whom I must respect and reproach.

MACHIAVELLI: Whom do you mean?

MARGARET: I will confess that I was deeply angry with Egmont today.

MACHIAVELLI: What did he do to anger you so?

MARGARET: Made his usual show of indifference and frivolity. The terrible news reached me just as I was leaving church; there were many with me, and he was among them. I did not attempt to restrain my grief; I cried out loud as I turned to him and said, 'See what is happening in your province! You, my lord, permit this, you from whom the King expected so much?'

MACHIAVELLI: And what did he answer?

MARGARET: As if it were nothing, as if it were a matter of no consequence, he said, 'If only the Netherlanders had a constitution to their liking! Then everything else would be well.'

MACHIAVELLI: Perhaps his words contained more of truth than of prudence or of piety. How will you win the Netherlander's lasting trust, when he sees that you are more interested in his worldly goods than in his well-being or the salvation of his soul? Are not the new bishops too busy living off the fat of the land to care about saving souls, and are not the most of them foreigners? True, all the Stadtholders are still Netherlanders, but do not the Spaniards make it all too plain for everyone to see that they will not be satisfied until they hold those positions too? Will a nation not rather be ruled in its own way, by its own people, than by strangers who have no sooner arrived in the country than they begin to suck its blood, who judge according to their foreign standards and rule harshly and without sympathy?

MARGARET: You take our enemies' part.

MACHIAVELLI: Assuredly not with my heart; and I wish my head could more unreservedly take our own.

MARGARET: If that is what you want, then I should have to hand over the regency to them; for Egmont and Orange did hold high hopes of taking my place. Once they were enemies, but now they are united against me; they have become friends, inseparable friends.

MACHIAVELLI: A dangerous pair!

MARGARET: If I am to speak my mind, then – I am afraid of Orange, but I am afraid for Egmont. Orange's plotting bodes no good, his thoughts reach into the distance, he is secretive, he seems to accept everything, never speaks out openly against me, and with the greatest show of reverence and prudence he does – just what he will.

MACHIAVELLI: While Egmont on the other hand walks as if the world belonged to him.

MARGARET: He carries his head so high that one would not think there was a king set above him.

MACHIAVELLI: All the people's eyes are turned to him, and all their hearts are his.

MARGARET: He has done nothing to avoid giving the impression that he is answerable to no man. He still uses the name Egmont. He likes to hear men call him Count Egmont, as if to remind him that his forefathers once owned Gelderland. Why does he not call himself by his rightful title, Prince of Gavre? Why does he do these things? Will he lay claim to rights that exist no longer?

MACHIAVELLI: I believe him to be a loyal servant of the King.

MARGARET: If he wanted, how he could put our government in his debt; instead he has chosen to make us endless trouble, and to no profit to himself. His feasts and banquets have brought the nobility together far more than the most dangerous secret meetings ever could. His toasts have gone to their heads, and intoxicated them beyond recovery. He can stir the people up with a mere word spoken in jest; and how the mob gaped at his new liveries, and the fool's badges he had made his servants wear!*

MACHIAVELLI: I am convinced there was nothing behind it.

MARGARET: Bad enough. I tell you, he harms us and does himself no good. He treats serious matters as trifles; and so if we would not appear idle and negligent we are forced to take his trifling seriously. One thing brings on another, and what we seek to avoid becomes all the more certain. He is more dangerous than a sworn leader of rebellion; and, if I am not greatly mistaken, every move he makes is noted at court. I must confess, a day scarcely goes by when I am not deeply troubled on account of him.

MACHIAVELLI: He seems to me to follow his conscience in all things.

MARGARET: His conscience is no hard task-master, then. His manner often gives offence. He often behaves like a man convinced that he was the master, sparing our feelings out

---

*In December 1563 Egmont had introduced a new livery for his servants, with a badge resembling a fool's cap or a monk's cowl. This was a gesture of ridicule aimed at the hated Cardinal Granvelle, the chief power behind Margaret's regency. Further reference is made to the new liveries in subsequent scenes. (*Translator's note.*)

of the kindness of his heart, not wanting to drive us out of the country, but ready one day to make his power felt.

MACHIAVELLI: He is frank and serene, the most earnest matters weigh but lightly on his shoulders. It is his nature; do not put too severe an interpretation upon it, you only harm him and yourself.

MARGARET: I put no interpretations on anything. I speak only of the inevitable consequences, and I know him. He belongs to the nobility of the Netherlands, and he wears the Golden Fleece; both protect him from any sudden, arbitrary disfavour of the King, and so his boldness and confidence are strengthened. Consider carefully, and you will see he is to blame for all the misfortunes of Flanders. He was too tolerant of these foreign preachers in the first place, turned a blind eye to them, was even glad, perhaps, that they made difficulties for us. No, I know what I am doing; I shall take this opportunity of setting my mind at rest. And I shall not waste my shots; I know where he is vulnerable. For he too is vulnerable.

MACHIAVELLI: Have you summoned the council? Will Orange be there too?

MARGARET: I have sent to Antwerp for him. I shall do all I can to make them accept responsibility; either they help me to stamp out this plague or they declare themselves rebels too. Hurry, see that the letters are finished, and bring them for me to sign! Then quickly send Vasca to Madrid; we know he is tireless and true. Let my brother hear the news first from him, and not by some hearsay. I will speak to him myself before he leaves.

MACHIAVELLI: Your orders shall be carried out promptly and to the letter.

Clara's house

[CLARA, *her* MOTHER *and* BRACKENBURG]

CLARA: Will you not hold my wool for me, Brackenburg?

BRACKENBURG: I beg you, Clara, leave me alone.

CLARA: What is it now? Why do you grudge me such a little favour?

BRACKENBURG: You sit me so close in front of you with the skein that I cannot avoid your eyes.

CLARA: What fancies! Come and hold it!

MOTHER [*in her chair, knitting*]: Let us have a song! Brackenburg sings so well with you. You always used to be so gay, and it made me laugh too.

BRACKENBURG: Yes, we used to be.

CLARA: Let us sing.

BRACKENBURG: Whatever you like.

CLARA: Come, then. But it must go cheerfully! It is a song about a soldier, and it is my favourite. [*She sings with* BRACKENBURG *as she winds her wool*]

> The drums they are beating,
> The fifes they do play,
> My lover is leading
> His men to the fray;
> With lance held aloft
> He will carry the day.
> O, hear my heart,
> How it beats true!
> Had I a buff jerkin
> I'd go with him too!
> Out through the gates
> So gaily I'd tread,
> All through the Provinces,
> Wherever he led.
> O, how we'd fire
> As the enemy ran;
> Joy of all joys
> To be a man!

[*As they sing,* BRACKENBURG *looks repeatedly at* CLARA; *at last his voice fails him, tears come into his eyes, he drops the skein and goes to the window.* CLARA *finishes the song alone, her* MOTHER *motions to her half reproachfully, she stands up,*

*takes a few steps towards him, hesitates, turns uncertainly round
and sits down again.*]

MOTHER: What is happening in the street, Brackenburg? I
can hear men marching.

BRACKENBURG: The Princess Regent's guard.

CLARA: At this hour of the day? What can it mean? [*She
stands up and joins* BRACKENBURG *at the window.*] But that
is not just the usual patrol; there are so many more! Almost
all the troops she has! Oh, Brackenburg, go and find out
what is happening! It must be something out of the ordin-
ary. Do go, dear Brackenburg, to please me.

BRACKENBURG: I will. I shall be back straight away! [*They
shake hands. Exit* BRACKENBURG.]

MOTHER: You have sent him away again.

CLARA: I want to know what is happening; and also, do not
be angry with me, but I would rather he went away. I
never know what to do when he is here; I know that I
wrong him, and it grieves me that he feels it so deeply; but
I cannot help it!

MOTHER: The lad is so faithful to you.

CLARA: I cannot stop it either, I have to be friendly to him
too. Often my fingers curl up against my will when he
takes my hand so gently, so lovingly in his. I reproach
myself for deceiving him, for giving him false hopes. I
suffer for it. Heaven knows I am not deceiving him. I do
not want him to go on hoping, but I cannot leave him in
despair.

MOTHER: It is wrong of you.

CLARA: I used to be fond of him, and still I can only wish him
well. I could have married him; and yet I believe I never
really loved him.

MOTHER: You would have been happy with him.

CLARA: I should have been well provided for and have led a
life of peace.

MOTHER: And all that you have thrown away.

CLARA: It is so strange. When I try to think of how it
happened, it is all so clear and yet so hard to remember.
But I only need to see Egmont again, and then I understand

it all – and it is as if I could understand so many other things. Oh, what a man he is! If all the Provinces worship him, how could I, in his arms, not be the happiest creature in the world?

MOTHER: But what of the future?

CLARA: I only ask whether he loves me, and can there be any question whether he does?

MOTHER: Children bring nothing but trouble. Where will it all end? Nothing but worries and sorrow! No good can come of it! You have destroyed your own happiness; you have destroyed mine.

CLARA [*calmly*]: When it began, you said nothing.

MOTHER: I am afraid I was too kind, I always am too kind.

CLARA: When Egmont rode by and I ran to the window, did you scold me then? Did you not come to the window too? When he looked up at us, smiled and nodded, greeted me, was it not to your liking? Did not you feel honoured too when compliments were paid to your daughter?

MOTHER: Go on, let me hear more reproaches!

CLARA [*with emotion*]: Then when he began to come this way more often, and we felt it must be because of me, were you not secretly glad of it yourself? Did you call me away when I stood at the window looking out for him?

MOTHER: Did I think it would come to this?

CLARA [*with faltering voice, holding back her tears*]: And then that evening when suddenly he was there, in the lamplight, wrapped in his cloak, who was it hurried to receive him, while I sat there dumbfounded as if I were tied to my chair?

MOTHER: And was there any reason for me to fear that my clever Clara would fall so soon, so helplessly in love? And now I have to sit by while my daughter –

CLARA [*bursting into tears*]: Mother! You want it to go on! You delight in making me so anxious.

MOTHER [*weeping*]: Yes, go on, weep too! make me even more wretched with your own unhappiness! Isn't it enough to bear that my daughter is a fallen creature?

CLARA [*coldly, standing up*]: Fallen! Egmont's love a fallen creature? What princess would not envy poor Clara her place in his heart? Oh, mother, mother, you used not to talk like that. Dear mother, be good to me! – Whatever people think, whatever your gossiping neighbours say – this room, this little house, has been a heaven of its own since Egmont found his love here.

MOTHER: I must admit, he is a man to win your heart. He is always so friendly, so frank and open.

CLARA: There is nothing false about him. And yet, mother, look, he is the great Egmont himself. And when he comes to see me, how kind and gentle he is! how gladly he would have me forget his rank and his bravery! how good he is to me! just a man, just a friend, just a lover.

MOTHER: Do you think he will come today?

CLARA: Have you not seen how often I have gone to the window? Have you not noticed how I listen every time there is a noise at the door? Oh, I know he will not come before evening, and yet I am looking for him every minute of the day, from the moment I get up in the morning. If only I were a boy, and could be with him all the time, go to court with him and everywhere, be his standard-bearer when he goes to war!

MOTHER: Oh! you always were such a madcap, even when you were a little child; so wild one minute, then brooding the next. Are you not going to put some better clothes on?

CLARA: Perhaps I will, mother, if the time goes too slowly. Think of it, yesterday some of his soldiers went past, and they were singing a song about what a fine man he is. At least I heard his name, though I could not catch the rest of the words. It made my heart beat so quickly; I would have called them back, but I was ashamed to.

MOTHER: Do take care! You will spoil everything with your impetuousness, even now; you give yourself away all the time. The other day at your cousin's, now, when you found that woodcut and the caption and cried out loud, 'Count Egmont!' It made me blush to the roots of my hair.

CLARA: Why should I not have cried out loud? It was the

battle of Gravelines, and there in the picture was letter C, and I look in the key underneath and there it says, 'C: Count Egmont, with his horse shot dead beneath him.' It sent shivers down my spine, and yet afterwards I had to laugh at the way Egmont was shown there, as big as the tower of Gravelines beside him and the English ships further over. Sometimes when I remember what I used to imagine a battle was like, and how I used to picture Count Egmont to myself when I was a girl and they talked about him, and all the counts and princes – and when I think of now!

[*Enter* BRACKENBURG.]

CLARA: What is happening?

BRACKENBURG: No one knows for certain. They say there has just been some disturbance in Flanders and the Princess is afraid it might spread here. There are lots of soldiers at the palace, crowds of citizens at the gates, people everywhere in the streets. – I must just hurry and see my old father. [*Making as if to go.*]

CLARA: Will you come tomorrow? I think I must find some better clothes; my cousin is coming, and I really am too untidy. Come and help me a moment, mother! – Take your book, Brackenburg, and bring me another story like it!

MOTHER: Good-bye.

BRACKENBURG [*holding out his hand*]: Your hand!

CLARA [*refusing hers*]: When you come again. [*Exeunt* CLARA *and* MOTHER.]

BRACKENBURG [*alone*]: I told myself I would not stay, but when she takes my going for granted, and says nothing, then I could go mad. Wretch! do you care nothing for your fatherland, and all this growing tumult? Is it all the same to you, Spaniard and fellow-countryman, who is in power and who is in the right? – I was a different lad when I was at school! If we had 'Brutus's speech in praise of Liberty' for our exercise, then it was always Fritz who won the prize, and our master said, if only it had been more orderly, and didn't all come out in such a rush! Yes, I was keen and sharp enough in those days! Now here I am always trailing after this girl. I won't leave her, and she won't love me!

Ah, no, she – she can't have turned me down for good – not for good – for indifferent, for bad! – I'll not bear it any longer! Might it be true, what one of my friends told me not so long ago? that there is a man who comes and visits her secretly at night, after she's turned me out so virtuously before it's even begun to get dark? No, it's not true, it's a lie, a shameful, slanderous lie! Clara is as innocent as I am unhappy. – She has rejected me, driven me out of her heart – and am I to go on like this? No, I'll bear it, I'll bear it no longer! – Here are all these troubles tearing our fatherland apart, and here am I in the thick of it all, just languishing away! I'll bear it no longer! – When the trumpet sounds, or I hear a shot, I tremble in every limb! Not for me the thrill, the challenge to join in, to help to save, to be bold and daring. – Wretched, shameful existence! Better to make an end of it at once. Not so long ago, I jumped into the water; I sank – but nature and fear were stronger; I found that I could swim, and saved myself against my will. If only I could forget the times when she loved me – when she seemed to love me! Such happiness – it warmed me through and through! Such hopes – they seemed to promise paradise waiting far off, and now they have driven every joy from my heart! And that first kiss – that one and only kiss! Here, [*laying his hand upon the table*] here we were, alone – she had always been kind and friendly to me – but then she seemed to melt – she looked at me – my senses were all in a whirl, and I felt her lips touch mine. And – and now? Die, wretch, why do you linger still? [*Taking a phial out of his pocket*] Sweet poison, it shall not be for nothing that I stole you from my brother's medicine chest. This fear, this sickness, this cold sweat, all at once you shall soothe them and take them away from me.

ACT II

A Square in Brussels

[*Enter* JETTER, *meeting* MASTER CARPENTER.]

CARPENTER: Didn't I say so? A week ago at the guild meeting I said there would be trouble.

JETTER: Is it true, then, that they have plundered the churches in Flanders?

CARPENTER: Stripped them, churches and chapels, to the bare walls. Nothing but rabble! And that gives our good cause a bad name. We should have claimed our rights from the Princess and insisted on them, firmly but like decent citizens. Now if we speak, or even meet, they'll say we are joining the rebels.

JETTER: Yes, then every man's first thought will be to keep his nose out of it, for fear of getting caught by the neck.

CARPENTER: I am afraid of what will happen when once the mob really begin to run wild, the ones that have nothing to lose. The rights we claim will be their pretext too, and they will ruin the whole country.

[*Enter* SOEST.]

SOEST: Good day to you, friends! What news is there? Is it true the image-breakers are heading this way?

CARPENTER: They shan't touch a thing here.

SOEST: A soldier came into my shop for tobacco, and I asked him about it. The Princess is usually a match for anything, but this time she is beside herself. It must be bad, for her to hide behind the guard like that. The palace is bristling with men. They even say she wants to leave the city.

CARPENTER: Leave? That she shall not! We are protected if she is here, and she will be safer with us than with those mustachios of hers. And if only she will guarantee our rights and freedoms, then we shall let no harm come to her.

[*Enter* SOAP-BOILER.]

SOAP-BOILER: A bad business, a wicked business! There is trouble brewing, things are heading for the worse. Be sure to keep silence, or they will take you for rebels.

SOEST: Here come the seven sages of Greece.

SOAP-BOILER: I know there are a lot of these secret Calvinists about, they blaspheme against the bishops, they have no respect for the King. But a loyal subject, a true Catholic –

[*Gradually more and more people are joining them and listening. Enter* VANSEN.]

VANSEN: God be with you, gentlemen! What news?

CARPENTER: Keep away from him, he's a ne'er-do-well.

JETTER: Isn't he Doctor Wiets's clerk?

CARPENTER: He's served many masters. First he was a clerk, lost one job after another on account of his mischief, and now he tries to teach the lawyers their job, and he's always at the brandy-bottle.

[*More people arrive and stand in groups.*]

VANSEN: I see you are meeting too, putting your heads together; yes, it's worth talking about.

SOEST: I think so too.

VANSEN: If now one or the other of you were bold enough, and one or the other clever enough, we could break the Spanish yoke at once.

SOEST: You must not speak like that, sir! We have sworn to be true to the King.

VANSEN: And the King has sworn to be true to us; did you know that?

JETTER: What's that you say? This is worth hearing!

OTHERS: Listen to him! He's no fool. He knows what he's talking about.

VANSEN: One of my masters was an old gentleman who had parchments and letters, deeds and contracts and legal papers from long, long ago; and he was a great lover of rare books. One of them had our whole constitution in it; how at one time different princes had ruled in the Netherlands, all according to established rights and privileges and customs; how our fathers had had every respect for their prince, if he ruled them as he should; but were always quick to stop him if he overstepped the mark. The Estates were after him straight away; for every province, however small, had its own Estates, its assembly.

CARPENTER: Hold your tongue! We've known that for a long time. Every honest citizen knows as much of the constitution as he needs to.

JETTER: Let him speak! We can always learn something more.

SOEST: He's right.

OTHERS: Tell us, tell us! You don't hear this sort of thing every day.

VANSEN: There's your good citizen for you. You go on just the same from day to day, and just as you carry on your fathers' trades without question, so you let the government do what it likes with you. You don't look into these traditions as you should, into history, into the rights of a regent! That's why the Spaniards have been able to catch you in their net.

SOEST: Who is going to think about all that, as long as he has his belly full?

JETTER: Damnation! why will no one stand up in time and say these things?

VANSEN: I am saying them, now. The King down in Spain, who by mere good fortune happens to possess all the Provinces at once, has no right to rule them in any other way than all the different princes did, when they belonged to them separately. Now do you understand?

JETTER: Explain it a bit more!

VANSEN: It's as plain as day! Must a man not be judged by the laws of his own Province? And what is the reason for that?

A CITIZEN: That's true!

VANSEN: Is there not one law in Brussels, and another in Antwerp? One law in Antwerp and another in Ghent? And what is the reason for that?

ANOTHER CITIZEN: By God!

VANSEN: But if you let things go on as they are going, they will change all that. Pah! What Charles the Bold could not do, Frederick the Third, Charles the Fifth could not do,

Philip will have done – and a woman will have done it for him.

SOEST: Yes, yes, the old princes tried it too.

VANSEN: Indeed they did! But our forefathers were on the watch for it. If they had reason to be displeased with their lord and master, then they did something about it, got hold of his son and heir, perhaps, kept him and only let him go on the strictest conditions. Our fathers had their wits about them! They knew what was good for them, and knew how to get what they wanted! They were real men! And that is why our privileges are so clearly set out and our liberties so plainly guaranteed.

SOAP-BOILER: What is all this talk of liberties?

THE PEOPLE: Our liberties, our privileges! Tell us more about our privileges!

VANSEN: We here in Brabant above all, although every one of the Provinces has its own advantages, we are the best off. I have read it all.

SOEST: Tell us!

JETTER: Let's hear!

A CITIZEN: Yes, tell us.

VANSEN: Firstly, it is written: The Duke of Brabant shall be a good and faithful master to us.

SOEST: Good? Does it say so?

JETTER: Faithful? Is that true?

VANSEN: As I am telling you. He has his duties to us just as we have ours to him. Secondly: He shall exercise no tyranny over us, nor seek to exercise, nor permit any other to exercise it, in any way.

JETTER: Fine, fine! Exercise no tyranny!

SOEST: Nor seek to exercise!

ANOTHER: Nor permit any other to exercise it! That's the most important part. Nor permit any other, in any way!

VANSEN: Those are the very words.

JETTER: Where is the book?

A CITIZEN: Yes, we must have it.

OTHERS: The book, the book!

ANOTHER: We'll go to the Princess with the book!

ANOTHER: You must speak for us, Doctor Vansen!

SOAP-BOILER: Oh, the fools!

OTHERS: More from the book!

SOAP-BOILER: I'll knock his teeth down his throat if he says another word!

PEOPLE: Just let us see anyone lay hands on him! Tell us about the privileges! Do we have any more privileges?

VANSEN: Many, and very fine and healthy they are. Another thing that's written there: The ruling prince shall in no way benefit or increase the number of the clergy without the consent of the nobility and the Estates! Take note of that! Nor shall he make any change in the constitution of the country.

SOEST: Is that true?

VANSEN: I can show you it in writing, two and three hundred years old.

CITIZENS: And we put up with the new bishops? The nobility must protect us! We must do something about it!

OTHERS: And we let the Inquisition plague us?

VANSEN: It is your own fault.

THE PEOPLE: We still have Egmont! still have Orange! They are on our side.

VANSEN: Your brothers in Flanders have begun the good work!

SOAP-BOILER: You dog! [*He strikes him.*]

OTHERS [*defending him*]: What, are you a Spaniard? Take your hands off him! He's a gentleman! A scholar! [*They attack the* SOAP-BOILER.]

CARPENTER: In God's name, stop! [*Others join in the struggle.*] Citizens, what is this? [*Boys whistle, throw stones and set their dogs on. Citizens stand and gape, more people come running, others walk up and down taking no notice, others play pranks of all kinds, shout and cheer.*]

OTHERS: Liberty and privileges! Privileges and liberty!
[*Enter* EGMONT *with soldiers.*]

EGMONT: Peace, peace, good people! What is it? Peace! Stop them fighting there!

CARPENTER: Oh, my lord, you have come like an angel sent

from heaven! Peace there, don't you see? Count Egmont!
Respect for Count Egmont!

EGMONT: Here too? What are you thinking of? Citizen
against citizen? Cannot even our Princess Regent's own
presence in the city restrain this madness? Let every man
go about his business! It is an evil sign when you make
holiday on a working day. What was it about? [*The tumult
gradually dies down, and all group themselves about him.*]

CARPENTER: They are fighting over their privileges.

EGMONT: That way they'll wantonly destroy them. And who
are you? You seem honest men to me.

CARPENTER: That is what we seek to be.

EGMONT: Your trade?

CARPENTER: Carpenter, and master of my guild.

EGMONT: And you?

SOEST: Shopkeeper.

EGMONT: And you?

JETTER: Tailor.

EGMONT: I remember: you were one of those that made the
new liveries for my men, your name is Jetter.

JETTER: I am honoured your lordship should remember it.

EGMONT: I do not easily forget a man, if I have once seen
him and spoken to him. Do everything you can to keep the
peace, good people; you have a bad enough name already.
Do not provoke the King any more; for when all is said
and done, it is he who has the power. A good citizen earning
his living by honest work will always enjoy all the liberty
he needs.

CARPENTER: Ah, that's just what is wrong these days! These
thieves and vagabonds, these ale-house idlers, with your
lordship's pardon, they make trouble for want of better
things to do, and instead of earning their bread they talk
about privileges, and there are always some who know no
better and will believe it; and so that someone will buy them
a jug of ale they stir up a disturbance, and thousands have
to suffer for it. That's what they want. Our money-boxes
are too well locked up in our houses for their liking, so they
try to set them alight over our heads.

EGMONT: The law is on your side; firm measures have been taken against this evil. Stand firm in the true faith, and do not think that revolt is the way to secure privileges. Stay in your houses, do not let these mobs gather. Sensible men can do a great deal. [*By this time most of the crowd has drifted away.*]

CARPENTER: Thank you, your excellence, thank you for your kindness. Everything we can do! [*Exit* EGMONT.] A true gentleman, and a true Netherlander; nothing of the Spaniard about him.

JETTER: If only we had him for our regent, everyone would be glad to obey him.

SOEST: That would be too much for the King; he always keeps that place for his own people.

JETTER: Did you see his clothes? They were the latest fashion, cut in the Spanish style.

CARPENTER: A fine man!

JETTER: That neck is just made for the block.

SOEST: Are you mad? What are you talking about?

JETTER: Oh, I know it's foolish, but these things keep coming to me. When I see a fine long neck, I can't help thinking, 'A good one for the axe!' It's all these damned executions! I can't take my mind off them. When the lads go swimming and I see a bare back, straight away I think of all the dozens I've seen flogged. If I meet a fat belly, I can see it roasting at the stake already. At night I dream they are torturing me in every limb; there's not a moment's peace and contentment. I've almost forgotten what it's like to be cheerful and gay; all the dreadful things I've seen are branded on my memory.

Egmont's room

[SECRETARY *at a table with papers. He stands up, impatiently.*]

SECRETARY: Not here yet! and two hours now I have been waiting, pen in hand and all the papers in front of me; and today of all days I wanted to be finished in good time. I can hardly wait to be away! 'Be punctual', he told me as he left, and now he will not come. There is so much to do, I shall not be finished before midnight. True, one's sometimes glad of his turning a blind eye, but I should be happier if he would be stricter, and then let me go at the proper time. You would know where you were then. It must be two hours since he left the Princess; who knows who may have got hold of him on the way.

[*Enter* EGMONT.]

EGMONT: Well?

SECRETARY: I am ready, and three messengers are waiting.

EGMONT: I have been too long coming, I suppose; I can see you are impatient by your face.

SECRETARY: I have been here a long time awaiting your orders.

EGMONT: Doña Elvira will be angry with me when she hears I have kept you.

SECRETARY: You are joking.

EGMONT: No, no! There is no need to be ashamed! You have good taste. She is pretty, and I like you to have a friend in the palace. What do the letters have to tell us?

SECRETARY: Many things, but little to comfort us.

EGMONT: A good thing, then, that we have our comforts at home and do not have to wait for them to come from somewhere else. Is there much?

SECRETARY: Enough, and there are three messengers waiting.

EGMONT: Tell me, then! The most essential.

SECRETARY: It is all essential.

EGMONT: Come then; one thing at a time, but quickly!

SECRETARY: Captain Breda reports on the further course of events in Ghent and the surrounding district. The disturbances have calmed down for the most part —

EGMONT: I suppose there are still alarms and incidents here and there?

SECRETARY: Yes, still quite a lot of that.

EGMONT: Spare me the details.

SECRETARY: He has caught six more of the ones that tore down Our Lady's statue at Wervik, and asks if he shall hang them like the rest.

EGMONT: I am tired of hangings. Let them be given a flogging and then go free.

SECRETARY: Two of them are women; shall they be flogged too?

EGMONT: They can be sent off with a caution.

SECRETARY: Brink from Breda's company wants to marry. The captain says he hopes you will refuse permission. He writes that there are so many women with the company that now when they are on the march they look more like a flock of gypsies than a troop of soldiers.

EGMONT: Just this one more! He's a handsome young fellow, and he begged me to give him permission before I went away. But from now on no more will be allowed; though it's hard on the poor devils to deny them their greatest pleasure, when they've enough to bear as it is.

SECRETARY: Two of your men, Seter and Hart, have got a girl into trouble, an innkeeper's daughter. They got her alone and the wench couldn't defend herself against them.

EGMONT: If she is an honest girl and they used force on her, tell him to have them whipped three days running, and if they have any property tell him to confiscate enough to set the girl up decently.

SECRETARY: One of the foreign preachers was caught going through Comines in secret. He swears he was on his way to France. According to orders he should be beheaded.

EGMONT: Tell them to take him quietly to the frontier and assure him he will not get away a second time.

SECRETARY: A letter from your tax-collector. He writes that there is so little money coming in that he will hardly be able to send you the sum you ask for this week; all these disturbances have turned everything upside-down.

EGMONT: I must have the money! How he finds it is his affair.

SECRETARY: He says he will do everything he can, and he

says he is going to have that Raymond who has owed you money for so long arrested and charged at last.

EGMONT: But he has promised to pay.

SECRETARY: The last time he said it would be within fourteen days.

EGMONT: Then give him another fourteen days, and after that take out proceedings.

SECRETARY: I think that would be right. It's not that he can't pay, but that he won't; and when he sees that you are in earnest he will take it seriously too. Your tax-collector also says he intends to stop the pensions you pay to the veterans and widows and so on, for a fortnight, while he decides what else can be done; they will have to manage as best they can.

EGMONT: Manage? Those people need the money more than I do. He is not to stop it.

SECRETARY: Where do you want him to find the money, then?

EGMONT: Let him think that out, as he was told in the last letter.

SECRETARY: But that is why he makes these proposals.

EGMONT: They are no good. Let him think of something better. Let him make proposals that are acceptable, and above all let him find the money.

SECRETARY: I have taken the liberty of putting Count Oliva's letter there again. I beg your pardon, but the old man does deserve an answer, more than anyone else. You said you would write to him yourself. He loves you like a father, you know.

EGMONT: I shall never find the time. And of all the things I hate, I hate writing the most. You can imitate my hand so well; write it for me. I am expecting Orange. I shall never find the time; but I should like him myself to have a comforting reply to his worries.

SECRETARY: Give me an idea of what to say; I will compose an answer and show you when it is ready. I shall write it so that anyone would swear on oath it was your own hand.

EGMONT: Let me see the letter! [*After looking at it*] Good, honest old man! Were you so cautious when you were young? Did you never climb a rampart? When you went to battle, did you stay where prudence commanded, in the rear? So loyal, so anxious! He wants me to live and be happy, and he does not realize that a man is already dead if he lives for his own safety. – Write to him that he is to have no fears; I shall do what I have to do, and I shall take good care of myself; if he will use his good name at court on my behalf, he shall be assured of all my gratitude.

SECRETARY: Is that all? But he is expecting much more than that!

EGMONT: What more am I to say? If you care to spin more words, I leave it in your hands. It is always the same: I ought to live as I do not care to live. That I am sanguine, take things lightly, live at a pace, is my good fortune; I will not change it for the safety of a funeral vault. The Spanish manner of living does not appeal to me; I have no desire to dance to the stately tunes they play at court these days. Do I only live to keep alive? Must I deny myself the enjoyment of one moment so as to be sure of the next? And let that again be eaten up with dismal fancies?

SECRETARY: I beg you, my lord, do not be so harsh and cruel to the good old man! You are always so considerate to others. Can you not find a kind word to soothe your noble friend? See how concerned he is, how gently he seeks your ear!

EGMONT: But he always harps on this one theme. He knows and always has known how I hate these admonitions; they only confuse me, they are of no help. Suppose I were a sleepwalker, wandering perilously along a rooftop; is it what a friend would do, to call out my name and warn me, waken me and kill me? Let every man go his own way, and look to himself as best he may.

SECRETARY: It is right that you should not worry; but those who know and love you –

EGMONT [looking at the letter]: Look, here is the old story again, of what we said and did that evening, when good company and wine had made us merry and bold, and what consequences and conclusions were drawn from it and dragged round the whole kingdom. Yes, we had a fool's cap and bells sewn on our servants' sleeves; then we changed that mad ornament for a bundle of arrows – an even more dangerous symbol, for those who will find meanings where meaning there is none. It was our folly, conceived and born in a merry moment; and so it is our fault that a whole company of nobles nicknamed themselves beggars* to remind the King of his obligations, in mock-humility? our fault that – what else is there? Is a carnival prank high treason now? Are we to be grudged a few gay rags our youthful high spirits, our cheerful fancy choose to deck our poor bare lives in? If you take life in such deadly earnest, what is there in it? If the morning no longer wakes us to new joys, if the evening leaves us no new delights to hope for, is it worth while dressing and undressing? Does the sun shine today for me to think of yesterday? to guess, to seek to bind what none can guess and none can bind, tomorrow's fate? No more of these philosophizings; we will leave them to scholars and courtiers. Let them plot and plan, go their tortuous ways and see where they may lead. – If any of this is of use to you, put it down, as long as your letter does not swell into a book. The good old man sees too much in everything. A friend who has held our hand a long time will tighten his grip once more before he lets it go.

SECRETARY: Forgive me; when one plods along on foot, it makes one giddy to see another hurtling by so swiftly.

EGMONT: Boy! boy! no more! Our destiny is like the sun; invisible spirits whip up time's swift horses, away with its light chariot they run, and all we can do is take courage, hold the reins in a firm grip, and keep the wheels clear of the rocks on one hand, the precipice on the other. Where we are going, who can tell? We scarcely know from whence we came.

---

*In 1566 the nobles in opposition to Margaret, who were petitioning against the powers of the Inquisition, adopted the name of *gueux* ('beggars'), originally applied to them in derision by Baron Berlaymont, one of Margaret's councillors of state. (*Translator's note.*)

SECRETARY: My lord, my lord!

EGMONT: I stand high, I can and must climb still higher; I feel hope, courage and strength in me. I have not yet reached the summit of my growth; and when I reach it, then I will stand firm, and know no fear. If I am to fall, let storm and thunderbolt, yes, let my own false step bring me low; then headlong into the abyss where thousands fell before me. I have never scorned to throw the bloody dice of war with my good companions, when the prize was small; shall I be miserly now, when all that makes life worth while to me is at stake?

SECRETARY: Oh, my lord! You do not know what you are saying! God preserve you!

EGMONT: Pick up your papers! Here comes Orange. See to it that the most essential letters are written so that the messengers can leave before the gates are shut. The rest can wait. Leave the letter to the Count until tomorrow; be sure to visit Elvira, and give her my good wishes. See if you can find out how the Princess Regent is; they say she is not well, although she seeks to hide it. [*Exit* SECRETARY.]

[*Enter* ORANGE.]

EGMONT: Welcome, Orange! But you do not seem at your ease.

ORANGE: What did you think of our conversation with the Princess?

EGMONT: I found nothing extraordinary in our reception. I have seen her like that many times. She seemed to me to be unwell.

ORANGE: Did you not notice that she was more reserved? At first it seemed that she would approve our reaction to the latest stirrings of the mob, and make no objection, but then it occurred to her that that too might be misinterpreted, and she went over to her old familiar theme: how her kindness, her mildness, her good-will towards us Netherlanders had never been appreciated, how they were taken for granted; how nothing she did would turn out as she would have it; how in the end she would grow tired of it, and the King would be forced to take other measures. Did you hear that?

EGMONT: Not all of it; I was thinking of something else. She is a woman, my dear Orange, and they always want everyone else to bear their gentle yoke without complaint; they want every Hercules to take off his lion's skin and sit down to spin; because their own ways are peaceful, they think that the ferment of a whole people, the storms of powerful rivals, should be stilled by a single word, and the most hostile elements unite in sweet harmony at their feet. So it is with her too, and since she cannot get her way, all she can do is turn moody, complain of ingratitude and lack of wisdom, threaten us with dreadful visions of the future, threaten – to go, and leave us.

ORANGE: Do you not believe that she will carry out her threat this time?

EGMONT: Never! How often I have seen her ready to depart! Where will she go? Here she is Stadtholder, Queen; do you think it will be enough for her to while away the days in insignificance at her brother's court, or go to Italy and pass the time stirring up old family quarrels?

ORANGE: Because you have seen her hesitate, seen her draw back when she was on the brink of deciding, no one will believe her capable of doing it; and yet she has it in her. New circumstances will force her to take the decision she has put off for so long. What if she did go, and the King sent someone else?

EGMONT: Then he would come, and he would find plenty to do. He would come with great plans, projects and ideas for setting all to rights, subjecting us, keeping a firm grip on things; and he would find himself occupied with one trifle today, and another tomorrow; the day after that there would be some new hindrance; he would spend one month in scheming, the next brooding over the failure of his designs, and six months worrying over the affairs of a single province. He too will find time passing, and his head spinning, and things going their own way as before, and instead of setting his course and following it smoothly across the ocean, he will thank God if only he can keep his ship off the rocks through this one storm.

ORANGE: But if the King were now advised to try an experiment?

EGMONT: Namely?

ORANGE: To see what the body would do without its head.

EGMONT: What?

ORANGE: Egmont, for many years I have watched carefully over our affairs like a game of chess, where I have to look for some significance in every move my opponent makes; and as some men while away their time studying all the secrets of nature, so I regard it as the duty, the profession of a ruler to know the moods and counsels of all parties. The King has for a long time acted according to certain principles. He sees that they will lead him nowhere; what is more probable than that he should decide to try another way?

EGMONT: I do not believe it. When a man grows old, and has tried so hard, and still the world will not be brought to order, then in the end he must decide that he has had enough.

ORANGE: One way he has not tried yet.

EGMONT: Well?

ORANGE: To spare the people and destroy the princes.

EGMONT: How many have worried about that, and for so long now! There is nothing to fear.

ORANGE: It is no longer a mere fear. I have long suspected, and now I am convinced, that it is going to happen.

EGMONT: Has the King more faithful servants than we are?

ORANGE: We serve him in our own way; and as one to another, we can admit that we know how to strike the balance between the King's rights and our own.

EGMONT: Who does not do that? We serve him and are subject to him in all that is his due.

ORANGE: But if now he were to claim more, and called disloyalty what we call insisting on our rights?

EGMONT: We shall be able to defend ourselves. Let him summon the Knights of the Golden Fleece, and we will be judged by them.

ORANGE: But a judgement without trial, a punishment without judgement?

EGMONT: That would be an injustice which Philip will never commit, and a folly which I would not believe of him or his advisers.

ORANGE: But if they should prove unjust and foolish?

EGMONT: No, Orange, it is not possible. Who would dare to lay hands on us? To take us prisoner would be a vain and futile venture. They will not dare to proclaim their tyranny so openly. The wind that news would raise in the land would blow up a tremendous fire. And what would they be trying to achieve? The King alone cannot judge or sentence; and would they set assassins to murder us? That they cannot intend. The people would instantly be united in a terrible alliance. Hatred and separation from the name of Spain for ever would be its battle-cry.

ORANGE: Then the flames would be raging over our graves, and all the blood of our enemies would not bring us back to life. Let us think, Egmont!

EGMONT: But how could they try?

ORANGE: Alva is on his way.

EGMONT: I do not believe it.

ORANGE: I know it.

EGMONT: The Princess said she knew nothing.

ORANGE: That convinces me all the more. The Princess will step down for him. I know his bloodthirsty ways; and he is bringing an army with him.

EGMONT: To burden the Provinces still more? The people will resist.

ORANGE: But their leaders will be taken in charge.

EGMONT: No, no!

ORANGE: Let us go, each to his own province, and gather our strength there. He will not begin with open violence.

EGMONT: Must we not greet him when he comes?

ORANGE: We will keep him waiting.

EGMONT: And if he summons us in the King's name as soon as he arrives?

ORANGE: We will find a way out of it.

EGMONT: And if he insists?

ORANGE: We will make excuses.

EGMONT: And if he orders us?

ORANGE: We shall be all the surer to stay away.

EGMONT: And war will be declared, and we shall be the rebels. Orange, do not be led astray by cleverness, for I know that fear will never make you yield. Think what it is you would have us do!

ORANGE: I have thought.

EGMONT: Think, if you are wrong, what you will be responsible for: the most fearful war that ever laid a country waste. Your refusal will be the signal for the Provinces to leap to arms, and every cruelty that Spain has so long and so greedily sought the pretext for will be justified. What we have so painstakingly sought to calm, you would stir up at once to the most frightful tumult. Think of the cities, the nobility, the people; trade, and the crafts of town and country; and think of the bloodshed and the destruction! The soldier may be calm on the battlefield when he sees his comrade fall dead beside him, but you will see the bodies of men, women and children floating down the river towards you, and you will stand horror-struck and know no longer whose cause you are defending, for those for whose freedom you took up arms will be destroyed. And what then, when you will have to admit: 'I did it for the safety of my skin'?

ORANGE: Egmont, our lives are not simply our own. If it is our duty to sacrifice ourselves for thousands, then it is our duty to spare ourselves for thousands.

EGMONT: He who spares himself must suspect himself.

ORANGE: He who knows himself can go surely, forward or back.

EGMONT: The evil that you fear will come about through what you do.

ORANGE: It is prudent and bold to go to meet evil when it is inescapable.

EGMONT: In such great danger one must cling to the last shred of hope.

ORANGE: We no longer have room to manoeuvre; the abyss is at our feet.

EGMONT: Is the King's favour such a narrow foothold?

ORANGE: Not narrow, no, but slippery.

EGMONT: By God, you do him an injustice. I cannot bear men to think ill of him. He is Charles's son, and could do nothing that was base.

ORANGE: What a king does cannot be base.

EGMONT: If men only knew him!

ORANGE: What we know tells us that it is dangerous to make further experiment.

EGMONT: No experiment is dangerous, if one has the courage for it.

ORANGE: Egmont, you are too heated.

EGMONT: I must see with my own eyes.

ORANGE: Oh, if only this once you could see with mine! My friend, because yours are open, you believe that you can see. I am going. Wait for Alva to arrive, and God be with you. Perhaps my refusal will save you. Perhaps the dragon will not think he has caught anything unless he can swallow us both at once. Perhaps he will delay, to be surer of his plan's succeeding, and perhaps in that time you will see things as they are. But then make haste, make haste! Save, save yourself! – Farewell. Take note of everything: how many men he has, how he disposes them in the city, what powers the Princess retains, what mind your friends are in. Send me word – Egmont!

EGMONT: What is it?

ORANGE [grasping him by the hand]: Be persuaded! Come with me!

EGMONT: What, Orange, tears?

ORANGE: A man too may weep for one who is lost.

EGMONT: You think I am lost?

ORANGE: You are. Think better of it! You have but a little time. Farewell! [Exit.]

EGMONT [alone]: That other men's thoughts should affect us so! It would never have occurred to me; and now this man makes me share his anxieties. Away with them! They are like drops of a stranger's blood that mingle with my own; kindly Nature, draw them out again! And still I think I know where I can bathe these fretful wrinkles from my brow.

ACT III

Palace of the Princess Regent

[MARGARET *alone*]

MARGARET: I ought to have suspected this would happen. Ah, we do our utmost here in toil and trouble, and think no man could do more; while he that looks on and gives his orders from afar thinks anyone could do the little that he asks. Oh, you kings! – I would never have believed it could vex me so. To rule is so splendid! – And to abdicate? – I do not know how my father could do it; but I will do it too.

[MACHIAVELLI *appears in the background.*]

MARGARET: Come closer, Machiavelli! You find me considering my brother's letter.

MACHIAVELLI: May I know what it contains?

MARGARET: As much tenderness and consideration for me as anxiety for his dominions. He praises the constancy, the loyalty and zeal with which I have guarded the prerogatives of royalty in these lands until now. He regrets that I have to endure so much from the unruly people. He is so completely convinced of my profound understanding, so exceptionally satisfied with the wisdom of my actions, that I must almost say this letter is too finely written for a king, let alone for a brother.

MACHIAVELLI: It is not the first time that he has expressed a proper satisfaction with your work.

MARGARET: But the first time that it is no more than honeyed words.

MACHIAVELLI: I do not understand.

MARGARET: You will. – For after this preamble he continues that without men, without some army I must always cut a poor figure here. He says that we were wrong to withdraw our soldiers from the Provinces because of the people's complaints. He thinks that if the citizen has to carry the burden of an army of occupation, the weight of it will make him less frisky.

MACHIAVELLI: It would be the greatest possible provocation.

MARGARET: But the King thinks, do you hear? – thinks that a general, a fighting man, one who will not listen to reason, could soon deal with people and nobility, peasants and citizens; and so he is sending, with a powerful army – the Duke of Alva.

MACHIAVELLI: Alva?

MARGARET: You are surprised?

MACHIAVELLI: You said he is sending Alva. You mean he asks if he is to send Alva?

MARGARET: The King does not ask. He is sending Alva.

MACHIAVELLI: Then – you will have an experienced soldier in your service.

MARGARET: In my service? Speak out, Machiavelli!

MACHIAVELLI: I would not anticipate your highness's thoughts.

MARGARET: And should I seek to hide them? I am grieved, Machiavelli, deeply grieved. I wish my brother would say what was in his mind, instead of signing these formal letters that some secretary has written for him.

MACHIAVELLI: But do they not see –?

MARGARET: And I know them through and through. They want the Netherlands swept clean; they will do nothing themselves, but will listen to anyone who comes to them with a broom in his hand. Oh, I can see the King and all his counsellors, as clearly as if they were here embroidered on this tapestry.

MACHIAVELLI: To the life?

MARGARET: To the last detail. Some of them are good men. Honest Rodrigo, so experienced and moderate, who would not fly too high, but would let nothing escape him; straight-forward Alonzo, hard-working Fresneda, solid Las Vargas and a few others who will go along with them when the good party is in the ascendant. But there is Toledo with his hollow eyes of fire and his brazen forehead, muttering between his teeth of woman's softness, of yielding too soon, and of how a woman can ride a well-broken horse, but makes a bad trainer, and quips of that kind, such as I have had to endure before from those political gentlemen.

MACHIAVELLI: You paint with a rich palette.

MARGARET: And yet you must admit it, Machiavelli: of all the colours to my hand there is not one as jaundiced or as black with gall as Alva's face or as the shades he paints with. He sees in every man a blasphemer and a traitor to the King; for call them that, and without more ado they are all ready for the axe and the sword, the wheel and the stake. – What good I have done here, at that distance no doubt seems nothing, just because it is good. – But he will seize on every stubbornness that is now past, recall every disturbance that is now quelled, and conjure up such desperate mutiny and rebellion before the king's eyes that he will believe every man here is at his neighbour's throat, when we have long forgotten a rough people's passing unruliness. Then he will begin to hate the poor wretches in earnest; they will seem repellent to him, like beasts and monsters; he will look to fire and sword, and fancy that that is the way to command men.

MACHIAVELLI: I think you go too far. You let yourself be carried away. Will not you remain Regent?

MARGARET: I know what will happen. He will have his orders. – I have grown old enough in public affairs to know how one can be permitted to keep one's position, and yet be elbowed out of it. To start with he will have his orders, imprecise and vague; then he will begin to take liberties, for he has the power; and if I complain, he will say he is acting on secret instructions; if I ask to see them, he will lead me some dance or other, and if I insist he will show me a paper with something quite different on it; and if that does

not satisfy me he will do no more than if I were beating the
air. Meanwhile he will have done all that I fear, and have
made impossible all that I desire.

MACHIAVELLI: I wish I could contradict you.

MARGARET: What I took such infinite pains to calm down,
his harshness and cruelty will stir up again; I shall see my
work destroyed before my eyes, and in addition have to
bear the responsibility for what he does.

MACHIAVELLI: Let your highness wait and see!

MARGARET: I have self-control enough to be silent. Let him
come; I shall step down for him as is fitting, before he
drives me out.

MACHIAVELLI: So soon, this fateful step?

MARGARET: It is harder than you think. When one is used to
rule, when one is accustomed to hold every day the fate of
thousands in one's hand, then to step from the throne is
like stepping into the grave. But rather that than remain a
ghost among the living, and seek to maintain with empty
show a place that has passed to another, who now occupies
it and enjoys its benefits.

Clara's house

[CLARA *and her* MOTHER]

MOTHER: I never saw a love the like of Brackenburg's; I
thought men only loved like that in the tales of old.

CLARA [*paces up and down the room, singing softly to herself*]:

> Only in love
> Can the soul draw its breath.

MOTHER: He suspects what there is between you and Egmont;
and yet, I do believe, if only you were a little friendly to
him, if you wanted him, he would still marry you.

CLARA [*sings*]:

> In joy and in sorrow,
> Pensive and gay,
> In fear and in longing
> Racked all the day,

> Rejoicing to heaven,
> Grieved unto death,
> Only in love
> Can the soul draw its breath.

MOTHER: Enough of that singsong!

CLARA: Do not scold me; there is power in that song. It has often lulled a great child to sleep for me.

MOTHER: You think of nothing but your love; if only it did not make you blind to everything else! Brackenburg deserves your respect, I tell you. He could still make you happy again.

CLARA: He?

MOTHER: Oh, yes, the time will come! You children see nothing of the future, and you will not listen to the voice of experience. Youth and the joys of love, it all comes to an end, and there comes a time when we thank God for a place to lay our head.

CLARA [*shudders, and is silent. Then starting up*]: Mother, let that time come when it comes, like death! To think of it before is terrible! And when it comes – when we have to – then – then let us bear it as best we can! Egmont! to be without you! [*In tears*] No, it cannot be, it cannot be.

> [*Enter* EGMONT *in a riding cloak, his hat pulled down over his face.*]

EGMONT: Clara!

CLARA [*cries out and draws back*]: Egmont! [*Rushing up to him*] Egmont! [*She embraces him and leans against him.*] Oh dear, good, sweet Egmont! Is it you? Have you come?

EGMONT: Good evening, mother.

MOTHER: God be with you, noble sir! My child has been pining away because you were so long coming; all day long again she's been talking and singing about you.

EGMONT: You'll give me some supper?

MOTHER: You do us too much honour. If only we had anything!

CLARA: Of course we will! Do not worry, mother, I have made something, everything is ready. Mother, don't give me away!

MOTHER: Poor enough.

CLARA: Just wait and see. And when I have him I am not hungry at all, so I think he should not have too big an appetite when he has me.

EGMONT: You think so?

CLARA [*stamps her foot and turns away as if offended.*]

EGMONT: What's the matter?

CLARA: How cold you are today! You have not even kissed me. Why are you wrapped up in your cloak like that, your arms too, like a baby? Soldiers and lovers need their arms free.

EGMONT: Not always, my sweet, not always. When a soldier is lying in wait for his enemy, hoping to win something from him by stealth, then he wraps his arms around himself tight and waits till the moment is ripe. And a lover –

MOTHER: Will you not sit down and make yourself comfortable? I must go to the kitchen; Clara can think of nothing when you are here. You will have to make do with what there is.

EGMONT: Good will is worth all the fine sauces in the world. [*Exit* MOTHER.]

CLARA: And what is my love worth, then?

EGMONT: As much as you will make it.

CLARA: Draw up the balance, if you have the heart to.

EGMONT: Firstly, then. [*He throws off his cloak and stands revealed magnificently dressed.*]

CLARA: Ohh!

EGMONT: Now I have my arms free. [*He embraces her.*]

CLARA: No, you will spoil it! [*Drawing back*] How magnificent you are! I would not dare to touch you.

EGMONT: Are you pleased? I promised you I would come in Spanish style one day.

CLARA: I had stopped asking you; I thought you did not want to. Ah, and the Golden Fleece!

EGMONT: There it is.

CLARA: The Emperor hung it round your neck?

EGMONT: Yes, my child; and this chain and this emblem give their wearer the noblest privileges. I admit no man in all the world to judge my actions but the Grand Master of the Order in session with all his knights.

CLARA: Oh, you could let the whole world judge you! The velvet is so wonderful, and the braid! and the embroidery! I do not know where to begin looking at it.

EGMONT: Look as much as you like!

CLARA: And the Golden Fleece. You told me the story of it, and said it was a sign of all that was great and precious, and earned and won through toil and labour. It is so precious – it is just like your love; I bear that next to my heart. But then –

EGMONT: What is it you want to say?

CLARA: But then they are unlike again.

EGMONT: In what way?

CLARA: I have not won it through toil and labour, I have not earned it.

EGMONT: Love is different. You deserve it because you do not seek to gain it; it is mostly only those who do not chase after it who find it.

CLARA: Are you speaking of yourself? Do you make such proud glosses on yourself, you whom all men love?

EGMONT: If only I had done something for them, if only I could do something for them! But no, they just see fit to love me.

CLARA: I suppose you have seen the Princess today?

EGMONT: I have.

CLARA: Are you in her confidence?

EGMONT: So it seems. We are friends and try to help each other.

CLARA: And in your heart?

EGMONT: I wish her well. Each of us is seeking his own ends; but that makes no difference. She is a fine woman, she knows her people and would see clearly enough if she were not suspicious too. I give her a great deal of trouble, because she is always looking behind what I do and say for secrets, and I have none.

CLARA: None at all?

EGMONT: Well – only a little hiding-place. Every wine makes

a crust in the barrel after a time. Orange is better entertainment for her, after all: always posing new problems. He has got himself the reputation of always hatching some secret plan; and she is always trying to read his mind, or to guess where his steps will take him.

CLARA: Is she frank?

EGMONT: She is our Regent. Need you ask?

CLARA: No; I should have said, is she deceitful?

EGMONT: No more and no less than any other who has his aims to achieve.

CLARA: I should be lost in a world like that. But then she has a man's spirit; she is not a woman like us cooks and seamstresses. She is great, courageous, determined.

EGMONT: Yes, if things do not move too fast for her. At the moment she is not quite herself.

CLARA: Why?

EGMONT: She has a little moustache, too, and sometimes she has the gout. A real Amazon!

CLARA: A noble lady! I should be afraid to show myself before her.

EGMONT: You do not usually lack courage. But it would not be fear, only a maiden's modesty.

[CLARA *lowers her eyes, takes his hand and presses close to him.*]

EGMONT: I understand. Dear Clara! Open your eyes. [*He kisses her eyelids.*]

CLARA: Let me be silent. Let me hold you, let me look into your eyes, let me find everything there, comfort and hope and joy and sorrow. [*She embraces him and looks at him.*] Tell me, tell me! I cannot understand it. Are you Egmont? Count Egmont, the great Egmont, the one who is always in the public eye, the one we are always hearing about, the one the Provinces are devoted to?

EGMONT: No, Clara, I am not.

CLARA: What?

EGMONT: Look, Clara! Let me sit down. [*He sits down, she kneels on a stool at his feet with her arms in his lap, looking at him.*] That Egmont is a stiff, cold, disagreeable Egmont, who has to keep himself in check, who has to wear this face today and that face tomorrow; plagued, misunderstood, turned in on himself, when men think he is cheerful and gay; loved by a people who do not know what they want, honoured and exalted by a mob one can get nowhere with, surrounded by men he cannot trust, spied on by men who would dearly love to lay their hands on him; working and straining himself often to no purpose, mostly without reward! Oh, let me not say how he feels, what life is like for him! But this one, Clara, is calm, free, happy, known and loved by the best of hearts, a heart he too knows through and through and can press to his own in perfect love and trust. [*He embraces her.*] And this is *your* Egmont!

CLARA: Then let me die! The world knows no joy beyond this!

ACT IV

A street

[*Enter* JETTER *and* CARPENTER.]

JETTER: Hey! Pst! Neighbour, a word in your ear!

CARPENTER: Go about your business, and be quiet!

JETTER: Just one word. Is there any news?

CARPENTER: Only that we are forbidden to talk about the news.

JETTER: What?

CARPENTER: Here, come close to this house! Watch out! The Duke of Alva, the moment he arrived, sent out an order saying that if two or three men speak together in the street they are guilty of high treason, without trial.

JETTER: Oh, ruin!

CARPENTER: To talk of public affairs means life imprisonment.

JETTER: Oh, our liberty!

CARPENTER: And to criticize the government is death.

JETTER: Oh, our heads!

CARPENTER: Fathers, mothers, children, relatives, friends and servants who will inform the special courts of what goes on in the privacy of their own houses, are promised a rich reward.

JETTER: Let's go home!

CARPENTER: And those who obey are assured that neither they nor their property shall come to any harm.

JETTER: That's gracious for you! I felt things were going to be bad as soon as the Duke came into town. Since then it's been as if there were black clouds all over the sky, and hanging down so low that you had to crawl under them all the time.

CARPENTER: And what did you think of his soldiers? Not like we're used to, are they? Quite a different kettle of fish!

JETTER: Ugh! It freezes your blood to see them marching down the street. Straight as a die, eyes front and never swerving, never a man a hair's breadth out of step. And when they are standing guard and you go past one of them, it's as if his eyes were boring into you, and they look so stiff and surly, you'd think there was a sergeant-major at every corner. It's not good to see. Our old militia was not so bad; they didn't take it all so seriously, stood easy with their hat down over one ear, lived and let live; but these fellows are like machines with a devil in them.

CARPENTER: If one of them shouts 'Halt!' and takes aim, what then? Do you stop?

JETTER: I should drop dead on the spot.

CARPENTER: Let's go home.

JETTER: It's a bad business. Adieu to you.

[*Enter* SOEST.]

SOEST: Friends! Comrades!

CARPENTER: Quiet! Let's be off!

SOEST: Have you heard?

JETTER: Too much already.

SOEST: The Princess has gone.

JETTER: God preserve us now!

CARPENTER: She was our last hope.

SOEST: Suddenly, and without a word. She couldn't get on with the Duke; sent word to the nobles that she would be coming back. No one believes it.

CARPENTER: God forgive the nobility for letting them send this new scourge on us. They could have stopped it. All our privileges have gone.

JETTER: For God's sake, not a word of privileges! Oh, I can smell it, like the morning of an execution; the sun doesn't want to rise, and the mists stink.

SOEST: Orange has gone too.

CARPENTER: So they have all left us, then!

SOEST: Count Egmont is here still.

JETTER: Thank God for that, and may the saints give him strength to do his best; he is the only one who can do anything.

[*Enter* VANSEN.]

VANSEN: At last, here are a few that haven't run away to hide yet!

JETTER: Will you be so good as to go about your business?

VANSEN: That is not polite.

CARPENTER: This is no time for politeness. Is your back itching for more punishment? Is it healed from the last time?

VANSEN: Ask a soldier about his wounds! If I had cared about a few blows, I should never be where I am today.

JETTER: Things might well get more serious.

VANSEN: The storm that's brewing seems to have given you all a sore head.

CARPENTER: Your head will be stuck up somewhere else if you are not more careful.

VANSEN: Look at the poor mice, in despair as soon as the master brings in a new cat! It's not quite the same, but we shall carry on as we did before, be sure of that!

CARPENTER: You are a daredevil good-for-nothing.

VANSEN: Come along, gaffer, just leave the Duke alone! The old tom-cat looks as though he'd eaten imps of hell instead of mice and found he couldn't stomach them. Let him be.

He has to eat and drink and sleep like other men. I'm not afraid, as long as we bide our time. At first things will be busy; but later on he'll find out that life is better in the larder where the sides of bacon are, than in the attic catching a mouse or two. I know these stadtholders, believe me.

CARPENTER: The things the man can get away with! If ever in my life I'd said such things I should never count myself safe.

VANSEN: There's nothing to worry about! God in his heaven will never get to hear of worms like you, let alone the Regent.

JETTER: Hold your blaspheming tongue!

VANSEN: There are others I know who would be better off with a yellow streak instead of all their courage.

CARPENTER: What do you mean by that?

VANSEN: Hm! I mean the Count.

JETTER: Egmont? What has he to fear?

VANSEN: A poor devil like me could live for a year on what he gambles away in an evening. But he might well give me his income for a whole year if only he could have my head for a quarter of an hour.

JETTER: A fine idea. Egmont has more brains in his little finger.

VANSEN: Maybe; but not better ones. These fine gentlemen are always the first to be fooled. He shouldn't be so trusting.

JETTER: What talk! A man like him!

VANSEN: Just because he isn't a tailor.

JETTER: Damn your insolence!

VANSEN: I wish he could have a tailor's courage just for an hour, just long enough to upset him, to poke him and prod him until he had to run away, out of the city.

JETTER: You are talking nonsense. He is as safe as the stars in heaven.

VANSEN: Have you never seen one fall? Phut, and it's gone!

CARPENTER: Who would do anything to him?

VANSEN: Who would? Who would stop them? You? Will you start a revolt when they arrest him?

JETTER: Eh?

VANSEN: You, would you risk your neck for him?

SOEST: B–b–

VANSEN [*mimicking them*]: C–c–c, D–d–d–d! You can gape
your way through the whole alphabet, but it will still be
the same. God preserve him!

JETTER: You astound me with your impudence. Can a fine
upstanding man like that have anything to fear?

VANSEN: A rogue will always have the advantage. Put him in
the dock, and he will make a fool of the judge; put him on
the bench, and he can turn any witness into a criminal, as
easily as you like. I once had to take down evidence from
some poor honest devil they were after, and the lawyer was
praised at court and well rewarded for proving that he was
a scoundrel.

CARPENTER: That's a lie again. If a man is innocent, what
can they hope to get out of him?

VANSEN: Blockhead! If they can't get anything out of him,
then they put it in. If he's honest, he doesn't think; he may
even be obstinate. At first, they just ask their questions, and
the prisoner protests his innocence, as they call it, and tells
them all sorts of things that a clever man would keep quiet
about. Then the inquisitor turns the answers into questions
again, and is always on the lookout for some little wee
contradiction; there he sets his snare, and the poor devil
puts his foot straight into it; he's said too much here, not
enough there, maybe even taken it into his head to suppress
some piece of information, let himself be intimidated somewhere or other; then we know where we are! And I can
promise you there's not a beggar-woman picks over rags
more carefully than one of these scoundrel-makers will look
you out tiny, half-forgotten, misbegotten, God-forsaken,
mistaken, misshapen, misleading and unheeding shreds and
tatters of evidence and patch them together into a scare-
crow so that he can at least hang his victim in effigy. And
the poor devil can thank God if he's still alive to see himself
hanged.

JETTER: What a tongue the fellow has!

CARPENTER: You may catch flies like that, but a wasp wouldn't be caught in your web; he would laugh at it.

VANSEN: That depends on the spider. Look, your lanky Duke is just like a spider; not one of the fat ones, they're not so dangerous, but one of those thin long-legged ones that never get any fatter, however much they eat; and the threads they spin are fine, but all the tougher for it.

JETTER: Egmont is a Knight of the Golden Fleece; who can dare to touch him? He can only be judged by his peers, by all the knights of the order. It's your long tongue and your bad conscience that make you talk so much nonsense.

VANSEN: What have I got against him? It's nothing to me. He is a fine man. Some good friends of mine, who would have been hanged anywhere else, he let off with a beating. Now go along, go along! Now I'm saying it myself. I can see some guards setting out on their rounds; they don't look as though they would sit down with us and drink our health. But I've some nieces, and an innkeeper in the family; if they're not quieter when they've tried them, then the beasts are untamable.

The Duke of Alva's rooms in the Culemburg Palace

[*Enter* SILVA *and* GOMEZ, *meeting.*]

SILVA: Have you carried out the Duke's orders?

GOMEZ: To the letter. All the patrols have been instructed to be in their prescribed places at the appointed time; meanwhile they are to keep order in the streets in the usual way. None of them knows that the others have received similar orders. We can close the cordon at a moment's notice, and all routes to the palace will be guarded. Do you know why these orders have been given?

SILVA: I am accustomed to obey without questioning. And whose orders are easier to obey than the Duke's? The results soon show that they were the right ones.

GOMEZ: Very well! I am not surprised that you are becoming as taciturn as he is, since you have to be with him all the time. It seems strange to me, now that I have grown used to the Italian service, where things are not so strict. Not that I am any less loyal or obedient; but I have taken to talking and discussing things. You are all so silent and never seem at ease. The Duke seems to me like a tower of bronze, without a door, so that the garrison must have wings. The other day at table I heard him say of some cheerful, friendly person that he was like a low tavern with its sign hung out to lure in beggars, thieves and idlers.

SILVA: And did he not bring us here in silence?

GOMEZ: I have nothing to say against that. Indeed not! The way he brought the army here from Italy was something worth seeing. How he wormed his way in between friend and foe, through all the French, King's men and heretics, and past the Swiss and their allies, and kept the strictest discipline, and completed a march that was supposed to be so dangerous without the least difficulty or trouble! That was a real lesson for anyone with eyes to see.

SILVA: So it is here! Is not everything as quiet and peaceful as if there had never been any revolt?

GOMEZ: Well, things had already calmed down for the most part when we arrived.

SILVA: It is much quieter in the Provinces now. If anyone stirs himself, it is to run away. But I expect he will soon have that stopped too.

GOMEZ: That will win the King's highest favour.

SILVA: And we must see to it that we stay in his. When the King comes here, you can be sure the Duke and those he recommends will not go unrewarded.

GOMEZ: Do you think the King will come?

SILVA: They are making so many preparations that it seems very likely.

GOMEZ: They do not convince me.

SILVA: Then do not speak about it. If the King should not intend to come, then at least he must intend us to believe he is coming.

[*Enter* FERDINAND.]

FERDINAND: Has my father not come out yet?

SILVA: We are waiting for him.

FERDINAND: The princes will soon be here.

GOMEZ: Are they coming today?

FERDINAND: Orange and Egmont.

GOMEZ [*softly to* SILVA]: I think I understand.

SILVA: Then keep it to yourself!

[*Enter the* DUKE OF ALVA. *The others draw back as he comes forward.*]

ALVA: Gomez!

GOMEZ [*coming forward*]: Your grace!

ALVA: You have sent out the patrols and given them their orders?

GOMEZ: To the letter. All the patrols –

ALVA: Enough. You will wait in the gallery. Silva will tell you when you are to close the cordon and man all approaches to the palace. The rest you know.

GOMEZ: Yes, your grace. [*Exit.*]

ALVA: Silva!

SILVA: Here.

ALVA: Everything I value and have always valued in you, courage, determination, unyielding tenacity of purpose, let me see it today.

SILVA: I thank your grace for the opportunity to show that I have not changed.

ALVA: As soon as the princes are here with us, have Egmont's private secretary arrested immediately. You have made all the preparations for the capture of the others I have named to you?

SILVA: You may rely on us. Their fate will be upon them like an eclipse of the sun, terrible and punctual to the minute.

ALVA: Have you had them carefully watched?

SILVA: All of them, especially Egmont. He is the only one who has behaved no differently since you arrived. The whole day long from one horse to another, sending out invitations, always merry and good company, shooting and dicing and slinking off to his girl at night. But the others have noticeably changed their style of living. They stay at home; go past their door and you would think it was a sick man's house.

ALVA: Quickly, then; we do not want them to recover.

SILVA: I have them at bay. On your orders we are overwhelming them with honours. They are afraid; anxiously, diplomatically, they thank us, but wonder whether they had not better run away; none of them dares to take the first step. They hesitate, they cannot agree on common action, but they have enough solidarity to prevent any one of them from risking anything on his own. They try to avoid doing anything suspicious, but only attract more and more suspicion. I am delighted: I can see your whole plan accomplished already.

ALVA: I am only delighted by what is accomplished, and not easily by that, for there is always enough left over to make more work and trouble for us. Fortune is wilful; so often it crowns the base and worthless with success and brings the most carefully planned actions to nothing. Wait until the princes are here, then give Gomez the order to man the streets, and hurry yourself to arrest Egmont's secretary and the others I have named. When it is done, come back here and inform my son, who will report to me in the council.

SILVA: I hope to be able to present myself to you this evening. [ALVA *withdraws to speak to his son, who has been standing in the gallery.*] I would not dare to say it, but my hope is wavering. I am afraid it will not turn out as he thinks. I see spirits before me, silent and brooding, weighing in their black scales the fates of the princes and of thousands more. Slowly the balance tips this way and that; deeply the judges seem to ponder; at last the one scale sinks, the other rises, tipped by the wilful breath of destiny, and it is decided. [*Exit.*]

ALVA [*coming forward with* FERDINAND]: How did you find the city?

FERDINAND: Everything is as we would have it. I rode as if to pass the time of day, up and down the streets. Your skilfully disposed guards have brought the townspeople's fear to such a pitch that there is not a whisper to be heard. The city is like a field when a thunderstorm is approaching;

not a bird or beast anywhere but is hurrying to find a place to hide.

ALVA: Was there nothing else?

FERDINAND: I met Egmont riding with a few followers into the market-place; he had a new, fiery horse; I had to praise his choice. 'Quickly, let us break our horses in,' he shouted to me, 'we shall soon be needing them!' He would be seeing me again today, he said; he was coming to confer with you as you had requested.

ALVA: He will be seeing you again.

FERDINAND: Of all the knights I know here I like him the most. I think we shall be friends.

ALVA: You are still too hasty and incautious; I recognize your mother's thoughtless nature, the same that made her surrender so easily to me. You have been lured by appearances into making many a dangerous acquaintance.

FERDINAND: I shall always bow to your will.

ALVA: I will forgive your youthful blood this frivolous generosity, this careless gaiety. But do not forget what work I have to do here, and what part of it I wish you to perform.

FERDINAND: Tell me again, and do not spare me, if you must be harsh.

ALVA [after a pause]: My son!

FERDINAND: Father!

ALVA: Soon the princes will be here; Orange and Egmont are coming. It is not because I do not trust you that I have not told you before what is to happen. They will not leave this place again.

FERDINAND: What is it you are planning?

ALVA: It has been decided to arrest them. — That surprises you! Hear what you have to do; when it is done you shall know the reason. Now is no time for explanations. With you alone I would discuss these most weighty secrets. A powerful bond unites us; I value you, and you are dear to me; all that I have I would pass on to you. I do not wish to teach you only to obey, but I would have you carry on the skill to plan, to command, to put into practice; to leave you a great inheritance, and to leave the King an accomplished servant; to furnish you with the best that I know, so that you need not be ashamed to be seen amongst your brothers.

FERDINAND: How much I owe you for this love that I alone enjoy, while a whole empire trembles before you!

ALVA: Now hear what is to be done. As soon as the princes are here, every way to the palace will be manned. Gomez is ordered to see to that. Silva will hasten to arrest Egmont's secretary and those whom we suspect the most. You will keep order among the guards at the gate and in the court-yards. Above all else, set the most trustworthy men to guard these rooms here; then wait in the gallery until Silva returns, and come in to me with some unimportant piece of paper, as a sign that he has performed his task. Then wait for Orange in the anteroom; follow him; I will keep Egmont here as if I had more to say to him. At the end of the gallery, demand Orange's sword, call the guards, quickly make sure of the most dangerous man; I will take Egmont, here.

FERDINAND: I will obey, father. For the first time it will be with a troubled, heavy heart.

ALVA: I pardon you for that; it is the first great moment in your life.

[*Enter* SILVA.]

SILVA: A messenger from Antwerp. Here is Orange's reply. He will not come.

ALVA: Did the messenger say so?

SILVA: No, my heart tells me so.

ALVA: I hear my evil genius in your words. [*He reads the letter, then motions to them both; they retire into the gallery, leaving him alone at the front of the stage.*] He will not come! He does not declare himself until the very last minute. He dares not to come! So this time, contrary to what I expected, the soul of prudence had the prudence to be rash! – Time presses! Before the hands of the clock have crept much further, a great work will have been accomplished – or the chance will have been lost for ever; for we can neither repeat it nor keep it secret. Long ago I had thought of everything, thought even of this happening and decided, firmly decided what was to be done if it did happen; and now that it must be done, I can hardly stop the arguments one way and another from crowding into my head anew. Is it wise to seize the others when *he* escapes? Shall I put it off, and let Egmont slip away with his followers, with so many who are now in my hands, today perhaps for the last time? So you, unbending one, you too must bend to fate! How long I had thought it out! How well it was prepared! How fine, how great a plan! How nearly my hopes had reached their goal! And now in the moment of decision you must choose between two evils. The future is a dark lottery. Whatever you draw, it is still folded tight and sealed; it may be a prize or a blank. [*He listens as if he heard a noise, and goes to the window*.] He has come! Egmont! Did your horse carry you here so lightly, did the smell of blood not frighten it, nor the spirit with the naked sword that received you at the gate? Step down! Now one foot is in the grave! now both! Yes, stroke him, pat his neck in thanks for the last time, the bold beast – And I, I have no choice. Blinded, as he comes today, Egmont will never come again! – Hear me! [FERDINAND *and* SILVA *hurry up to him*.] You will carry out my orders. I shall not alter my purpose. I shall delay Egmont as best I can until you bring me word from Silva. Then stay close at hand. Fate has robbed you too of the glory of taking the King's greatest enemy prisoner with your own hand. [*To* SILVA] Hurry! [*To* FERDINAND] Go to meet him! [*They go, leaving* ALVA *alone for a few moments. He paces up and down in silence*.]

[*Enter* EGMONT.]

EGMONT: I have come to hear the King's commands, to hear what service we, who remain devoted to him in perfect loyalty, are to perform.

ALVA: He desires above all to hear your advice.

EGMONT: On what matters? Is Orange coming too? I thought he would be here.

ALVA: I am sorry that we are to lack his presence on this most important occasion. The King desires your advice, your opinions as to how these dominions are to be pacified again.

Indeed he hopes that you will lend your strength to calm these troubles and to establish sound and lasting order in the Provinces.

EGMONT: But you know better than I that everything is calm enough again; indeed it was calmer still before the appearance of these new soldiers troubled men's hearts with fear and anxiety once more.

ALVA: It seems you would imply the wisest course would have been for the King not to have sent me here to ask you.

EGMONT: Your pardon. Whether the King should have sent the army, or whether perhaps the power of his own royal presence alone might have been the stronger, is not for me to judge. The army is here, he is not. But it would be most unmindful and ungrateful of us not to remember what we owe the Princess Regent. We must admit it: she, as skilful as she is brave, by her power and her presence, with persuasion and with cunning brought the rebels to order and astonished the whole world by leading an unruly people back into the path of duty within the space of a few months.

ALVA: I do not deny it. The tumult has died down and all seem to be confined within the bounds of obedience again. But is not each man free to break them at his will? Who can restrain the people? What power have we to prevent them? Who is our surety that they will continue to be loyal and faithful subjects? Their good will is the only pledge we have.

EGMONT: And is not a people's good will the surest and noblest of pledges? In God's name! When may a King feel safer than when all stand for one and one for all? Safer from enemies within and without?

ALVA: But you would not have us persuade ourselves that that is the case here?

EGMONT: Let the King proclaim a general amnesty, and set men's hearts at rest; soon he will see that trust will bring back loyalty and love.

ALVA: And every man who had insulted the King's majesty and blasphemed against religion should go free and do as he pleased, a living example to others of the most monstrous crime going unpunished?

EGMONT: And should not a crime committed in madness or drunkenness be pardoned rather than cruelly punished? Especially where there is hope, indeed certainty, that the evil will not happen again? Were not those kings the safer for it, are they not praised now and for ever, who could forgive, regret, ignore an insult to their majesty? Is that not why kings are likened to God, who is far too great to be touched by any blasphemy?

ALVA: And because of that, the King must fight for the glory of God and of religion, and we must fight for the King's majesty. What to the mighty is beneath contempt, we must avenge. If my word is to count for anything, then no guilty man shall go unpunished.

EGMONT: Do you believe that you will catch them all? Do we not hear every day that fear is driving them away, up and out of the land? The rich will take with them their goods, their families and friends; the poor man will take his hands to work for another master.

ALVA: They will, if we cannot stop them. Therefore the King demands support in word and deed from every prince, action from every stadtholder; he does not want to hear how things are, how things could be if everything were left to run its own course. To sit idly by watching this evil, flattering oneself with hopes, trusting to time, striking a blow now and then like a harlequin, so that it makes a noise and it seems as if one were doing something, when one would rather do nothing – is that not merely inviting the suspicion that this rebellion suits one very well, that one would not wish to stir it up but is happy to keep it simmering?

EGMONT [*is about to burst out angrily, but checks himself and speaks calmly after a short pause*]: Intentions are not always clear, and many a man's intentions may be misinterpreted. For every day one must hear it said on all sides that the King's intention is not to rule the Provinces by uniform and unambiguous laws, to guarantee the majesty of religion and to allow his peoples to enjoy universal peace, but rather to crush and subjugate them, to rob them of their ancient rights, to make himself master of their possessions and to curtail the fine privileges of the nobility, for whose sake alone the true nobleman will serve the King with all his strength. Religion, one hears it said, is nothing but a sham, a gorgeous veil to cover dangerous plots and plans. The people kneel and adore the sacred images woven upon it and behind it lurks the fowler ready to snare them.

ALVA: Must I hear this from you?

EGMONT: These are not my opinions! Only what is spoken, spread abroad, here one day, there the next, amongst great and humble, by wise men and by fools. The Netherlands fear a double yoke; who will guarantee their freedom?

ALVA: Freedom? A fine word! What does it mean? What sort of freedom do they want? What is the freest man free to do? What is right! And the King will hinder no man from doing that. No, no, they will not believe they are free unless they can do themselves and others mischief. Would it not be better to abdicate than to rule a people like that? When enemies gather from abroad, enemies the common citizen does not think of, too busy with his everyday affairs, and the King demands support, then they begin to disagree amongst themselves, and as good as conspire with the enemy. It is much better to keep them confined, hold them close like children, lead them like children for their own good. Believe me, the people will never grow up, will never grow wise; they will always be children.

EGMONT: How rarely a king attains to reason! And should not the many rather trust the many than the one? And if it only were the one; but it is the many who gather round that one, the company that grows up with its master. Perhaps only they have the right to grow wise.

ALVA: Perhaps indeed, because they are not left to themselves.

EGMONT: And therefore will not leave others to themselves. Do what you will; I have answered your question, and I repeat, it will not succeed, it cannot succeed! I know my countrymen. They are men, fit to walk God's earth; every man standing on his own feet, a little king in his own right, solid, industrious, capable, true, devoted to their old ways. It is hard to win their trust, but easy to keep it. Stiff and obstinate! You may bend them, but you will not break their spirit.

ALVA [who has looked round several times during this speech]: Would you repeat those words before the King?

EGMONT: The worse for me if I were frightened by his presence! The better for him, for his people, if he gave me the courage and the confidence to say much more.

ALVA: What is profitable to hear, I can hear as well as he.

EGMONT: I would say to him: a shepherd can easily drive a whole flock of sheep, and the ox draws his plough un-resisting, but if you would ride the noble horse, then you must learn his thoughts, you must ask nothing foolish of him and you must ask nothing foolishly. That is why the citizen desires to keep his old constitution, and to be ruled by his fellow-countrymen; because he knows how he will be led and can expect from them unselfishness and sym-pathy with his lot.

ALVA: And should a ruler not have power to alter these traditions? Is this not rather his finest privilege? What is lasting on this earth? Can any institution, any state remain for ever? Must not everything change in time, and will not then an outdated constitution only cause a thousand evils, because it takes no account of the new condition of the people? I am afraid it is because they leave so many gaps that these old rights are so beloved, so many loopholes where a clever man, a powerful man can hide or slip through, against the interest of the people and of the whole.

EGMONT: And these arbitrary changes, these unchecked interventions from above, do they not announce that one man claims the right to do what thousands may not? He alone will set himself free to satisfy all his desires, to carry out all his wishes. And if we were to trust him completely, a good and wise king, can his promise bind his successors? Will none of them be able to rule unsparingly and merci-lessly? Who will save us from tyranny when he sends us his servants, his kinsmen, to reign and to rule as they will with no knowledge of the country or its needs, meeting no resistance, knowing they are answerable to no man?

ALVA [*who has been looking round again*]: There is nothing more natural than that a king should seek to rule in his own right and should give the execution of his commands to those above all who understand him best, who will understand him, and who will carry out his will without demur.

EGMONT: And it is just as natural that the citizen should wish to be ruled by a man born and bred beside him, who has the same ideas of right and wrong, and whom he can look on as his brother.

ALVA: And yet the nobility has given its brothers a very unequal portion.

EGMONT: All that is centuries past, and no one bears us any grudge for it. But if new men were sent unnecessarily, who sought to enrich themselves at the nation's expense a second time, if the people were exposed to fierce, bold, absolute rapacity, then a tumult would arise that would not easily die down of its own accord.

ALVA: I should not tolerate these words: I too am a stranger in this country.

EGMONT: That I say them to you shows that it is not you I mean.

ALVA: And even so I would not wish to hear them from you. The King sent me in the hope that I should find the nobles ready to support me. The King will have his will. The King has seen, after careful consideration, what is best for the people; things cannot go on as before. The King's intention is to constrain them for their own good, to force salvation on them if it must be so, to sacrifice the troublesome citizens so that the others may enjoy peace and the good fortune that wise government brings. This is his decision; I am commanded to make it known to the nobility, and in his name I ask advice *how* it is to be done; I do not ask *what* is to be done, for that he has decided.

EGMONT: Your words unhappily justify the people's fear, the general fear! Then he has decided what no prince ought to decide. The strength of his people, their spirit, their own vision of themselves, these he will weaken, oppress, destroy, so that he may rule them at his ease. He will crush the very marrow of their character, to be sure – with the intention of making them happy. To make something of them, he will sweep them away and put something else in their place. Oh, if his intention is good, then it is misguided! We are not rebels against the King, we only resist when the King would take the first unhappy steps on a road that leads to ruin.

ALVA: It seems useless to try to reach agreement with you when you are in this frame of mind. You must have a poor opinion of the King, and a worse one of his advisers, if you can doubt that all these things have been thought of and said and weighed against each other long ago. It is no part of my mission to rehearse it all again. I demand obedience from the people; and from you, first in rank and dignity, I demand help in word and deed, as tokens of your absolute loyalty.

EGMONT: Demand our heads, and have done with it. No man of spirit will care whether he is to bow his neck beneath this yoke or before the headsman's axe. All that I have said has been wasted; I have done no more than disturb the air.

[*Enter* FERDINAND.]

FERDINAND: Excuse me for interrupting your conversation. Here is a letter which the messenger said required immediate attention.

ALVA: Allow me to see what it contains. [*He turns aside.*]

FERDINAND: It is a magnificent horse your men have brought for you.

EGMONT: It is not bad. I have had it some time, and was thinking of letting it go. If it takes your fancy, perhaps we might talk about it.

FERDINAND: Good, we will see.

[ALVA *motions to his son, who withdraws upstage.*]

EGMONT: Good-bye! Let me go, for in God's name there is nothing more that I can say.

ALVA: You are fortunate that fate prevents you from giving away any more of the secrets of your heart. Imprudently you have laid it bare, and it is more evidence against you than the most malicious of your enemies could offer.

EGMONT: Your reproaches do not touch me; I know myself well enough, and I know my duty to the King better than many who serve him only to serve themselves. But I am sorry to leave this quarrel unresolved, and I only hope we may soon be united in the service of our master and for the country's good. Perhaps a happier occasion, and the presence of the other princes who are not here today, will see us reach that agreement which now seems so impossible. With this hope, I will take my leave.

ALVA [*with a sign to his son*]: Stop, Egmont! – Your sword! [*The central door opens, and the gallery is seen to be full of armed guards, standing motionless.*]

EGMONT [*is silent in astonishment a while before he speaks*]: So that was your intention? That was why I was summoned? [*Seizing his sword as if to defend himself*] Am I defenceless, then?

ALVA: The King commands it: you are my prisoner. [*Armed men enter from both sides.*]

EGMONT [*after a pause*]: The King? – Orange! Orange! [*After another pause, giving up his sword*] Take it then! It has more often fought in the King's name than to defend this breast. [*Exit through the central door, escorted by the armed men,* FERDINAND *following.* ALVA *remains standing where he is. The curtain falls.*]

ACT V

A street, twilight

[CLARA, BRACKENBURG *and* CITIZENS]

BRACKENBURG: Dearest, in God's name! what are you doing?

CLARA: Come with us, Brackenburg! Do you not know what

men can do? We shall be sure to set him free. For what can compare with their love for him? Every man, I swear it, is burning with desire to save him, to turn aside danger from his precious life and to give the freest of men his freedom again. Come, they only lack the voice to summon them. What they owe to him must still be alive in their souls; and they know it is his strong arm alone that wards off destruction from them. For his sake and for their own, they must risk everything; and what is it then that we risk? At most our lives, and they are not worth living if he dies.

BRACKENBURG: My poor Clara, you do not see the power that holds us bound in brazen fetters.

CLARA: I do not believe it is invincible. Let us not waste time with idle words! Here come some of the men we know, honest and true! Listen, friends and neighbours, listen! Tell us, what of Egmont?

CARPENTER: What does the child want? Tell her to be quiet!

CLARA: Come closer, let us speak more softly till we are united in strength! There is not a moment to lose! The insolent tyranny that has dared to take him prisoner already holds its dagger poised to murder him. Oh, my friends! with every step of the advancing dusk I grow more anxious. This night fills me with fear. Come, let us separate. We will run quickly from one ward to another and call out the citizens. Let every man take up his trusty arms. We will meet again in the market-place, and carry all before us. Our enemies will find themselves surrounded, overwhelmed; we shall crush them. How can a handful of slaves resist us? And in our midst he will return, will see that he is freed; this once he can thank us, who owe him so much. Shall he not see the dawn once more free to the open skies?

CARPENTER: What is it, girl?

CLARA: Do you not understand? It is the Count I speak of, it is Egmont!

JETTER: Do not mention that name! It is death!

CLARA: Not that name? What, not that name of all names? Who will not seize every chance to mention it? Where can it not be read? There in the stars I have often seen it spelt out. Not mention it? What can this mean? Friends, dear, good neighbours, you are dreaming; awake! Do not stare at me so fearfully! Do not cast down your eyes and look so timidly away! What I am saying is only what you all long to hear. Is not my voice the voice of your own hearts? In this dreadful night, who would not kneel before his restless sleep and pray that heaven might save him? Ask each other, let each man ask himself, and who will not say with me: Egmont's freedom, or death!

JETTER: God preserve us, here is trouble.

CLARA: Stay! Stay, do not run and hide from his name, the name that used to call you out so happy to meet him! When they cried that he was coming, when you heard, 'Egmont is here! Egmont has come from Ghent!' – then the happiest of men were those that lived in the streets through which he passed. And when you heard his horse's hooves, you all threw down your work, and the joy and hope in his face lit up your poor faces at the windows like a ray of the sun. Then you lifted up your children at the doors and showed them: 'Look, that is Egmont, the greatest of men! That is the man who one day will give you a better life than your wretched fathers lived!' Do not let your children ask you one day, 'Where is he gone? Where are the better days you promised us?' – And here we are bandying words, idling, betraying him.

SOEST: Brackenburg, are you not ashamed? Take her in hand, don't let her go on like that!

BRACKENBURG: Clara, my dear, let us go. What will your mother say? Perhaps –

CLARA: Do you think I am a child, or mad? Perhaps, what perhaps? No hope can dim this awful certainty. You must hear me, and you shall, for I see that you are taken aback, and do not know your own selves. In this present hour of danger, cast just one glance back into the past, into the most recent past! And then turn your thoughts to the future! Can you go on living? Will you, when he has perished? His last breath will be the last breath of freedom. What did he mean to you? Who was it for whose sakes he faced the most terrible danger? His wounds bled and were healed again for you alone. That great soul that was your bulwark is now shut up in a dungeon, and vile, cowardly murder creeps about him. Perhaps he is thinking of you, pinning his hopes on you, he who was only used to giving, to fulfilling others' hopes!

CARPENTER: Come along, friends.

CLARA: And I have not strong arms and sinews like you, but I have what you all lack, courage and scorn for danger. If only my breath could fire you! If only my embrace could give you warmth and vigour! Come, let me go in your midst! Just as a waving banner, itself defenceless, leads a noble army of warriors, so let my spirit flame about your heads, and let love and courage unite the people now scattered and irresolute, into a terrible army!

JETTER: Take her away. I am sorry for her. [*Exeunt* CITIZENS.]

BRACKENBURG: Clara! Do you not see where we are?

CLARA: Where? Beneath God's heaven, that so often seemed more splendid when *he* rode beneath it in all his glory. They have thronged these very windows four and five deep to look out, crowded these very doors, nodding when he looked down to them, the cowards! Oh, I loved them so when they honoured him! If he had been a tyrant, then they might pass by as he fell. But they loved him! Their hands could tug their caps to him, but could not draw a sword. – And we, Brackenburg, can we rebuke them? These arms that held him tight so often, what are they doing for him now? – Cunning has done so much in this world. You know the paths and alleyways, you know the palace. Nothing is impossible; tell me what we can do!

BRACKENBURG: Let us go home.

CLARA: Oh, yes!

BRACKENBURG: I can see Alva's guards there at the corner; let your heart listen to the voice of reason! Do you think I am a coward? Do you not believe that I could die for you? But to stay here is madness, for me as well as for you. Do you not see that it is impossible? If you would only come to your senses. You are not yourself.

CLARA: Not myself! Oh, it is horrible, Brackenburg; it is you, you who are not yourself! When you all shouted your praises of the hero, called him friend, protector and hope, cried out 'Long may he live!' when he came by, then I stood quietly listening in my corner, with the window ajar, and my heart beat faster than any of yours. Now again it beats faster than any of yours! You run and hide when you are needed, you deny him and do not realize that you are all lost if he perishes.

BRACKENBURG: Come home!

CLARA: Home?

BRACKENBURG: Be sensible, and look about you. These are the streets you only used to pass through on a Sunday, going modestly to church; where you used to make a great show of offended virtue if I as much as spoke a friendly word of greeting to you. Here everyone can see you, here all the world will know what you say and what you do. Be sensible, my love, what use is it to us?

CLARA: Home! Yes, I will be sensible. Come, Brackenburg. Home! Do you know where my place is? [*Exeunt.*]

Prison, lit by a lamp, with a bed

EGMONT [*alone*]: Old friend, faithful sleep! Do you desert me too, like all my other friends? How willingly you would bend over my head in the days of my freedom and cool my brow like the sweet myrtle wreath of love. In the midst of battle, on the rough waves of life you rocked me gently in your arms, breathing softly like a child. When stormy winds howled through leaves and branches, when boughs and treetops bent and groaned, my heart stood firm within and was not swayed. What shakes it now? What can disturb my steadfast spirit? I know: it is the ringing of the axe that the murderers have laid at my root. Still I stand upright, but a shudder runs through me. Yes, they will conquer with their treacherous power, this firm tall trunk will be laid low; before the bark has withered, your crown with destruction will come crashing down.

But why, you who have so often blown away the greatest cares as if they were no more than soap-bubbles, why can you now no longer dismiss that foreboding that stirs and whispers to you in a thousand voices? How can it be that death seems terrible to you, you who have lived with his many guises as calmly as with all the other familiar things of this world? Yet it is not he, the swift enemy that the sound heart longs to meet face to face; it is the dungeon, image and foretaste of the grave, hateful alike to hero and to coward. I used to be uneasy even in my cushioned chair, when the princes in solemn assembly debated with endless words and repetitions some matter so simple to decide; in the hall, surrounded by the gloomy walls, I felt the roof-beams weighing down upon me. Then I would hurry out, as soon as I could, to leap on my horse with a deep breath, and away! Away, where we belong, into the open fields, where we scent the benefits of nature like an exhalation of the earth, and feel the blessings of the stars in the free air that envelops us; where like the earth-born giant we rise with new strength and vigour from our mother's touch; where in our veins we feel that we are men, and feel the desires of men, and the young huntsman's soul glows with ambition to press onward, to capture and to vanquish, to feel the power of his fist, to conquer and possess; where the soldier with swift step asserts his native right to all the world, and in terrible freedom like the hail lays waste the meadows, woods and fields, and knows no limits drawn by hand of man!

It is but a vision, a memory and a dream of the happiness I enjoyed so long; where is it treacherous fate has led me now? Does it deny me the swift death under the sun that I have feared, to let me first taste the grave in this dank mouldering dungeon? How these stones' evil breath portends it! Already life grows numb; I fear to lie upon my couch no less than I fear the grave.

Oh, care, care, must you begin my murderers' work already? How long has Egmont been alone, alone in all the world? It is not fate, but doubt that makes you weaken. Is the King's justice you have always trusted, is the Princess's friendship – almost love for you, do not deny it – are these no more, have they vanished suddenly like will-o'-the-wisps at night, and left you alone to find your way? Will not Orange lead your friends in some bold plan? Will not the people gather in ever-increasing might to save and avenge their friend of old? Oh, you walls that shut me in, do not bar the way to so many eager spirits; and whatever courage they have drawn from my quickening glance, let it now flow back from their hearts into mine! Yes, yes, they are coming, thousands of them, they run to stand beside me. Their pious wishes speed urgently to heaven, to beg for a miracle. And if no angel will descend to save me, then I shall see them take up lance and sword. The doors are opened and the iron bars burst, the stone walls crumble at their touch, and Egmont rises joyfully to meet the new dawn of freedom. How many familiar faces are there to greet me with their shouts of jubilation! Ah, Clara, if you were a man, then surely I should see you here before all the others, and thank you for that gift one does not gladly thank a king for: freedom!

Clara's house

[*Enter* CLARA *from her room with a lamp and a glass of water; she puts the glass on the table and goes to the window.*]

CLARA: Brackenburg? Is it you? What was it then I heard? No one yet? No one! I will put the lamp in the window, so that he can see I am still awake and watching for him. He promised to bring me news. News? Dreadful certainty! Egmont condemned! What court dare summon him? And now they condemn him! The King, or the Duke? And the Princess leaves him to his fate; Orange hesitates, and all his friends – ! – Is this the world, of whose inconstancy and fickleness I have heard so much, and known nothing? Is this the world? – Who could be so wicked as to be his enemy? Could wickedness be powerful enough swiftly to overthrow the man all recognize and love? But it is so, it is! Oh, Egmont, I thought you were safe before God and men, as safe as in my arms! What was I to you? You called me yours, I vowed my whole life to your life. What am I now? In vain I stretch out my hand towards the snare that holds you fast. You are helpless, and I am free! – There is the key to my door. Just as I please I may come and go, and for you I can do nothing? – Oh, bind me, so that I may despair, throw me into the deepest dungeon, let me beat my head against the damp walls, whine for freedom, dream of how I would help him if I were not lamed by fetters, how I would run to help him. – Now I am free, and in my freedom know the fear of helplessness. I know I cannot lift a finger to save him. Oh, I am afraid your lesser self, your Clara, is a prisoner like you and, parted from you, flutters her last strength in the agony of death. – I hear someone creeping along, a cough – yes, it is Brackenburg! Good, wretched Brackenburg! Your fate will never change; your love opens the door to you at night, and oh, to what unhappy meeting!

[*Enter* BRACKENBURG.]

CLARA: So pale and frightened you are, Brackenburg. What is it?

BRACKENBURG: I have come through dangers, round about, to tell you. All the main streets are guarded. I have had to steal through alleyways and byways.

CLARA: Tell me, what is it?

BRACKENBURG [*sitting down*]: Oh, Clara, let me weep! I did not love him; he was the rich man, I was the poor man whose one little lamb he lured to better pasture. I have never cursed him; God made me true and gentle. I lived my life away in sorrow, every day I hoped that I should perish of grief.

CLARA: Forget these things, Brackenburg, forget yourself! Tell me about him. Is it true? Is he condemned?

BRACKENBURG: He is. I know for sure.

CLARA: But is he still alive?

BRACKENBURG: Yes, he is still alive.

CLARA: How can you be sure of that? – The tyrants are murdering the great man now, at dead of night, his blood is flowing hidden from all eyes. The people, numbed, lie in their anxious sleep and dream of rescue, dream that their powerless wish may be fulfilled; meanwhile his soul departs the earth in anger with us who have failed him. He is dead! Do not deceive me, do not deceive yourself.

BRACKENBURG: No, he is alive, I am sure! And I am afraid the Spaniards are preparing a terrible spectacle for the people they seek to crush, one that will shatter every heart that longs for freedom.

CLARA: Tell me everything, speak my death-sentence too. Already my steps take me ever closer to the fields of eternal bliss, and I feel the breath of heavenly peace already come to comfort me. Speak!

BRACKENBURG: I could tell by the guards, and from things I heard said, here and there, that some horror was being prepared in secret in the market-place. I crept through alleyways and paths I know to my cousin's house, that backs onto the market, and looked out through a window. – There was a great circle of Spanish soldiers, with torches flaring to and fro. I sharpened my uncertain eyes and peered through the darkness, and there I saw a scaffold, black, tall and spacious; the very sight filled me with terror. Many men were busy all around, hiding any woodwork that still showed white, covering it with black cloth. At last I saw them covering the steps in black as well. They seemed to be dedicating it for some dreadful sacrifice. At one side they put up a crucifix, tall and white, shining like silver in the darkness. There were still torches waving here and there, they went out one by one – till suddenly the fearful thing had disappeared, gone back into the womb of night from where it had come.

CLARA: Hush, Brackenburg, be still now! Let this veil rest upon my soul. The ghosts have disappeared, and you, sweet night, lend earth your mantle in her ferment; she will no longer bear this hideous burden, shuddering she opens her deep fissures and swallows up the instrument of murder. And the God who in shame has witnessed their fury will send his angel, bolts and fetters will be loosed at the holy envoy's touch, and he will bathe our friend in his mild radiance, and lead him silently and gently through the night to freedom. And I too must go in secret through this darkness to meet him.

BRACKENBURG [*holding her back*]: My child, where are you going? What foolhardiness is this?

CLARA: Quiet, dear Brackenburg, do not wake anyone! We must not wake ourselves! Do you recognize this phial? I took it from you, joking, when you so often threatened hasty death; and now, my friend –

BRACKENBURG: By all the saints!

CLARA: You cannot save me. Death must be my part, and let it be the swift and gentle death you had prepared for yourself. Give me your hand! At this moment, as I open this door from which there can be no turning back, I could say to you as I press your hand how I loved you, how I grieved for you! My brother died when he was young; I chose you to take his place. Your heart rebelled, tormented itself and me, you demanded ever more ardently what could never be. Forgive me, and farewell! Let me call you brother! It is a name that holds so many others in itself. From me as I depart take this last fair flower with a faithful heart: here, take this kiss. – Death will unite all, Brackenburg; we too shall be united.

BRACKENBURG: Then let me die with you! Share it, share it! There is enough to end two lives.

CLARA: Stay! You shall live, you can live. Help my mother, who without you would waste away in poverty. Be to her what I can no longer be, stay with her, and both of you, weep for me! Weep for our fatherland, and for him who alone had the power to save it! Our generation will always have this grief to bear, even the fury of revenge cannot purge it. Live, unhappy people, through this time when time has stopped. The world stands still, stayed in its course; and my pulse will not beat many minutes more. Farewell!

BRACKENBURG: Oh, live, live with us; we shall live only for you! If you kill yourself you will kill us too; stay and suffer with us! We shall stand beside you, inseparable from you, and ever-mindful love shall offer sweet consolation in its living arms. Be ours, be ours – I may not say be mine.

CLARA: Softly, Brackenburg, you do not know what chords you touch. Where you see hope, I only see despair.

BRACKENBURG: Let the living share their hopes with you! Stop at the precipice, cast your eyes down, and then look back to where we stand!

CLARA: I have conquered; do not call me into battle again!

BRACKENBURG: You are numbed and blinded thus to see the depths. Still there is light, still many a day –

CLARA: Unhappy man! Alas! Cruelly you tear the veil from my eyes. Yes, the day will dawn, will draw the mists about itself in vain and dawn against its will! Timidly the citizens will peer from their windows and see that night has left a black spot behind it; look and see the scaffold rear up in the light. Suffering anew, God's desecrated image turns his face imploring to his Father. The sun will not come out; it will not mark the hour in which he dies. Slowly the clocks tick on, the hours strike one after the other. Stop, stop – the time has come! The thought of morning sends me to my grave. [*She goes to the window and drinks secretly.*]

BRACKENBURG: Clara! Clara!

CLARA [*goes to the table and drinks the water*]: Here is what is left. I shall not invite you to follow me. Do what is right, and farewell! Put out the light, quietly and without delay; I shall go to bed. Creep softly away, pull the door to after you. Quiet! Do not wake my mother. Go, save yourself, save yourself, if you do not want men to think you are my murderer. [*Exit.*]

BRACKENBURG: She leaves me for the last time, and it is the same as always. Oh, if only soul of man could feel how she can tear a loving heart to shreds! She leaves me here to live my life alone; and life and death are hateful to me alike. –

To die alone! Oh, weep, lovers, there is no harsher fate than mine! She shares the poison with me, and sends me away, away from her side! Oh, Egmont, what enviable lot is yours! She goes before you; the victor's wreath you shall receive from her hand, all heaven she will bring to welcome you. And I, am I to follow? again to stand to one side, to carry my unquenchable envy with me into those realms? — There is no place on earth for me now, and heaven and hell promise equal torment. Wretch that I am, how welcome to me would be the terrors of destruction's hand! [*Exit.*]

[*The scene remains unchanged for some time.*

Music, representing CLARA'S *death. The lamp, which* BRACKENBURG *had forgotten to extinguish, flickers a few times and goes out.*]

Prison

[EGMONT *sleeping on the bed. The rattle of keys is heard, the door opens; enter* SERVANTS *with torches, after them* FERDINAND *and* SILVA *with an armed escort.* EGMONT *starts up from his sleep.*]

EGMONT: Who are you, come to drive sleep so roughly from my eyes? What do I read in these uncertain, sullen looks? Why this parade of fearful power? What lying visions of horror do you come to summon up before my drowsy soul?

SILVA: The Duke has sent us to pronounce your sentence to you.

EGMONT: Have you brought the hangman too, to carry it out?

SILVA: Listen, and you shall hear what fate awaits you.

EGMONT: Yes, that is fitting for you and for your shameful schemes! Hatched out at night, at dead of night performed. Thus may injustice seek to hide its insolence. Come forward boldly, you there with the sword hidden beneath your cloak; here is my head, the freest head that ever tyranny had severed from its body.

SILVA: You are mistaken. What just judges have decreed shall not be hidden from the sight of day.

EGMONT: Then insolence has passed all understanding.

SILVA [*takes the sentence from one of his men, opens it and reads*]: 'In the King's name, and by virtue of the especial power conferred upon us by his majesty to judge all his subjects of what rank soever they may be, the Knights of the Golden Fleece not excepted; after –'

EGMONT: Can the King confer that power?

SILVA: '– After previous just examination according to the law, we find you, Henry, Count Egmont, Prince of Gavre, guilty of high treason, and pronounce sentence: that you be taken from this place at dawn tomorrow, brought to the market-place, and there before the people put to death by the sword, as an example to all traitors. Delivered at Brussels, this [*the date is read inaudibly*]; Ferdinand, Duke of Alva, President of the Council of Twelve.' – You now know your fate; there is a little time for you to reconcile yourself, to put your affairs in order and to take your farewells. [*Exeunt* SILVA *and all except* FERDINAND. *Two torches remain; the scene is half-lit.*]

EGMONT [*stands still brooding, and does not look round when* SILVA *goes. He believes himself alone, but raising his eyes he sees* FERDINAND]: You, still here? Do you seek to increase my astonishment and my horror still further by your presence? Perhaps your father hopes you will bring him news of my unmanly despair? Go! Tell him, tell him that he shall not deceive me, nor the world with his greedy ambition. First he will hear it whispered behind his back; then louder and louder; and when one day he climbs down from the summit of his fame, a thousand voices will shout it to his face: not the good of the state, nor the King's majesty, nor the peace of the Provinces brought him here. For his own selfish ends he counselled war, so that he, the warrior, should have his place; he himself stirred up this terrible tumult, so that he should be needed. And I fall a victim to his base hatred and his petty jealousy. Yes, I know it, and dying, fatally wounded, I may say it: in his conceit he envied me; he has long sought and planned to destroy me. Even when we were young and played at dice, and the piles of gold sped one by one from his side to mine, he stood furious, in spite of his pretended calm, and eaten up with rage within, more at my good luck than at his own loss. I still remember how he turned pale and how his eyes flashed, betraying him, one day when we were shooting against each other, before thousands at a public festival. He challenged me, and the two nations, Spain and the Netherlands, stood wagering and making their wishes. I won; his bullet went astray, mine hit the mark; a cry of joy burst from my countrymen. Now he has brought me down. Tell him that I know it, that I know him, that the world will despise the trophies that a petty spirit sets up for itself by stealth. And you, if a son may learn better ways than his father, learn in time to feel shame, and be ashamed now of him you would wish to honour with all your heart.

FERDINAND: I hear you, and I will not interrupt you. Your reproaches are like heavy blows raining down on a helmet; I feel their force, but I am armed against them. They find their mark, but they do not wound; the only pain I feel is that which tears at my heart. Oh that I should have grown up to witness this day, oh that I should be sent to see these things come to pass!

EGMONT: You break out into lamentation? What is it that moves you, grieves you? Is it belated repentance for lending your arm to this shameful conspiracy? You are so young, and there is good fortune in your face. You were so frank and friendly towards me; when I saw you I was reconciled with your father. And you, as deceitful, more deceitful still than he, lure me into the net. It is you who are beneath contempt! Any man who would trust *him* knows what risk he is taking; who would suspect danger in trusting *you*? Go! Go! Do not rob me of these last few moments! Go, let me collect my thoughts, let me forget the world and you above all!

FERDINAND: What am I to say to you? I stand here looking at you and I do not see you, and cannot believe that I am here. Am I to make excuses, am I to assure you that it was only at the last moment I discovered what my father purposed, that I acted as a lifeless instrument, bent to his will? What does it matter what you think of me? You are lost, and I can only stand here in my misery to tell you of it and to grieve for you.

EGMONT: What strange voice is this I hear, bringing me unexpected comfort on my way to the grave? You, son of my greatest, almost my only enemy, you pity me, you are not one of my murderers? Speak, tell me, what am I to think of you?

FERDINAND: Cruel father! Yes, this command is like you. You knew my heart, my thoughts – my weakness, as you so often called it, inherited from my mother. To make me hard like you, you sent me here. You force me to see this man at the edge of the yawning grave, victim of an arbitrary death, to make me feel the keenest pain, to make me deaf to fate, indifferent to what may happen to me.

EGMONT: I am amazed! Do not give way! Speak like a man!

FERDINAND: Would that I were a woman, so that men could say, 'What is it moves you so? What is the matter?' Tell me a greater, a more monstrous evil, make me witness a more dreadful deed than this, and I will thank you and say that it was nothing.

EGMONT: You forget yourself. Where are you?

FERDINAND: Let this passion rage, let me be free to weep! I will not seem brave when everything is breaking up within me. To see you here? You? It is terrible! You do not understand me. Will you not understand me? Egmont! Egmont! [*Falling about* EGMONT's *neck.*]

EGMONT: Explain this mystery!

FERDINAND: It is no mystery.

EGMONT: How can you be so moved by a stranger's fate?

FERDINAND: No, not a stranger's. You are no stranger to me. It was your name that shone bright as a star for me when I was young. How often did I listen, ask for news of you. The boy's hope is the youth, the youth's the man; so you went before me always, and without envy I saw and followed in your wake, onward and onward. And now at last I hoped to meet you, and I met you, and my heart was yours. I had chosen you to be my guiding light, and I chose you again when I saw you. Now I hoped to be by your side, to live with you, to hold fast to you, to – but all that has been cut off, and I see you here!

EGMONT: My friend, if it will comfort you, then be assured that in that first moment my heart went out to you. And now hear me; let us exchange a word in calm. Tell me, is your father in earnest? Will he have me killed?

FERDINAND: He will.

EGMONT: Might not this sentence be an empty threat, to terrify me, to punish me with fear, to humble me only to let the King's mercy raise me up again?

FERDINAND: No, I am afraid it is not! At first I flattered myself with that elusive hope; and even then it grieved and terrified me to see you come to this. But now it is certain, it is real. No, I cannot help myself. Who can help me, tell me how I can escape the inevitable?

EGMONT: Listen to me. If your soul longs so desperately to save me, if you abhor the power that holds me captive, then – save me! Every moment is precious. You are the all-powerful one's son, you have power yourself – let us flee! I know the ways, and the means cannot be unknown to you. Only these walls, only a few leagues separate me from my friends. Loose these fetters; take me to them and be one of us! One day the King will surely thank you for saving me. Now he has been taken by surprise, he may even know nothing of it. Your father dares to act, and the King must approve what has happened, even if it horrifies him. – You pause to think? Think me the way to freedom! Speak, give nourishment to the hopes of my living soul!

FERDINAND: Be silent, oh, be silent! Every word you speak deepens my despair. There is no escape, no way out, nothing we can do. It is that which torments me, seizes and tears my heart as if with claws. I myself drew in the net, I know how fast and tight its knots are tied; I know how the ways are blocked for every deed of daring or of cunning, I feel myself bound with you and with all the others. Would I be here lamenting if I had not tried everything? I lay at his feet, I pleaded with him, begged him; he sent me here to destroy in this moment all the joy and gladness that I have ever known.

EGMONT: And nothing we can do?

FERDINAND: No, nothing!

EGMONT [*stamping his foot*]: Nothing! – Sweet life, existence, action, we are such good and faithful friends; must we be parted? And must I take my leave of you so calmly, may we not bid each other a hasty farewell in the tumult of battle, amidst the clash of arms, in the confusion of the fighting, to speed our parting, to cut short the bitter moment? No, I am to take your hand, to look into your eyes once more, to feel your worth and beauty most keenly before I tear myself away and say: go your way, and leave me!

FERDINAND: And I am to stand by and watch, unable to hold you back or hinder you. Oh, what voice could grieve enough! What heart would not be filled to overflowing by this sorrow!

EGMONT: Stand firm!

FERDINAND: You can stand firm, you can renounce, go like a hero, hand in hand with grim necessity. What can I do? What must I do? You will overcome yourself and us; you will conquer, but I shall outlive you and outlive myself. I have lost my light to light me at the feast; I have lost my banner to lead me on the battlefield. Drab, gloomy and confused I see the future before me.

EGMONT: My young friend, you whom a strange destiny in one and the same moment gives and takes away from me, you who feel the pains of death for me, who suffer for me, look at me now; you shall not lose me. If in my life you saw the mirror of what you wished to be, let it not be otherwise with my death. Men need not be face to face to be together; even one who is far away, even one who is dead can live in us. I shall live in you, and I have lived long enough in myself; I have rejoiced in every day, done my duty vigorously every day according to my conscience.

Now my life is ending; as it could have done long ago, as long ago as on the sands of Gravelines. Now I shall cease to live, but I *have* lived. Live like me, my friend, gladly and with joy, and do not fear death!

FERDINAND: You could, you should have stayed alive for us. You have killed yourself. Often I heard clever men speaking about you, enemies and friends; they would argue long about your worth, but in the end they would agree, none could deny it, every one admitted it: yes, it is a dangerous path he treads. How often I wished that I could warn you! Had you no friends?

EGMONT: I was warned.

FERDINAND: And all their accusations were there again, every one, in the charge against you; and your answers. They were good enough to excuse you, but not to free you from all stain of guilt.

EGMONT: Let us forget that. Man believes he lives his own life, is his own master, and deep down within he is dragged on inexorably to meet his destiny. Let us not consider that. I can shrug off such thoughts with ease. Harder to rid myself of anxious cares for this country; but that too will be cared for. If my blood can flow for many, bringing peace to my people, then I shed it willingly. I fear it will not be so. But man should not brood on things he cannot change. If you can stay or steer your father's ruinous violence, then do so. But what man is there who can do that? – Farewell!

FERDINAND: I cannot go.

EGMONT: Let me commend my people to you, my servants; they are good men, keep them together and do not let them come to harm. What has happened to Richard, my secretary?

FERDINAND: He has gone before you. They have beheaded him as an accessory to high treason.

EGMONT: Poor wretch! – One thing more, and then farewell, I cannot go on. Though there may be so much to busy our mind, nature at last insists upon her due, and just as a child in the coils of a snake is refreshed with sleep, so the weary man lies down once more on the threshold of death and rests as if he had a long way still to go. – One thing more. I know a young girl; you will not despise her because she was mine. Now that I commend her to you I can die in peace. You are a fine young man; a woman will be safe in such a haven. Is my old Adolf still alive, and free?

FERDINAND: That cheerful old man who always rode with you?

EGMONT: The same.

FERDINAND: He is alive, and free.

EGMONT: He knows where she lives, let him take you there and reward him to the end of his days for showing you the way to such a jewel. – Farewell.

FERDINAND: I will not go.

EGMONT [*pushing him to the door*]: Farewell.

FERDINAND: Oh let me –

EGMONT: No, my friend, no last embrace! [*He goes with* FERDINAND *to the door and breaks away from him.* FERDINAND *hurries away as if dazed.*]

EGMONT [*alone*]: Oh my enemy! You did not think you would be granting me this boon through your own son. Through him I am freed of all my cares and my grief, freed from fear and all anxieties. Gently insistent, nature demands her last tribute. It is finished, it is decided! And what last night kept me awake, uncertain, on my bed, now lulls my senses in unconquerable certainty. [*He sits down on the bed. Music.*]

Sweet sleep! You come like the purest of blessings, most willingly when unsought and unimplored. You loose the knots of earnest thought, you blend all visions of joy and sorrow; unhindered turn the spheres of inner harmony, and wrapped in fancies of delight we sink down and are no more. [*He falls asleep. As he sleeps, the music plays. Behind his bed the wall seems to open, and a dazzling vision appears.* FREE-DOM *is seen clad in heavenly robes and bathed in light, resting on a cloud; her features are those of* CLARA. *She bends over the sleeping hero. She wears an expression of pity, and seems to be grieving for him; but soon she composes herself, and with gestures of encourage-*

ment shows him first the bundle of arrows, then the hat and staff.* *She bids him be cheerful, and giving him to understand that his death will bring freedom to the Provinces, holds out a laurel wreath to him in token of victory. As she approaches him with the wreath,* EGMONT *stirs in his sleep, turning his face upwards to her. She holds the wreath suspended above his head. Very distant martial music is heard, with fifes and drums; at its first sound the vision disappears. It grows louder.* EGMONT *awakes; the prison is dimly lit by the light of dawn.* EGMONT's *first action is to put one hand to his head; still holding it there, he stands up and looks around.*]

EGMONT: The victor's wreath is gone! Beautiful vision, the light of morning has driven you away. Yes, those two it was, my heart's two dearest joys united: divine Freedom took the shape of my dear one, and my love was clad in the heavenly robes of my spirit's companion. In that solemn moment they appeared as one, more solemn than lovely. With bloodstained feet she stepped before me, the rippling folds of her dress stained too with blood. It was my blood, the blood of many noble men. No, it was not shed in vain. Onward! Brave people! The goddess of victory leads you on! And as the sea breaks through your dykes, so break, tear down and sweep away the barriers of usurping tyranny!

[*Drums, nearer.*]

Hark! Hark! How often that sound called me out to stride freely to the field of battle and of victory! How boldly my comrades trod the path of danger and of fame! But I too step forth from this prison to an honourable death. I die for freedom; the goal for which I lived and fought I now attain, in suffering as a sacrifice!

[*Enter a row of* SPANISH SOLDIERS, *with halberds, occupying the back of the stage.*]

Yes, bring them up there, close your ranks! You will not

---

*Symbols of the unity and freedom of the Provinces. It was, of course, only the northern provinces (the modern Kingdom of the Netherlands) whose revolt was successful. Their independence was recognised *de facto* by Spain in 1609, over forty years after the events portrayed in Goethe's play, while the southern provinces, scene of these crucial events, remained under Spanish rule for another century and more. (*Translator's note.*)

frighten me. I am used to stand with spears behind me and before, and surrounded on all sides by threatening death, to feel the bold pulse of life beat all the stronger!

[*Drums.*]

The enemy draws in on every side! Their swords are flashing – come, more courage, friends! Your families and loved ones stand behind you! [*Pointing at the guards*] And these are spurred on by a tyrant's hollow word, not by their own true spirit. Protect what is your own! Save what you love, by falling joyously; and follow the example that I give!

[*Drums.* EGMONT *strides out boldly towards the guards and the door at the rear. The curtain falls, and the orchestra concludes the play with a symphony of victory.*]

MARY STUART

Friedrich Schiller

A tragedy
1800

CHARACTERS

ELIZABETH, Queen of England
MARY STUART, Queen of Scotland, a prisoner in England
ROBERT DUDLEY, Earl of Leicester
GEORGE TALBOT, Earl of Shrewsbury
WILLIAM CECIL, LORD BURGHLEY, Lord Treasurer of England
EARL OF KENT
WILLIAM DAVISON, Secretary of State
SIR AMYAS PAULET, Mary's gaoler
MORTIMER, his nephew
COUNT AUBESPINE, French Ambassador
COUNT BELLIÈVRE, French envoy extraordinary
O'KELLY, friend of Mortimer
DRUDGEON DRURY, assistant to Paulet
MELVIL, Mary's former steward
BURGOYNE, her physician
HANNAH KENNEDY, her nurse
MARGARET CURLE, her maid
SHERIFF of Northamptonshire
AN OFFICER of the Queen's guard
HERALDS
SERVANTS

ACT I

A room in the Castle of Fotheringhay

SCENE I

[HANNAH KENNEDY, *the Queen of Scotland's nurse, is angrily trying to prevent* PAULET *from opening a chest.* DRURY, *his assistant, with tools.*]

KENNEDY: What is this, sir – this latest insolence?
  That chest – you shall not touch it!

PAULET: And the jewels?
  The jewels I saw thrown from this upper floor
  To bribe the gardener? Damn your woman's cunning!
  For all my vigilance, for all my searching, still
  You've valuables, still you've secret treasures!
  And where that came from, there'll be more! [*Breaks it open.*]

KENNEDY: You shall not touch it!
  My lady's secrets!

PAULET: Just what I am looking for. [*Takes out papers.*]

KENNEDY: Papers of no importance, jottings made
  To while away these idle hours in prison.

PAULET: The devil finds work for idle hands to do.

KENNEDY: Letters in French –

PAULET: What's that? So much the worse,
  The language of my country's enemy.

KENNEDY: Letters intended for your country's queen.

PAULET: Then I'll deliver them. – But look at this,
    [*He has found a secret compartment, from which he takes out jewellery.*]
  A jewelled band, made for a queenly brow,
  With lilies woven in – the badge of France!
  Here, Drury, take it. Put it with the rest. [*Exit* DRURY.]

KENNEDY: O must we still endure this cruel shame!

PAULET: Until her hands are empty, they can harm,
  For anything they hold she'll use against us.

KENNEDY: O sir, be kind, and leave us this last joy
    To brighten our sad life! Unhappy lady,
    This memory of the past is all she has,
    For you have taken all the rest away.
PAULET: Into safe keeping; and I promise you
    That in due time these things will be restored.
KENNEDY: Look at these cold bare walls! O who could tell
    That this might be the lodging of a queen?
    Where is the canopy above her chair?
    Her feet, accustomed to a softer floor,
    Must tread upon these rough hard common stones;
    Coarse pewter – fit not for the meanest lady –
    Is set upon her table –
PAULET: As it was
    Upon her husband's, there in Stirling, while
    She drank from gold, she and her paramour.
KENNEDY: She may not even have a looking-glass.
PAULET: A looking-glass would serve her vanity,
    Inspire her hopes, encourage her intrigues.
KENNEDY: She has no books to entertain her spirit.
PAULET: She has the Bible to improve her heart.
KENNEDY: You even dared to take her lute away.
PAULET: It was but wanton songs she played upon it.
KENNEDY: Is this a fate for one so delicate,
    Already in her cradle crowned a queen,
    Who grew up at the court of Medici,
    Surrounded there by every earthly joy?
    Why was it not enough to take her power,
    Must you begrudge her these small pleasures too?
    A noble heart can bear a great affliction,
    To lose these lesser comforts though is bitter.
PAULET: They only turn the heart to vanity;
    She should repent, and seek to mend her soul.
    A life of sin can only be atoned
    In chastisement of fleshly lusts, and hardship.
KENNEDY: If in the tenderness of youth she erred,
    Then she must seek her own way back to God;
    But England cannot sit in judgement on her.

PAULET: The land she wronged will judge the wrongs she did.

KENNEDY: How could she wrong you, here a prisoner?

PAULET: A prisoner; and yet her arm could reach
Out far enough to stir up civil war,
To set this realm alight, to arm a pack
Of murderers against our Queen – God save her!
Was it not from within these walls that she
Set evil Parry on, and Babington,
To lay their wicked plots of regicide?
And could these bolts and bars of iron prevent her
From snaring Norfolk's noble heart as well?
Because of her, he had to lay his head,
The best in all this island, on the block.
A terrible example – but it could
Not hold the madmen back, they raced each other
Over the precipices for her sake,
For her the scaffolds fill, and drip with blood,
And it will never end until the day
That she, who bears the guilt for all of them,
Goes to her death upon the block herself.
– I curse the day that our fair land received
This Helen with its hospitality.

KENNEDY: What English hospitality is this?
O wretched lady, since the very day
She first set foot in your fair land, an exile,
Begging for help and succour from her kin,
Against the laws of nations and against
The dignity of kings, she has been kept
A prisoner, to mourn away her youth
Shut in this dungeon like a criminal.
And now that she has suffered all this grief,
She is accused most shamefully, and must
Stand trial and answer for her life – a queen!

PAULET: She came into this land a murderess,
Deposed and exiled by the Scottish people,
Whose throne she had dishonoured with her crimes.
She came conspired with England's enemies
To bring back Spanish Mary's bloody times,

Make England Papist, sell us to the French.
Why else did she refuse to sign the treaty
Of Edinburgh, to renounce her claim
To England's throne, and open up the door
To freedom with a swift stroke of the pen?
No, she would rather stay a prisoner,
Suffer ill-treatment even, than give up
Her empty, foolish claim to England's crown.
Why does she do it? Why, because she trusts
To intrigue and to black conspiracy,
And hopes by weaving webs of treachery
To conquer all this island from her prison.

KENNEDY: You mock her, sir – you are not satisfied
With harshness, you must taunt her too! She, dream
Of conquest, walled up here in living death,
Far from the sound of comfort, where no voice
Of friendship from her native land can reach her,
She who so long has seen no human face
But of her gaolers with their frosty looks;
Who but a short while since received new torment,
Your boorish nephew added to their ranks;
Who finds herself surrounded by new bars –

PAULET: No bars of iron can keep her guile in check.
How do I know she has not filed them through,
How do I know these floors, these walls of stone,
So hard they seem, have not been hollowed out
To make a path for traitors while I sleep?
I curse the task that is entrusted to me,
To keep this scheming vixen in my care.
I wake in terror in the night, I walk
About the castle like a ghost in torment,
Try all the locks, spy on the guards, and wait
In fear and trembling for the day to dawn
And show me that she's fled. But no! At last,
Now I can hope this dread will soon be over.
For I would rather stand before the gates
Of Hell to guard the legions of the damned,
Than keep my watch on this deceitful queen!

KENNEDY: See where she comes!

PAULET: The Lord God in her hand,
   And pride and worldly vices in her heart.

SCENE 2

   [*Enter* MARY, *veiled, a crucifix in her hand.*]
KENNEDY [*hurrying to meet her*]:
   My queen! They trample us beneath their feet;
   There is no end to what the tyrants dare!
   Each day they cruelly heap some new disgrace,
   Some new affront upon your royal head.
MARY: Be calm, and tell me what has happened.
KENNEDY: Look!
   Your chest is broken open, and your letters,
   Your only treasure, saved with bitter woe,
   That single remnant of your bridal jewels
   From France is in his hand. Now all is gone,
   Your royal state; you have been robbed of all.
MARY: Peace, Hannah. It is not these trinkets make
   A queen; though we be basely treated, this
   Cannot debase us. I have learnt to bear
   So much in England, I can bear this too.
   – Sir, you have taken from me, and by force,
   What I had of my own free will resolved
   To give to you today. Amongst these letters
   Is one intended for my royal sister,
   The Queen of England. Give me now your word
   That you will honestly deliver it
   To her, and not to Burghley's faithless hand.
PAULET: I shall decide what it is right to do.
MARY: Sir, you shall know what it contains. I ask
   A gracious favour of her in this letter –
   That I may meet and speak with her, whom I
   Have never seen with my own eyes. I have
   Been summoned to appear before a court
   Of men who cannot judge me: they are not
   My peers, I cannot bear to face them. She,

Elizabeth, is of my house, my sex,
My rank – to her alone, my sister, Queen
Of England, and a woman, I will speak.
PAULET: My lady, you have often put yourself,
Yes, and your honour, in the hands of men
Who less deserved respect and trust than these.
MARY: A second favour I would beg of her,
Which it would be inhuman to refuse.
Here in this prison I have been without
The comfort of the holy sacraments,
And though she rob me of my crown, my freedom,
Even perhaps my life, she cannot wish
To bar the way to Heaven to my soul.
PAULET: If you desire, the Dean of Peterborough –
MARY [*interrupting forcefully*]:
I do not want your dean. I wish to see
A priest of my own church. And I would have
A notary and clerks, to make my will.
This grief, this endless prison gloom is like
A worm that gnaws my very life. My days
I fear are numbered, and I count myself
As one already dying.
PAULET: Well you may,
Such thoughts as these are right and proper in you.
MARY: And can I tell, perhaps a swifter hand
Will speed this sorrow's slow and painful work.
So I will write my testament, will make
My dispositions over what is mine.
PAULET: That you are free to do: for England's queen
Will not enrich herself with robber's spoils.
MARY: My faithful women you have taken from me,
My servants too. Where are they? Will you not
Tell me what has become of them? I do
Not need their service here, but I would be
Assured they do not suffer for my sake.
PAULET: They will be taken care of. [*Going*]
MARY: You go, sir? You are leaving me again,
And will not free my fearful anxious heart

Of this cruel burden of uncertainty?
Your zealous spies have cut me off from all
The world that lies beyond these prison walls,
No news can reach me, and my enemies
Do with me what they will. A painful month
Has passed since England's forty commissaries
Fell on me in this castle, set their bench
Up with unseemly haste, and dragged me forth
To face their trumped-up charge and stand without
An advocate, or time to be prepared,
Surprised and in a daze, out of my head
To answer accusations of great weight.
They came like ghosts, the next day they were gone,
And now the lips of men are sealed to me.
In vain I seek to read it in your face,
Whether my innocence, my friends' support,
Or others' evil counsel won the day.
Will you not break your silence, let me know
What I may hope, or what I have to fear?

PAULET [*after a pause*]: My lady, make your peace with
     God above.

MARY: I hope to know His mercy, sir – and hope
     For justice from my judges here on earth.

PAULET: You shall have justice, that you need not doubt.

MARY: Sir, am I judged already?

PAULET: I do not know.

MARY: Condemned?

PAULET: My lady, I know nothing of it.

MARY: They're quick about their work here. Will perhaps
     My murderer surprise me like my judges?

PAULET: Believe it, and he'll find you, if he comes,
     Better prepared for Heaven than you were then.

MARY: Sir, nothing could astonish me that came
     From a tribunal sat in Westminster,
     Urged on by Burghley's hatred, Hatton's zeal.
     They would say anything in their presumption;
     But will the Queen of England dare to *do* it?

PAULET: The Queen of England fears no voice but that

Of her own conscience and her Parliament.
When judgement has been spoken, fearlessly
The world will see the sentence carried out.

SCENE 3

[*Enter* MORTIMER. *He addresses* PAULET, *taking no notice of* MARY.]

MORTIMER: Uncle, I'm sent to find you. [*He goes out in the same manner.* MARY *observes with displeasure, and turns to* PAULET, *who is following him.*]

MARY: One thing more.
   Sir, what *you* have to tell me I can bear,
   Your age commands respect, but sir, I beg,
   I cannot bear this youth's impertinence,
   Spare me the sight and sound of his ill manners.

PAULET: What you find hateful in him, I find good.
   Indeed he's no soft-hearted fool, I grant you,
   Easily melted by a woman's tears –
   He's been abroad, to Paris and to Rheims,
   And yet has kept his trusty English heart.
   No, boy, this lady's wiles will not enchant you! [*Exit.*]

SCENE 4

KENNEDY: To think the boor dare say it to your face!
   O, it is hard to bear!

MARY [*pensively*]: In times more fortunate we lent our ear
   Too willingly to flattery and praise,
   And therefore, Hannah, it is just that now
   We should endure these harsh reproachful tones.

KENNEDY: Dear lady, have you now become so meek?
   You who were once so gay, you used to comfort me,
   And if I had to scold you, then it was
   For fickle joy, not melancholy.

MARY: Yes!
   See, rising from its vault comes Darnley's ghost,
   Bloodied and angry, to confront me now;

And he will never make his peace with me
Until my cup of sorrow overflows.

KENNEDY: What thoughts are these?

MARY: Good Hannah, you forget;
My memory is faithful to the death.
Today it is the anniversary
Of that black deed; and so I fast and pray.

KENNEDY: O, send this evil ghost back to his tomb!
The deed has been atoned in penitence,
Long years of suffering have made your peace.
The Church, that has the power of absolution
From every guilt, and Heaven itself forgive you.

MARY: Guilt long forgiven rises from its grave
Bleeding as if it were but yesterday!
My husband's spirit, crying for revenge,
Cannot be banished to its vault by prayers
And bells, nor by the sacred Host itself.

KENNEDY: It was not you who killed him! Others did it!

MARY: I knew; I bade them do it; it was I,
With flattery, who lured him to his death.

KENNEDY: But you were still so young. Your tender years
Lighten your guilt.

MARY: So tender, yet I took
That heavy weight of guilt upon my youth.

KENNEDY: But you had been insulted and provoked
To what you did by that man's vanity,
Who by your love had risen from the darkness,
As if the hand of God had drawn him forth,
Whom you had taken for your husband and
Our King, who had enjoyed such precious gifts:
Yourself to be his bride, and Scotland's crown.
Could he forget that all his splendid state
He owed to you and your ungrudging love?
And yet he did forget, he was so vile!
With base suspicions and with boorish ways
He met your tenderness, and bruised your heart;
The magic that had charmed your eye was gone,
And so you shunned in horror his embrace,

And let him feel the weight of scorn. – And he –
He, did he seek to win you back again?
Did he repent, and swear to mend his ways,
And beg your favour on his bended knee?
He offered you – defiance; he, your creature,
He sought to be your master and your king;
Before your eyes he had your favourite,
The handsome singer, Rizzio, struck down –
You only sought his blood in just revenge.

MARY: And he will have his just revenge on mine;
You speak my sentence in your words of comfort.

KENNEDY: But when you let him die, then you were not
Yourself, you did not know what you were doing.
Blind passion had enslaved your will, you were
Beneath the yoke of Bothwell, the seducer –
Would you had never seen that fearful man!
He had imposed his violent will upon you,
Bewitched you with black arts, and turned your head
With wicked potions brewed in hell –

MARY: He had no arts
But those of manly strength, and I was weak.

KENNEDY: It is not true! The spirits of the damned
He called to weave his spells, and blind your senses.
You could no longer hear my warning voice,
Nor see the bounds of what was right and good.
Your tender, timid modesty was gone,
Your cheeks no longer blushed in purity,
But glowed with hectic fires. You threw the veil
Of secrecy away, his shameless vice
Had conquered you, you flaunted openly
Your degradation, let the murderer,
Amongst the curses of the people, bear
The royal sword of Scotland through the streets
Of Edinburgh triumphing before you,
Surrounded by the arms of Parliament;
In justice's own temple made the law
In shameless farce pronounce him innocent,
The murderer – and more! O God!

MARY: Say on!
  – And gave my hand to him before the altar!
KENNEDY: O let eternal silence help us to
  Forget that deed, that terrible disgrace,
  Worthy of one for ever lost, – but no,
  I know you are not lost, for it was I
  Who taught you. No, your heart is tender, knows
  True modesty and shame – but it is weak.
  We must be ever watchful, or the fiends
  At once will make their dwelling in our breast
  Unguarded, in our name commit their crime,
  Then flee to hell from whence they came, and leave
  The horror of it there to stain our heart.
  – But since that deed that tarnishes your life,
  I know that you have never sinned again.
  And so be brave! Make peace with your own soul.
  For that be penitent; but England knows
  No wrong of you, and not Elizabeth,
  Nor England's Parliament can be your judge.
  They hold you here by force; before this court
  They have set up, that knows no name in law,
  You can proclaim your innocence with courage.
MARY: Who's there?
    [MORTIMER appears at the door.]
KENNEDY: The nephew. Do not speak to him.

SCENE 5

    [Enter MORTIMER, cautiously.]
MORTIMER [to KENNEDY]: Go, leave us here, and guard
        the door with care,
  For I must speak in private with the queen.
MARY [with dignity]: Hannah, you stay.
MORTIMER: My lady, have no fear.
    [He gives MARY a card. She reads it and cries out in
    surprise.]
MARY: But what is this?

MORTIMER: Go, Mistress Kennedy,
  And see my uncle does not find me here!
MARY [*to* KENNEDY, *who hesitates and looks questioningly at
    her*]: Go, as he says!

SCENE 6

  [*Exit* KENNEDY, *with signs of bewilderment.*]
MARY: But this is from my uncle,
  The Cardinal of Lorraine, written from France! [*Reading*]
  'Trust Mortimer, who bears this message to you,
  You have no truer friend in England now!'
  [*Gazing in astonishment at* MORTIMER]
  Can this be true? Is it not some delusion?
  I find a friend so near, and when I thought
  That all the world had left me – find him in
  My gaoler's nephew, you, whom I believed
  The bitterest of enemies?
MORTIMER [*throwing himself at her feet*]: Forgive
  This hateful mask, my queen, which I must wear
  With so much pain, and yet which I must thank
  For bringing me to you, to help and save you!
MARY: O do not kneel – Sir, you surprise me – I
  Cannot so quickly trust in hope again
  After such deep despair – Now tell me, sir,
  What does this mean? Let me believe this joy!
MORTIMER [*standing up*]: Time presses; soon my uncle will
      be here,
  And with him there will come a hateful man.
  Before their fearful errand reaches you,
  Listen to Heaven's own plan for your deliverance.
MARY: A miracle of Heaven's omnipotence!
MORTIMER: Allow me to speak first –
MARY: Sir?
MORTIMER: – Of myself.
  At twenty years of age, your majesty,
  Brought up to serve in strict obedience,
  And taught to loathe all taint of Popery,

I found my heart consumed with longing for
Another land – And so I left these shores,
Their gloomy Puritan conventicles,
And sped through France to Italy, the land
Of my desires, of which I heard such praise.
– It was the greatest feast-day of the Church,
The roads were thronged with countless bands of
    pilgrims,
And every image was bedecked; it seemed
That all mankind was making its procession,
That led to Heaven's gate. And I myself,
Caught up amidst the faithful multitudes,
Found myself swept along to Rome –
And O, my queen!
When splendid column and triumphal arch
Arose before my eyes, and when I gazed
In wonder at the Colosseum's might, it was
As if a lofty spirit opened up
A glorious realm of wonders to my soul!
For I had never known the power of art,
The Church in which I grew knows only hate
For beauty, tolerates no images,
Adores the immaterial Word alone.
But now, imagine, as I stepped inside
The churches, how the heavenly sound of music
Descended, and a host of figures burst
From every ceiling and from every wall;
The noblest and the highest that we worship
Was there to ravish my enchanted senses.
I saw myself the saints in glory shining,
The angel's salutation and the birth
Of the Lord God, His holy Mother too,
The Trinity descended, Christ transfigured –
I saw the Pope in all his majesty
Say Mass, and bless the peoples of the world.
O, what is all the pomp of gold and jewels
With which our earthly kings adorn their state!
His house is like the courts of Heaven itself,

For everything about him is divine,
These beauties are not like the works of men!

MARY: O spare me, sir, I beg you, do not spread
This tapestry of life before my eyes!
No more! I am an exile and a captive.

MORTIMER: As I was too, my queen! But now my prison
Was opened wide; my soul took wing in freedom,
To greet the glorious day of new-found life.
I swore to hate the crabbed and gloomy Book,
I ran to set a garland on my head,
Joyful I mingled with the joyful throng.
And many noble Scotsmen there I found,
And Frenchmen too, a merry company.
They took me to the Cardinal de Guise,
Your noble uncle – such a man, my queen!
An upright spirit, generous and sure!
O, he was born to rule the hearts of men,
A kingly priest, the wonder of the world,
Prince of the Church whose like I never saw!

MARY: You who have seen that face so dear to me,
That noble and beloved man, who was
The guardian and the teacher of my youth,
Speak to me of him. Does he think of me?
Does fortune favour him, does life still bloom,
Does he still stand a rock of Christendom?

MORTIMER: Excellent man! Himself he undertook
To teach me in the doctrines of true faith,
And banished doubt entirely from my heart.
He showed me that a man is led astray
By brooding reason; that his eyes must see,
And then his heart believe; that there must be
A head to lead the Church that all can know;
That truth inspired the counsels of the Fathers.
The vain delusions of my childish soul
Fled from his reasons and his eloquence;
He was victorious, and I returned
Into the bosom of the holy Church,
And in his hands abjured my false beliefs.

MARY: And so you count yourself among the thousands
    That he with heavenly gift of speech has touched,
    Like Him who preached upon the mount, and brought
    Them back to the salvation of their souls.

MORTIMER: When shortly afterwards his duty called
    Him back to France, he sent me on to Rheims,
    Where Jesuits with pious zeal are schooling
    The priests who will return to England's Church.
    I found the noble Scotsman Morgan there,
    Your loyal Lesley too, the learned bishop
    Of Ross, in joyless exile now in France.
    I sought these worthy men in company,
    My faith grew stronger. – Looking round one day
    Within the Bishop's house, a woman's portrait
    Of wondrous moving beauty caught my gaze,
    My soul was seized, into its very depths,
    And overwhelmed, I knew not what to do.
    The bishop said to me: Well may you gaze
    In wonder at this portrait; for you see
    The loveliest of ladies on this earth,
    The saddest too, a martyr for our faith,
    And in your fatherland it is she suffers.

MARY: O worthy man! No, all is not yet lost,
    If I have such a friend in need as this.

MORTIMER: Then he began to speak, to break my heart
    With eloquent account of all your grief
    And of the blood-lust of your enemies.
    He showed me too the tree of your descent
    From the great house of Tudor, proved to me
    That you alone should sit on England's throne,
    Not this usurping queen, the child of an
    Adulterous bed, whom her own father Henry
    Himself rejected as a bastard daughter!
    Still I did not believe his words alone;
    I sought out men of learning in the law,
    Read many ancient genealogies;
    And every man of knowledge that I asked
    Confirmed the strength and justice of your claim.

And now I know the only wrong you do
Is that you have the right to England's crown,
And that this kingdom, where in innocence
You lie imprisoned, is your own to rule.

MARY: O this unhappy right! It is the source,
The single cause of all my sufferings.

MORTIMER: At this same time I heard the news that you
Had been removed from Talbot's custody,
And handed over to my uncle here;
In this I thought I saw the hand of Heaven,
A miracle, designed for your salvation.
I heard in it the voice of destiny,
That summoned me to free you with my arm.
My joyful friends assent, the Cardinal
Gives me his blessing and his good advice,
My first hard lessons in deceitfulness.
The plan was quickly made, and I return
To my own country, where ten days ago
I landed, as you know. [*He pauses.*]
                               Your majesty, my queen!
Now it was you I saw, and not your portrait!
O, what a treasure this dark castle holds!
No dungeon, but a palace of the gods!
More splendid than the royal court itself
Of England – O, what happiness is mine,
That I may breathe this prison air with you!
– Yes, she is right to keep you hidden so!
For every youth in England would rebel,
Never a sword would rest within its sheath,
And civil war, an ogre, would stride through
This peaceful land, if only Albion's sons
Could see their queen!

MARY: O would that every son
Of Albion saw her with such eyes as yours!

MORTIMER: O could he be a witness here with me
To see your sorrows, and the noble patience
With which you bear this most unworthy shame!
For does not every test of suffering

Prove that you are a queen? Can the disgrace
Of this dank prison rob you of your beauty?
You have not one of life's adornments here,
And yet I see you shine with light and life.
I never set my foot within this door,
But I am torn with grief within my heart,
Enraptured with the joy of seeing you!
But reckoning draws near, with every hour
Danger approaches closer, menacing,
I can delay no longer – hide from you
The dreadful truth no longer –

MARY: Is my sentence
Pronounced? Tell me, I beg, for I can bear it.

MORTIMER: It is pronounced. The Forty-two have judged
You guilty. Lords and Commons, and the City
Of London urge that it be carried out
Without delay, the Queen alone holds back –
Cunningly hoping they will force her hand,
Not out of pity or humanity.

MARY [*with dignity*]: Sir Mortimer, your news does not
    surprise,
No, nor alarm me. Long I have expected
This message, for I know the men who judge me.
After the treatment I have suffered here,
I understand they cannot grant my freedom –
No, I can see what they will do with me.
Imprisoned here for ever; and my hopes
Of vengeance and my lawful claims will all
Be buried with me in this endless night.

MORTIMER: No, no, my queen! It is not that. That could
Not satisfy their tyranny, for it
Would leave their work half done. While yet you live,
So too lives on the Queen of England's fear.
There is no prison deep enough to hide you,
Only your death secures her on her throne.

MARY: What, could she lay a queen's anointed head
Upon the shameful block? She would not dare!

MORTIMER: She will. Be sure of that, your majesty.

MARY: To roll it in the dust, the name *she* bears,
  The dignity and state of every king?
  And does she not fear the revenge of France?
MORTIMER: With France she means to sign eternal peace,
  And to bestow her throne and hand on Anjou.
MARY: And will the king of Spain not rise in arms?
MORTIMER: She does not fear the might of all the world,
  As long as she has peace with her own people.
MARY: And would she give them such a spectacle?
MORTIMER: This land, my lady, has in recent years
  Seen other royal ladies make their way
  Down from the throne and up the scaffold's steps.
  Elizabeth's own mother; Catherine Howard;
  Lady Jane Grey – she too had worn a crown.
MARY [*after a pause*]: No, Mortimer! These are imagined
    fears.
  Your loyal heart is filled with cares for me
  Which make you think such horrors could be true.
  No, sir, I do not fear the headsman's block,
  For there are other and more private means
  For England's mistress to be rid of me,
  And of my claims that trouble her so sorely.
  Sooner than find an executioner,
  She'll hire a common murderer for me.
  That makes me tremble, sir; and never can
  I raise my cup to drink, but I am seized
  With terror, for I always fear perhaps
  My sister's loving hand has poured it for me.
MORTIMER: Neither in public nor in secret shall
  The murderess lay hand upon your life.
  You shall not fear. All is in readiness.
  Twelve noble English youths, in league with me,
  Have sworn this morning on the sacrament
  To carry you away from Fotheringhay.
  The French ambassador, Count Aubespine,
  Knows of our oath, himself has sworn his aid,
  And it is in his palace that we meet.
MARY: O sir, I tremble – not for joy, I fear,

But ill foreboding weighs upon my heart.
What are you seeking? Are you not dismayed
By Babington's and Tichbourne's bleeding heads,
Spiked upon London Bridge in grim example,
Nor by the fate of countless other men,
Who in a like adventure found their deaths,
And made my fetters heavier to bear?
Unhappy, foolish youth, flee while there's time!
If Burghley has not spied you out already,
Set an informer in your midst – go, flee
While still you may! No man has served the Queen
Of Scots and prospered.

MORTIMER: I am not dismayed
By Babington's and Tichbourne's bleeding heads,
Spiked upon London Bridge in grim example,
Nor by the fate of all those countless others,
Who in a like adventure found their deaths;
They found eternal glory too and fame,
And it is joy to die for your salvation.

MARY: In vain! Boldness and cunning will not save me,
My enemy is vigilant and mighty.
Not only Paulet and his men-at-arms,
All England watches at my prison gates,
Elizabeth, and of her own free will,
Alone can open them.

MORTIMER: There is no hope!

MARY: One man there lives with power to unlock them.

MORTIMER: What is his name?

MARY: The Earl of Leicester.

MORTIMER [drawing back in astonishment]:   Leicester!
The Earl of Leicester! Chief of your tormentors,
Favourite of Elizabeth! From him –

MARY: In him my only hope of rescue lies.
Go to him. Tell him what is in your mind,
And as a pledge that you have come from me,
Give him this letter. It contains my portrait.
[She takes a paper from her bosom. MORTIMER draws back,
and hesitates to accept it.]

Here! I have guarded it for many days,
Your uncle's vigilance has barred the way
To him for me. But now you have been sent
By my good angel.

MORTIMER: But, your majesty,
Explain this riddle –

MARY: Leicester will do that.
Trust him, and he will trust in you. – Who's there?
[*Enter* KENNEDY, *in haste.*]

KENNEDY: Paulet is here, and some great lord is with him.

MORTIMER: Burghley it is, your majesty. Have courage!
Listen with calm to what he has to tell you.
[*Exit* MORTIMER *by a side door.* KENNEDY *follows him.*]

SCENE 7

[*Enter* BURGHLEY, *Lord Treasurer of England, with him*
PAULET.]

PAULET: You wished to learn your fate with certainty;
The certainty you ask, his excellency
Lord Burghley brings you. Bear it as is fitting.

MARY: With fortitude, as I am innocent.

BURGHLEY: I come as envoy of the Commissaries.

MARY: The court that Burghley served with reasons, now
Enjoys the service of his busy tongue.

BURGHLEY: You speak as if you knew what was its verdict.

MARY: As it is brought by Burghley, yes, I know it.
My lord, to business.

BURGHLEY: As you did submit
To judgment by the Court of Forty-two –

MARY: Forgive, my lord, that I must interrupt
Your words so soon. Did I submit myself
To that court's judgement? That I did not do.
I could not do it, not in any way.
I know the due I owe to my own rank,
The pride I owe my nation and my son,
And all the princes of this world, too well.

For it is written, sir, in England's law,
That no man may be judged but by his peers.
There is not one among the Commissaries
Can be my judge – or are they kings?

BURGHLEY: And yet
You heard the articles of accusation,
Gave evidence –

MARY: I let myself be swayed
By Hatton's evil cunning, for my honour,
And trusting in the rightness of my cause,
To listen to those articles, and answer to
Their falsehood; this I did out of respect
For those their lordships' persons, not their office,
For that I could and would not recognize.

BURGHLEY: My lady, whether you will choose or not
To recognise their office, is a trifle
Which cannot halt the course of England's justice.
You breathe the air of England, you enjoy
Benefit and protection of her laws,
And so you must submit to them.

MARY: I breathe
The vapours of an English prison, sir.
Is this a benefit, is this the life
Which England's laws protect? I scarcely know them,
And I have never sworn obedience to them.
My lord, I am no subject of this land,
I am a queen who rules another country.

BURGHLEY: And do you think the name of queen can be
Excuse to stir up civil war and strife
In other kingdoms, and to go unpunished?
Could any nation ever sleep at peace
If justice with her righteous sword could not
Reach out to strike a stranger's guilty head,
Whether he be a monarch or a beggar?

MARY: I do not seek to flee just punishment,
These judges only I will not accept.

BURGHLEY: These judges? What, my lady? Are they then
The meanest rabble of the common crowd,

Unworthy babblers, who would willingly
Sell truth and justice to the highest bidder,
The eager servants of a tyrant's whim?
Are not these men the foremost in the land,
Free to speak truth, noble and bold enough
To count themselves above the fear of princes,
Beyond the reach of furtive bribery?
Do they not rule in justice and in freedom
A noble race, are not their names enough
To conquer doubt, to make suspicion idle?
First in their number comes my lord Archbishop
Of Canterbury, shepherd of the people;
Talbot, Lord Privy Seal, famed for his wisdom,
And Howard, Admiral of England's fleet.
What, could the Queen of England have done more
Than choose the finest men in all this kingdom
To judge this royal cause? And even if
One man were swayed by partiality,
Can forty chosen men speak with one voice
A verdict prejudiced by hate?

MARY [*after a moment's silence*]: Amazed I hear the power of
    this tongue,
That never spoke but brought ill-luck to me.
How can I hope, a poor unlearned woman,
To match myself with such an orator!
– Sir, if these lords were as you have portrayed them,
Then I should hold my peace, for I must know
My cause was lost if they should speak me guilty.
But, sir, these names which you pronounce with pride,
Thinking to crush me with their glorious weight,
Tell me a different story of the part
That they have played in England's history.
I see this kingdom's high nobility,
The senate of this empire, flattering
Like Turkish harem slaves the Sultan's whim
Of Henry Tudor, my great-uncle; see
The noble House of Lords, as venal as
The meanest commoners, make and unmake

The laws, and at the tyrant's word proclaim
Divorce and marriage; disinherit now
His daughters, brand them with the name of bastard,
The next day raise them up and crown them queens.
I see these worthy peers converted with
Such servile haste that in four reigns four times
They can betray the faith that they profess.

BURGHLEY: You say that England's laws are strange to you;
England's misfortunes you know well, it seems.

MARY: And I am to be judged by men like these!
My lord, I will not be unjust to you.
Will you be just with me? Men say your heart
Is loyal to England and your queen, that you
Are incorruptible and vigilant –
I will believe it. You may not be swayed
By thought of your own profit, nothing but
The good of England and her ruler moves you.
But for that selfsame reason, sir, beware
That you do not mistake the cause you serve
For justice. And I cannot doubt that there
Are other worthy men among my judges.
But they are Protestants, and zealous in
The name of England, and pronounce upon
The Queen of Scotland and a Catholic.
An Englishman will never fairly judge
A Scot – so it is always said, my lord;
And therefore it has been the custom of
Our nations since the very dawn of time,
That in a court of law an Englishman
May not be heard in evidence against
A Scot, nor Scot against an Englishman.
And it was right that this strange rule should be;
There is good reason for such ancient customs,
And we must honour them. For Nature cast
Two fiery peoples on this ocean raft
Adrift, and gave them their unequal shares,
And bade them fight to hold what was their own.
The narrow bed of Tweed alone divides

Their jealousies, and often red with blood
Its waters flowed between their hostile fronts.
With sword in hand, and menacing, they watched
From banks opposed, a thousand years and more.
No enemy has ever threatened England
That could not count on Scotland as his friend,
And Scotland's cities knew no civil strife
But it was kindled by an English torch.
And never will this hatred cease until
One Parliament in brotherhood unites them,
One sceptre rules this island undivided.

BURGHLEY: And it should be a Stuart who bestowed
This blessing on our kingdom?

MARY: Why should I
Deny that I have cherished hope that this
Might be, that these two noble nations might
Through my own hand unite in peace and joy?
I did not think to be the victim of
Their hatred; rather did I hope that I
Might stifle age-old jealousies for ever,
Put out the fires of ancient enmity,
And, as my ancestor of Richmond made
Two Roses bloom together side by side
In peace, and ended long and bloody war,
So I might join the Scots and English crowns.

BURGHLEY: You chose a wicked path to your desires:
To raise rebellion, and to climb the steps
Of England's throne through bitter civil strife.

MARY: Great God in Heaven, that was not what I chose!
Where is your proof that such was my intent?

BURGHLEY: I did not come to bandy words. There is
No room for argument in this case more.
The court has judged by forty votes to two
That you have broken England's law, laid down
By England's Parliament a year ago:
'If in this kingdom there shall be rebellion
Raised in the name and in the interest
Of any person claiming England's crown,

That guilty person shall be brought to justice,
Tried and condemned to suffer execution.'
As it is proved –

MARY: My noble lord of Burghley!
I do not doubt that laws expressly made
To prove me guilty and to ruin me
Can well be used against me. – O, alas
For the unhappy victim, when the tongue
That spoke this law gives judgement under it!
My lord, can you deny that Parliament
Devised this Act solely for my destruction?

BURGHLEY: It was intended only as a warning,
But you yourself have made a snare of it.
You saw the pit that gaped before your feet,
You did not heed our warning, and you fell.
You plotted with the traitor Babington
And with his fellow-murderers, you knew
Of their conspiracy, and cunningly
Contrived to lead them, in your prison cell.

MARY: I plotted, led conspiracy? Show me
Your proof.

BURGHLEY: We did produce the documents
Before the court.

MARY: Copies by other hands!
Bring me your proof that I dictated them,
Dictated every word just as you read it.

BURGHLEY: These letters were the same that Babington
Received, as he confessed before he died.

MARY: And why was he not brought before me while
He lived? And why were you in so much haste
To rid the world of him, before he could
Be made to answer face to face with me?

BURGHLEY: Your secretaries, Curle and Nau, confirmed
On oath those letters were the very same
That they had written down at your dictation.

MARY: And so upon the evidence of servants
I am condemned? Upon the oath of men
Who broke their oath of loyalty to me,

Their queen, in that same moment when they gave
Their evidence against me and betrayed me?
BURGHLEY: But you yourself have said that Curle the Scot
Was steadfast and would always speak the truth.
MARY: And so I knew him; but the final test
Of steadfastness is how it faces danger.
Under the torture he grew faint, and then
Spoke and confessed things he knew nothing of!
He thought false evidence would save himself,
And be of little harm to me, his queen.
BURGHLEY: He freely swore his evidence was true.
MARY: But not before my face! What then, my lord?
Those are two witnesses are still alive.
Bring them before me here and make them speak
Their evidence again before my face!
This favour you may not withhold – this right
That every murderer enjoys! I know,
For Talbot told me, when he was my gaoler,
That by decree of this same government,
Accused may see accuser face to face.
Or am I wrong? Paulet! Is this not so?
You I have always thought an honest man,
Prove it to me, and tell me, on your conscience,
Is it not so? Is this the law of England?
PAULET: It is, my lady. Yes, we have this law,
I must admit the truth.
MARY: You see, my lord!
If I am to be subject to the law
Of England when it is no friend to me,
Why is this law denied when it could prove
To my advantage? Will you answer me?
Why was not Babington brought face to face
With me, according to the law? Nor my
Two secretaries, who are still alive?
BURGHLEY: My lady, calm your passion. It is not
Your plot with Babington alone –
MARY: It is
No other thing which threatens me with death,

If I cannot disprove your accusations.
It is, my lord! Do not evade me, sir!

BURGHLEY: It has been proved that you have bargained
with
Mendoza, the ambassador of Spain –

MARY [*vigorously*]: Do not evade me, sir!

BURGHLEY: – That you have schemed
To overthrow the worship which has been
Established in this land, have urged all Europe's
Kings to make war on England –

MARY: And what if
I have? And I have not. But if I have,
What then? My lord, you keep me prisoner
Against the sacred laws which bind all nations.
It was not sword in hand I came to England,
I came in supplication to your country,
Claiming the right of hospitality.
I hoped for comfort from my sister queen,
And I was seized with force and thrown in chains
Where I had sought protection – tell me then,
What obligations have I to your state?
What debts of conscience do I owe to England?
It is my sacred right to answer force
With force, and seek to break my prison bars,
And gather Europe's nations to my cause.
Whatever is legitimate in war,
And honourable, I may undertake.
Murder alone, a secret bloody deed,
My conscience and my pride forbid to me,
For murder would dishonour and besmirch me.
I say besmirch me – it would not condemn me,
Nor make me answerable to your justice,
For between me and England it is force
Alone, it is not justice will decide.

BURGHLEY [*gravely*]: Do not invoke the right of force, my
lady!
It will not favour you, a prisoner!

MARY: The power is in her hand, not mine. So be it!

Let her use all her might against me, kill me,
Sacrifice me for her security.
But let her then admit it is by force
Of arms alone, not by the law I die.
I am her hated enemy, she will
Be rid of me, but let her not disguise
Her bloody enterprise in robes of justice,
And borrow Themis' sword to strike me down.
Let not this masquerade deceive the world!
Kill me she may, my judge she cannot be!
Let her not seek to eat in secrecy
The fruits of crime, and yet escape the blame,
But dare to give her deed its rightful name! [*Exit.*]

SCENE 8

BURGHLEY: Defiance, Paulet – and she will defy us
Upon the scaffold! This proud heart will not
Be broken – Did she show the least surprise
To hear the verdict? Did you see her weep
Or change complexion? No, she will not try
To move our pity. All too well she knows
The doubts and fears that trouble England's queen,
And that which makes us weak is strength to her.
PAULET: My lord, this vain defiant pride will soon
Be gone, if we can banish its excuse.
The conduct of this case, sir, by your leave,
Has not been free of impropriety.
Tichbourne and Babington should have been brought
To speak before her face, and Curle and Nau
To testify here in her presence.
BURGHLEY [*quickly*]: No!
No, Paulet, that we could not dare to do!
She can bewitch the mind of any man,
And wield the power of a woman's tears.
Her secretary, if he stood before her,
If he should have at last to speak the word
Her life depended on, he would grow faint,

Take back his own confession and recant –

PAULET: The enemies of England now will spread
Vile slander through all nations of the world,
And make the solemn pomp of these proceedings
Seem nothing but the flaunting of a crime.

BURGHLEY: This is what agitates and grieves our queen. –
O would this woman, cause of all our troubles,
Had died before she ever set her foot
On England's soil!

PAULET: To that I say Amen.

BURGHLEY: That sickness had consumed her here in prison!

PAULET: It would have spared our land these miseries.

BURGHLEY: And yet, if by some chance of nature she
Had died, men still would call us murderers.

PAULET: That may be so. You cannot hinder men
From thinking what they will.

BURGHLEY: There could have been
No proof, and it had passed without such noise.

PAULET: Let there be noise, I say! Not loud reproach,
But just reproach alone a man should fear.

BURGHLEY: Not even Heaven's own justice can escape
Men's blame: the sufferer will always win
Their favour, and the fortunate, the victor,
With jealousy and hatred they pursue.
The sword of justice is the pride of man,
But hated in a woman's hand. The world
Will not believe a woman can be just
When woman is her victim. No, in vain
Have we pronounced according to our conscience!
She has the royal prerogative of mercy,
And she must use it, for it may not be
That she will let stern justice take its course!

PAULET: And so –

BURGHLEY [interrupting quickly]: And so she will be
    pardoned? No!
She shall not live! She may not! This alone
Causes our queen all her anxieties.
She cannot close her eyes in sleep – I read

In them the fearful struggles of her soul;
Her lips dare not give utterance to her wish,
And yet her silent gaze is ever asking:
'Is there not one of all my servants here
Will take from me this hateful choice: to sit
In everlasting terror on my throne,
Or cruelly send a queen, and my own cousin,
Beneath the headsman's axe?'

PAULET: It must be so;
Necessity commands, there is no other way.

BURGHLEY: There might be, so her majesty believes,
If only she had more attentive servants.

PAULET: Attentive?

BURGHLEY: Servants who would hear commands
Although they were unspoken.

PAULET: What? unspoken?

BURGHLEY: Who, when entrusted with the custody
Of poisonous snakes, would not protect their charge
As if it were a sacred precious jewel!

PAULET [*gravely*]: A jewel indeed is the unspotted name,
The precious reputation of our queen.
One cannot guard too closely such a treasure!

BURGHLEY: When Mary was removed from Talbot's house
And given into Paulet's custody,
It was because –

PAULET: I hope, my lord, it was
Because this charge was thought to be too great
For any but the purest hands to hold!
By God in Heaven! This gaoler's office I
Would not have taken, had I not believed
This task would tax the best of Englishmen.
Let me not think that I was chosen, sir,
For any reason but my honesty.

BURGHLEY: Let it be known that she is sick, then let
Her weaken, fade away at last in quiet –
So she is dead in memory already,
And Paulet's name is clear.

PAULET: But not my conscience.

BURGHLEY: But if you will not lend your own hand to it,
  You would not keep another's hand away –
PAULET [*interrupting him*]: No murderer shall enter at her
    door
  As long as she is kept beneath this roof.
  Her life is sacred to me, not more sacred
  I hold the head of England's majesty.
  You are her judges! Judge her! Speak her sentence!
  And when the time is come, the carpenter
  May bring his axe and saw and build her scaffold;
  The sheriff and the executioner
  Shall find this castle open to admit them.
  But now I am her guardian, and be sure
  That I will guard her, safe from all alarm,
  And she shall neither do, nor suffer harm! [*Exeunt.*]

ACT II

The Palace of Westminster

SCENE I

[*Enter the* EARL OF KENT *and* SIR WILLIAM
DAVISON, *meeting.*]

DAVISON: My lord of Kent! Already you return?
  Are the festivities so quickly over?
KENT: Were you not there to see the tournament?
DAVISON: My duty kept me here.
KENT: Then you have missed
  The finest spectacle, most skilfully
  Devised and nobly executed, sir.
  We saw a fortress, held by Chastity
  And Beauty, and assaulted by Desire.
  Burghley and Talbot, Leicester and ten more
  Of the Queen's knights made up its garrison,
  And cavaliers of France were the besiegers.

A herald first appeared, in madrigal
Demanding its surrender. From the walls
The Treasurer replied, and then the guns
Were touched, and from this sweet artillery
The finest perfumes fired, with wreaths of flowers.
In vain! for every charge was beaten back,
And bold Desire was forced to sound retreat.

DAVISON: My lord, this was no favourable omen
For those that come from France to woo our Queen.

KENT: Come, this was but a jest; I think in truth
The fortress will be yielded at the last.

DAVISON: Do you believe it will, my lord? I cannot.

KENT: The articles that caused the most delay
Are now amended and agreed by France.
Monsieur will undertake to hear his Mass
In his own private chapel, and to guard
And honour publicly the Church of England.
If you had seen the people's joy when they
Received this news! For this was what they feared,
That she might die and leave no heir, and England
Be forced to bear the Roman yoke once more,
If Mary Stuart should ascend the throne.

DAVISON: No, that they need not fear; *she* goes to be
A bride, and Mary Stuart to her death.

KENT: Her majesty the Queen!

SCENE 2

[*Enter* ELIZABETH, *escorted by* LEICESTER; COUNT
AUBESPINE, BELLIÈVRE, *the* EARL OF SHREWSBURY,
LORD BURGHLEY *and other* FRENCH *and* ENGLISH
GENTLEMEN.]

ELIZABETH [*to* AUBESPINE]: Monsieur le comte! I fear
these gentlemen
Whom zealous gallantry has brought across
The sea to us, will find our court is lacking
In the magnificence of St Germain.
I cannot match the splendid festivals

The Queen of France can give, for all I have
To show you is a virtuous, happy people,
That every time I go amongst them, throng
The path about my chair, and shout their blessings.
This is the spectacle that I can offer
With modest pride. If I were to appear
Amidst the glittering beauties of the court
Of Catherine de Medici, I fear
No man would notice my more humble worth.

AUBESPINE: There is but one so fair at Westminster,
To charm the stranger's eye – but everything
Her sex possesses to enrapture us
In her own single person is united.

BELLIÈVRE: Your gracious majesty of England, grant
That we may take our leave and hasten home
To greet our royal master with the message
That all the joys he longs for shall be his.
His heart's impatience would not let him stay
In Paris, he has gone to Amiens
There to await the news of his good fortune,
And he has sent his messengers to Calais,
To speed as swiftly as on wings the word
That you will give, back to his ravished ear.

ELIZABETH: Monsieur de Bellièvre, do not press me,
It is not time, I must repeat to you,
As yet to light the merry nuptial torch.
Black are the clouds that brood above this land,
And mourning garments would become me more
Than all the gay apparel of a bride.
For I must fear a grievous blow will fall
Too soon upon my heart and on my house.

BELLIÈVRE: My queen, will you but give us now your
promise,
Let its fulfilment wait for happier days.

ELIZABETH: We monarchs are the slaves of our condition,
We may not heed the promptings of our heart.
I only wished that I might die unmarried,
And that my everlasting fame might be

That men should come and read upon my grave,
'Here lie the bones of England's virgin queen'.
But no, my subjects do not wish it so;
Already they are thinking of the time
When I am dead, and not enough for them
The present blessings that this land enjoys,
But for their future I must yield myself,
And sacrifice the freedom of a maid,
My greatest treasure, for my people's good;
And they will find a husband to command me,
To prove to me that I am but a woman,
Who thought to govern like a man, a king.
Indeed, I know that God is not well pleased
When Nature's laws are broken, and it was
A meritorious deed of those before me
To raze the convents, and to turn back thousands
Of victims of misguided piety
To the observance of their natural duty.
And yet a queen, not one who spends her days
In idle, fruitless contemplation, but
Untiringly has laboured to perform
The most exacting of all duties, she
Should be exempted from this natural law
That binds one half of our humanity
In bondage to the other –

AUBESPINE: Your majesty, upon your throne you have
Exalted every virtue. What remains,
But that the sex of which you are the pearl
Should learn from you observance of its own
Vocation? True, there is no man on earth
Fit to receive this sacrifice from you;
But if high birth, nobility, and courage,
And handsome manliness could make a mortal
Worthy of this, then –

ELIZABETH: Sir ambassador,
I cannot doubt that it would honour me
To seal a marriage-treaty with a son
Of France's royal house! Yes, I confess

Unfeignedly, that if this thing must be,
If I am forced to yield to the entreaties
Of these my people – and I fear that they
Will at the last be stronger than my wishes –
Then there is not a prince I know in Europe
To whom with less reluctance I would yield
My maiden freedom, my most precious jewel.
Let this confession be enough for you.

BELLIÈVRE: O fairest hope, and yet it is no more
  Than hope, and my good master had desired –

ELIZABETH: What then? [*She takes a ring from her finger
    and gazes thoughtfully at it.*]
                    A queen has nothing, after all,
More than the meanest of her subjects' wives!
Like tokens mark a like obedience,
A like devotion: rings make marriages,
And ring is joined to ring to make a chain.
– Monsieur shall have this present. It is not
A chain as yet, I will not yet be bound,
But it may be a ring one day to bind me.

BELLIÈVRE [*kneeling to receive it*]: Your majesty, I kneel to
    take this gift,
  Receive it in my master's name, and press
  Upon my sovereign's hand a kiss of loyalty!

ELIZABETH [*to* LEICESTER, *whom she has been watching
    uninterruptedly throughout the last speech*]: My lord,
    permit me! [*She takes his sash of the Garter and hangs
    it round* BELLIÈVRE'*s neck.*] Give this ribbon to
His highness, as I give it here to you,
Admitting you to my most noble Order.
Sir! *Honi soit qui mal y pense!* Between
Our nations let suspicion fade and die,
And from this moment let a bond of peace
And friendship join the crowns of France and England!

AUBESPINE: Your gracious majesty, this is a day
Of joy! Let all men share it and let none
Upon this island be denied a part.
Your countenance is radiant with grace,

O that one beam could touch with its glad mercy
A noble lady, weighted down with sorrow,
Whose fate affects in equal measure France
And England –

ELIZABETH: Sir, no more! Do not confuse
Two matters which do not concern each other.
If France in earnest seeks with me alliance,
Then France must share my cares, and not befriend
My enemies –

AUBESPINE: But France would be unworthy
Even in your own eyes, if she forgot
In this alliance that unhappy lady,
Our sister Catholic, and widow of
Our King! Our honour, our humanity
Demand no less!

ELIZABETH: And in their name the word
Of France on her behalf shall be esteemed.
It is the duty of a friend; but I
Must exercise the office of a queen. [*She bows to the*
        FRENCH LORDS, *who withdraw followed by the other*
        GENTLEMEN, *leaving the* QUEEN *behind with*
        BURGHLEY, SHREWSBURY *and* LEICESTER *only.*
        She sits down.]

SCENE 3

BURGHLEY: Most glorious majesty! Today you crown
The people's dearest wishes. Now at last
We may enjoy these blessed days of peace
That you bestow on us, since we no more
Need fear a troubled future for this land.
There is but one anxiety remaining,
One sacrifice which every voice demands.
Grant what we ask, and from this happy day
England shall flourish till the end of time.

ELIZABETH: What do my people still desire?

BURGHLEY: They ask
For Mary Stuart's head. – If you would have

Your people keep the precious gift of freedom,
And hard-won truth, then she must die. – If we
Are not to tremble for your precious life
In all eternity, your enemy
Must breathe no more! – You know it all too well,
Not every Englishman has seen the light,
And many still serve Rome's idolatry
Within this island, though in secrecy.
These men know only enmity to you,
Their hearts are faithful to the Stuart woman,
And allied with the brothers of Lorraine,
Who bear undying hatred to your name.
These desperate men have sworn to drive you out
With bloody war, waged with the arms of Hell.
The palace of the cardinal at Rheims,
That is their arsenal, there they forge their bolts,
There plan their regicide; from there they send
Their busy missionaries to this island,
Zealous fanatics, masked in many guises.
From there three murderers have come already,
And hidden enemies unceasingly
Pour forth like vermin from the teeming pit.
And in the castle there at Fotheringhay
She sits, the Ate of this endless war,
Who sets this realm on fire with brands of love.
For her, who feeds their hopes with flattery,
So many giddy youths seek certain death –
To free her is their cry, to set her on
Your throne the purpose of their enterprise.
The sons of Guise will never recognize
Your right to England's throne, they say that you
Are a usurper, crowned by trick of fortune!
They led the foolish creature on to call
Herself our queen. And there can never be
Peace between you and her, or with their house!
Unless you strike the blow, it falls on you!
Her life is death to you, her death your life.

ELIZABETH: My lord, a thankless office you perform.

I know that zealous loyalty inspires it,
I know that wisdom and experience
Dictate the words you speak – and yet I hate
This bloody wisdom in my very soul.
Is there no milder remedy? – My lord
Of Shrewsbury, tell us what is your counsel.

SHREWSBURY: Justly and generously you have praised
The zeal that speaks in Burghley's heart. I too,
Though I may lack his skill in eloquence,
Know that a loyal heart beats in my breast.
Long may you live to govern us, my queen,
To be your people's joy, and grant this land
The benefits of peace for years to come.
This island has not known such prosperous days
In all its native princes' many reigns.
But may this land's good fortune not be bought
With its good name! Let Talbot's eyes at least
Be shut, if ever this should come to be.

ELIZABETH: May God forbid we should besmirch our
name.

SHREWSBURY: Then you must find another, better means
To save this kingdom – for to execute
The Queen of Scots in truth would be unjust.
You cannot sit in judgement over her,
For she is not your subject.

ELIZABETH: Parliament
And Privy Council then have spoken wrong,
And all the courts of justice in this island,
Who with one voice acknowledge it my right.

SHREWSBURY: Their voices are no test of right and wrong.
England is not the world, your Parliament
Not the assembly of humanity.
England today is not what she will be
In future years, nor what she has been – Just
As inclinations change, so do the scales
Of justice and of judgement rise and fall.
Do not protest it is necessity
You must obey, or popular demand.

At any moment, if you wish it, you
May prove the sovereign freedom of your will.
Let it be so! Say you abhor this bloodshed,
And will not let her die who is your cousin;
Show those who would advise you otherwise
The open features of your royal displeasure;
This feigned necessity will disappear,
And what is now called justice seem unjust.
You, you alone must judge. You cannot lean
Upon this feeble reed swayed by the wind.
Do not refuse to hear the voice of mercy.
God did not make severity the stuff
Of woman's heart; and those who made the law
That England's throne should not be barred to woman
Proved that severity should never be
A virtue in the ruler of this kingdom.

ELIZABETH: My lord of Shrewsbury, you speak with
        warmth
For England's enemy and mine. I must
Prefer the counsels of my better friends.

SHREWSBURY: She has no advocate, and none will dare
To brave your anger, speaking in her part.
But I am old, and earthly hopes will not
Lead me astray, for death I know is near.
So let me speak for her whom all have fled.
Men shall not say that selfish interest
And passion in your counsels had their voice,
But there was none to speak for clemency.
All circumstances have conspired against her;
Your majesty has never seen her face,
So to your heart she must remain a stranger.
– I do not plead her innocence. Men say
That it was she who had her husband murdered,
And it is true she wed the murderer.
A fearful crime! – But it was in a day
Of grim misfortune and of civil war
With all its terrors that black deed was done,
When she in weakness saw herself surrounded

By vassals pressing urgently, and threw
Herself upon the boldest and most daring.
Who knows by what black arts she was beguiled?
For woman is a frail and tender creature.

ELIZABETH: Woman is not weak. There are mighty souls
Amongst our sex. I will not hear one word
Of woman's weakness spoken in my presence.

SHREWSBURY: You were brought up in harsh adversity.
Life hid its joyous face from you; you saw
No throne awaiting, but an open grave.
At Woodstock and within the Tower's gloom
The gracious father of this kingdom let
You find your way through suffering to duty.
No flatterers could reach you there. You learnt,
Beyond distraction of the giddy world,
In youth to gather up your inward strength,
To seek true peace of mind within yourself
And know what lasting good life has to give.
– No God preserved that wretched lady. She
Was sent, a tender child, to France, and to
The court of folly and of frivolous joy.
There in eternal drunken gaiety
She never heard the sterner voice of truth,
And dazzled by the glittering show of vice
Was carried on the flood that leads to ruin.
The idle gift of beauty she enjoyed,
She was the foremost woman in the land,
Not less by radiance than by right of birth –

ELIZABETH: Will you not cease, my lord of Shrewsbury!
Pray spare our Privy Council these enchantments.
They must indeed be peerless, to inflame
Such ardent passion in your old grey head!
– My lord of Leicester! You alone are silent?
What fires his eloquence has struck you dumb?

LEICESTER: Dumb with astonishment, your majesty,
That men should fill your ears with idle terrors,
That rumours that affright the foolish mob
In London's streets should climb so high that they

Disturb your Council's calm serenity,
And occupy the thoughts of these wise men.
Amazement seizes me, I must confess,
To find that this poor landless Queen of Scots,
Who could not keep her place upon her own
Far lesser throne, the butt of all her vassals,
Rejected and expelled by her own country,
Now frightens you, whose prisoner she is!
What in the name of God makes *you* fear *her*?
That she lays claim to England, that the Guises
Do not acknowledge you this kingdom's queen?
Can their denial rob you of the right
You have by birth, and which has been confirmed
By resolution of your Parliament?
Was she not silently dismissed by Henry,
By his last will, and is this island now,
So happy in the new-found light, to turn
And throw itself into a Papist's arms,
Forget its adoration of its queen,
And kiss the feet of Darnley's murderess?
Why do these hasty men, while you still live,
Torment you with the fear of her succession,
Why are they so impatient to betroth you,
And save our nation and our Church from danger?
Do you not still enjoy the bloom of youth,
While she must fade and droop from day to day?
By heaven, I hope that you for many years
Will walk upon her grave, without the need
Of hastening her death by your own hand.

BURGHLEY: Lord Leicester was not always of this mind.

LEICESTER: No, it is true, I spoke and gave my vote
For execution, when we sat in judgement,
But here in Council I say otherwise.
Here we are not concerned with justice, but
With what is advantageous to the state.
Is this a time to be afraid of her,
When France, her sole protector, quits her cause,
When you will give your hand to bless a son

Of France's royal house, and men may hope
To see a new proud race of English kings?
Why should you kill her? She is dead already!
Scorn and contempt are death to her. Beware,
And do not let her be revived by pity!
So therefore I advise: allow the sentence
Of death upon her head to stay in force,
And let her live – beneath the shadow of
The axe, and if but one man arm himself
To fight for her, then let it swiftly fall.

ELIZABETH [*rising*]: My lords, I have attended to your
    counsels,
And thank you for your loyalty to me.
With God's assistance, who illuminates
The heart of kings, I will consider what
You have advised, and choose what seems the best.

SCENE 4

[*Enter* PAULET *with* MORTIMER.]

ELIZABETH: Our loyal knight, Sir Amyas Paulet. Sir,
  What do you bring?

PAULET: Most glorious majesty!
My nephew, who has travelled far, and now
Returned, has come to kneel here at your feet
And swear a young man's loyal oath to you.
Receive it graciously, and let him grow
In the bright sunshine of your royal favour.

MORTIMER [*falling on one knee*]: Long may my royal lady
    live and flourish,
Fame and good fortune crown her brow for ever!

ELIZABETH: Rise, and be welcome back in England, sir!
So you have made that famous journey: France
And Italy are known to you, and Rheims.
Tell me, what are our enemies contriving?

MORTIMER: May God confound them with His hand, and
  make

The arrows they would loose upon my queen
Return to wound the treacherous archer's breast.

ELIZABETH: Did you see Morgan and that cunning schemer,
His grace of Ross?

MORTIMER: I saw the company
Of Scotsmen banished from their native country,
Who sit at Rheims and plot against this island;
I stole into their confidence, to see
What I could find to tell you of their schemes.

PAULET: They have entrusted him with secret letters,
Meant for the Queen of Scotland, all in cipher,
Which he has loyally put into our hands.

ELIZABETH: What can you tell me of their latest plans?

MORTIMER: I found them thunderstruck to hear the news
That France abandons them to make this bond
With England; they will turn their hopes instead
To Spain.

ELIZABETH: Yes, that I learnt from Walsingham.

MORTIMER: Pope Sixtus sends a Bull against you, which
Arrived in Rheims the day I left the city.
The ship that next leaves France will bring it here.

LEICESTER: Weapons like these we fear no more in England.

BURGHLEY: But they are fearsome in a zealot's hand.

ELIZABETH [with a searching look at MORTIMER]: It is
alleged that you received instruction
From Roman priests in Rheims, and changed your faith!

MORTIMER: I feigned conversion, I do not deny,
Yes, even this, in eagerness to serve you!

ELIZABETH [to PAULET, who is handing her a paper]: What
have you there for me?

PAULET: It is a letter
The Queen of Scots desired that I should give you.

BURGHLEY [reaching quickly for it]: Give it to me.

PAULET [giving it to ELIZABETH]: Your pardon, Treasurer!
She asked that I should put this letter in
The Queen's own hands, and in none other, sir.

She says I am her enemy, but I
Hate nothing in her but her vice, and if
My duty will allow it I will serve her.

[*The* QUEEN *takes the letter. While she is reading it,* MORTI-
MER *and* LEICESTER *exchange a few words in private.*]

BURGHLEY [*to* PAULET]: What can this letter hold but vain
complaints?

Should we not spare our monarch's noble heart
Entreaties such as these?

PAULET: What it contains
She did not keep from me. She begs the favour
That she may see the Queen's own face.

BURGHLEY [*quickly*]:   No, never!

SHREWSBURY: Why not? What she requests is not unjust.

BURGHLEY: The grace of royal countenance is not
For one who has encouraged murderers
And thirsted for the life-blood of our queen.
No loyal subject of his sovereign
Can give such false and treacherous advice.

SHREWSBURY: But if our Queen will grant her what she
asks,
Would you forbid an act of grace and mercy?

BURGHLEY: She is condemned! Her head is forfeit to
The axe. It is not fitting for the Queen
To see the face of one who is to die.
The sentence may not be performed if once
The Queen has favoured her with her own presence;
The presence of the sovereign brings pardon!

ELIZABETH [*drying her tears after reading the letter*]: O what
is man, and what is earthly fortune!
How lowly she is sunk, this once proud queen,
Who wore the oldest crown in Christendom,
Who thought herself already queen thrice over!
How altered are her present words, from when
She bore the arms of England as her own,
And let the flatterers about her court
Proclaim her queen of both these island realms!
– My lords, forgive me, but it sears my heart,

Draws my soul's blood and grieves me bitterly,
That destiny can be so treacherous,
That I must see the fearful lot of all
Humanity pass me so closely by!

SHREWSBURY: Your majesty, if God has moved your
          heart,
Obey these promptings of His heavenly mercy.
With grievous suffering she has atoned
For grievous sin. Let this hard penance cease:
Give her your hand, to raise her up again,
And like a vision of angelic light
Scatter the darkness of her prison grave –

BURGHLEY: Be constant, mighty queen, and do not let
Generous feelings of humanity
Lead you astray. Do not deprive yourself
Of liberty to do what must be done.
You cannot pardon her, you may not spare her;
Do not incur just hatred and reproach
By cruelly feasting with triumphant scorn
Upon the sight of your defeated victim.

LEICESTER: My lords, let us not overstep our duty.
Our Queen is wise and will not need advice
From us to choose what it is right to do.
A meeting, face to face, of these two queens
Affects the course of justice not the least.
The law of England, not our sovereign's will,
Condemns the Stuart. It is worthy of
Elizabeth's own magnanimity
To follow where her noble heart commands,
While England's law maintains its rightful course.

ELIZABETH: Leave us, my lords. We shall yet find a way
To satisfy and fittingly unite
Both mercy's and necessity's demands.
Now – leave us. [*Exeunt* LORDS. *She calls* MORTIMER
          back from the door.] Mortimer – a word with you!

SCENE 5

ELIZABETH [*after a long, searching look at him*]:
Sir, you have courage and self-mastery
Not often to be seen in one so young.
One who can practise in such tender years
The taxing art of self-disguise is ripe
Before his time, and wins the test of manhood.
– Fate summons you to great and glorious deeds,
I make this prophecy, and I, to your
Good fortune, can myself help you fulfil it.
MORTIMER: My noble mistress, what is in my power
And what I am I place at your command.
ELIZABETH: Sir, you have met the enemies of England.
Irreconcilably they hate my name,
And they will never cease to plot my death.
God has protected me, until this day,
But never is my crown safe on my head
While *she* still lives to stir fanatic zeal
On her behalf, and nourish its ambition.
MORTIMER: If you but say the word, she lives no more.
ELIZABETH: Ah, sir! I thought that I had reached my goal,
And yet in truth I scarcely am set out.
I wanted to allow the law to act,
Yet keep the stain of blood from my own hand.
The sentence is pronounced. What have I gained?
It must be carried out, good Mortimer!
And I must give the order for her death.
I shall be hated for this deed; I must
Admit it, and I cannot save my name.
That is the worst of it!
MORTIMER: How can you fear
Appearances, if but your cause is just?
ELIZABETH: You do not know the world. Appearance, sir,
Is judged by every man, and truth by none.
None will believe that I am in the right,
So I must always fear that men will doubt
What was the part I bore in Mary's death.

Such deeds as this cast shadows either way,
Unless themselves they are concealed in darkness.
The fatal step's the one that we admit,
What is not given up is never lost.

MORTIMER [*inquiringly*]: The best thing then would be –
ELIZABETH [*quickly*]:   Indeed, sir, *that*
Would be the best. O, it is my good angel
That speaks in you! Say on, sir, and be finished.
You are in earnest, you can take my meaning,
You are not like your uncle in the least!

MORTIMER [*taken aback*]: Did you reveal your wishes to
       Sir Amyas?
ELIZABETH: I wish I had not done.
MORTIMER: You must excuse
His age; the caution which advancing years
Bring with them. Such a deed as this demands
The fiery gallantry of youth.
ELIZABETH [*quickly*]:   May I –
MORTIMER: I will lend you my hand, and you may save
Your name as best you can –
ELIZABETH: Yes, sir! If you
One morning came to wake me with the message
That Mary, Queen of Scots, our enemy,
Was dead that very night –
MORTIMER: Rely on me!
ELIZABETH: When will my head lie peaceful on its pillow?
MORTIMER: Before the next new moon your fears shall
       sleep.
ELIZABETH: And now farewell, sir! You will not regret
That I must lend my gratitude the veil
Of darkness – Silence is the god adored
By happy men; and those are intimate
And tender bonds are sealed in secrecy! [*Exit.*]

SCENE 6

MORTIMER [*alone*]: Hypocrite queen! Go on your evil way,
I will trick you as you would trick the world;

It is a good man's duty to betray you.
Do I look like a murderer? Could you
Detect the mark of evil in my face?
If you will only trust my arm and stay
Your own, and seek to make the world believe
This pious show of mercy, while in secret
You hope that I will do your murderous work,
The axe is stayed, and time is won to save her!
– You would advance me; show me from afar
A glimpse of great reward – And if the prize
Should even be yourself, your woman's favour,
Who are you, wretched creature that I see?
I am not lured by dreams of idle fame,
She only bears delight's true name –
About her in unending melody
Hover the gods of grace and youthful joys;
There at her breast is bliss that never cloys,
But you have only death to offer me!
The highest ornament that life can show,
When heart and heart only each other know,
In sweet delight all selfishness forbear,
The crown of womanhood, you cannot wear,
Never on man did you true love bestow!
– I must await my lord of Leicester, give
This letter to him. How I hate my task!
This courtier is a stranger to my heart,
I can deliver her, my spirit cries,
Danger and fame be mine, and mine the prize!

SCENE 7

[*As he turns to go, enter* PAULET.]

PAULET: What had the Queen to say to you?
MORTIMER: Why, nothing –
 Of any consequence.
PAULET [*looking fixedly and severely at him*]: Hear, Mortimer!
 It is a slippery slope that you have set
 Your foot upon. The royal favour is

A tempting prize, and youth is greedy for
Such honours. But do not be led astray!

MORTIMER: Was it not you yourself who brought me
here?

PAULET: I wish I had not. It was not at court
The honour of *our* house's name was won.
Nephew, stand firm! And do not buy too dear,
Do nothing that your conscience would forbid!

MORTIMER: What thoughts are these, what vain
anxieties?

PAULET: Whatever greatness you are promised by
The Queen – do not believe her flattery.
If you obey her wish she will deny you,
And wash her own good name clean in your blood,
Avenging what herself she bid you do.

MORTIMER: She bid me do?

PAULET: Away with your pretence!
I know the plan the Queen has put to you.
She hopes your youth, athirst for fame, will be
More pliable than my unyielding age.
Have you agreed to do it? Have you?

MORTIMER: Uncle!

PAULET: If you agreed, then hear my curse on you:
I cast you out –
    [*Enter* LEICESTER.]

LEICESTER: Good sir, allow me, pray,
A word with Mortimer. Her majesty
Is graciously disposed to him, and wishes
That he be given unrestricted freedom
To see the Lady Stuart – She relies
Upon his honesty –

PAULET: Relies on – good!

LEICESTER: What is it, sir?

PAULET: The Queen relies on him,
And I rely, my lord, upon myself,
And on my own two eyes – and they are open. [*Exit.*]

SCENE 8

LEICESTER: I am amazed! What could your uncle mean?

MORTIMER: I do not know – the unexpected trust
And confidence the Queen has placed in me –

LEICESTER [*with a searching look at him*]: Do you deserve so
great a confidence?

MORTIMER [*returning it*]: I ask the same of you, my lord of
Leicester.

LEICESTER: You had a message for my ear in secret.

MORTIMER: First let me be assured I dare to speak.

LEICESTER: Sir, how am I to be assured of you?
– You will not be affronted by my caution!
At court I see you show two faces: one
Is false, but which am I to think is true?

MORTIMER: I see the same in you, my lord of Leicester.

LEICESTER: Come then, who shall be first in confidence?

MORTIMER: Let it be he who has the less to lose.

LEICESTER: You then, sir.

MORTIMER: No sir, you! The evidence
Of such a great and mighty lord as you
For me could mean destruction; mine would prove
Nothing against your rank and influence.

LEICESTER: You are mistaken. In all else I have
Great power here, but in this tender spot,
Which now I must betray in trust to you,
I am the weakest man in all this court,
The meanest beggar's evidence would damn me.

MORTIMER: If then the mighty Leicester stoops so low
To favour me with this confession, I
May rather think more highly of myself
And set him a more generous example.

LEICESTER: Lead me in confidence, and I will follow.

MORTIMER [*quickly producing the letter*]: The Queen of
Scotland sends to you this letter.

LEICESTER [*startled, seizing it hurriedly*]: Speak softly, sir!
What do I see? It is
Her portrait! [*He kisses it and gazes at it with silent rapture.*]

MORTIMER [*watching him closely while he reads*]: Now, my
    lord, I will believe you!
LEICESTER [*after scanning through the letter*]: Sir Mortimer,
    you know what this contains?
MORTIMER: No, I know nothing.
LEICESTER: Did she not entrust
  You with –
MORTIMER: With nothing. You, she said, would tell
  Me what this riddle's meaning was, my lord.
  It is a riddle that the Earl of Leicester,
  Favourite of Elizabeth, sworn foe
  Of Mary, one of those who have condemned her,
  Should be the very man from whom the Queen
  Now hopes for rescue in her grief – and yet
  It must be so, for in your eyes I read
  Too clearly what your feelings are for her.
LEICESTER: But first you must explain to me how you
  Have come to take her part with such devotion,
  How she could put her trust in you.
MORTIMER: My lord,
  I can explain it in a few brief words.
  I have renounced my faith and taken that
  Of Rome, and I am allied with the Guises.
  A letter sent with me by the Archbishop
  Of Rheims was my credential to the Queen.
LEICESTER: Yes, I had heard that you had changed your faith,
  And that it was that made me trust in you.
  Give me your hand. Forgive my doubts, I beg.
  I cannot be too cautious in this place,
  For Walsingham and Burghley hate me so,
  I know that they have laid their snares for me.
  You might have been their creature and their lure
  To catch me in their net –
MORTIMER: What timid steps
  So great a lord must take at England's court!
  Your grace, I pity you.
LEICESTER: With joy I throw
  Myself upon the bosom of a friend,

Where I at last am free from this constraint.
You are surprised to see this sudden change
Of feelings in my breast to Mary, sir.
Truly I never hated her – but force
Of circumstance made me her enemy.
You know she was intended to be mine,
Long years ago, before she married Darnley,
While still she sat upon her throne in splendour.
But coldly I refused that happiness.
Now in her prison, at the gates of death,
I long for her, and at my own life's risk.

MORTIMER: What magnanimity is this!

LEICESTER: The shape
Of things has altered with the passing years.
I was ambitious, and it made me blind
To youth and beauty. Then I thought the hand
Of Mary was too mean for me, I hoped
That I might yet possess the queen of England.

MORTIMER: It is well known she favoured you above
All men –

LEICESTER: Sir, thus it seemed – and now, with ten
Lost years of tireless courtship and of base
Constraint behind me – O, my heart can breathe!
I must unbosom this long misery –
Men think that I am happy – if they knew
What chains these were that they so envy me –
For ten long bitter years, sir, I have bowed
Before the idol of her vanity,
Obeyed each fancy of her despot's mood
As if I were an Eastern slave, a toy
For each new petty selfish whim to play with,
One day caressed in tenderness and love,
The next repulsed with frigid haughtiness.
Watched like a captive by the Argus eyes
Of jealousy, interrogated like
A naughty boy, and scolded like a servant.
There is no word in all our tongue for this,
It is the pain of hell!

MORTIMER: I pity you.

LEICESTER: And cheated at the last! Another comes
   To rob me of the prize of patient courtship,
   A young and handsome bridegroom takes the rights
   That I have earned and owned these many years,
   And I must pack my bags and quit this stage
   Where I so long have played the leading part.
   I fear this new arrival comes to rob me
   Not of her hand alone, but of her favour.
   She is a woman; he is skilled in love.

MORTIMER: Catherine's son. It is the best of schools
   Where he has learnt the arts of flattery.

LEICESTER: Then every hope is gone – I try to grasp
   A single plank in this, the shipwreck of
   My happiness – and now my eye returns
   To those fair hopes it cherished long ago.
   Mary I saw in all her radiant grace
   Once more before me, youth and beauty came
   Restored once more into their lawful rights,
   Usurped by cold ambition, and I knew,
   When I compared, that I had lost a jewel.
   With horror now I see her plunged into
   The depths of misery – and through my fault.
   And then the hope awakes in me that I
   Might still contrive to save her and possess her.
   A faithful hand enables me to show
   Her that my heart has changed, that it is hers,
   And by this letter which you bring to me
   I am assured that she forgives me, and
   That if I rescue her she will be mine.

MORTIMER: You, my lord, rescue her? But you did nothing!
   You let her be condemned without resistance,
   Voted yourself that she be put to death!
   There had to be a miracle – the light
   Of truth must touch myself, her gaoler's nephew,
   And Heaven within the Vatican at Rome
   Prepare for her an unexpected saviour,
   Or she had never found this way to you!

LEICESTER: O sir, it cost me suffering enough!
At that same time they took her from the castle
Of Talbot; she was sent to Fotheringhay,
Under your uncle's ever-watchful guard.
All ways to her were barred, and I was forced
To carry on my persecutor's role.
But do not think that I had calmly let
Her go to execution! No, I hoped
And still I hope to save her from that end,
And at the last to find a way to rescue.

MORTIMER: That way is found. My noble lord of Leicester,
Your trust in me deserves a like response.
I will deliver her, for that I come,
The plan is made, and with your powerful
Support we are assured of our success.

LEICESTER: What, sir? You make me anxious. What is
this?

MORTIMER: I will break down the prison bars that hold
her,
I have my helpers, all has been prepared –

LEICESTER: You have accomplices? The worse for me!
What risks are these that you would have me run?
Your friends and helpers know my secret too?

MORTIMER: You need not fear. Our plan was made
without you,
And had been carried out without you; she
Alone would owe deliverance to you.

LEICESTER: Then you can swear to me with certainty
My name will not be mentioned in your schemes?

MORTIMER: You may be sure! Your grace, are you so
cautious,
When what we bring is help in your own cause?
You wish to save the lady and possess her,
You find such sudden, unexpected friends,
The means you seek are sent to you from Heaven,
And yet you show embarrassment, not joy!

LEICESTER: Force can do nothing. This adventure is
Too dangerous.

MORTIMER: So also is delay!

LEICESTER: I tell you, sir, it is too great a risk.

MORTIMER [*bitterly*]: O yes, too great for you who would
    possess her!
  We only seek to save her, and are not
  So chary –

LEICESTER: My young man, you are too rash
  In such a dangerous and thorny errand.

MORTIMER: You very cautious in the cause of honour.

LEICESTER: I see the nets and snares laid round about us.

MORTIMER: And I have courage to destroy them all.

LEICESTER: Your courage is foolhardiness and madness.

MORTIMER: Your caution is not bravery, my lord.

LEICESTER: Is it your wish to end like Babington?

MORTIMER: It is not yours to follow Norfolk's greatness.

LEICESTER: Did Norfolk win the bride that he desired?

MORTIMER: He proved that he was worthy of her hand.

LEICESTER: But if we fail, we shall destroy her too.

MORTIMER: Yet spare ourselves, and she will not be saved.

LEICESTER: You do not think, you do not listen, you
  Will wreck with your blind headlong violence
  All that has been so carefully prepared.

MORTIMER: So carefully prepared – by you, my lord?
  What is it you have done to rescue her?
  – And if I had been reprobate enough
  To murder her, as I was ordered by
  The Queen, and as she confidently waits
  For me to do – tell me what preparations
  You will have taken to preserve her life?

LEICESTER [*in astonishment*]: The Queen commanded you
    to murder her?

MORTIMER: In me she was mistaken, just as Mary
  In you.

LEICESTER: And you agreed to do it? Did you?

MORTIMER: So that she would not look for other hands,
  I offered mine.

LEICESTER: And it was well you did.
  This gives us breathing-space. She will rely

On you to do the deed for her, the sentence
Remains, but in suspension, time is won –
MORTIMER [*impatiently*]: No, time is lost!
LEICESTER: But if she counts on you,
She need no longer fear to show the world
She can be merciful – or seem to be.
Perhaps with cunning I can then persuade her
To see her adversary face to face,
And if she takes that step then she is bound.
Burghley is right. The sentence can no longer
Be carried out if she has seen her person.
– Yes, I will try it, seek by every means –
MORTIMER: And what will be accomplished? If her hopes
In me are disappointed, Mary still
Alive – is everything not just the same?
Never will she be free! The best that she
May hope for is imprisonment for life.
Only a deed of bravery can end it,
Why will you not begin, and do it now?
The power is in your hands; why, you could raise
A regiment from all the gentry in
Your countless castles, if you would but arm them!
Mary has many friends in secret still,
The families of Percy and of Howard,
Although their heads are taken from them, yet
Are rich in heroes, only waiting for
A mighty lord to set them an example!
Away with this disguise! Show your true face!
Defend your lady as a true knight should,
And fight the noble fight for her. You can
Be master of the Queen of England, if
You only will. Entice her to your castles,
Where she so often followed you; and there,
Speak as a man! Command her! Do not let
Her go, till Mary Stuart has her freedom!
LEICESTER: I am amazed, I tremble – Will you let
Yourself be swept away? Where are you? Do
You know how matters stand at England's court,

And how this woman's rule has cramped our spirits?
Look for the noble spirit that this land
Knew in the days of old – now all is subject,
The kingdom's keys are in a woman's hand,
Slack are the springs that drove our courage on.
Follow my lead, and take no heedless risk!
– Go, I hear someone coming.

MORTIMER: Mary hopes!
Shall I return to her with empty comfort?

LEICESTER: Bring her my oath of everlasting love!

MORTIMER: Bring that yourself! I promised I would be
Her saviour, not your messenger of love! [*Exit.*]

SCENE 9

[*Enter* ELIZABETH.]

ELIZABETH: Who was it went away? I heard your voices.

LEICESTER [*starting at her voice and turning quickly to face her*]:
        Sir Mortimer.

ELIZABETH: What is it? Why are you
So startled, sir?

LEICESTER [*recovering his self-possession*]: Elizabeth! – To
        see you!
Never were you so beautiful before,
And I am dazzled by your loveliness.
– Ah!

ELIZABETH: Why this sigh?

LEICESTER: Have I not then good cause
To sigh? For when I look upon your beauty
I feel again the nameless agony
Of loss that threatens me.

ELIZABETH: What will you lose?

LEICESTER: Your heart, and your dear person I am losing.
Soon you will know the passionate embrace
Of your new youthful bridegroom, and be happy,
And he will be sole master of your heart.
He is of royal blood, and I am not,
But I am willing to defy the world

That there is not one man upon this globe
Adores you more devotedly than I.
The Duke of Anjou has not even seen you,
Your glorious name is all he knows to love.
But I love *you*. If you were poor and lowly,
And I the greatest prince of all the earth,
I would abase myself to your estate,
And lay my diadem before your feet.

ELIZABETH: Pity me, Robert, do not scold me – I
May not consult my heart. Ah! it would choose
A different man. I envy other women,
Who may raise up the object of their love.
I do not have the happy privilege
Of giving him who is most dear to me
The crown! The Stuart could permit herself
To give her hand away as she desired,
She was allowed all she could wish for, she
Has drunk and drained the cup of earthly joys.

LEICESTER: But now she drinks the bitter cup of sorrow.

ELIZABETH: She took no notice of the world's opinion.
She went by easy paths, she never felt
The heavy yoke to which I bent my neck.
I too could just as well as she have claimed
The right to earthly joys and happiness,
But I preferred the duties of a king.
And yet she won the heart of every man
Because she only strove to be a woman,
And youth and age are rivals at her feet.
That is the way of men. All dissolute!
They all rush headlong to their dizzy pleasures,
And have no eyes for what they should revere.
Why, did not Shrewsbury himself grow young,
As he began to tell us of her charms!

LEICESTER: Forgive him. She was once his prisoner,
With skilful flattery she won his heart.

ELIZABETH: And is it true she is so beautiful?
So often I have heard her features praised,
And I would gladly know, should I believe it?

A portrait flatters, and descriptions lie,
I would trust nothing but my own two eyes.
– Why do you look so strangely?

LEICESTER: I compare
You in imagination with the Stuart.
–I do not hide that I would dearly love,
If it could be contrived in secrecy,
To see yourself and Mary side by side!
Then you would be assured of victory
At last! And I would let her feel the shame,
To see with her own eyes – for envy's eyes
Are sharp – herself convinced she falls as far
Behind you in nobility of feature
As she remains in every other grace.

ELIZABETH: She is the younger of us two.

LEICESTER: The younger!
It does not show. Of course, her suffering –
She may indeed have aged beyond her years.
And she would feel more bitterly disgraced
If she could see you as a bride! Each one
Of life's glad hopes lies far behind her now,
But you are going on to happiness,
To be the bride of France's royal son,
While she has always been so proud, proclaiming
That she was married to the King of France,
And still insists that France will send her aid!

ELIZABETH [casually]: They harass me to see her.

LEICESTER [eagerly]:   What she asks
As favour, grant it as a punishment!
You can submit her to the headsman's axe,
But it will pain her less than if she sees
Herself extinguished by your loveliness!
Do this, and you will murder her, as she
Would murder you. O, when she sees your beauty,
Guarded by purity and crowned with rays
Of heavenly glory by unblemished virtue,
When hers was thrown away in wantonness;
Exalted by your royal state, and now

Adorned with bridal tenderness – then will
Her hour have struck, and she will be destroyed.
– And when I cast my eye upon you now,
Never before, no, never were you armed
With such all-conquering beauty. When you came
Into this room, a radiant brightness spread
Its beams about me, and I was aglow.
What if you were to go, just as you are,
To her this hour? There could not be a better!

ELIZABETH: This hour? No, Leicester, no – not now, –
    I must
Consider carefully – ask Burghley –

LEICESTER [*interrupting vigorously*]: Burghley!
He only thinks of what will serve the state,
Your womanhood has other rights than those.
This tender issue must be judged by you,
Not by the statesman – yes, and statesmanship
Itself demands you see her, win good will
By such an act of generosity!
And after that you may be rid of her,
Your hated rival, by what means you will.

ELIZABETH: She is my cousin. It would not be proper
For me to see her want and shame. They say
She is not kept as would befit a queen,
And I would feel her wants as a reproach.

LEICESTER: You need not even enter at her door.
Hear my advice. It seems that fate would have
It as we wish. Today there is a hunt,
The way we follow passes Fotheringhay.
They may allow her out into the park,
You come that way by chance, as it must seem,
For nothing shall appear to be prepared –
And if you do not wish, you need not speak
To her at all –

ELIZABETH: If this is folly, Leicester,
Then let it be your folly, not my own.
Today I can deny no wish of yours,
For I today have injured you of all

My subjects most. [*Looking tenderly at him*]
– Let it be just a whim of yours. Affection
May show itself in granting a request
In generous grace, which to refuse were best.
　　[*As* LEICESTER *throws himself at her feet, the curtain
　　falls.*]

ACT III

A park
with trees, and a wide open view to the rear

SCENE I

　　[*Enter* MARY, *hurrying between the trees, with* KENNEDY
　　following slowly.]

KENNEDY: You run as fast as if your feet had wings,
　　I cannot keep this pace. Pray wait for me!
MARY: Liberty! O how I feel it so sweetly!
　　Let me be young, be young with me!
　　Step like a child so swiftly and fleetly
　　Over the green of the meadow and lea!
　　Am I escaped from the prison that bound me?
　　Am I no longer to stifle there?
　　O how I thirst for this freedom around me,
　　Let me drink deep of the heavenly air!
KENNEDY: O dearest lady! You are still in prison;
　　This is but small relief that you are granted.
　　Only the trees with their thick branches mask
　　The castle walls that hold us still confined.
MARY: O let me thank these green and friendly trees
　　That hide this loathsome prison from my sight.
　　When happiness my spirit frees,
　　Why wake me from this dream of sweet delight?
　　Only the vault of Heaven roofs this park,
　　My eyes, long used to prison dark,

Are free to look, and wander as they please.
There where the misty mountains rise
My kingdom lies,
Those clouds that southward swift advance
They seek the shores of France.
   Hurrying clouds like the ships of the sky!
   O could I sail with you as you fly!
   Greet me the land of my youth as you pass!
   I am a captive, I have no friend,
   There is no other whom I can send!
   Free in the heavens you go on your way,
   You are not under this queen's sway!

KENNEDY: You are beside yourself, my dearest lady,
  This freedom long denied awakes such fancies!

MARY: See over there, where the fisherman lands!
  His simple boat could be my salvation,
  Speed me away to a friendly nation.
  Wretched the life he earns on these strands,
  But I would load his nets with treasure,
  A draught he should draw that would burst their bands,
  Joy and good fortune beyond all measure,
  If he would take me to other lands!

KENNEDY: O these vain wishes! Look, do you not see
  The spies who follow every step we take?
  A cruel and fearful ban frightens away
  All creatures who might take some pity on us.

MARY: No, my dear Hannah. It is not for nothing,
  Believe me, that my prison door is opened.
  This lesser favour is the herald of
  A greater blessing. I am not mistaken.
  To love's own hand I owe my gratitude:
  I see in this Lord Leicester's mighty arm.
  Little by little I shall be accustomed
  To relaxation of my strict confinement,
  Until at last I see the face of him
  Who comes to free me from my bonds for ever.

KENNEDY: I cannot understand these contradictions!
  But yesterday they told you you must die,

And suddenly today they set you free.
O, I have heard it said that their chains too
Were loosed, who soon should know eternal freedom!
MARY: Hear the horn so merrily sounding,
    Echoing over spinney and mead!
    O to be on my horse, and bounding,
    Following where the huntsmen lead!
    Often I heard that voice on the mountains,
    Bitter and sweet to remember today:
    O how joyously we would gather,
    Gallop across the purple heather,
    While the noisy hounds would bay!

SCENE 2

    [*Enter* PAULET.]

PAULET: Well now, my lady, is it right at last?
  Have I this once deserved your thanks?
MARY: What, sir?
  Can it be you have gained this favour for me?
  Can it be you?
PAULET: Why not? I was at court,
  I gave your letter to her majesty –
MARY: You gave it to her, sir? In truth, you did?
  So I must think this freedom is the fruit
  Of my own letter?
PAULET [*meaningfully*]: Not the only one!
  Prepare yourself to hear a greater yet.
MARY: A greater, sir? What can you mean by this?
PAULET: You heard the hunting-horns –
MARY [*starting back as if guessing his meaning*]: You frighten
    me!
PAULET: The Queen is hunting in this district –
MARY: What?
PAULET: In a few minutes she will stand before you.
KENNEDY [*hurrying to* MARY, *who trembles, and appears to be
    about to faint*]: My, lady, what is this? You turn so
    pale!

PAULET: Is it not right? Did you not ask this favour?
  Now it is granted, sooner than you thought.
  You always had a lively tongue before,
  Now you will need your words, now is the time
  For talking!
MARY: O why could I not be prepared for this?
  I am not ready for it now, not now!
  What I requested as the greatest favour,
  It now seems frightful, terrible – come, Hannah!
  Take me into the house, and let me gather
  My wits –
PAULET: Stay here. You must attend the Queen.
  Yes, yes, I understand you are afraid,
  Now that you must appear before your judge.
MARY: No, not because of that! By Heaven, such thoughts
  Are far from me!

SCENE 3

  [*Enter* SHREWSBURY.]
MARY: – Ah, noble Shrewsbury!
  You are an angel sent to me from Heaven!
  I cannot see her. Save me, save me from
  The hateful sight of her –
SHREWSBURY: Come, come, your majesty, and gather up
  Your courage. Now it is the fateful moment.
MARY: How I have waited for it – and for years
  Prepared myself, rehearsed my every word,
  Implanted deep within my memory
  How I would seek to touch and move her heart!
  All gone, forgotten now so suddenly,
  Nothing remains alive in me this moment
  But burning consciousness of what I suffer.
  My heart is turned with hate against her, all
  My gentle thoughts are flown, and Gorgons shake
  Their heads of serpent locks on every side.
SHREWSBURY: You must command your wild rebellious
    blood,

Fight down the bitterness within your heart!
If hate meets hate, the fruit cannot be good.
However much your spirit may resist,
You must obey the law that rules this hour.
She is all-powerful: submit yourself!

MARY: To her? I cannot! Never!

SHREWSBURY: Yet you must!
Speak to her with respect and resignation,
Appeal to her humanity; do not
Insist upon your rights – not in this hour.

MARY: O what I have entreated is my ruin,
To curse me she has granted my entreaty!
Never should we have seen each other, never!
For nothing, nothing good can come of it!
Sooner may fire and water in true love
Be mingled, and the lamb embrace the tiger.
Too deep my wounds, too heavy are the blows
That she has dealt – we cannot live at peace!

SHREWSBURY: But see her first, and face to face!
I saw how deeply she was moved to read
Your letter, when the tears flowed down her cheeks.
No, she is not unfeeling, if you will
But trust her more – and for that very reason
I hurried on before, to warn you to
Be calm, and to prepare you for this meeting.

MARY [grasping his hand]: O Talbot! you have always been
        my friend,
Might I have stayed in your mild custody!
But I was harshly met, good Shrewsbury!

SHREWSBURY: Forget it all today, and only think
How to receive her in humility.

MARY: Is Burghley with her too, my evil angel?

SHREWSBURY: No one is with her but the Earl of Leicester.

MARY: Lord Leicester!

SHREWSBURY: Him you need not fear. It is
Not he desires your end. He has persuaded
The Queen to grant your wish and meet you here
Today.

MARY: O, but I knew –
SHREWSBURY: What do you say?
PAULET: Her majesty the Queen!
  [*All draw back except* MARY, *who remains leaning on*
  KENNEDY.]

SCENE 4

  [*Enter* ELIZABETH *and* LEICESTER, *with attendants.*]
ELIZABETH [*to* LEICESTER]: What is this place?
LEICESTER: It is called Fotheringhay.
ELIZABETH [*to* SHREWSBURY]: The hunting-party shall
      return to London;
  There are such crowds of people by the way,
  We'll rest awhile in this quiet pleasant park.
    [SHREWSBURY *dismisses the attendants.* ELIZABETH *fixes
    her gaze on* MARY, *and goes on speaking to* PAULET.]
  They love me, these good people, to excess.
  They pay me such immoderate reverence,
  Idolatrous, as if I were a god.
MARY [*has been leaning, as if in a faint, upon her nurse; she now
    stands on her own feet, and her eyes meet* ELIZABETH's
    *fixed stare. She shudders, and collapses onto her nurse's
    breast once more*]: O heavens, these looks – she surely
      has no heart!
ELIZABETH: Who is the lady?
  [*General silence*]
LEICESTER: Your majesty, you are at Fotheringhay.
ELIZABETH [*feigning surprise, with a dark look at* LEICESTER]:
      Who has done this to me? Explain it, Leicester!
LEICESTER: It happened so, your majesty – and now
  That Heaven has brought you to this place, let pity
  And magnanimity command the day.
SHREWSBURY: Let us persuade your gracious majesty
  To look upon this wretched lady here,
  Who faints before your gaze.
    [MARY *gathers her strength and approaches* ELIZABETH, *but
    stops halfway, trembling; her gestures express a violent conflict
    of emotions.*]

ELIZABETH: What's this, my lords?
 Who was it then, who told me I should find
 Her humble? Look at her! Misfortune has
 Not bowed this stubborn pride the least.
MARY: So be it!
 To this as well I must submit myself.
 Farewell, my noble spirit's useless pride.
 I will forget my queenly rank, and all
 My sufferings, and kneel before this woman,
 Who cast me down into my present shame.
     [*Turning to* ELIZABETH]
 It seems that Heaven is on your side, my sister!
 Your head is crowned with victory and fortune,
 I praise the God who has exalted you.
     [*Falling on her knees before her*]
 But now you too be generous, my sister!
 You will not let me kneel in shame before you.
 Give me your hand, give me your royal right hand,
 To raise me from the depths of wretchedness.
ELIZABETH [*drawing back*]: My lady Mary, you are in your
         place!
 And I give thanks to God above, that in
 His goodness He did not desire that I
 Should kneel to you, as you do now to me.
MARY [*with increasing emotion*]: Remember all our human
         fortunes change!
 And there are gods who take revenge on pride!
 Honour and fear them; they are dreadful; they
 Have cast me down to lie before your feet.
 And there are others here; on their account
 Give me the dignity I share with you,
 Do not dishonour and profane the blood
 Of Tudor, which is mine as well as yours –
 O God in Heaven! how can you stand so hard
 And merciless – you're like a rock, and I
 A stranded wretch who's struggling to be saved!
 My life, my fate, and all I have depend
 Upon the power of my words, my tears;

Set free my heart, and let me speak to yours!
But when you look at me so icily,
My heart shuts tight in fear and trembling, tears
Dry up their stream, and cold black horror binds
My words of pleading fast within my breast.

ELIZABETH [*coldly and severely*]: Come, Lady Stuart, what
    have you to say?
You asked to speak with me. I put aside
The queen in me, who has been so insulted,
To do the gentle duty of a sister,
And let you see me and be comforted.
These impulses of generosity
Will bring just censure on me; I should not
Have stooped so far – as you well know,
You have made plots and schemes to have me murdered.

MARY: O, how shall I begin, how can I choose
My words so skilfully that they will touch
Your heart and yet not injure it as well?
O God, give strength to my poor speech, but take
Away its sting, so that it cannot hurt!
Indeed, I cannot speak in my own cause
Without accusing you, and that I do not wish.
– You have behaved unjustly to me, sister,
For I, like you yourself, am called a queen,
And you have held me like a common captive.
I came to England as a suppliant,
And you, in scorn both of the sacred laws
Of hospitality and of the rights of nations,
Imprisoned me within these walls; my friends
And servants have been cruelly taken from me;
I suffer the indignities of want,
Am made to answer to a trumped-up court –
No more of this. Let all this be forgotten
For ever, all the pain that I have suffered.
See! I will call it all the hand of fate.
Not yours the guilt, but neither is it mine.
An evil spirit rose up from the pit,
To kindle fires of hatred in our hearts,

That even in our youth drove us apart.
They grew with us, and evil men were there
To fan the flames, and madmen armed themselves
With swords, in zeal for an imagined cause –
This is the fate and curse that kings must bear,
That their estrangement tears the world with hate
And looses all imaginable strife.
No stranger's slander comes between us now –
   [*approaching* ELIZABETH, *flatteringly*]
We two are now alone, and face to face,
Now, sister, speak! Tell me what I have done,
And I will make you recompense in full.
O, if you only had but heard me then,
When I besought so urgently of you!
It never would have come to this: we should
Not be in this unhappy place today,
We should not meet at this unhappy meeting.
ELIZABETH: My favourable star protected me
  From nourishing a serpent in my bosom.
  Do not accuse the hand of fate, but your
  Black heart, the wild ambition of your house.
  There never had been enmity between us;
  But then your uncle, that proud priest, drunk with
  His dreams of power, stretching greedy hands
  To grasp all Europe's crowns – he challenged me,
  Persuaded you to take my coat-of-arms,
  My royal titles, claim them as your own,
  To ride in battle to the death against me.
  Whom did he not stir up to fight with me?
  The tongues of priests, the swords of peoples, all
  The fearful armoury of pious madness –
  Here in the peaceful heart of my own kingdom
  He kindled revolution's fiery flames;
  But God is on my side, and that proud priest
  Will not prevail; the blow that threatened me
  Is turned aside, yours is the head that falls!
MARY: God holds me in His hand, and you will not
  So cruelly overstep your rightful powers.

ELIZABETH: Who will prevent me? It was your own uncle
 Who showed the kings of all the world how best
 To make their peace with enemies – let me
 Learn in the school of Saint Bartholomew!
 Kinship, the laws of nations, what are these?
 The Church can sever any bond of duty,
 Make treason sacrosanct, and regicide;
 I only practise what your priests have taught.
 Tell me what pledge I should retain for you,
 If I in generosity should free you?
 What padlock could I set on your good faith,
 That would not open to Saint Peter's keys?
 Force is my one and only guarantee,
 For there can be no treaty with a viper.

MARY: Why must you always nurse these black suspicions?
 Never could you see me but as a stranger,
 And as your enemy. But if you had
 Declared me heir to you, as is my right,
 Then gratitude and love had made of me
 Your truest friend and cousin.

ELIZABETH: Lady Stuart,
 Elsewhere you have your friends, your house is Rome,
 The monk your brother – I, declare you heir
 To me! This snare, this noose, this treachery!
 That in my lifetime you already have
 Seduced my people, tangled in your net
 Of wantonness the noblest youths within
 This kingdom, like a cunning Armida –
 That all men's eyes were turned towards this sun
 New rising, and that I must –

MARY: Reign in peace!
 I do renounce all claim to England's throne.
 Alas, the pinions of my soul are lamed,
 Greatness no more can tempt me – you have won,
 And I am nothing more than Mary's shadow.
 The shame of long imprisonment has broken
 My noble spirit – you have done your worst
 To me, destroyed me in the bloom of life!

– Now make an end of this, my sister. Speak
The word which you have come to say to me,
For I cannot, will not believe you came
To gloat in cruelty upon your victim.
Speak it, that word! Say to me, 'You are free,
Mary! You have endured and known my power,
Now learn to honour my nobility!'
Say it, and I will take my life, my freedom
Gratefully as a present from your hand.
– One word, and none of this has been. I wait
To hear it. Do not keep it back too long!
But if you will not speak it, woe to you!
For if you do not leave me with your blessing,
A heavenly messenger – o sister, then
I would not for the riches of this island,
No, not for all the lands the sea surrounds,
Stand before you as you appear to me!

ELIZABETH: Do you at last admit yourself defeated?
Are your plots done with? Is no murderer
Still on his way? Will no adventurer
Dare a last sorry enterprise for you?
– Yes, it is done with, Lady Mary. You
Will lure no others from me. Other cares
Busy the world. There is no man desires
To be your fourth – unlucky consort, for
You kill your suitors as you kill your husbands!

MARY [*starting up*]: Sister! Sister! O God, grant me
    restraint!

ELIZABETH [*with a long, proud, contemptuous stare at her*]:
So these, my lord of Leicester, are the charms
Which no man can behold unscathed, no woman
May ever dare to set herself beside!
Indeed! I think this fame is cheaply bought.
To rank as most *uncommon* beauty costs
Nothing but to be *common* to all men!

MARY: This is too much!

ELIZABETH [*laughing scornfully*]: Now we shall see your
    true

Complexion, what we saw till now was sham.

MARY [*with passionate anger, but maintaining her dignity*]:
My faults were human faults, the faults of youth.
Power led me astray, I have not sought
To hide it, I have scorned all secrecy
And show of virtue with a royal frankness.
The world knows all the worst of me and I
Can say that I am better than my name.
But woe to you, that day when all your deeds
Are stripped of their disguise, the virtuous cloak
That you have cast about your secret lusts!
It was not virtue that your mother left
To you: all know the honour for whose sake
Anne Boleyn met her death upon the block!

SHREWSBURY: O God in Heaven! Must it come to this?
Is this humility, is this restraint,
My lady Mary?

MARY: This, restraint! I have
Endured as much as any may endure.
And now farewell, meek lamb-like resignation,
Fly to the heavens, patient suffering,
Break from your bonds, come out from your dark lair,
Bitter resentment, all too long confined, –
And you who gave the angry basilisk
The look that kills, lay now upon my tongue
The poisoned dart! –

SHREWSBURY: She is beside herself!
She is provoked, she rages, o forgive her!

[ELIZABETH, *speechless with rage, glares furiously at* MARY.]

LEICESTER [*in great agitation, trying to lead* ELIZABETH
away]: O do not listen to this fury! Go,
Go, leave this place! Would you had never come!

MARY: A bastard sits on England's throne, and dupes
This noble race with cunning and deceit.
If right was might, then you would crawl before
My feet this moment, for I am your Queen.

[*Exit* ELIZABETH *in haste, the* LORDS *following her in
great confusion.*]

SCENE 5

HANNAH: What have you done? She goes away enraged!
  It is the end, and all our hopes are vanished.
MARY: She goes, enraged, and death is in her heart!
    [*Throwing her arms around* KENNEDY]
  O Hannah, this is joy! At last, at last,
  After the years of misery and shame,
  A single moment of revenge and triumph!
  A mountain's weight is lifted from my heart,
  I thrust the knife into my enemy!
KENNEDY: Alas, in madness you have wounded her
  Beyond all hope of reconciliation!
  She wields the thunderbolt, for she is queen,
  Before her paramour you have disgraced her!
MARY: In Leicester's sight I have degraded her,
  He saw my victory, he was my witness!
  And as I brought her crashing to her fall
  He stood there, and his presence gave me strength!

SCENE 6

    [*Enter* MORTIMER.]
KENNEDY: O sir! How this turned out –
MORTIMER: I heard it all.
    [*He motions to the nurse to withdraw, and approaches*
      MARY, *glowing with violent passion.*]
  The victory is yours! You laid her low,
  You were the queen, and she the criminal.
  I am enraptured at your courage, I
  Adore you. Like a great and wondrous goddess
  You seem to stand before me in this moment.
MARY: You spoke to Leicester, took my letter to him,
  Gave him my present – tell me everything!
MORTIMER [*gazing ardently at her*]: O, how this noble, regal
      anger shone
  About you, and your beauty was transfigured!
  You are the loveliest woman on this earth!

MARY: I beg you, tell me, sir, in my impatience,
    What has my lord to say? What can I hope?

MORTIMER: From whom? From him? That wretch, that
      coward? No!
  Hope not in him, despise him and forget him!

MARY: What do you say?

MORTIMER: He, save you and possess you?
  He, you? But let him so presume, and I
  Will challenge him, and fight him to the last!

MARY: You did not give my letter to him, then?
  – It is the end!

MORTIMER: The coward loves his life;
  He who would rescue you and call you his,
  He must be willing to embrace his death.

MARY: He will do nothing for me?

MORTIMER: What of him?
  No more. What can *he* do? We do not need him,
  I will save you, yes, I alone!

MARY: What can you do?

MORTIMER: Do not deceive yourself,
  And think that all is still as yesterday!
  For as I saw the Queen depart from here,
  And as I heard your words, so all is lost,
  All paths to grace and clemency are barred.
  Now we must act, and boldness will decide;
  Let all be staked, for all is to be won,
  You shall be free before the night is done.

MARY: What do you say? Tonight? How can it be?

MORTIMER: Hear what has been decided. In a chapel
  In secret I assembled all my friends.
  A priest was there to hear us make confession,
  And grant us absolution for the sins
  We have committed, absolution too
  For every sin that we may yet commit.
  On this we took the holy sacrament,
  And we are ready now for our last journey.

MARY: What can this fearful preparation mean?

MORTIMER: This very night we shall invade the castle,

I have the keys. The sentries will be killed,
We shall abduct you from your prison cell
By force, and so that not a living soul
Be left to tell that we have taken you,
Each single one must perish by our hand.

MARY: And Drury, Paulet, what of them, my gaolers?
O, they will rather shed their life's last blood –

MORTIMER: My knife shall strike them down the first of
all!

MARY: What's that? Your uncle, sir, your second father?

MORTIMER: By my hand he shall die. Yes, I will kill him.

MARY: O bloody crime!

MORTIMER: What crimes we may commit
Already are absolved. I can commit
The worst; yes, and I will!

MARY: O fearful, fearful!

MORTIMER: And if I must strike down the Queen herself –
Upon the Host I swore that I would do it.

MARY: No, Mortimer! Before I let this blood –

MORTIMER: And what is life to me compared with you,
And with my love! Let all the universe
Dissolve, and let a second deluge rise
And swallow all that breathes beneath its waves!
I care for nothing more! Before I yield
My love, let earth's foundation be repealed!

MARY [drawing back]: God, what is this? These words, sir –
and these looks!
They terrify me, they repel me.

MORTIMER: What is life
But one brief moment, death another like it?
Let me be dragged to Tyburn, let them tear
Me limb from limb with tongs of red-hot steel – [Rushing
towards her with outstretched arms]
When I embrace you, o my love, I feel –

MARY [drawing back]: What is this madness, sir?

MORTIMER: Upon this breast,
Upon these lips that breathe of love –

MARY: In God's name, leave me, sir! Let me go in!

MORTIMER: A madman he who would not hold his fortune
    Close to his heart and never let it go,
    When God had given it to him to know!
    Let thousands die, but I have sworn your rescue,
    You shall be rescued, and by me, but then,
    True as God lives, you shall be mine, I vow!

MARY: O will no god, no angel save me now?
    Merciless fate! Relentlessly you cast me
    Upon new horrors when the old have passed me!
    Was I but born to rouse these raging fires?
    For my destruction love with hate conspires.

MORTIMER: Yes, fierce as all their hatred is, my love,
    They would behead you, cut this lovely throat,
    So dazzling white, with their accursed axe.
    Dedicate to the living god of joy
    What soon must be a sacrifice to hatred!
    Bestow this beauty, now no longer yours,
    In blessed happiness upon your lover!
    These beauteous locks, these silken tresses fair,
    Are doomed to fall to darkness and to death;
    O let them bind your slave till his last breath!

MARY: What are these ravings, sir, that I must hear?
    You should respect my grief, my suffering,
    Even if you do not respect my crown.

MORTIMER: The crown has fallen from your head, my
        queen,
    Nothing remains of earthly majesty.
    Try, let your royal command resound, and see,
    Will any friend or saviour intervene?
    You have no more but what is in your face,
    Beauty that moves us with a godlike grace,
    Urging me on to dare and venture all,
    Even though at the last my head must fall!

MARY: O, who will save me from this raging flood?

MORTIMER: Shall the reward of danger be so small?
    Why should a brave man shed his precious blood?
    Is not this earthly life our highest good?
    A madman, who would quit it all for nothing!

First let me lay my head upon this breast – [*He embraces her violently.*]

MARY: O must I call for help against the man
Who came to save me –

MORTIMER: You are not unfeeling,
It is not coldness men condemn in you.
Love holds your heart beneath his ardent sway;
You gave the singer Rizzio your favours,
And then let Bothwell carry you away.

MARY: You dare!

MORTIMER: He was the tyrant of your heart;
When you loved him you trembled in his presence.
If only fear can win you to my part,
Then, by the Prince of Hell! –

MARY: Madman, let be!

MORTIMER: I swear that you shall tremble before me!
[*Enter* KENNEDY, *in haste.*]

KENNEDY: They will be here! The park is full of men,
Of soldiers, everywhere!

MORTIMER [*starting, and seizing his sword*]: I will protect you!

MARY: O Hannah, from this man deliver me!
Where shall I fly from this unhappy state?
Which of the saints will hear my helpless plea?
Here violence threatens, there my murderers wait. [*She hurries away towards the castle:* KENNEDY *follows.*]

SCENE 7

[PAULET *and* DRURY *come rushing furiously in. Attendants run across the stage.*]

PAULET: Close up the gates, and raise the drawbridges!

MORTIMER: What is it, uncle?

PAULET: Where's the murderess?
Down with her to the deepest of the dungeons!

MORTIMER: What is it? What has happened? Speak!

PAULET: The Queen!
Accursed hands! Audacity of hell!

MORTIMER: The Queen? What queen?

PAULET: Of England! She is dead!
  She has been murdered on the road to London!
    [*Exit, hurrying into the castle.*]

SCENE 8

MORTIMER [*alone*]: What, am I mad? Did someone not
      this minute
  Come running by and cry the Queen was dead?
  No, no, it was a dream. A fit of fever
  Brings thoughts of terrors that oppress my mind
  Before my eyes as clear as they were real.
  Who is it comes? O'Kelly! In such fright?
    [*Enter* O'KELLY, *rushing in.*]
O'KELLY: Flee, Mortimer, flee! Everything is lost!
MORTIMER: Lost? What?
O'KELLY: Stop not to ask, but only think
  Of speedy flight.
MORTIMER: What is it?
O'KELLY: Sauvage struck
  The blow, the madman!
MORTIMER: What, then it is true?
O'KELLY: True, true! Flee, save yourself!
MORTIMER: Then she is murdered,
  And Mary will ascend the throne of England!
O'KELLY: Murdered? Who says it?
MORTIMER: You yourself!
O'KELLY: She lives!
  And you, and I, each one of us is dead!
MORTIMER: She lives!
O'KELLY: He missed his mark, and struck her cloak,
  And Shrewsbury disarmed the murderer.
MORTIMER: She lives!
O'KELLY: Lives to destroy us, every one.
  Come, or the park will be surrounded!
MORTIMER: Who
  Did this insanity?
O'KELLY: The Barnabite

From Toulon, whom you saw there in the chapel
Sit brooding while we heard the monk pronounce
The Pope's anathema upon the Queen.
He only sought the nearest, quickest way,
Wanted to free the Church of God with one
Swift stroke, and win himself a martyr's crown.
Only the priest he told what he would do,
And struck the blow here on the road to London.

MORTIMER [*after a long silent pause*]: It is a cruel, relentless
    fate pursues you,
Unhappy lady! Yes, now you must die,
It was your angel brought you to your fall.

O'KELLY: Tell me which way you think to flee. I'll go
To hide myself amid the northern forests.

MORTIMER: Go, then, and God preserve you in your flight!
I'll stay. My queen once more I'll try to save,
And if I fail, seek rest upon her grave.

    [*Exeunt to opposite sides.*]

ACT IV

Antechamber

SCENE I

    [*Enter* AUBESPINE, KENT *and* LEICESTER.]

AUBESPINE: How is it with her majesty? My lords,
You see that I am still distraught with terror.
How did it happen? How could this occur
Amongst her loyal people?

LEICESTER: It was not
One of her people; he who struck the blow
Was subject to your king, a Frenchman, sir.

AUBESPINE: He must have been a man insane.

KENT: A Papist,
Count Aubespine!

SCENE 2

[*Enter* BURGHLEY, *talking to* DAVISON.]

BURGHLEY: The warrant for her death
  Must be drawn up immediately, and
  The seal set on it – When you have it ready,
  Present it to the Queen for signature.
  Go, Davison. We have no time to lose.

DAVISON: It shall be done. [*Exit.*]

AUBESPINE [*going to meet* BURGHLEY]: My lord, my loyal
          heart
  Shares in the just rejoicing of this island.
  Praise be to God, who turned away the blow
  That would have murdered England's sovereign!

BURGHLEY: Praise be to Him, who brought the wicked
          schemes
  Of England's enemies to nought!

AUBESPINE: May he be damned,
  The doer of this most accursed deed!

BURGHLEY: The doer, and the shameful author too.

AUBESPINE [*to* KENT]: If it will please your grace, my
          lord of Kent,
  Now to conduct me to her majesty,
  Then I may humbly lay before her feet
  Congratulations from the King my master.

BURGHLEY: You need not take the trouble, sir.

AUBESPINE [*pompously*]:   I know,
  Lord Burghley, what my duty is.

BURGHLEY: It is
  To quit our shores as quickly as you may.

AUBESPINE [*drawing back in astonishment*]: Ha! what is this?

BURGHLEY: You still enjoy today
  Your privilege; tomorrow you will not.

AUBESPINE: And may I know what is my crime?

BURGHLEY: Once it
  Is named, it can no longer be forgiven.

AUBESPINE: My lord, the rights of an ambassador –

BURGHLEY: Will not protect – a traitor.

LEICESTER *and* KENT: What is this?

AUBESPINE: My lord, think what you say –

BURGHLEY: A passport in
  Your hand was found upon the murderer.

KENT: Can this be true?

AUBESPINE: I write so many passports,
  I cannot read the thoughts of every man.

BURGHLEY: The murderer made confession in your house.

AUBESPINE: My house is open.

BURGHLEY: To our enemies.

AUBESPINE: I shall demand inquiry!

BURGHLEY: Fear it rather!

AUBESPINE: In me you do offence to France's king.
  He will tear up the treaty we have signed.

BURGHLEY: The Queen has torn your treaty up already,
  England and France will not be married now.
  My lord of Kent! I charge you to conduct
  Count Aubespine in safety to the coast.
  The people in their anger have attacked
  His embassy, and found an arsenal
  Of weapons; they will tear him limb from limb
  If they but see him; hide him well until
  Their rage is spent – you answer for his life!

AUBESPINE: Yes, I will go, and leave this land, whose
      queen
  Tramples the rights of nations underfoot,
  And takes a treaty for a toy – my king
  Will demand vengeance!

BURGHLEY: Let him come and take it!

  [*Exeunt* KENT *and* AUBESPINE.]

SCENE 3

LEICESTER: So you yourself have broken this same treaty
  That you alone so zealously cemented.
  You have done little to earn England's thanks,
  My lord, you could have spared yourself this trouble.

BURGHLEY: My ends were good. God wished it otherwise.

Many a worse thing other men have done.

LEICESTER: Burghley, we know this ominous demeanour,
When you are smelling out some crime of state.
– These times, my lord, are after your own heart.
A monstrous wickedness has been committed,
Its authors hidden still in secrecy.
Now a committee of investigation
Will sit; men's words, their looks will all be weighed,
Even their thoughts arraigned before the court.
Then it is Cecil, Atlas of the state,
Who bears all England on his mighty shoulders.

BURGHLEY: My lord, I must acknowledge you my master.
Your eloquence has won a victory
Which mine could never hope to have achieved.

LEICESTER: What do you mean, my lord?

BURGHLEY: Was it not you,
Behind my back, persuaded, lured the Queen
To go to Fotheringhay?

LEICESTER: Behind your back!
When did I fear to act before your face?

BURGHLEY: And it was *you* took *her* to Fotheringhay?
No, sir, you did not take the Queen with you,
No, sir, it was the Queen who was so gracious,
And *she* took *you* where *you* desired to go.

LEICESTER: What do you mean, my lord?

BURGHLEY: The noble part
In which you let her majesty appear!
The glorious triumph you prepared for her,
Who trusted your good faith – O gracious queen!
With shameless impudence how you were mocked,
Subjected to this merciless contempt!
– So this is that humanity and pity
Which suddenly affected you in Council?
And so this Stuart is an enemy
So paltry and contemptible that we
Should not demean ourselves to shed her blood?
– A cunning plan! Sharp as a needle! But
Unhappily so sharp it broke its point!

LEICESTER: You shall support these base and wicked
    charges
  With evidence before the Queen herself!
BURGHLEY: I shall be there! And see to it, my lord,
  Your eloquence does not abandon you. [*Exit.*]

SCENE 4

LEICESTER [*alone*]: I am betrayed, my secret is no more,
  How did this sorry villain come upon it?
  Alas for me, if he has proof! If once
  The Queen discovers what has passed between
  Myself and Mary – God! how guilty then
  I shall appear to her, how treacherous
  And cunning my advice, my luckless thought
  To lead her majesty to Fotheringhay!
  By me she will have been so cruelly mocked,
  Betrayed to her detested enemy!
  Never will she forgive it, never more!
  Now everything will seem a wicked plot,
  The bitter words that she was forced to hear,
  The scorn and triumph of her enemy,
  Yes, even that last fearful trick of fate,
  The dagger the assassin raised against her –
  I shall have pressed the weapon in his hand!
  I see no hope for me – Ha! Who comes there?
    [*Enter* MORTIMER *in great agitation, looking anxiously about
    him.*]
MORTIMER: My lord of Leicester! Are we two alone?
LEICESTER: Unhappy wretch, what brings you here? Away!
MORTIMER: They are upon our track, and yours as well,
  Beware!
LEICESTER: Begone, begone!
MORTIMER: They have found out
  There was a secret meeting in the house
  Of Aubespine –
LEICESTER: What's that to me?

MORTIMER: That the assassin
   Was there —
LEICESTER: But that is your affair! What means
   This insolence? How dare you seek to make
   Me party to your bloody schemes of treason?
   You may defend your villainies yourself!
MORTIMER: But you must hear me, sir.
LEICESTER [*furiously*]:   Go, and to hell!
   Why do you dog my footsteps like a devil?
   Away, away, I say! I do not know you,
   I keep no company with murderers.
MORTIMER: You will not hear me. I have come to warn
      you,
   Your steps have been betrayed as well —
LEICESTER: What's that?
MORTIMER: The Treasurer went too to Fotheringhay,
   The moment this ill-fated deed was done.
   He made a thorough search of Mary's rooms,
   And found there —
LEICESTER: What?
MORTIMER: A letter she was writing
   To you —
LEICESTER: O ill-starred queen!
MORTIMER: Demanding that
   You keep your word, promising you her hand,
   And making mention of the portrait which
   You sent her —
LEICESTER: Death and all the pains of hell!
MORTIMER: Lord Burghley has the letter.
LEICESTER: I am lost!
   [*During the following speech, he paces up and down despairingly*.]
MORTIMER: Come, take your chance! Strike the first blow
      yourself.
   Save yourself, save her too — You can invent
   Excuses, swear an oath, at least avert
   The worst! I can do nothing more myself.
   My friends and comrades are dispersed, our whole
   Alliance shattered. I shall make my way

To Scotland, there to win new friends for her.
Now you must try what your prestige, what your
Effrontery can do.

LEICESTER [*standing still, suddenly calm*]: That I will try.
   [*He goes to the door, opens it and calls out.*]
Here, guards!
   [*Enter an* OFFICER *with armed guards.*]
                    This man is guilty of high treason.
Seize him and keep him under close arrest!
A vile conspiracy has been revealed,
I'll go myself to tell the Queen this news. [*Exit.*]

MORTIMER [*after standing still for a moment in amazement,
      calmly and with a contemptuous glance at* LEICESTER *as
      he goes*]: This was a shameful trick – but I deserve it!
In this vile coward who bade me confide?
My fall has opened him the way to safety,
Over my neck as on a bridge he'll ride.
Go, then! My lips shall speak no treachery,
I will not drag you down in my disgrace;
Even in death you shall not share with me,
Life is the only good to one so base. [*To the* OFFICER,
      who advances to arrest him]
What would you then, hired slave of tyranny?
You I despise, for I am free! [*Drawing a dagger*]

OFFICER: He has a weapon. Take the dagger from him!
   [*They press in upon him; he defends himself.*]

MORTIMER: And free in this last moment shall my heart
Be opened, and my tongue be loosed to speak!
Ruin and curses fall on you, who have
Betrayed your God and your undoubted queen!
Who have deserted Mary here on earth
As faithlessly as Her who rules in Heaven,
And sold your service to this bastard queen –

OFFICER: Do you not hear his blasphemies? Come, seize
      him!

MORTIMER: Beloved! Though I could not set you free,
Yet I will show you what a man can do.
O holy Mary, pray for me,

Take me to Heaven that I may dwell with you! [*He stabs
himself with the dagger, and falls into the soldiers' arms.*]

The Queen's Room

SCENE 5

[ELIZABETH, *holding a letter;* BURGHLEY]

ELIZABETH: To take me there to her! To play such tricks
With me! The traitor! To display me to
His mistress there in triumph! Never was
A woman so betrayed, good Burghley, never!

BURGHLEY: I cannot grasp it yet, how he succeeded,
What power could aid him, or what magic arts,
So that my Queen in all her wisdom was
So overwhelmed!

ELIZABETH: O I shall die of shame!
O how he must have gloated at my weakness!
I thought to humble her, and I myself
Had to endure her gloating mockery!

BURGHLEY: Now you must see how truly I advised you.

ELIZABETH: O I am punished, I am sorely punished,
For not attending to your wise advice!
And was *he* not to be believed? Should I
Have feared a snare in oaths of truest love?
Whom could I trust, if he was faithless to me?
He whom I made the greatest of the great,
Who always stood the closest to my heart,
Whom I permitted to conduct himself
As master at this court, yes, as a king!

BURGHLEY: And all the while he was betraying you
To her, to that perfidious Queen of Scots!

ELIZABETH: O let her pay me for it with her blood!
Speak, is the warrant for her death prepared?

BURGHLEY: Ready, as you commanded.

ELIZABETH: She shall die!
And he shall see her fall, then fall himself.
I cast him from my heart in banishment,

My love is gone, I only long for vengeance;
He stood so high, now let him fall so low,
And show men how I can be unrelenting,
Just as he showed them how I could be weak.
Let him be taken to the Tower; I shall
Name peers to be his judges, let him know
The full severity of England's law.

BURGHLEY: He'll force his way to you, and make excuses –

ELIZABETH: And what excuses can there be? Does not
The letter speak against him? O, his guilt
Is clear as day!

BURGHLEY: You are so mild and gracious,
The sight of him, his presence, all his power –

ELIZABETH: I will not see him. Never, never more!
Have you not given orders that he be
Refused admittance if he comes?

BURGHLEY: I have!

[*Enter a* PAGE.]

PAGE: My lord of Leicester!

ELIZABETH: Vile impertinence!
I will not see him. Tell him that I will
Not see him.

PAGE: That I do not dare to tell
My lord, and he would not believe me.

ELIZABETH: So I have set him up, that my own servants
Fear his displeasure more than they fear mine!

BURGHLEY [*to the* PAGE]: The Queen forbids him to
approach her presence.

[*Exit* PAGE, *hesitantly.*]

ELIZABETH [*after a pause*]: And yet, if it were possible, if he
Could make excuse! Tell me, could it not be
Some snare that Mary had prepared for me,
To separate me from my truest friend?
O she is skilled in every villainy –
That letter! – if she wrote it to implant
A poisonous suspicion in my heart,
To ruin him she hates –

BURGHLEY: My queen, consider –

SCENE 6

[LEICESTER *tears open the door by force and enters in a commanding manner*.]

LEICESTER: Let me now see whose insolence this is,
　To bar me from the presence of my Queen.

ELIZABETH: O this audacity!

LEICESTER:　　　　　　　　To bid me go!
　If she will not refuse to see a Burghley,
　She'll not refuse *me*!

BURGHLEY:　　　　　You are very bold,
　My lord, to enter here without our leave.

LEICESTER: And you are brazen, sir, to speak for her.
　Your leave, indeed! There is no man at court
　Whose leave or whose refusal Leicester heeds!
　　[*Approaching* ELIZABETH, *humbly*.]
　No, from my queen's own lips alone I'll hear –

ELIZABETH [*without looking at him*]: Despicable deceiver,
　　leave my sight!

LEICESTER: I do not hear my sweet Elizabeth,
　In these harsh words, but him, my enemy.
　I make appeal to *my* Elizabeth!
　You lent that lord your ear; I must demand
　The same attention.

ELIZABETH:　　　　Speak then, renegade!
　And magnify your crime, if you deny it!

LEICESTER: But let this burdensome intruder first
　Be gone – Leave us, my lord. The things I have
　To speak of with my Queen can do without
　Your witness. Go.

ELIZABETH [*to* BURGHLEY]: Remain! It is my order!

LEICESTER: Why should a third intrude between us two?
　What I would speak of is of no concern
　To any but the monarch I adore,
　And I insist upon my rights, for they
　Are sacred rights, and I demand my lord
　Withdraw!

ELIZABETH: These haughty words befit your tongue.

LEICESTER: In truth they do, for I enjoy your favour,
That sets me up above all other men!
Your heart it was that granted this proud rank,
And what was given me by love, I swear
I will defend it, should it cost my life.
Let him be gone – and two brief moments will
Suffice for us to make our peace again.

ELIZABETH: You trust the cunning of your lips in vain.

LEICESTER: No, he it was could win you with his cunning,
But I would only seek to touch your heart.
And what because I trusted in your favour
I dared to do, I will defend before
Your heart alone! It is the only judge
I will acknowledge to pronounce on me.

ELIZABETH: Have you no shame? It is this very heart
Condemns you first! – My lord, the letter!

BURGHLEY: Here!

LEICESTER [*looking quickly through the letter without losing his
         composure*]: The Stuart's hand.

ELIZABETH: Read it, and then be silent!

LEICESTER [*after reading it, calmly*]: Appearance is against
me, but I hope
I am not to be judged by mere appearance!

ELIZABETH: Can you deny that you have secretly
Communicated with the Stuart, fed
Her hopes of freedom, and received her portrait?

LEICESTER: How easily, if I were guilty, might
I say my enemy had borne false witness!
But I am innocent, and I admit
That what she writes is true!

ELIZABETH: What then,
Vile wretch!

BURGHLEY: He is condemned by his own lips.

ELIZABETH: Out of my sight, the traitor! To the Tower!

LEICESTER: I am no traitor. I did wrong to keep
The secret of my actions hidden from you;
But it was done with good intent. I hoped
To spy her out, your foe, and be her ruin.

ELIZABETH: Contemptible excuses –
BURGHLEY: Do you think –
LEICESTER: It was a game of deadly risk I played,
I know; and no one but the Earl of Leicester,
Of all your noblemen, would dare to do it.
My hatred of the Stuart all men know,
The rank I hold, the trust with which my Queen
Has honoured me, must banish any doubt
That might be entertained in my allegiance.
May not the man whom you have singled out
Above all others with your favour, choose
His own bold way to do his duty?
BURGHLEY: Why
Did you not tell us, if the cause was good?
LEICESTER: My lord, you always talk before you act,
Loudly proclaim what you will do. That is
Your way, my lord. It is not mine. With me,
Actions come first, then words!
BURGHLEY: You do not spare
Your words when once you need them, sir.
LEICESTER [*measuring* BURGHLEY *with a proud and
     contemptuous look*]:   And you
Would claim the credit for a splendid deed,
For rescuing your queen, and laying bare
A traitorous conspiracy. There is
Nothing you do not know, nothing that can
Escape your eagle eye, your bloodhound's nose.
Poor fool! Despite your boasting, Mary Stuart
Were free today, if I had not forestalled it.
BURGHLEY: If *you* –
LEICESTER: Yes, I, my lord. The Queen had pinned
Her hopes on Mortimer, revealed to him
Her dearest wishes, yes, had gone so far
As to entrust him with a bloody deed,
Since uncle Paulet turned away, repelled,
And would not carry out this mission for her –
Speak now! Is it not so? [ELIZABETH *and* BURGHLEY
     exchange glances of surprise.]

BURGHLEY: And where did you
Learn this?

LEICESTER: Is it not so? My lord! Where were
Your thousand eyes, that you could fail to see
That Mortimer was playing false with you?
That he was a fanatic Papist, tool
Of Guise and creature of the Stuart woman,
A bold, determined madman, come to set
The Stuart free and kill the Queen –

ELIZABETH [*in amazement*]: What, Mortimer!

LEICESTER: He was the messenger between myself
And Mary; that is how I came to know him.
This very day they planned to tear her from
Her prison cell; I heard it from his lips
This minute; I arrested him, and he,
Despairing when he saw himself unmasked,
His treason thwarted – killed himself!

ELIZABETH: O, shamefully
I am betrayed – this villain Mortimer!

BURGHLEY: This minute, did you say? When I had left
you!

LEICESTER: For my own sake, most deeply I regret
That this should be his end. His evidence,
If he still lived, would be my sure acquittal,
It would have rescued me from all suspicion.
And so I wished to give him up to justice;
With strictest form the law should set its seal
Upon my innocence before the world.

BURGHLEY: He killed himself, you say. With his own hand?
Or did you kill him?

LEICESTER: Base suspicion! Hear
The captain of the guard I called to seize him! [*He goes
to the door and calls in the* OFFICER *of the guard.*]
The Queen desires to hear you give account
Of Mortimer, and how he met his death.

OFFICER: I had the watch within the antechamber.
The door flew open, and my lord appeared,
Commanding us to seize this man, a traitor.

But then we saw him fly into a rage
And draw his dagger, utter curses on
The Queen, and then before we could prevent it
He stabbed himself, and fell dead to the ground –

LEICESTER: The Queen has heard enough, sir. You may
go.

   [*Exit* OFFICER.]

ELIZABETH: O bottomless abyss of crime and horror!

LEICESTER: Who was it then delivered you? Was it
My lord of Burghley? Did he know the danger
That threatened you? And was it he who turned
The blow aside? Your angel Leicester saved you!

BURGHLEY: My Lord, this Mortimer could not have died
More opportunely.

ELIZABETH: What am I to say?
I do not know. I think I must believe you,
And I do not. I think you must be guilty,
And you are not. O, she it is who brings
These miseries upon me; how I hate her!

LEICESTER: Then she must die, and now myself I vote
For death. I had advised you that the sentence
Should be suspended till another arm
Be raised for her. Now it has happened, and
I must insist she dies without delay.

BURGHLEY: You had advised it! You!

LEICESTER: As much as I
Deplore that we should take this fateful step,
I now believe and recognize that it
Is necessary for the welfare of
Our Queen to make this bloody sacrifice.
I therefore recommend the warrant for
Her execution be prepared at once.

BURGHLEY [*to* ELIZABETH]: What true and loyal concern
my lord has shown!
I therefore recommend that *he* be charged
To see the sentence carried out upon her.

LEICESTER: I!

BURGHLEY: You. There is no better way to clear

Yourself of all suspicion that remains,
Than by yourself presiding at the death
Upon the block of her men said you loved.

ELIZABETH [*fixing her eyes on* LEICESTER]: My lord's
  advice is good. So let it be.
LEICESTER: It would be fitting that my lofty rank
  Should bring exemption from such sorry duties
  As this, which is a task in every way
  More suited to a Burghley than to me.
  Who stands as near as I do to his queen
  Should never be a bringer of ill fortune.
  And yet, to prove my zealous loyalty,
  And offer satisfaction to my queen,
  I will give up the privilege I cherish,
  And undertake to do this hateful duty.
ELIZABETH: My lord of Burghley will perform it with you.
  [*To* BURGHLEY] See that the warrant is drawn up at
    once.

  [*Exit* BURGHLEY. *A confused noise is heard outside.*]

SCENE 7

  [*Enter* KENT.]

ELIZABETH: My lord of Kent, what is this tumult in
  The city? What is happening?
KENT: My queen,
  It is the people, swarming round the palace,
  Demanding urgently that they should see you.
ELIZABETH: What is my people's wish?
KENT: London's in terror,
  They say you are in danger, murderers
  Sent by the Pope against you are abroad,
  The Catholics are plotting to release
  The Stuart woman from her prison with
  A deed of violence, and proclaim her Queen.
  The mob believe it; they are raging, and
  Will not be pacified unless the head
  Of Mary Stuart falls this very day.

ELIZABETH: What? Am I then to be compelled to do it?
KENT: They are determined, and they will not go
    Until you sign the warrant for her death.

SCENE 8

[*Enter* BURGHLEY *and* DAVISON *with a document.*]
ELIZABETH: What have you brought me, Davison?
DAVISON: My queen,
    You ordered –
ELIZABETH: What? [*She reaches out for the paper, but
        starts back, shuddering.*]
                        O God in Heaven!
BURGHLEY: Obey
    The people's voice, it is the voice of God.
ELIZABETH [*struggling with herself in indecision*]: O, but my
        lords! How can I know if this
    Is truly all my people's voice, the voice
    Of all the world I hear? I am afraid
    That if I now yield to the mob's desire,
    Another voice, and in a different tone,
    Will then be raised – yes, that the very men
    Who now so hotly urge me to this deed,
    When it is done, will censure me most harshly!

SCENE 9

[*Enter* SHREWSBURY.]
SHREWSBURY: O do not act in haste, your majesty!
    Stand firm, do not be driven! [*Seeing* DAVISON *with the
        paper.*]
                            What, or is it
    Too late? Already done? I see a paper
    In this man's hand that tells an evil tale.
    Let it not come this day before my queen.
ELIZABETH: O noble Shrewsbury! They will compel me.
SHREWSBURY: Who can compel you? You are sovereign,
    You must make manifest your sovereignty!

Command those rude harsh voices to be silent
That would presume to force your royal will,
And overrule the wisdom of your judgement.
Fear and blind rage have overcome the people,
And you yourself are smarting from this blow,
Are not yourself – you cannot judge her now.

BURGHLEY: She has been judged. No sentence is to be
Decided, it must now be carried out.

KENT [*who had left on* SHREWSBURY's *arrival, returning*]:
The people can be checked no longer; more
And more they press.

ELIZABETH [*to* SHREWSBURY]: You see how I am driven!

SHREWSBURY: Wait, that is all I ask. On this one stroke
The peace and happiness of your life hang.
For years you have been weighing it, and shall
This moment's storm now carry you away?
Wait but a while. Stay, and collect yourself,
Until a more propitious hour has come.

BURGHLEY [*forcefully*]: Wait, hesitate, delay, until the
kingdom
Goes up in flames, until success at last
Has crowned the Stuart's murderous attempts.
Three times has God delivered you from her;
Today the blow struck close; to hope for yet
Another miracle is tempting God.

SHREWSBURY: The God who by his miracles four times
Delivered you, who gave the feeble arm
Of an old man the strength to overcome
A raving murderer – deserves your trust!
I will not seek to make the voice of justice
Heard at this time, the storm will drown it now.
Hear this one thing! You tremble now with dread
Of Mary while she lives. You need not fear
Her while she is alive. But tremble at
The thought of Mary dead, beheaded. She
Will rise up from her grave, a fearful goddess
Of strife and vengeance, to bestride your kingdom,
And turn the hearts of your own people from you.

The Englishman now hates her, for he fears her,
But when she is no more he will avenge her,
For he will pity her and see in her
No more the enemy of his religion,
Only the daughter of his own royal house,
Victim of hatred and of jealousy.
Soon, all too soon you will perceive the change.
Go on your way through London, when the deed
Is done, and greet your people, who were used
To throng with joy about you; you will see
Another England and another people,
For you no longer then will wear the crown
Of justice, which must always win the hearts
Of men; but fear, the dreadful escort of
The tyrant, will go everywhere before you,
To blight and wither every path you tread.
If you did this then you would shrink from nothing,
What head is safe if hers, anointed, fell?

ELIZABETH: Ah, Shrewsbury! You saved my life today,
You turned aside the dagger that was meant
To kill me; why did you not let it find
Its mark? Then all my struggles would be ended,
And free of doubt and innocent of crime
My peaceful grave would cover me. In truth,
The cares of life and kingship weary me.
If it is true that one of us two queens
Must fall to let the other live – and it
Is true, I know – then why should I not be
The one to yield? My people shall decide,
I will restore to them their sovereignty.
God is my witness that I have not lived
For my own ends, but for my people's good.
If they believe the Stuart flatterer,
Younger than I, will be the better queen,
Then gladly I will quit this throne and go
Back to my quiet and lonely life at Woodstock,
Where in all modesty my youth was spent,
Where far from earthly power and idle pomp

I was a sovereign to myself – I am
Not made to govern others! Who would rule,
He must be hard, and I – my heart is tender.
Long and in happiness I governed here,
When I but sought to make my people happy;
Now comes the first cruel duty of a king,
And I am faint before it –

BURGHLEY: God in Heaven!
If I must hear such words, unworthy of
A sovereign, upon my queen's own lips,
I should betray my duty and betray
My motherland, if I kept silent longer.
– You say you love your people, not yourself;
Then show it now! Do not choose your own peace
And let your kingdom suffer hostile storms.
Think of the Church! Are we to see with her
The old idolatry return again?
The monk will lord it here, the legate come
In priestly pomp from Rome to shut our churches
And turn our rulers from their lawful throne.
– It is the souls of all your subjects that
I ask of you! For as you now decide,
Accordingly they live or they are lost.
This is no time for gentleness and mercy,
The nation's good is duty above all;
Though Shrewsbury it was who saved your life,
I will save England – that is worth the more!

ELIZABETH: Let me be left alone. I shall not find
Advice or comfort in the voice of men.
The greater Judge shall be my guide – I will
Submit myself to him. Go, leave me now,
My lords. [*To* DAVISON] You, sir, do not go far away.

> [*Exeunt* LORDS. SHREWSBURY *remains a few moments after
> the others have gone, standing before* ELIZABETH *with his
> looks fixed meaningfully upon her; then he too withdraws, slowly
> and with an expression of deep sorrow.*]

SCENE 10

ELIZABETH [*alone*]: My people's slave! O shameful
      servitude!
O how it galls me, still to grovel at
The feet of this dumb idol I despise!
When shall I sit in freedom on my throne?
I must conciliate their wishes, seek
Their praise with flattery, and please a mob
Only a mountebank will satisfy.
O, he is not yet king who still must please
The world! No, only he who need not ask
Consent of any man for what he'd do.
    Why have I heeded all my life the voice
Of justice, scorned the act of tyranny,
Only to find that when I can no longer
Abstain from violence my hands are bound?
Men will condemn me by my own example!
If I had been a tyrant like my sister,
Mary, who sat before me on this throne, then now
I could shed royal blood, with none to blame me!
But did I choose it of my own free will,
When I was just? Necessity, that rules
Our every act, yes, even those of kings,
Inexorable, forced this virtue on me.
    Surrounded by my enemies, I owe
My kingdom to the favour of my people.
For all the powers of the continent
Seek to destroy me. With unceasing hate
The Pope from Rome hurls curses at my head,
With kisses of false friendship France betrays me,
And on the seas the Spaniard openly
And unrelentingly makes war upon me.
So I must stand, and fight against a world,
I, a defenceless woman! With my virtue
I must attempt to patch my tattered rights
And cover up the stain upon my birth,
The shame that my own father laid upon me.

I cannot cover it – my enemies
With hate have laid it bare, and set her up,
The Stuart, like a ghost to threaten me.
   No, I must make an end to fears!
Her head shall fall. I must have peace from her!
She is a Fury in my life, a spirit
Sent by my fate to plague and torture me.
Wherever I have cherished any joy
Or hope, I find this serpent lurking in
My path! She tears away the man I love,
She robs me of a husband! Mary Stuart,
The name of every evil blow that strikes me!
When she no longer walks upon the earth,
I shall be free, as is the mountain air.
   [*Pause*]
With what contempt she looked upon me then,
As if her eyes could scorch me with their gaze!
– But you are powerless! I have better weapons,
Their blow is death, and you will be no more! [*She goes
    quickly to the table and takes up the pen.*]
A bastard am I, then? Unlucky wretch,
Only as long as you are living still!
What doubts remain upon my princely birth,
They are stamped out, when I have stamped on you!
As soon as England can no longer choose,
My blood is pure, my birth legitimate! [*She signs the
    warrant with swift, firm strokes of the pen, then drops the
    pen and steps back with an expression of horror. After a
    pause, she rings.*]

SCENE II

   [*Enter* DAVISON.]
ELIZABETH: Where are the lords? Not here?
DAVISON: They have gone out
To calm the furious temper of the people.
Their ragings were immediately stilled
When once they saw the Earl of Shrewsbury.

That's he, that's he, they cried, a hundred voices,
The man that saved the Queen! Let's hear him speak!
The finest man in England! – He began
To speak to them, the noble Talbot, and
With gentle words reproached the people for
Their violence, with such powerful persuasion
That they were calmed, and quietly, one by one,
They went their ways.

ELIZABETH: The idle, fickle mob,
Swayed by the slightest breeze! Yes, woe to him
That leans upon that broken reed! – My thanks,
Good Davison. You may retire again. [*As he turns to the
        door*]
This paper – take it back – I place it in
Your hands.

DAVISON [*glances at the paper and starts in horror*]: Your
        majesty! It is – I see
Your name – you have decided?

ELIZABETH: It was meant
For me to sign. I have. A piece of paper
Is no decision, and no name can kill.

DAVISON: *Your* name, my queen, beneath this document
Does decide all, it kills, it is the flash
Of lightning winged to strike – This piece of paper
Orders the commissaries and the sheriff
To make all haste to Fotheringhay castle,
Present themselves before the Queen of Scots,
Inform her that she is to die, and then,
When morning breaks, to execute the sentence.
There can be no delay, her life is done
When once my hands part with this document.

ELIZABETH: Yes, sir! It is a weighty matter God
Has placed in your weak hands. You must implore Him
To grant you guidance of His heavenly wisdom.
I leave you now, to carry out your duty.

DAVISON [*stepping in front of her as she is about to go*]: No, no,
        your majesty! You must not go
Before you have informed me of your will.

Do I need any other wisdom than
To carry out your orders to the letter?
– You place this paper in my hands, that I
Should pass it swiftly on for execution?
ELIZABETH: Your own judiciousness will guide you –
DAVISON [*terrified, hastily interrupting*]: No,
Not mine! May God forbid! Obedience
Is my judiciousness! You may not leave
Your servant to decide this fearful step.
The merest error would be regicide,
Fearful disaster and unending woe.
Grant that I may remain in this affair
Your instrument, blind and without a will
Speak your desire in plain and simple words,
What is this warrant for her death to mean?
ELIZABETH: – Its name must tell you that.
DAVISON: It is your wish it shall be carried out?
ELIZABETH [*hesitantly*]: I do not say so, and I fear to
    think it.
DAVISON: You wish that I should keep it longer yet?
ELIZABETH [*quickly*]: At your own risk! You answer for it
    then.
DAVISON: I? God in Heaven! My queen! O, speak your
    will!
ELIZABETH [*impatiently*]: My will is that this sorry matter
    shall
No more be thought of, and that at the last
I may be free of it in peace for ever.
DAVISON: It costs you but a single word. O speak,
This paper, say what must become of it.
ELIZABETH: That I have said. Now go, plague me no
    more.
DAVISON: That you have said? But no, you have said
    nothing
To me! O let your majesty be pleased
To think of it –
ELIZABETH [*stamping her foot*]: Intolerable!
DAVISON: O,

Have mercy on me! But a few short months
Ago I took this office, and I do
Not know the tongue of courts and kings – I learnt
The manners of a humbler, simpler station.
And so I pray, have patience with your servant!
Do not begrudge a word for my instruction,
To tell me how I best may do my duty – [*He approaches
    her in supplication; she turns her back on him. He stands
    in despair, then speaks in a tone of decision.*]
Take back this paper! Take it back from me!
It burns my hands as if it were on fire.
Do not choose me to be your servant in
This fearful business.

ELIZABETH: Do your duty, sir. [*Exit.*]

SCENE 12

DAVISON [*alone*]: She goes! She leaves me helpless, in
    despair,
Here with this paper – What am I to do?
Am I to keep it, or to pass it on?
    [*Enter* BURGHLEY.]
My lord, how good that you have come! You brought
Me here and introduced me to this office.
Take it from me, I beg. I undertook it
Not knowing all its workings. Let me go
Back to the humbler life from which I came,
From which you took me, this is not my place –
BURGHLEY: What is the matter, sir? Where is the warrant?
The Queen – she called for you.
DAVISON: She went away
In anger. O I beg you, help, advise me!
Rescue me from this doubt that sears my soul.
Here is the warrant – with her signature.
BURGHLEY [*quickly*]: It's signed? Give it to me!
DAVISON: I may not.
BURGHLEY: What?
DAVISON: She has not clearly told me what her will –

BURGHLEY: Not clearly! She has signed it. Give it here!
DAVISON: I am to see it carried out – am not
  To see it carried out – O God! I know not.
BURGHLEY [*with increasing urgency*]: Straightway you are to
    see it carried out.
  Give it to me! Delay, and you are lost.
DAVISON: If I am over-hasty I am lost!
BURGHLEY: You are a fool, I say. Give it to me! [*He
    seizes the warrant and hurries off with it.*]
DAVISON [*hurrying after him*]: What are you doing? Stay!
    I shall be ruined! [*Exit.*]

ACT V

Fotheringhay
The scene is as in Act I

SCENE 1

[HANNAH KENNEDY *in deep mourning, her eyes red with
weeping and in great though silent grief, is occupied in sealing
letters and packages. From time to time her sorrow overcomes
her, and she pauses occasionally to pray silently. Enter* PAULET
and DRURY, *also in black, followed by numerous* SERVANTS
*carrying gold and silver vessels, mirrors, paintings and other
precious things with which they fill the back of the room.*
PAULET *gives* KENNEDY *a jewel-casket and a paper which,
as he indicates to her by signs, is an inventory of the articles they
have brought. At the sight of these riches the nurse again sinks
into deep sorrow and grief.* PAULET *and* DRURY *leave again
without speaking. Enter* MELVIL.]

KENNEDY [*crying out as soon as she sees him*]: O Melvil, is it you
    I see again?
MELVIL: Yes, faithful Kennedy, we meet again!
KENNEDY: After a long and grievous time of parting!
MELVIL: Yet full of grief, and fearful is our meeting!
KENNEDY: O God in Heaven! You come –

MELVIL: To take my last
  Farewell, for ever, from her majesty.
KENNEDY: Now, on the very morning of her death,
  At last they grant that she may see again
  Those she has missed so long – O, I will not,
  Good Melvil, ask how you have fared, nor tell
  You all the sorrows we have had to bear
  Since you were torn from us by those rude hands.
  Another time will come to tell of that!
  O Melvil, Melvil! Did we have to live
  To see the dawning of this day?
MELVIL: We must
  Not make each other weaken! I will weep
  Until I die, and never shall a smile
  Lighten the pallid sorrow of these cheeks,
  Nor will I shed these clothes of deepest black
  While I yet live, for I will mourn for ever;
  But this day I will not be bowed – and you
  Must promise me to moderate your grief –
  And should all others plunge into despair
  Inconsolate, let us still not give way,
  But with a manly courage go before her
  And be a staff to her on this last journey.
KENNEDY: Melvil! You are mistaken if you think
  The Queen has need of any help from us,
  To go to meet her death unbowed. She is
  Herself a fit example to us all.
  You need not fear, for Mary Stuart knows
  How like a hero and a queen to die.
MELVIL: Did she receive the news with dignity?
  Men say that she was not prepared to hear it.
KENNEDY: No, she was not. But it was other fears
  That moved my lady; Mary did not quake
  To think of death, but of her liberty.
  – We had been promised freedom. This same night,
  Mortimer swore that he would rescue us,
  And midway between hope and fear, in doubt
  Whether she might entrust her honour and

Her royal person to this hasty youth,
Her majesty lay waiting for the dawn.
– Then we hear people coming, and a knocking
Affrights our ears, the blows of many hammers.
We think we hear our rescuers at work,
Hope waves to us, the sweet desire for life
Awakes unbidden and omnipotent –
Then the door opens wide – and it is Paulet,
Come to announce to us – the carpenters
Are putting up the scaffold here below us! [*She turns
away, overcome by violent grief.*]

MELVIL: Almighty God! O tell me, how did Mary
Endure this fearful blow to all her hopes?

KENNEDY [*collecting herself somewhat, after a pause*]: We cannot
ease ourselves away from life!
But in a moment, swiftly, we must make
The change between this life below and life
Eternal; and my lady was vouchsafed
By God to cast all earthly hopes away
With fortitude, and in this moment set
Her faith in Heaven with a courageous soul.
No sign of fear, no word of lamentation
Dishonoured her – But only when she heard
Of Leicester's shameful treachery, and of
The wretched fate of that poor noble youth
Who sacrificed himself for her, and when
She saw the bitter grief of his old uncle,
Whose only hope was dead, and in her cause,
Then did she weep, for not her own misfortune,
Only the grief of others drew her tears.

MELVIL: Where is she now? And can you bring me to her?

KENNEDY: She stayed awake all through the night in prayer,
Wrote letters of farewell to all her friends,
And made her testament with her own hand.
Now she is sleeping for a moment, that
In rest her strength may be renewed.

MELVIL: Who's with her?

KENNEDY: Burgoyne, her own physician, and her women.

SCENE 2

[*Enter* MARGARET CURLE.]

KENNEDY: What is it, mistress? Is the Queen awake?

CURLE [*drying her tears*]: Already dressed, and she is asking
    for you.

KENNEDY: I'm coming. [*To* MELVIL, *who makes as if to*
    accompany her] Do not follow me, until
My lady is prepared to see you. [*Exit.*]

CURLE: Melvil!
Once master of our household!

MELVIL: I am he.

CURLE: O, Mary's household needs no master now!
– Melvil! You come from London, have you then
No news to tell me of my husband's fate?

MELVIL: They say he will be set at liberty,
As soon –

CURLE: As soon as Mary is no more!
O shameful wretch and traitor to his queen!
He is the murderer of our dear lady,
Was it not his, the evidence that damned her?

MELVIL: It was.

CURLE: O may his soul be cursed in hell
For that! His evidence was false, I know –

MELVIL: Come, Mistress Curle! Think what it is you say.

CURLE: Yes, I will swear it to a court of law,
Repeat it to him, to his very face;
The whole world shall give echo to the truth
That she dies guiltless –

MELVIL: God, let this be true!

SCENE 3

[*Enter* BURGOYNE.]

BURGOYNE: O Melvil!

MELVIL: O Burgoyne!

BURGOYNE [*to* CURLE]:   A cup of wine,
Now, for my lady. Haste, attend to it. [*Exit* CURLE.]

MELVIL: What is it? Is her majesty not well?
BURGOYNE: Her courage flatters her, she thinks that she
  Is strong, and has no need of nourishment.
  But there is still a fierce ordeal awaits her,
  And never shall her enemies make boast
  That fear of death sat ashen on her cheek,
  Though nature should at last give way to weakness.
    [*Enter* KENNEDY.]
MELVIL [*to* KENNEDY]: May I go in?
KENNEDY: She will be here herself.
  – You seem to look about you, sir, with wonder,
  And ask me with your looks, what means this show
  Of earthly pomp, here in the place of death?
  O, while we lived we suffered deprivation,
  Only in death our riches all return.

SCENE 4

    [*Enter two more* MAIDS *of Mary's, also in mourning costume.
    At the sight of* MELVIL, *they burst into loud weeping.*]
MELVIL: What is this sight? Must we endure this meeting?
  Rosamund! Gertrude!
SECOND MAID: She has sent us out!
  She will remain alone to speak with God
  For the last time!
    [*Two more* MAIDS *enter, in mourning like the others, with
    silent gestures of grief.*]

SCENE 5

    [*Enter* MARGARET CURLE *with a golden goblet of wine,
    which she places on the table, as she does so leaning pale and
    trembling upon a chair.*]
MELVIL: What is the matter? What appals you so?
CURLE: O God!
BURGOYNE: What is the matter?
CURLE: Such a sight!
MELVIL: Be calm, and tell us what it is.

CURLE: As I
  Came up the staircase with this cup of wine,
  Past the great hall below, the doors flew open;
  I saw – O God!

MELVIL: What did you see? Have courage!

CURLE: Covered in black were all the walls about,
  A scaffold, tall, and carpeted with black,
  Rose up, and in the middle of it there
  A black block, and a hassock, and beside them
  An axe of glittering steel. – The hall was filled
  With people crowding round the stage of death,
  And waiting for the sacrifice, with lust
  For blood in all their eyes.

THE WOMEN: God spare our lady!

MELVIL: Courage! She comes.

SCENE 6

[*Enter* MARY. *She is clad in white as for some festivity; around her neck she wears an Agnus Dei on a necklace of small beads, and a rosary hangs at her waist; she has a crucifix in her hand and a diadem on her head, and wears a long black veil, thrown back. As she enters all those present draw back on either side with expressions of violent grief.* MELVIL *sinks to his knees with an involuntary gesture.*]

MARY [*looking about her with calm dignity*]: Why do you weep?
      What is this grief? You should
  Rejoice with me, that all my sufferings
  Are now to end, my fetters to be loosed,
  My prison opened and my joyous soul
  On angel's wings soar to eternal freedom.
  Then, when I was surrendered to the power
  Of my proud enemy, and suffered insults
  Unfitting for a free and noble queen
  To bear, then was the time to weep for me!
  – Kindly and soothing, death approaches now,
  Grave-featured friend! He spreads his sable wings
  Over my shame – all men, though they may be

So lowly sunk, are noble in this last.
I feel the crown once more upon my head,
And seemly pride within my noble soul! [*Advancing a few
    steps*]
What, Melvil here? No, sir, you shall not kneel!
Arise! It is the triumph of your queen,
And not her death that you have come to see.
This is a blessing I had never hoped
To know, that not my enemies alone
Shall speak of me, and that I have at least
One friend and one believer of my faith
To be the witness of my hour of death.
– Speak, noble sir! How did it fare with you
In this unfriendly and unkindly land
After you had been torn away from us?
Often my heart has grieved with care for you.
MELVIL: I knew no wants, and suffered only pain
For you, and that I could not come to aid you!
MARY: How is my good old chamberlain, Didier?
But no, that faithful friend must long be sleeping
Eternal sleep, for he was rich in years.
MELVIL: God has not been so merciful to him;
He lives, to bury you who are still young.
MARY: Would only that before I died, I might
Embrace but one of my beloved kinsmen!
But I must meet my end here among strangers,
Yours are the only tears that I may see!
– Melvil, your loyal breast shall be the keeper
Of my last wishes for my own. – My blessing
Upon my brother, the Most Christian King,
And all the royal house of France; upon
The Cardinal, my uncle, and my cousin
Henry of Guise, the noble, valiant man.
My blessings on the Pope, the holy vicar
Of Christ on earth, who blesses me in turn,
And the Most Catholic King, who nobly strove
To rescue me and to avenge my wrongs –
Each one is named in my last testament,

They shall receive the presents of my love,
And will not spurn them, though they may be poor.
　　[Turning to her SERVANTS]
I have commended you into the care
Of France's king, my royal brother; he
Will make his land a second home for you.
And if you would obey my one last wish,
Then do not stay in England; do not let
Albion's sons gloat at your misery
And see my faithful servants in the dust.
Come, swear to me upon this crucifix
To leave this sorry land when I am gone!

MELVIL [*touching the crucifix*]: I swear it in the name of each
　　of these.

MARY: What I still have, poor though I am and robbed,
What I am still permitted to bestow,
I have divided up among you and
I hope that my last wishes will be honoured.
All that I shall be wearing at my death,
This too is yours; but grant me now once more
These earthly glories, on my way to Heaven! [*To the
　　women*]
To you, my Alice, Gertrude, Rosamund,
I give my pearls, and all my clothes; for you
Are young, and youth enjoys such ornament.
You, Margaret, must have the greatest claim
Upon me, for I leave you here behind
Of all of these the most disconsolate.
You shall not suffer for your husband's guilt,
My testament will make it plain. – And you,
My faithful Hannah; you, who are not swayed
By gold, for all its worth, nor splendid jewels:
Here, take this kerchief! I embroidered it
With my own hand for you in hours of sorrow,
And wove into it my most bitter tears.
I beg you with this kerchief bind my eyes,
When it must come to that – for I would have
My Hannah to perform this final service.

KENNEDY: O Melvil! I cannot endure it!

MARY: Come!
    Come, all of you, and take this last farewell! [*She
    stretches out her hands, and one by one they fall at her feet and
        kiss her hand, weeping bitterly.*]
    Farewell, good Margaret – Alice, farewell –
    My thanks, Burgoyne, for all your faithful service –
    Your lips are burning, Gertrude – I have been
    Much hated, but as well most dearly loved!
    O may my Gertrude find a worthy husband,
    For it is love this ardent heart desires –
    Bertha! It is a better way you choose,
    To be the bride of Heaven in chastity!
    Go, hasten to perform your sacred vows!
    Know that all earthly good is treacherous,
    Learn this by the example of your queen.
    No more! Farewell! Farewell! For ever more! [*She turns
    quickly away from them. Exeunt all except* MELVIL.]

SCENE 7

MARY: All my affairs of this life I have settled,
    And hope I am in no man's debt when I
    Must leave the world; but there is one thing more,
    Melvil, which bars the passage of the soul
    Seeking to rise in freedom and in joy.

MELVIL: Tell me what that may be. Lighten your breast.
    Entrust your cares to me, your faithful friend.

MARY: I look upon eternity today,
    Soon I shall stand before the Judge of all;
    And still I am not reconciled with Him.
    No priest of my own church will they allow me,
    I scorn to take the blessed sacrament
    From their false priests, by whom it is defiled.
    For I will die faithful to my own church,
    The only one that can remit our sins.

MELVIL: Be calm, for Heaven will hear your ardent wish
    And know that it could not be carried out.

The tyrant's power can only bind our hands,
The pious heart is lifted up to God;
The word is dead, the spirit gives us life.
MARY: Ah, Melvil! Faithful heart is not enough,
But there must be an earthly pledge, or we
Can never hope to see the light of Heaven.
It was for this that God became a man,
And sealed invisible and heavenly gifts
Within a human body to be seen.
It is the Church, the holy and exalted,
That builds the ladder we must climb to Heaven;
The universal, Catholic we call it,
Only the faith of all can make faith strong.
When thousands worship and adore their God,
A mighty flame is kindled, and on wings
The spirit soars, and Heaven is opened wide.
– O happy they who share their cheerful prayer
Assembled in the house of their own God!
The altar is adorned, the candles glow,
The bells are rung and incense spread about,
The bishop stands in vestments gleaming white,
He takes the chalice, blesses it, proclaims
The miracle, the presence of their Lord;
And on their knees before their God the people
In faithful adoration fall – But I
Alone may not be with them, and the blessing
Of Heaven may never reach my prison cell.
MELVIL: Yes, it is here, and near to you! But trust
In the Omnipotent – the withered staff
May branch and blossom in the hand of faith!
And He who struck the rock and brought forth springs
Can make an altar of this prison cell,
Can take this cup, that quenches earthly thirst,
And with it swiftly quench your thirst for Heaven.
[*He takes the goblet from the table.*]
MARY: Melvil! Can this be true? O yes, it can!
Here is no church, here is no priest, here is
No Host – but our Redeemer spoke these words:

304

Where two are gathered in My name together,
There I am also present in their midst.
What gives a priest the right to speak for God?
A blameless life, and purity of heart.
Then you may be my priest, though not ordained,
A messenger of God to bring me peace.
To you now will I make my last confession,
And hear forgiveness spoken from your lips.

MELVIL: If with such zeal your heart demands this blessing,
Then know, my queen, that God to comfort you
Can work a miracle upon His servant.
Here is no priest, you say, here is no church,
No sacred Host? But you are wrong. Here is
A priest, and God is present in this place. [*He bares his
head, and also reveals to her a Host in a golden dish.*]
— I am a priest, and I have taken on
My head the seven orders, that I might
Hear from your lips your last confession, and
Grant peace to you when you must go to die.
And I have brought this consecrated Host
The Holy Father sends to you himself.

MARY: O then upon death's very threshold yet
I shall enjoy a heavenly blessedness!
Like an immortal soaring down on clouds
Of gold, like that fair angel sent to free
The good apostle from his prison cell —
Stayed not by bars, nor by the soldiers' swords,
Through bolted doors striding in majesty,
He stands within the dungeon shining bright.
So too Heaven's messenger has come to me
When every earthly rescuer has failed me!
And you who served me once are now the servant
Of God on high, and speak His holy word!
And as before me once you bent your knee,
So now I kneel to you. [*She sinks down on her knees before
him.*]

MELVIL [*making the sign of the cross over her*]: And in the name
Of Father, Son and Holy Ghost, Amen!

305

Queen Mary! Have you spoken with your heart
To know its secrets, do you swear that you
Before the God of truth the truth confess?

MARY: My heart from you hides nothing, nor from Him.

MELVIL: Say now what sins you have committed since
You last did make your peace with God above.

MARY: My heart was filled with envy and with hatred,
And thoughts of vengeance raged within my breast.
I dared to hope that God forgave my sins,
But I could not forgive my enemy.

MELVIL: Do you repent your guilt, and are you now
Resolved to leave this world at peace with her?

MARY: As truly as I hope for God's forgiveness.

MELVIL: What other sins must you confess to Him?

MARY: Ah, not by hate alone, by sinful love
Still more have I abused His highest gift.
My heart betrayed me in its vanity
To him who faithlessly abandoned me!

MELVIL: Do you repent your guilt, and does your heart
Shun this idolatry and turn to God?

MARY: It was a fearful struggle to withstand,
But I have broken every earthly band.

MELVIL: What other guilt still weighs upon your soul?

MARY: Ah, guilt of blood, long past and long confessed,
Returns, and all its terrors freshly mount,
Now when I must prepare my last account,
And grimly lowering bar my heavenward way.
The king, my husband, I gave word to slay,
And offered heart and hand to my seducer!
I have done bitter penance for these deeds,
But still the worm upon my spirit feeds.

MELVIL: Is there no other sin your heart accuses,
Which you have not repented and confessed?

MARY: Now you know all that weighs upon my heart.

MELVIL: Remember the Omniscient is near!
Remember all the pains with which the Church
Threatens the penitent who does not make
Full and complete confession of his faults!

That brings eternal punishment and death,
For it is sin against the Holy Ghost!

MARY: Then may I be assured of victory
In this last struggle, for my conscience now is free.

MELVIL: But would you seek to cover from God's sight
The very crime for which you are to die?
Nothing you have to tell me of your share
In Babington and Parry's bloody treason?
For that this day you suffer punishment.
Would you be punished in eternity?

MARY: To face eternity I am prepared;
So shall before the minute-hand has turned
My soul before its Judge's throne be bared,
But all my sins I swear that you have learned.

MELVIL: Think on it well. Our heart deceives us often.
Perhaps with cunning trickery you did
Keep back the word that would proclaim your guilt,
Although your will was party to the crime.
But know you will not trick with juggler's arts
The eye of fire that looks into our hearts.

MARY: I called upon the princes of the world
To free me from this base captivity;
But I have never sought in will or deed
To take the life of her that keeps me here.

MELVIL: Then did your secretaries bear false witness?

MARY: What I have said is true; as for their witness,
God is their judge.

MELVIL: Then you set foot, convinced
Of your own innocence, upon the scaffold?

MARY: God has vouchsafed me through a guiltless death
To pay an ancient, heavy debt of blood.

MELVIL [*making the sign of the cross over her*]: Go then, and
make atonement by your death!
Fall as a sacrifice upon the altar;
Blood washes out the crimes that blood designed,
A woman's weakness was your only fault,
And when the spirit soars to heavenly bliss,
This life's infirmities are left behind.

Now I declare, by virtue of the power
To bind and loose, the Church confers on me,
That you from every taint of sin are free!
As you believe, so let it be to you! [*Giving her the Host.*]
Take this, the body of Christ who died for you! [*He takes
     the goblet standing on the table, blesses it with a silent
     prayer, and offers it to her. She hesitates to accept it, and
     waves it away with her hand.*]
Take this, the blood that Christ did shed for you!
Take it! The Pope has granted you this favour.
In death the noblest privilege of kings,
The right of priesthood, shall be yours to know! [*She
     takes the goblet.*]
And as you now, in this your earthly body,
Are joined with God, by this great mystery,
So in that realm of everlasting joy,
Where sin shall be no longer, neither weeping,
You shall be changed, and take on heavenly shape,
An angel, safe for ever in His keeping. [*He puts down the
     goblet. A noise is heard; he covers his head and goes to the
     door.* MARY *remains kneeling in silent prayer.* MELVIL
     returns.]
A grim ordeal remains for you to bear.
Are you now strong enough to overcome
The stirrings of past bitterness and hatred?
MARY: There shall be no relapse. My hatred and
My love are sacrificed to God in Heaven.
MELVIL: Then you must be prepared to meet my lords
Of Leicester and of Burghley. They are here.

SCENE 8

     [*Enter* BURGHLEY, LEICESTER *and* PAULET. LEICESTER
     remains standing at a distance with averted gaze. BURGHLEY,
     observing this, comes between him and MARY.]
BURGHLEY: I come, my lady Stuart, to receive
Your last commands.
MARY: For that, my lord, I thank you.

BURGHLEY: It is the will and order of my Queen
  That what you ask, if just, be not refused.

MARY: My testament will tell you my last wishes.
  It is delivered into Paulet's hand,
  And I request that it be carried out.

BURGHLEY: You may be sure it will.

MARY: I ask that all my servants be allowed
  To pass unharmed to Scotland, or to France,
  Wherever they themselves desire to go.

BURGHLEY: It shall be as you wish.

MARY: And as my body
  May not be laid in consecrated ground,
  Permit this man, who is my faithful servant,
  To take my heart to France, to my own people –
  Ah, there it always dwelt!

BURGHLEY: It shall be done.
  And is there more?

MARY: Take to the Queen of England
  The greetings of her sister – Say to her,
  I do forgive her truly for my death,
  And grieve that yesterday I pained her with
  My hasty words – May God in Heaven preserve her,
  And grant her years to reign in happiness!

BURGHLEY: But have you not yet made a wiser choice,
  Do you still scorn the presence of the Dean?

MARY: My peace with God is made. – O good Sir Amyas!
  Though guiltless, I have brought you bitter grief,
  And robbed your age of comfort – let me hope
  That when you think of me it will not be
  With hatred –

PAULET [giving her his hand]: Go in peace, and God be with
      you!

SCENE 9

  [Enter KENNEDY and the Queen's other WOMEN with
  expressions of horror, followed by the SHERIFF with a white
  staff in his hand. Behind him through the open door armed men
  can be seen.]

MARY: What is it, Hannah? Yes, the hour has struck,
The sheriff comes to lead us out to death.
Now it is time to part. Farewell, farewell! [*The* WOMEN
cling to her with passionate grief. To MELVIL]
But you, good sir, and you, my faithful Hannah,
Shall bear me company on my last journey.
My lord will not deny me this one favour!
BURGHLEY: It is not in my power to grant it.
MARY: What?
It is a small request. Could you refuse it?
I am a woman: that you must respect.
Who shall perform the final service for me?
It cannot be my sister's will that men
Should lay rough hands upon me, that my sex
Should suffer degradation when I die!
BURGHLEY: No woman may accompany you on
The scaffold's steps – their screaming and their cries –
MARY: She shall not scream! I will be surety
That Hannah will be valiant of soul.
My lord, be gracious. Do not part me from
My faithful nurse when I must meet my end.
She brought me in her arms into this life,
Let her with gentle hand guide me to death.
PAULET [*to* BURGHLEY]: Let it be so.
BURGHLEY: It shall.
MARY: Now I have nothing
More in this world – [*Taking her crucifix and kissing it*]
                         My saviour, my redeemer!
As you spread wide your arms upon the cross,
So let them now be opened to receive me! [*She turns to go.
At this moment her eyes meet those of* LEICESTER, *who
at her turning has involuntarily started and looked round at
her. On seeing him she trembles, her knees give way and she
seems about to collapse;* LEICESTER *takes hold of her and
receives her in his arms. She turns on him a long, earnest
and silent gaze, which he cannot bear. At last she speaks.*]
I see you keep your word, my lord of Leicester!
You promised you would lend your arm to lead

Me from my prison, and you do so now! [*He stands as if
    annihilated. She continues, softly.*]
Yes, Leicester, and not only
Freedom it was that I should owe your hand.
My freedom should be dear to me through you,
And at your hand, made happy by your love,
I hoped I should enjoy my new-found life.
But now, when I am on my way to leave
This world, and to become a blessed spirit,
Beyond temptation of all earthly love,
Now, Leicester, without blushing I confess
To you that weakness I have overcome –
Farewell, and if you can, be happy now!
Fortune made you the suitor of two queens;
A loving, tender heart you cast aside,
Betrayed it for another cold with pride.
Go then, and kneel before Elizabeth!
May your reward not turn to punishment!
Farewell. There is no more – my life is spent.
    [*Exeunt* MARY *preceded by the* SHERIFF, MELVIL *and*
    KENNEDY *at her side,* BURGHLEY *and* PAULET. *The
    others gaze sorrowfully after her; when she is out of sight they
    leave by the other doors, leaving* LEICESTER *alone behind.*]

SCENE 10

LEICESTER: And I still live! I can endure to live!
    Will not this roof collapse upon my head?
    Will the abyss not open to engulf
    The wretchedest of creatures? O, what have
    I lost! O what a pearl I cast away!
    What heavenly joy I spurned and threw aside!
    She's gone; her soul already is transfigured,
    And I am left the torments of the damned.
    Where is the firm resolve with which I came,
    To stifle all the promptings of my heart,
    To watch her die, and coldly stand apart?
    The sight of her awakes forgotten shame,

Can she in death still pierce me with love's dart?
Accursed wretch, it is no longer yours
To yield in meekness to this piteous shock:
Your path is turned for ever from love's shores,
Within your breast for ever close the doors
Of mercy, let your brow be like a rock!
If you would still enjoy your treason's fruit,
You must not shrink back now; be resolute!
Pity, be silent; turn to stone, my eye;
I will be witness, I will see her die. [*He goes determinedly
    towards the door by which* MARY *left, but stops halfway.*]
In vain, in vain! With horror I am racked,
I cannot, cannot see this fearful act,
I cannot see her fall – Hark! what was that?
They are already there below, preparing
To do their dreadful work beneath my feet.
Voices I hear – No, no! Away, away
Out of this house of terror and of death! [*He attempts to
    leave by another door, but finds it locked, and starts back.*]
What? Am I bound here by a god's command
To hear that thing I cannot bear to see?
The Dean of Peterborough – he exhorts her –
She interrupts him – Hark! She prays aloud,
Her voice is firm – Now silence – utter silence!
I only hear the women weep and sob,
They are unrobing her – Hark! Now they move
The stool for her – she kneels – she lays her head – [*The
    last words have been spoken in a tone of increasing terror.
    There is a pause; then suddenly, with a convulsive movement,
    he collapses in a faint. At the same time a muffled, long
    drawn out murmur of voices is heard from below.*]

The Queen's Room
Scene as in latter part of Act IV

SCENE 11

ELIZABETH [*alone*]: None here as yet – no messenger – O will
    The evening never come? Is the sun fixed

In its position? Yes, I am to lie
Yet longer on this rack of expectation.
– Is the deed done, or is it not? – I fear
For either case, and do not dare to ask!
Leicester and Burghley nowhere to be found,
These whom I named to carry out the sentence;
If they are gone from London – then the deed
Is done, the arrow has been loosed, it flies,
It strikes its mark, I cannot bring it back,
And must I for my kingdom's sake – Who's there?

SCENE 12

    [*Enter a* PAGE.]
You have returned alone – where are my lords?
PAGE: My lord of Leicester and the Treasurer –
ELIZABETH [*in extreme excitement*]: Where are they?
PAGE: They are not in London.
ELIZABETH: Not?
Where are they, then?
PAGE: There was no man could tell me that.
Before the break of day, in secrecy
And haste, my lords had both, so I was told,
Departed London.
ELIZABETH [*bursts out forcefully*]: I am Queen of England!
    [*Pacing up and down in great agitation*]
Go! Call me – no, stay here! – Then she is dead!
At last now there is room for me on earth.
– Why do I tremble? Why this sudden dread?
My fears are in their grave, and who can say
I did it? I shall not lack tears to weep
For her, now she is dead. [*To the* PAGE] Are you still
    here?
Go, bid my secretary Davison
Present himself to me immediately.
Send for the Earl of Shrewsbury – But see,
He comes! [*Exit* PAGE.]

SCENE 13

[*Enter* SHREWSBURY.]

ELIZABETH: Welcome, my noble lord! What is it?
It cannot be a trifle that brings you
To me so late.

SHREWSBURY: Your noble majesty,
My heart, weighed down with anxious fears for your
Good name, today compelled me to the Tower,
Where Mary's secretaries, Curle and Nau,
Are prisoners, wishing to test once more
If what they said in evidence was true.
Embarrassed, the Lieutenant of the Tower
Refused to let me see the prisoners;
At last with threats I forced him to admit me.
O God, it was a fearful sight I saw!
With hair all wild, with madness in his eye
Like one tormented by the Furies, lay
The Scotsman Curle upon his bed – Scarce had
The wretch seen who I was, he threw himself
Down at my feet, and seized my knees with screams
Of terrible despair, and writhed before me like
A stricken snake, to beg me and implore me
To speak, and say what fate befell his Queen;
For rumour that she was condemned to death
Had reached the nooks and crannies of the Tower.
When I had told him that it was the truth,
And added that it was his evidence
That damned her, raving up he sprang and leapt
Upon his fellow-prisoner, knocked him down
Before us with a madman's strength, and tried
To strangle him. We scarcely could deliver
The other from his rage, unhappy wretch.
But then he turned his ravings on himself,
Beat on his breast with angry fists and cursed
Himself and his companion, wished they both
Might be the victims of the fiends of hell.
His evidence was false, the fateful letters

To Babington, that he had sworn were true,
Were false, and he had written other words
Than those the queen herself dictated to him;
The villain Nau had led him on to do it.
He ran then to the window, tore it open
With fearful violence, and cried into
The streets, that all the people flocked to hear,
That he was Mary's secretary, he
The villain who had made false accusations,
He was accursed, for he had borne false witness!

ELIZABETH: You said yourself that he had lost his wits;
Words spoken by a madman in his ravings
Prove nothing.

SHREWSBURY: But his madness proves itself
The more! O do not act in haste, my queen.
I urge you to command a new inquiry.

ELIZABETH: It shall be so – because you ask it, sir,
And not because I can believe the peers
Gave judgement in this case too hastily.
To satisfy your doubts, let them renew
Inquiry. It is good there is still time!
Our royal honour shall not be impugned,
Not by the slightest shadow of a doubt.

SCENE 14

   [*Enter* DAVISON.]

ELIZABETH: The warrant, sir, that I put in your hand –
Where is it?

DAVISON: – Warrant?

ELIZABETH: That I placed in your
Safe keeping, yesterday –

DAVISON: In my safe keeping?

ELIZABETH: The people clamoured for my signing it,
I had to grant them what they asked, I did it,
They forced me to, and so I put the paper
Into your hands for keeping, to gain time.
You know well what I told you; give it to me!

SHREWSBURY: Come, sir, let's have it; matters now have
    changed,
  Inquiries must begin again anew.
DAVISON: Anew? – O God have mercy on my soul!
ELIZABETH: Why do you hesitate? Where is the paper?
DAVISON [*in despair*]: This is the end of me, I am destroyed!
ELIZABETH [*interrupting quickly*]: I hope, good sir, you
    have not –
DAVISON: I am lost!
  The paper's gone –
ELIZABETH: What's that?
SHREWSBURY: O God in Heaven!
DAVISON: It is in Burghley's hands – since yesterday.
ELIZABETH: What does this mean? Is this obedience?
  Did I not order you to keep it safe?
DAVISON: You did not order so, your majesty.
ELIZABETH: What, wretch, would you accuse me of a lie?
  When did I tell you Burghley should receive it?
DAVISON: You never said it in those words – and yet –
ELIZABETH: Scoundrel! My words you venture to
    interpret?
  Read into them your own bloodthirsty meanings?
  O woe to you, if this high-handed deed
  Of yours has brought upon us some misfortune!
  If so, you pay me for it with your life.
  – My lord of Shrewsbury, you see my name
  Is shamefully abused.
SHREWSBURY: I see – O God!
ELIZABETH: What do you say?
SHREWSBURY: If truly on his own
  Account this gentleman has so presumed
  To do this deed without your knowing of it,
  Then he must be accused and stand his trial
  Before the peers, for he has caused your name
  To be abhorred for all eternity.

SCENE 15

[*Enter* BURGHLEY.]

BURGHLEY [*falling on one knee before the* QUEEN]: Long live
    my gracious and most royal lady,
And may all enemies of England's realm
End like the Stuart!

    [SHREWSBURY *hides his face,* DAVISON *wrings his hands
    despairingly.*]

ELIZABETH: Tell us now, my lord!
Did you receive the warrant for her death
From my own hands?

BURGHLEY: No, majesty. I had it
From Davison.

ELIZABETH: Did Davison give you
The warrant in my name?

BURGHLEY: Why no, he did
Not so –

ELIZABETH: And you have had it carried out
In haste, and did not ascertain my will?
The sentence was a just one, and the world
Cannot reproach me, but it was not yours
So to prevent the mercy of our heart –
And therefore you are banished from our presence!
[*To* DAVISON]
You, sir, shall know a harsher punishment,
Who wickedly have overreached your powers,
And so betrayed a sacred royal trust.
Let him be taken to the Tower! He shall
Be tried, and for his life – it is my will!
– My noble Talbot! You alone of all
My counsellors I find are just and true.
From now on you shall be my friend and guide. –

SHREWSBURY: You should not banish your most loyal
        friends,
Nor cast those into prison who have acted
For you, and who for you now keep their silence.
– But me, most mighty queen, grant this request:

The seal that you entrusted twelve long years
To me, receive it back into your hands.
ELIZABETH [*taken aback*]: No, Shrewsbury! You will not
    leave me now,
    At such a time –
SHREWSBURY: Forgive me, I am old;
    My hand is honest, but it is too stiff
    To set the seal upon such deeds as this.
ELIZABETH: What, does the man who saved my life now wish
    To leave me?
SHREWSBURY: It is little I have done.
    I could not save your nobler self. So live,
    And reign in happiness. Your foe is dead.
    There is no more that you need fear, or care for. [*Exit.*]
        [*Enter* KENT.]
ELIZABETH: Send for my Lord of Leicester!
KENT: He regrets
    He cannot come, he is embarked for France.
        [ELIZABETH *conquers her emotions and stands calm, as the
        curtain falls.*]

PENTHESILEA

Heinrich von Kleist

A tragedy
1808

CHARACTERS

PENTHESILEA, Queen of the Amazons
PROTHOE ⎫
MEROE ⎬ Amazon princesses
ASTERIA ⎭
HIGH PRIESTESS of Diana
ACHILLES ⎫
ODYSSEUS ⎪
DIOMEDES ⎬ Kings of the Greeks
ANTILOCHUS ⎭
Greeks and Amazons

Scene: A Battlefield near Troy.

NOTE ON NAMES. Kleist varies his characters' names, as in classical epic, by the use of epithets, patronymics and other equivalents. Thus Achilles is called Aeginian, Dolopian, Peleid (son of Peleus), son of Thetis; Odysseus is called Larissan (wrongly, since it was Achilles who came from Larissa) and Laertiad (son of Laertes), and Diomedes is called son of Tydeus. The Atrides (sons of Atreus) are the Greek leaders Agamemnon and Menelaus; 'great Priam's greatest son' is Hector, son of Priam king of Troy, whom Achilles killed and dragged round the walls of Troy at his chariot-tail. The Greeks are also called Achaeans, Argives and Danaans (all of which names, like Aetolian and Myrmidon, were originally the names of individual nations or tribes), and the Trojans Dardanians and Teucrians; Ilium and Pergamon are names of Troy itself. Kleist also uses Latin and Greek equivalent names side by side: Diana/Artemis, Mars/Ares, Jupiter/Zeus, Ulysses/Odysseus.

SCENE I

[*Enter* ODYSSEUS *and* DIOMEDES *from one side,* ANTI-
LOCHUS *from the other, with soldiers.*]

ANTILOCHUS: My greetings to you, kings! How do you fare,
Since last we saw each other there at Troy?

ODYSSEUS: Badly, Antilochus. You see before you
The armies of the Greeks and Amazons,
Tearing each other like two angry wolves;
By Jupiter! they could not tell you why.
If angry Mars, or if Apollo will
Not seize his rod, or He that shakes the clouds
Will not despatch his thunderbolts to part them:
Still they are fighting, doggedly, today,
Their teeth clenched tightly in each other's throats. –
Fetch water in a helmet!

ANTILOCHUS: By the gods!
What is it that these Amazons want from us?

ODYSSEUS: We, as the sons of Atreus advised,
Set out with all the Myrmidons in force,
Achilles and myself; Penthesilea,
We heard, had risen in the Scythian forests,
And at the head of Amazonian armies,
Clad in the skins of serpents, hot for blood,
Came toiling through the mountain passes, down
To Troy, to raise the siege of Priam's city.
And on Scamander's banks we heard it said,
Deiphobus, the son of Priam, had
Set out from Ilium with men in force
To meet the queen, who came to him with help,
And greet her as a friend. Our men devour
The roads, to make a barrier between
Our foes, and to forestall this ill alliance;
All through the night we make our winding march.

But, when the morning first begins to dawn,
With what amazement then, Antilochus,
We see before us in an open valley
Deiphobus's Trojans fighting with
The horde of Amazons! Penthesilea,
As stormy winds disperse the jagged clouds,
Sweeps all the Trojan ranks away before her,
As if to scatter them beyond the sea
Of Hellespont, and from the very earth!

ANTILOCHUS: Strange, by our gods!

ODYSSEUS: We gather up our strength,
To meet the Trojans now, who come in flight
Like an attacking thunderbolt upon us;
And like a bristling wall our spears are ranged.
The son of Priam wavers at the sight,
And we in council quickly are resolved
To greet the princess of the Amazons;
She too has checked the rush of victory.
Was ever simpler, better resolution?
If I had asked Athene, could her tongue
Have whispered me more evident advice?
By Hades! after all, this maiden, there,
Who suddenly, as if from heaven, drops
Into our battle, armed for strife herself,
She must ally herself to one or other;
And we must think she comes to be our friend,
As she is hostile to the sons of Troy.

ANTILOCHUS: Of course. Why, by the Styx! what
     else?

ODYSSEUS: Well, then.
We spy her out, the Scythian conqueress,
Achilles and myself: – in warlike pomp
Planted erect before her warrior maids,
Her skirts girt up, her helmet's crest afloat;
And with a stir of gold and purple harness
Her palfrey stamps and pounds the ground beneath her.
So, for a moment with a thoughtful gaze,
She scans our army's ranks, expressionless,

As if we stood before her carved in stone;
My open hand – see here – I swear to you,
Bears more expression than her countenance;
Until she lights upon the son of Peleus.
A sudden glow, enveloping her throat,
Colours her face, as if about her head
The world were roaring up in flames of fire.
Then with a shock and quiver, down she leaps
– And angry is the look she turns on him –
Down from her horse's back to us, and asks,
Giving the bridle to a slave to hold,
What brings us to her in such splendid state.
I tell her how it gladdens Argive hearts
To meet a foe of Dardanus's race,
What hatred of the sons of Priam long
Has burned in Grecian hearts, how useful,
To her and us, alliances would be;
And anything that comes into my head.
But with astonishment, while yet I speak,
I notice that she does not hear. She turns,
With wonderment upon her face, just like
A girl of sixteen summers, suddenly,
Returning from Olympic sports, and cries
Out to a friend that stands beside her there:
O such a man as this, my Prothoe,
Otrere, my dear mother, never saw!
Her friend is silent, moved by these strange words,
Achilles eyes me with a smile, I him.
She for her part is gazing rapt again
Upon the glittering Aeginian;
Until the other, shyly drawing near,
Reminds her that she owes me still an answer.
Upon this, with that flush – of rage or shame? –
Reflected in her armour to her waist,
Confused and proud and wild at once: she was
Penthesilea – turning as she spoke –
The Queen of Amazons, and I should have
My answer sent to me from bows and quivers!

ANTILOCHUS: Thus, word for word, the messenger you sent;
But there was none in all the Grecian camp who could
Divine his meaning.

ODYSSEUS: Now, in ignorance
Of what we were to think of this encounter,
In shame and anger, we are turning home,
And see the Teucrians, guessing our disgrace,
Though from afar, and smiling in their scorn,
Gathering as in triumph. They decide,
Deluded it is they who have her favour,
And only some mistake, now realized,
Had caused the Amazons to fly at them,
That they will quickly send another herald
To offer her the friendship she despises.
But now, before their chosen messenger
Has time to shake the dust off from his armour,
Loosing her reins this female Centaur charges
Down upon us and them, on Greek and Trojan,
And like a raging torrent of the forest
Sweeps all the men on either side before her.

ANTILOCHUS: This is unheard of, Danaans!

ODYSSEUS: A fight
Begins the like of which has not been seen
On earth, not since the Furies came to reign.
As far as I have heard, in nature there
Is only force and counter-force, no third.
What puts out coals of fire does not dissolve
Water that boils in steam, nor the reverse.
But here we see a savage foe of both,
And when she strikes the fire cannot be sure
If with the water it should run, the water
If with the fire it should assault the sky.
The Trojan hurries, pressed by Amazons,
To hide behind a Grecian shield, the Greek
Delivers him from her that pressed upon him,
And now it almost seems that Greek and Trojan,
Despite the rape of Helen, must unite

In common cause against this enemy.
  [*Water is brought for him.*]
Thanks! How my throat is dry.

DIOMEDES: And since that day
  Uninterrupted rages on this plain
  The battle, ever with fresh fury, like
  A thunderstorm confined between the peaks
  Of wooded cliffs. As I came yesterday
  With the Aetolians to swell our ranks,
  She launched a new and furious attack,
  As if she would destroy the race of Greeks,
  Down to the ground, as thunder splits a tree.
  Its finest fruit lies scattered there – Ariston,
  Astyanax, plucked by the storm unripe,
  Menandros – on the battlefield, and feed
  The laurels now for Ares' reckless daughter,
  Their fine young bodies nothing more than dung.
  She took more prisoners away with her
  Than she left eyes to us to count their loss,
  Or arms to give them back their liberty.

ANTILOCHUS: And what she wants with us no man can
    guess?

DIOMEDES: No, not a soul; that's it; however we
  Have tried to probe and sound her in our thoughts.
  Often, to judge by that especial rage
  With which she seeks the son of Thetis in
  The battle, we must think that it is hate
  For him above all else that fills her breast.
  A she-wolf does not follow with such hunger,
  Through forests thickly wrapped in snow, the prey
  That she has chosen with her cruel eye,
  As she, through all our battle-ranks, Achilles.
  And yet, just now, when for a moment she
  Already held the power of his life,
  She gave it smiling back to him, a present;
  He went to Orcus, if she did not save him.

ANTILOCHUS: What? Who save him? The queen herself?
DIOMEDES: Indeed!

For when last night as darkness fell, those two,
Fighting, Penthesilea and Achilles,
Met with each other, comes Deiphobus;
And, rushing to the maiden's side himself,
The Teucrian, he strikes at Peleus' son;
His armour rattles from the cunning blow;
It echoes from the tops of elms around.
The queen turns pale, and for a moment lets
Her arms drop down; and then she shakes her locks
In rage about her cheeks of fiery red,
Then rises high above her horse's back
And plunges, as it came from heaven above,
A thunderbolt, her sword into his neck,
So that he rolls, the poor presuming wretch,
Before the feet of Thetis' godly son.
In gratitude for this, the Peleid
Would do the same for her; but crouching on
Her dapple's neck, who with his flowing mane
Champs at his golden bit and wheels about,
She ducks his blow, and gives the horse his head;
She looks around, she smiles, and she is gone.

ANTILOCHUS: How strange!

ODYSSEUS: What news have you for us from Troy?

ANTILOCHUS: I come from Agamemnon, and he asks,
  If prudence does not, now that matters stand
  So differently, urge you to retreat.
  We are concerned to breach the walls of Troy,
  Not to prevent a free princess from leading
  Her army – where, we do not seek to know.
  If you have ascertained beyond all doubt
  That it is not with help for Ilium
  Penthesilea comes, he wishes you
  At once, and cost it what it may, to throw
  Yourselves again behind the Argive lines.
  If she comes after you, then he himself,
  The son of Atreus, with his men will come
  To see what then this enigmatic sphinx
  Will do before the very face of Troy.

ODYSSEUS: By Jupiter! That is my counsel too.
  Do you believe Laertes' son can take
  The slightest pleasure in this senseless fight?
  Get him away from here, the Peleid!
  For when the mastiff bitch let off the leash
  Springs baying at the antlers of the stag,
  The anxious huntsman calls her off, but she,
  Her teeth clenched tightly in his mighty neck,
  Up hill, down dale, and through the stream beside him
  She dances through the forest night; so he,
  The madman, ever since he spied this rare
  And royal beast within the glades of war.
  Shoot arrows through his thighs, and pin him down;
  For he has sworn that he will never quit
  This Amazon's pursuit until he shall
  Have torn her by her silken locks of hair
  Down from that tiger-dappled horse she rides.
  Antilochus, try, if you have a mind,
  And see what all your eloquence and skill
  Can do with him when he is raving so.
DIOMEDES: Come, kings, and let us once again unite,
  And calmly set our reason like a wedge
  Upon this madness of determination.
  I know that you, ingenious Larissan,
  Will soon discover where it first will crack.
  If you do not succeed, then I and two
  Aetolians will lift him on our backs,
  And like the senseless block he has become
  Take him and drop him in the Argive camp.
ODYSSEUS: Follow!
ANTILOCHUS: But who is this comes running here?
DIOMEDES: It is Adrastes; see how pale he looks!

SCENE 2

  [*Enter a* CAPTAIN.]
ODYSSEUS: What do you bring?
DIOMEDES: A message?

CAPTAIN: And the worst
  Your ears have ever heard.
DIOMEDES: What?
ODYSSEUS: Speak!
CAPTAIN: Achilles –
  He has been captured by the Amazons,
  The walls of Pergamon will never fall.
DIOMEDES: Gods of Olympus!
ODYSSEUS: Bringer of ill news!
ANTILOCHUS: Say when, and how, did this disaster happen?
CAPTAIN: A new attack, that scorched like lightning blast,
  From Ares' angry daughters, laid the ranks
  Of the Aetolians before us low.
  Then like a torrent over us they poured,
  The Myrmidons, who never knew defeat.
  In vain we press against the surging wave
  Our strength; for like a raging flood it tears
  Us in a whirlpool from the battlefield.
  And not before we have been swept away,
  Far from the Peleid, can we stand firm.
  Now he at last, with spears set all about him,
  Emerges from the battle's night; he drives
  Down from a lofty hilltop, cautiously;
  He turns towards us, is approaching, we
  Already greet him with our joyful cry;
  But our rejoicing dies within our breast
  When suddenly his chariot-horses shy
  Before a precipice, and from the clouds
  Above look down into a giddy deep.
  They rear; in vain he shows his mastery
  Of every practice of the Isthmian art;
  The frightened team of horses turn their heads
  Against the whip, and tangle up the harness,
  And crashing down with chariot and horses,
  The son of our own gods lies in the wreck,
  As if he had been captured in a snare.
ANTILOCHUS: The madman! But where was he –
CAPTAIN: Now there comes

Automedon, the nimble charioteer,
Leaping into the tangle of the horses;
He helps the four upon their feet again.
But while he struggles still to free their legs
Out of the knots and twistings of the harness,
The queen already charges with a horde
Of Amazons victorious through the rocks
And bars him every way to his salvation.

ANTILOCHUS: Olympians!

CAPTAIN: She checks, in clouds of dust,
The palfrey's charge, and lifting to the peak
Her face all sparkling, scans the mountain wall;
Her helmet's crest itself, as if affrighted,
Seems to rear up and pull her down again.
Then suddenly she lays the reins aside;
We see her, swift as if she feared to faint,
Pressing her forehead in her slender hands
Beneath the flowing locks of silken hair.
At this strange sight her maidens stand amazed;
They crowd about her, gesturing and pleading;
The one that seems the nearest kin to her
Puts her own arm about her, while another,
More resolute, would seize the horse's reins;
By force they seek to keep her from pursuit,
But she –

DIOMEDES: What, dare she?

ANTILOCHUS: Tell us!

CAPTAIN: You shall hear.
In vain is their attempt to hold her back;
With gentle strength she presses them away
On either side, and, trotting nervously
Along the rocky valleys, up and down,
She looks if there is not some narrow path
By which a wish might climb that had no wings;
Then like a woman raving mad we see
Her clambering upon the rocky walls,
Now here, in fiery longing and desire,
Now there, in yet more senseless hope to reach

By such a route the prey that lies enmeshed.
Now every gentler valley she has tried
That in the cliffs the rain has washed away;
She sees the precipice cannot be scaled;
And yet as if bereft of reason turns
And starts to climb again from the beginning.
In truth, she ventures tireless upon paths
Where never wanderer would set his foot;
Climbs nearer to the mountain's highest ridge
An elm-tree's height; and now she stands upon
A block of granite, barely large enough
Its surface for a mountain antelope,
Repulsed by jagged rocks on every side,
Forward or backward cannot move a step;
The women's cry of terror fills the air;
She plunges suddenly, upon her horse,
Amidst the clatter of an avalanche,
As if she rode to Orcus, crashing down
Back to the very bottom of the cliff –
And neither breaks her neck, nor learns good sense;
She only gathers strength to climb again.

ANTILOCHUS: O, this hyena in her mindless rage!

ODYSSEUS: What of Automedon?

CAPTAIN: At last he leaps –
Chariot and horses set to rights again –
Though in the time Hephaestus almost could
Have forged a whole new chariot of bronze –
Leaps in the driver's seat, and takes the reins;
A weight is lifted from our Argive hearts.
But even now, just as he turns the horses,
The Amazons at last espy a path
That gently climbs the peak, and cry aloud,
Filling the valley with their wild rejoicing,
To call their queen, who in her madness still
Attempts to climb the rocky precipice.
Upon the word, she, reining in her horse,
Explores the pathway with a rapid glance,
And like the supple panther follows where

Her glance has led; meanwhile, the Peleid,
True, with his horses made a swift withdrawal,
But in the valleys soon escaped my view,
And what became of him I do not know.

ANTILOCHUS: Lost, he must be!

DIOMEDES: Come, friends, what shall we do?

ODYSSEUS: Obey the order of our heart, you kings!
Come! Let us go, and save him from the queen!
And though it were a battle to the death,
I'll answer for it to the Atrides.

SCENE 3

[*Exeunt* ODYSSEUS, DIOMEDES *and* ANTILOCHUS.
Meanwhile a party of GREEKS *have climbed a hill.*]

A MYRMIDON [*looking into the distance*]:
Look! do you see, above that mountain ridge,
The head of – is it not? a man in armour,
A helmet with a lofty feathered crest?
The neck, the powerful, that bears it up?
The shoulders and the arms, in shining steel?
The breast, the body, look, O look, my friends,
The waist encircled by its belt of gold?

CAPTAIN: But whose?

MYRMIDON: But whose! O Argives, do I dream?
And now the heads, each with its blaze of white,
Of chariot horses! Nothing but their legs,
Their hoofs, still hidden by the mountain top!
And now on the horizon, chariot
And team entire are there! Just as the sun
In glory rises on a fair spring day!

THE GREEKS: Triumph! Achilles, see! Son of the gods!
Driving himself the four-horse chariot!
He is delivered!

CAPTAIN: Great Olympians!
Eternal fame be yours for this! – Odysseus!
– Fly, one of you, and find the Argive princes!
Is he approaching, Danaans?

MYRMIDON: O look!
CAPTAIN: What is it?
MYRMIDON: Captain, o it takes my breath!
CAPTAIN: Speak then!
MYRMIDON: O see, how his left hand flies out
    And swings the whip above his horses' backs!
    How, urged along as by its very sound,
    Beasts fit for gods to drive, they pound the earth!
    How in the harness, by the living Zeus,
    They draw the chariot with steaming breath!
    The flight of hunted stags is not so swift.
    The whirling spokes cut off the eye that seeks
    To look beyond the wheels, the flying discs!
AN AETOLIAN: And yet, behind him –
CAPTAIN: What?
MYRMIDON: There, on the ridge –
AETOLIAN: Dust –
MYRMIDON: Dust like swirling thunderclouds arising!
    And like the lightning flash –
AETOLIAN: Eternal gods!
MYRMIDON: Penthesilea.
CAPTAIN: Who?
AETOLIAN: The queen it is!
    Hot on the heels of Peleus' son she flies,
    With all her band of women following.
CAPTAIN: Raging Megaera!
GREEKS [calling]:   Come, this way your course!
    This way, divine Achilles, set your course!
    Your course to us!
AETOLIAN: See how between her thighs
    She clasps her tiger horse with furious passion!
    How leaning forward, clinging to his mane,
    She drinks with greedy gulps the air that checks her!
    She flies as if the bowstring sped her on;
    Swifter than arrows of Numidia!
    Her army pants along behind like curs
    That cannot match the mastiff when she speeds!
    Her helmet's crest can scarcely keep her pace!

CAPTAIN: Does she draw near?

A DOLOPIAN: Draws near!

MYRMIDON: Draws near – not yet!

DOLOPIAN: Draws near to him, you Greeks! With every
    beat
Of hoofs she swallows as if hunger-crazed
The yards that keep her from the Peleid!

MYRMIDON: By all the gods above that do protect us!
Already she draws level with him now!
Already breathes the dust, borne in the wind,
That he stirs up in all too sluggish flight!
The wind-swift palfrey that she rides throws up
The clods of earth he scatters in his course
Back on the floor of his own chariot!

AETOLIAN: And now – this is not courage, this is madness!
He steers a curve, as if in sport – Take care!
The Amazon will cut him off –

MYRMIDON: Zeus, help us!
Already at his side she flies! Her shadow,
Gigantic in the morning sun, already
Devours him!

AETOLIAN: See, but suddenly he swings –

DOLOPIAN: Swings all four horses suddenly about
And comes this way!

AETOLIAN: He flies towards us now!

MYRMIDON: Ha, this is cunning! How he tricked her!

DOLOPIAN: Ho!
How she unchecked in her assault shoots past
The chariot –

MYRMIDON: Collides, leaps in the saddle,
And stumbles –

DOLOPIAN: Falls!

CAPTAIN: What?

MYRMIDON: Falls! The queen is down!
And now a maiden, blindly, over her –

DOLOPIAN: And now one more –

MYRMIDON: Another –

DOLOPIAN: And another –

CAPTAIN: What, friends, they fall?

DOLOPIAN: They fall!

MYRMIDON: They fall, my captain!
  As in a furnace melted down together,
  All in a heap, the horses and their riders!

CAPTAIN: Would they were burnt to ashes!

DOLOPIAN: Dust about them,
  The glint of armour through the clouds, and weapons;
  The eye can see no more, however keen.
  A knot, a twisted knot of warrior maids,
  With horses tangled in it; Chaos, when
  The world was first formed out of it, was clearer.

AETOLIAN: But now – a wind; they see the light again.
  One of the maidens scrambles to her feet.

DOLOPIAN: Ha! How they stir themselves to life again,
  See how they seek their helmets and their spears,
  Scattered about the field on every side!

MYRMIDON: Three horses still, and one horsewoman lie
  Stretched out, as they were dead –

CAPTAIN: Is it the queen?

AETOLIAN: Penthesilea, do you mean?

MYRMIDON: The queen?
  – O that my eyes refused to see this sight!
  There she is!

DOLOPIAN: Where?

CAPTAIN: No, tell us!

MYRMIDON: There, by Zeus,
  Where she had fallen, in that oak-tree's shadow!
  I see her clutching at her horse's neck,
  Her head is bare – her helmet on the ground.
  See how with feeble hand she pulls her locks,
  Wipes – is it dust or blood? – upon her brow.

DOLOPIAN: You gods, it is her!

CAPTAIN: Indestructible!

AETOLIAN: That headlong fall had killed a cat; not her!

CAPTAIN: And Peleus' son?

DOLOPIAN: Him all the gods protect!
  Three arrow-shots away he sped beyond her,

Her eye can scarcely reach him any more;
Even her thoughts, pursuing without cease,
Are halted in her breathless bosom now!

MYRMIDON: Triumph! See where Odysseus now advances!
The army of the Greeks, beneath the sun,
Suddenly from the forest's night strides forth!

CAPTAIN: Odysseus? Diomedes too? O gods!
– How far off is he still upon the field?

DOLOPIAN: Hardly a stone's throw, captain! On the heights
Above Scamander see his chariot flies;
Where rapidly the army is drawn up.
Along the ranks he thunders now –

VOICES [*from the distance*]: Hail, hail!

DOLOPIAN: They cry to him, the Argive host –

VOICES: Hail, hail!
Achilles! Son of gods! Hail, Peleid!
Hail, hail, Achilles, hail!

DOLOPIAN: He checks his course!
Before the Argive princes gathered there
He checks his course! Odysseus welcomes him!
Down from his seat, covered in dust, he springs!
He lays aside the reins! He turns around!
Takes off the helmet that weighs down his head!
And all the kings are gathered round about him!
The Greeks with cries of exultation bear
Him on, and swarm in throngs about his knees;
While, step by step, Automedon leads on
The horses, steaming in the sun, beside him!
Here comes the whole triumphant throng already
Upon us! Hail to you, o son of gods!
O look, o look upon him – here he is!

SCENE 4

[*Enter* ACHILLES, ODYSSEUS, DIOMEDES, ANTILO-
CHUS, AUTOMEDON *with the quadriga, and the* GREEK
ARMY.]

ODYSSEUS: With all my heart, o hero of Aegina,

I greet you! Victor even while in flight!
By Jupiter! If you, behind your back,
By virtue of your spirit's greater strength,
Cast in the dust your enemy, what then,
When once, divine Achilles, you succeed
At last in meeting with her face to face!

ACHILLES [*he holds his helmet in his hand, and is wiping the
sweat from his forehead. Without his noticing,* TWO GREEKS
have taken hold of his arm, which is wounded, and are bandaging it]:
What is it? What's the matter?

ANTILOCHUS: You have been,
O son of Thetis, victor in a trial
Of speed, a struggle such as storms of thunder,
That roar afar across the plane of heaven,
Have never shown to the astonished world.
Now, by the Furies! From my guilt I should
Be able with your flying team to flee,
If on my heavy creaking way through life
My breast had taken up to bear the load
Of all the sins of Ilium's citadel.

ACHILLES [*to the* TWO GREEKS, *who seem to be annoying him
with their attentions*]: Fools.

ONE OF THE PRINCES: Who?

ACHILLES: Why bother me –

FIRST GREEK [*binding up his arm*]:   But you are bleeding!

ACHILLES: O, well.

SECOND GREEK: Then stay.

FIRST GREEK: Then let us bind it up.

SECOND GREEK: See, soon we shall be done.

DIOMEDES: At first we heard
My men by their retreat had made you take
This sudden flight; as I was occupied
Here, with Ulysses, and Antilochus
Who brought a message from the Atrides,
I was not present at the scene myself.
But everything I see now has convinced me
This masterly display sprang from your own
Determined plan. Yes, one might even wonder

If at the dawn, while all the rest of us
Began to arm ourselves to fight this battle,
You had already chosen on which stone
The queen in her pursuit should trip and fall;
So surely, by the everlasting gods,
Did you to that same boulder lead her on.

ODYSSEUS: But now, Dolopian hero, may we hope,
If you do not prefer another plan,
That you will seek with us the Argive camp.
The sons of Atreus urge us to return;
With feigned retreat we shall attempt to draw
Them on into the valley of Scamander,
Where Agamemnon, in an ambuscade,
Prepares to meet them in decisive battle.
There, by the Thunderer! or not at all,
You'll slake this thirst that drives you ever onward,
Hunting you like a stag, relentlessly;
And you shall have my blessing in that hour,
For hateful to me, loathsome to the death,
This Harpy sweeps, destroying all our work,
About this battlefield, and I for one
Would gladly, I confess it, see your foot
Imprinted on her fair and rosy cheek.

ACHILLES [*noticing the horses*]:
They're sweating.

ANTILOCHUS: Who?

AUTOMEDON [*feeling their necks with his hand*]:
                    Like lead.

ACHILLES: Good. Take them, then,
And when the air has cooled them off, wash down
Their chests for them and both their flanks with wine.

AUTOMEDON: Here are the skins already.

DIOMEDES: You will see
That we are fighting at a disadvantage.
Covered as far as sharpest eyes can see
With bands of women all the hills around;
Not locusts on a field of ripened corn
Were ever seen to light more thickly down.

Was ever victory an easy thing?
Is there another man but you can say
He even caught a glimpse of her, this centaur?
Useless for us, in shining golden armour,
To make advance, proclaim our princely rank
To her with noisy trumpets' brazen clang;
She will not budge from her assured position;
And who would hear, borne on the distant wind,
Even the echo of her silver tongue,
Must first have fought a doubtful, furtive battle,
That brings no glory, with the scattered bands
By whom, like dogs at hell-gate, she is guarded.

ACHILLES [*gazing into the distance*]:
Is she still there?

DIOMEDES: You ask – ?

ANTILOCHUS: Is it the queen?

CAPTAIN: Nothing to see. Make way! These helmets,
    down!

FIRST GREEK [*binding* ACHILLES' *arm*]:
Wait, just a moment.

ONE OF THE PRINCES: There, why yes, indeed!

DIOMEDES: Where?

THE PRINCE: By the oak-tree, there just where
    she fell.
Her crest once more is waving from her head,
She seems to have won through her pain.

FIRST GREEK: At last!

SECOND GREEK: Now you can use your arm just as you
    will.

FIRST GREEK: You can go now. [*They tie one more knot,
    then let his arm go.*]

ODYSSEUS: Did you hear, son of Peleus,
What we have said to you?

ACHILLES: Have said to me?
No, nothing. Why, what do you want?

ODYSSEUS: – We want?
Strange, this! – The orders we were telling you
Of Atreus' sons! The will of Agamemnon

Is, we return straight to the Grecian camp;
Antilochus he sent – look, do you see him? –
To tell us of the generals' decision.
The plan of battle is, the Amazon
Should be enticed before the walls of Troy,
Where she, once in between the hostile armies,
And driven on by urgent circumstance,
Must now declare herself, whose friend she be;
We then, be her decision what it may,
We at the least shall know what we must do.
I trust you have the wisdom, Peleid,
To follow with us in this prudent plan.
For it would be insane, by all the gods,
When urgent summons calls us on to Troy,
To waste our time in fighting with these women,
Before we know, *what* do they want of us,
Or *is* there anything they want of us?

ACHILLES [*putting his helmet on again*]:
Go then, and fight like eunuchs, if you will;
I feel I am a man, and with these women
I will do battle, if I stand alone!
Whether you stay beneath these shady pines,
Helpless, evading her attack, or not,
Far from the battle when it rages round her,
Is no concern of mine; for, by the Styx,
I would not stop you going back to Troy.
But what she wants of me I know full well;
She sends me messengers of love, swift-feathered,
In plenty through the air, to whisper in
My ear of her desires with notes of death.
In all my life I never yet was bashful;
Since first my beard grew, why, my friends, you know
No beauty looked on me with hopes in vain;
And if this one so far has not been met,
It is, by Zeus the Thunderer, because
I could not find a quiet and bushy place
To take her, even as her heart would wish,
And on this fiery bed of brass embrace her.

Go; in the Grecian camp I will be with you;
These tender moments are not far off now.
But should it be for months and months again,
For years, that I must woo her; not before
Will I drive back my chariot to my friends,
I swear it, nor return to Pergamon,
No, not before I have made her my bride,
And she, her forehead decked with wounds of death,
Drags headlong through the streets of Troy with me!
Follow!

[*Enter a* GREEK SOLDIER.]

SOLDIER: Penthesilea is at hand!

ACHILLES: I too. Is she astride the Persian horse?

SOLDIER: Not yet. On foot she is approaching us,
But at her side the Persian paws the ground.

ACHILLES: Good! Then a horse for me as well, my friends!
Come, my brave Myrmidons, and follow me!

[*The army breaks up.*]

ANTILOCHUS: The madman!

ODYSSEUS: Why then, will you try and use
Your eloquence, Antilochus, upon him?

ANTILOCHUS: But let us see what force –

DIOMEDES: No, he is gone!

ODYSSEUS: Curses upon this Amazon campaign! [*Exeunt*
GREEKS.]

SCENE 5

[*Enter* PENTHESILEA, PROTHOE, MEROE, ASTERIA *and
retinue; the* AMAZON ARMY.]

THE AMAZONS: Hail, conqueror! Victorious! Hail and
triumph!
Queen of the festival of roses, hail!

PENTHESILEA: No triumph and no festival of roses!
The fight calls me once more into the field.
That young defiant war-god I will conquer,
My comrades, for ten thousand suns would seem,

All melted in a ball of fire, to me
Never so fine as victory over him.

PROTHOE: Dearest, I beg of you –

PENTHESILEA: Leave me alone!
You hear my resolution; sooner would
You stem the flood that pours from mountain tops
Than calm the thunders rolling in my heart.
I at my feet will see him ground to dust,
Foolhardy man, who on this glorious day
Of war and victory, like none before,
Disturbs the pride of battle in my heart.
Is this the conqueror, the terrible,
The Queen of Amazons, that now I see,
When I draw near to him, reflected in
The gleaming plates of bronze that guard his breast?
Do I not feel, accursed of all the gods,
When Grecian soldiers flee on every side,
That I am crippled by this one man's sight
As if I had been dealt a deadly blow?
I, I the vanquished, I the one to fall?
Where then should I, that have no bosom, find
In me the feeling that can conquer me?
Into the battle's turmoil I will plunge,
Where he, contemptuously smiling, waits
For me, and conquer him, or will not live!

PROTHOE: If you would lay your head, my dearest queen,
Upon this faithful bosom here and rest!
Your fall, that bruised your breast with violence,
Has set your blood on fire, confused your mind;
Why, see how all your youthful limbs are trembling!
Decide on nothing, we implore you all,
Until your spirit has returned in calm.
Come, sit by me and rest a little while.

PENTHESILEA: Why? What has happened? What? What did
   I say?
Did I – What have I done?

PROTHOE: For this one conquest,
This one temptation to your youthful soul,

341

You would begin the battle all anew?
Because some wish, I know not what, remains
Deep in your heart unsatisfied, you'd throw
Away, just like a moody child, the blessing
The gods have sent to crown your people's prayers?

PENTHESILEA: Ah, see! My curses fall on this day's
    fortune!
How on this day with spiteful destiny
These my own soul's most precious friends conspire
To injure me and do my heart offence!
If ever but my hand in eagerness,
When fame comes flying by me in his course,
Would snatch him by his golden locks of hair,
My way is barred by this malicious power –
And in my soul defiance, enmity!
Away!

PROTHOE [aside]: O all you gods above, protect her!

PENTHESILEA: Is it myself, my wishes then alone
That call me back upon the battlefield?
The people, is it not, and the destruction
That in the frenzied joy of victory,
With wing-beats loud to hear, comes from afar?
How can it be that in the afternoon
We rest already, as if we had done?
Our harvest reaped and bound up into sheaves,
Bounteous crop, lies piled high to the skies;
But yet there hover evil clouds above us,
Threatening with a flash of swift destruction.
This band of Grecian youths that you have conquered,
You will not lead them, garlanded with flowers,
With joyous sound of trumpets and of cymbals,
Back to the fragrant valleys of your home.
Wherever there is chance of treachery
And ambush, there I see the Peleid
Leap out upon your gay, rejoicing train;
Pursue you and your band of prisoners
Up to the ramparts of Themiscyra;
Yes, in the very temple of Diana,

Tear off the chains of roses from their limbs
And fetter ours with heavy links of bronze.
Am I to draw back now from mad pursuit,
I, now, who while the sun did rise and sink
Five times in sweat, so nearly brought him low?
When from a single stroke he soon must fall,
As by the wind, beneath my horses' hooves,
Blown down, a rare ripe fruit, upon the ground?
No, if what I so nobly have begun,
So great, do not accomplish, if I do
Not grasp the wreath that brushes at my brow,
If I do not, as I have promised, lead
Mars' daughters joyous to the peak of glory,
Then let his pyramid bring crashing down
Utter destruction upon me and them!
I curse the tender heart that cannot wait.

PROTHOE: This fearful glitter in your eye, my queen,
I never saw, and black my thoughts are stirred,
As if arisen from eternal night,
To tumult and foreboding in my breast.
The army that your soul so strangely fears
Fled on all sides like chaff before the wind;
Hardly a spear-point is there to be seen.
Achilles, by this placing of your army,
Is quite cut off here from Scamander's banks;
Do not provoke him more; evade his sight;
Then he will turn, I swear by Jupiter,
His step once more into the Grecian camp.
I, I will guard the army's flank for you.
See, by the gods of great Olympus, not
One captive shall he rescue from you! All
The glitter, even far-off, of his arms
Shall not affright your army, nor his horses
Disturb the laughter of one maiden here;
With my own head I'll be your surety!

PENTHESILEA [*turning suddenly to* ASTERIA]:
Can this be done, Asteria?

ASTERIA: My mistress —

PENTHESILEA: Can I, as Prothoe demands, lead back
  My army to Themiscyra? Come, say.

ASTERIA: Forgive, if for my part, o my princess –

PENTHESILEA: Speak openly, I say!

PROTHOE: If you would ask
  Of your princesses here assembled counsel,
  All of them –

PENTHESILEA: *This* one's counsel I would know!
  What is become of me, in these few hours?
    [*Pause, she calms herself.*]
  – Can I lead back, tell me, Asteria,
  The army, can I lead it home again?

ASTERIA: If it should be your will, o mistress, let
  Me tell you how the sight amazes me,
  That greets my unbelieving senses here.
  With my own nation from the Caucasus
  Later set out one circuit of the sun,
  I could not catch your army as it sped
  Before me like a torrent from the hills.
  No, not until this morning, as you know,
  Did I arrive, prepared for battle, here;
  And from a thousand throats the cry goes up
  To greet me, that the victory is won;
  Concluded, all we sought already gained,
  The Amazons' campaign. With greatest joy,
  I do assure you, that your people's prayers
  Had been, without my aid, so swiftly answered,
  I make my preparations to return;
  But yet for curiosity I go
  To see the band acclaimed the prize of war;
  And slaves, a handful, pale and quivering,
  Dregs of the Greeks, are all that meet my eye;
  Swept up in jubilation by your forces
  Upon the shields they had thrown down in flight.
  Before the mighty walls of Troy there stands
  The Hellenes' army still, stands Agamemnon,
  Ajax and Palamedes, Menelaus;
  Antilochus, Ulysses, Diomede,

They stand there still, and laugh before your face,
Yes, that young son of Peleus and of Thetis,
Who by your hand with roses should be decked,
He dares with reckless courage still to spite you;
He'll set his foot – so loudly he proclaims –
With armoured step upon your royal neck;
And Ares' noble daughter asks of me
If she may celebrate the victory?

PROTHOE [*passionately*]: O, you are false! Before the queen
    there sank
Such heroes, noble, brave and handsome –

PENTHESILEA: Silence!
Asteria feels as I, there is but one
Fit here to sink before me; and that one,
There is he in the field defiant still!

PROTHOE: O noble mistress, you will not permit
This passion –

PENTHESILEA: Viper! Hold your spiteful tongue!
Or would you dare to face your queen in anger!
Away!

PROTHOE: I dare the anger of my queen!
O let me never see your face again
If in this moment cowardly I stand
A traitress and a flatterer beside you.
This fiery passion cannot make you fit
To lead the maidens on in their campaign;
No more than is the lion to meet the spears,
When he has drunk the huntsman's cunning poison.
No, you will not, by the eternal gods,
Conquer the son of Peleus in this temper;
Rather before the sun has set, I swear it,
Be sure to see the youths our arms have conquered,
The prize of so much bravery and toil,
By this your madness lost to us again.

PENTHESILEA: This is so strange, I do not understand!
What makes you suddenly a coward?

PROTHOE: What – ?

PENTHESILEA: Who was it that you conquered, say?

PROTHOE: Lycaon,
  The youthful prince of the Arcadians.
  I think you saw him.
PENTHESILEA: Yes. Was that the one
  That stood crestfallen, trembling, when I went
  To see the captives yesterday –
PROTHOE: He, trembling!
  He stood as firm as ever Peleus' son!
  In battle by my arrows sorely wounded,
  He sank before my feet, and proudly I
  Will lead him at the festival of roses,
  Proudly into the temple of our god.
PENTHESILEA: Indeed? How taken with him you must
    be.
  Well then – why, he shall not be torn from you!
  – Take from the band of prisoners Lycaon,
  Him, the Arcadian, and bring him here!
  – Take him, unwarlike maiden, flee from here,
  So that you do not lose him, go away,
  Far from the noise of battle, hide yourselves
  Beneath the scented lilac-blossom's shade,
  In distant mountain valleys, where with sweet
  Lascivious song the nightingale will greet you,
  And celebrate the festival of lust
  Your tender soul impatiently desires.
  But never come before my face again,
  Be banished from my capital, and let
  Your paramour console you with his kisses,
  When you have lost all else, your motherland,
  Your honour and your love, your queen, your friend.
  Go and release – I do not want to hear! –
  Release me from the hateful sight of you!
MEROE: O queen!
ANOTHER PRINCESS: What are these words?
PENTHESILEA: Silence, I say!
  I swear revenge, if any speak for her!
    [*Enter an* AMAZON.]
THE AMAZON: Achilles is approaching, noble mistress!

PENTHESILEA: He comes! – To battle, then, my maidens,
  on!
Give me the spear that's surest of its mark,
The sword whose blade vies with the lightning-flash!
This joy, o gods, it must be granted me,
In victory to trample in the dust
This youth, so hotly longed for, at my feet.
Then I will give up every happiness
That destiny has fashioned for my life.
– Asteria! You shall command the armies.
See that the Greeks are occupied, and do
Not let the battle reach me with its tumult.
Of all you maids not one, who she may be,
May strike the Peleid herself! An arrow waits,
Sharpened with death, for any who would touch
His head – what do I say? – one lock of hair!
I, I alone can fell the son of gods.
This steel you see, my comrades, it shall be,
That with the tenderest embrace shall draw
Him (since it *must* be an embrace of steel!)
To rest upon my bosom, without pain.
Bear up, you blossoms of the spring, his fall,
That of his limbs not one shall come to harm.
My own heart's blood I'd rather shed than his.
I will not rest until I have brought down
This bird of gorgeous plumage from the skies;
But if, you maidens, I may see him lie
With broken pinions at my feet, but with
No drop of purple essence spilt, why, then
May all the blessed ones above descend
To us, to celebrate our victory;
Then home rejoicing we will go, then I
Will crown for you the festival of roses!
Now come!
  [*About to go, she sees* PROTHOE *weeping, and turns away, in
  agitation. Then suddenly she falls about* PROTHOE'*s neck.*]
        O Prothoe! My soul's own sister!
Will you come with me?

PROTHOE: To the depths of Orcus!
  Could I go to Elysium without you?
PENTHESILEA: O, finer than all mortals! You will come?
  Then we will fight and conquer side by side,
  We both, or neither, and the cry shall be:
  Pluck roses to adorn our heroes' brows,
  Or cypresses to cover up our own. [*Exeunt omnes.*]

SCENE 6

[*Enter the* HIGH PRIESTESS *of Diana, with* PRIEST-
ESSES, *followed by* GIRLS *with baskets of roses on their heads,
and the* GREEK PRISONERS, *led by* AMAZON WARRIORS.]

HIGH PRIESTESS: Come now, you sweet rose-maidens, let
        me see
  What fruits your wanderings have borne today.
  Here where this lonely mountain spring bursts forth,
  Beneath this pine-tree's shadow, we are safe;
  And you may tip your harvest out before me.
FIRST GIRL [*tipping out her basket*]:
  These roses here are mine, o holy mother!
SECOND GIRL [*likewise*]: And here this lapful mine!
THIRD GIRL: And here are mine!
FOURTH GIRL: And here, a whole spring's crop of
        blossoms, mine!
  [*The others follow.*]
HIGH PRIESTESS: Why, this is like the summit of Hymetta!
  A day of blessings never, o Diana!
  Like this was seen before, by all your people.
  The mothers bring me, and the daughters, gifts;
  This twofold glory dazzles me; I do
  Not know which have deserved the greater thanks.
  But is this all you have to bring me, children?
FIRST GIRL: No more than now you see were to be found.
HIGH PRIESTESS: Then I must say your mothers have
        sought harder.
SECOND GIRL: On these fields, holy priestess, truly are
  More captives to be gathered in than roses.

When thickly on the hills on every side
The young Greeks stand like corn, awaiting but
The sickle of the eager reaping-maid,
In valleys round about so sparsely blooms,
I swear, the rose, and girt with such defence
That rather might one fight through spears and arrows,
Than battle through the fearsome mesh of thorns.
– O look upon my fingers here, I beg!

THIRD GIRL: Upon a beetling rock I dared to step,
Only to pluck for you a single rose,
Where palely through the leaves of darkest green
I saw it gleaming, but a tender bud,
And for the joys of love not blossomed yet;
But I would pluck it; suddenly I slip
And fall into a deep abyss, the night
Of death I thought had wrapped about my head.
But it was my good fortune, for a blaze
Of roses here in bloom I found, enough
To celebrate ten victories again!

FOURTH GIRL: I plucked for you, Diana's great priestess,
I plucked for you one rose alone, but one;
But such a rose it is, o look and see!
Fit to adorn the temples of a king;
No finer rose desires Penthesilea
When she brings home Achilles, son of gods.

HIGH PRIESTESS: It shall be so; Penthesilea, when
She brings him home, shall have this royal rose.
Keep it then carefully, until she comes.

FIRST GIRL: But when in years to come the cymbals call
The army of the Amazons to war,
We shall go with them, but no more, o promise,
Only to pick our roses and to wind
Our garlands for our mothers' victory.
See, my arm throws the javelin already,
And with the whirling sling I strike my mark;
Why, for myself a wreath of roses blooms,
– And may he well acquit himself in battle,
The youth for whom it is I draw my bow.

HIGH PRIESTESS: Do you think so? – But you must
    know, indeed.
  – And have you picked your roses then already?
  – Next spring when once they blossom forth again,
  You shall in battle seek your young man out.
  But now your mothers' eager hearts rejoice:
  These roses quickly gather into garlands!

THE GIRLS [*all together*]: Come, to our task! How may we
    best begin?

FIRST GIRL [*to* SECOND]:
  Come here, Glaucothoe!

THIRD GIRL [*to* FOURTH]: Come, Charmion!
   [*They sit down in pairs.*]

FIRST GIRL: We weave this wreath of roses for – Ornythia,
  Who won Alcestis, with his lofty crest.

THIRD GIRL: This, sisters, for – Parthenion, to bind
  Her Athenaeus of the Gorgon shield.

HIGH PRIESTESS [*to the* AMAZON WARRIORS]:
  Come now, will you not entertain your guests?
  Why, do not stand so helpless there, you maidens,
  As if you still must learn the ways of love!
  Will you not venture them a friendly word?
  Not hear what they, exhausted from the battle,
  Would ask of you? Their wishes? What they lack?

FIRST AMAZON WARRIOR: They say that they want
    nothing, lofty one.

SECOND: We feel their anger.

THIRD: When we go to them,
  Defiantly they turn away in scorn.

HIGH PRIESTESS: If they are angry with you, by our
    goddess,
  Then make them friends again! Why did you have
  To strike them with such violence in battle?
  Tell them what is to happen, to console them;
  They will no longer be unyielding then.

FIRST AMAZON WARRIOR [*to one of the* GREEK PRISONERS]:
  O noble youth, will you not rest your limbs
  On carpets soft? Shall I not make a couch

Of flowers of spring for you who seem so weary,
Beneath the shadow of the laurel tree?
SECOND AMAZON [*similarly*]:
Shall I not mix you sweetest Persian oils
In water fresh-drawn from the clearest spring,
To bathe your dusty and exhausted feet?
THIRD: You will not scorn the juice of oranges
I bring you with a tender, loving hand?
ALL THREE: Speak! Tell us! What then may we bring you?
ONE OF THE GREEKS: Nothing!
FIRST AMAZON: You strangers, why this angry bitterness?
Why, now our arrows rest within the quiver,
Do you still turn in horror from our sight?
Is it our lionskins that frighten you?
You, with the belt! Speak, tell us what you fear.
THE GREEK [*after a searching look at her*]:
Who is it that those wreaths are made for? Say!
FIRST AMAZON: Why, you! Who else?
THE GREEK: And that you say to us?
Inhuman creatures! Will you lead us on
In flowers wreathed like beasts to sacrifice?
FIRST AMAZON: To Artemis we lead you, to her temple!
What do you think? To her dark oaken grove,
Where joys beyond all measure shall be yours!
THE GREEK [*astonished, in a low voice to the other* PRISONERS]:
Was ever dream so strange as here the truth?

SCENE 7

[*Enter an* AMAZON CAPTAIN.]
CAPTAIN: Here in this place I find you, o great priestess!
While yet the army, but a stone's throw distant,
Prepares for bloody and decisive battle!
HIGH PRIESTESS: The army? Where? It cannot be!
CAPTAIN: Below,
There in the valleys that Scamander carved.
Give ear to what the wind bears from the hills;
A voice of thunder you can hear, the queen's,

The clash of weapons drawn, the neigh of horses,
The trumpet, bugle, clarion and cymbal,
And all the brazen tongues that speak of war.

A PRIESTESS: Who quickly now will climb that hill?

THE GIRLS: I! I!
   [*They climb the hill.*]

HIGH PRIESTESS: The queen's voice! Tell me, I cannot
       believe it! –
   Why, when the battle had not run its course,
   Did she command the festival of roses?

CAPTAIN: The festival? – Did she give word – to whom?

HIGH PRIESTESS: To me!

CAPTAIN: Where, when?

HIGH PRIESTESS: A minute past,
   I stood in shade beneath that obelisk,
   When Peleus' son, and she upon his heels,
   Swift as the winds themselves, sped by before me.
   How does it go? I asked her as she flew.
   'Why, I am going to the festival!'
   She cried, and whirled on still rejoicing past me,
   'Let roses not be lacking, holy mother!'

FIRST PRIESTESS [*to the* GIRLS *on the hill*]:
   Speak, do you see her?

THE GIRLS: Nothing, we see nothing!
   No, not a single crest can be distinguished.
   The shadow of a thundercloud is spread
   Over the fields around; we only hear
   Armed warriors in confusion pressing on,
   Seeking each other on the field of death.

SECOND PRIESTESS: Surely she seeks to cover our retreat.

FIRST: I think so too.

CAPTAIN: No, armed for deadly battle,
   I tell you, grim to meet the Peleid,
   The queen stands fresh as her own Persian horse,
   That rears up skywards as it bears her on.
   Brighter than ever now her eyes they flash,
   Now jubilant and free she draws her breath,
   As if her proud young warrior's bosom had

Not known the air of battlefields before.

HIGH PRIESTESS: By the Olympians, what will she do?
What is it, now that in their thousands all
About us here the captives fill the forests,
She lacks to make her victory complete?

CAPTAIN: – She lacks to make her victory complete?

GIRLS [*on the hill*]: O gods!

FIRST PRIESTESS: What is it? Is the shadow gone?

FIRST GIRL: O holy ones, come here!

SECOND PRIESTESS: But tell us what –

CAPTAIN: – She lacks to make her victory complete?

FIRST GIRL: O see, o see, how through the thunderclouds
The sun comes streaming forth in brilliance bright
To shed its light upon the Peleid!

HIGH PRIESTESS: On whom?

FIRST GIRL: On him, I said! Upon what
    other?
High on a hilltop shining there he stands,
His horse is cased in steel and he – the sapphire,
The chrysolite shed not such radiant beams!
The earth around, with all its bloom and colour,
Is hidden still in black and stormy night;
A sombre background only and a foil
To show him glorious like a single jewel!

HIGH PRIESTESS: What business is the Peleid of ours?
– Does it become a daughter of great Mars,
O queen, to take her stand upon a name?
    [*To one of the* AMAZONS]
Go with all haste, Arsinoe, before her,
And tell her in the name of Artemis,
That Mars has shown himself to these his brides;
And by Her anger whom I serve, I charge her
To take him back with garlands to our home,
And straightway in her temple to begin
The festival of roses in his honour!
    [*Exit* ARSINOE.]
Was ever of such madness heard as this?

FIRST PRIESTESS: You children! Can you not yet see the queen?

FIRST GIRL [*on the hill*]: Yes, yes! The whole field glitters –
    there she is!
FIRST PRIESTESS: Where is she?
FIRST GIRL: At the head of all the maidens!
  See how a-sparkle in her golden armour
  She dances eagerly to fight with him!
  It is as if, spurred on by jealousy,
  She strove to overtake the sun in flight,
  That strokes his fair young head! O see, o see!
  As if she strove to scale the heights of heaven,
  To look her lofty rival in the face!
  The Persian, slave to her desires, could not
  More Pegasus-like rise into the air!
HIGH PRIESTESS [*to the* CAPTAIN]:
  Was there not even one among the maidens
  Who warned her or who sought to hold her back?
CAPTAIN: Her princely following entire opposed
  Her here; in this place where we stand
  Prothoe used her utmost art to move her,
  And every eloquence was tried in vain
  To make her turn back to Themiscyra.
  To reason's voice it seemed that she was deaf;
  And it is said that by the sharpest dart
  From Cupid's quiver her young heart is poisoned.
HIGH PRIESTESS: What do you say?
FIRST GIRL [*on the hill*]:   Ha, they are face to face!
  You gods! Now let your earth stand firm for them!
  Now, now, just as I say it, like two stars
  They crash and hurl themselves upon each other!
HIGH PRIESTESS [*to the* CAPTAIN]:
  The queen, you say? It cannot be, my friend!
  By Cupid's arrow stricken? When and where?
  The wearer of the diamond girdle – she?
  Mars' daughter, she who lacks that very bosom
  The poison-feathered darts first make their target?
CAPTAIN: So at the least the people's voice would have it;
  I learnt it now from Meroe herself.
HIGH PRIESTESS: O, this is fearful!

[*Re-enter* ARSINOE.]

FIRST PRIESTESS: Well, what news? Come, say!

HIGH PRIESTESS: May we begin? Speak, did you ask the
    queen?

ARSINOE: It was too late, o holy one, forgive.
    Amidst the bands of women here and there
    I glimpsed her, but I could not come to her.
    But for a moment Prothoe I met,
    And told her of your will and your command;
    But she replied in words – I do not know
    If I could hear aright in the confusion –

HIGH PRIESTESS: In what words, pray?

ARSINOE: She rested on her horse,
    And looked, I thought, with eyes that filled with tears
    Towards the queen. And when she heard from me
    How you were angered that in madness she
    Still for one man alone prolonged the struggle,
    She said to me: go back to your priestess,
    And bid her fall upon her knees and pray
    That this one man might yet succumb to her,
    For else all will be lost, for her and us.

HIGH PRIESTESS: O, headlong down to Orcus she will fall!
    And not her enemy, if once she meet him,
    But that in her own heart will conquer her.
    And she will drag us all down to our doom;
    I see the ship that bears us prisoners
    To Greece, and mocks us with its festive flags,
    As if it ploughed the Hellespont already.

FIRST PRIESTESS: Is this so soon the news of our defeat?

SCENE 8

[*Enter an* AMAZON COLONEL.]

COLONEL: Flee! Save the prisoners, priestess, away!
    All the Greek army rushes to engulf us.

HIGH PRIESTESS: Gods of Olympus! What is this has
    happened?

FIRST PRIESTESS: Where is the queen?

COLONEL: She's fallen in the fight,
And all the Amazonian army scattered.

HIGH PRIESTESS: What, have you lost your wits? What is
this news?

FIRST PRIESTESS [*to the* AMAZON WARRIORS]:
Remove the prisoners! [*They are led away.*]

HIGH PRIESTESS: Speak, where and when?

COLONEL: Let me then quickly tell this fearful tale.
She and Achilles, with their lances set,
Fly at each other like two thunderbolts,
That from the storm-clouds hurl into collision;
Their lances, weaker than their breasts, are shivered;
He stands, the Peleid; Penthesilea
Sinks down, by death enveloped, from her horse.
And as she now, laid bare to his revenge,
Rolls in the dust before him, all believe
That he will cast her down at last to Orcus;
But pale himself, incomprehensible,
Like death's own shadow stands; o gods! he cries,
How with these dying looks she strikes my heart!
And from his horse now swiftly down he leaps;
And while all paralysed with horror still
The maidens stand, remembering the word
She gave, and do not dare to lift their swords,
Boldly he nears her, pale to death; he bends
Down over her; Penthesilea! calls,
And lifts her up to him in his own arms,
And cursing his own deed with fearful cries
Of grief he seeks to woo her back to life!

HIGH PRIESTESS: He, he himself?

COLONEL: Away, detested one!
The army cries with voice of thunder; let
Death be his thanks, cries Prothoe, if he
Refuse to yield; come, send your sharpest arrows!
And spurring on her horse to trample him,
She tears the queen away from his embrace.
Now she awakes, in fearful grief and pain,
And gasping she is led with bleeding breast

Behind the army's lines, where she recovers;
But he, incredible, the great Dolopian –
– His breast was forged with thunderbolts of bronze,
But now a god within him, suddenly,
Has melted down his heart with flames of love –
– He calls to us: no, stay, my friends, o stay!
Achilles greets you with eternal peace!
And throws away his sword, away, his shield,
Loosens his armour, tears it from his breast,
And follows us – with clubs, or with our hands,
If we might touch him, we could strike him down –
Us and the queen, with sturdy, fearless step;
As if he knew in his foolhardiness
We with our arrows may not harm his life.

HIGH PRIESTESS: Who was it gave you such insane command?

COLONEL: The queen! What other could it be?

HIGH PRIESTESS: O horror!

FIRST PRIESTESS: Look, look! See, Prothoe leads her
    faltering step!
See how she comes, image of grief, herself!

SECOND PRIESTESS: O dreadful sight, eternal gods in
    heaven!

SCENE 9

[*Enter* PENTHESILEA, *led by* PROTHOE *and* MEROE, *with
retinue.*]

PENTHESILEA [*in a feeble voice*]:
Set all the dogs on him! With brands of fire
Whip on the elephants to trample him!
Arm chariots with scythes and drive them on
To tear his lordly limbs and mow them down!

PROTHOE: Beloved queen! O, we implore you –

MEROE: Hear us!

PROTHOE: He comes upon your heels, the Peleid;
If ever your own life you cherish, flee!

PENTHESILEA: To shatter this my bosom, Prothoe!
Is it not thus, as if I were to smash
A lyre in anger when it whispers soft

And still, touched by the winds of night, my name?
O, I would cower at the bear's own feet,
And stroke the spotted panther that would come
To me with such a will as I to him.

MEROE: Then you will not escape?

PROTHOE: You will not flee?

MEROE: You will not save yourself?

PROTHOE: You would have that
Which knows no name befall you in this place?

PENTHESILEA: Is it my fault, that on the battlefield
And with the sword I must assault his heart?
What is it that I seek when I attack him?
Would I then send him headlong down to Orcus?
I would, o you eternal gods, I would
But draw him down upon this tender breast!

PROTHOE: She raves!

HIGH PRIESTESS: Unhappy wretch!

PROTHOE: She is deranged!

HIGH PRIESTESS: She has no thought but of that one.

PROTHOE: Her fall
Has robbed her of her wits, o hateful sight!

PENTHESILEA [*with forced calm*]:
Good. As you will. Let it be so. I will
Compel my heart with force, since it must be,
And with good grace obey necessity.
And you are right. Why should I, like a child,
Because one fleeting wish was not vouchsafed me,
Break with my gods? Come, let us leave this place.
I do confess, it would have brought me joy,
But if it will not drop down from the clouds,
To storm the heavens for it is too much.
Help me to rise, and find a horse for me,
Then I will lead you home again from here.

PROTHOE: O mistress, threefold be the blessings on
A word so worthy of a queen as this.
Come, for our flight all is prepared –

PENTHESILEA [*seeing the garlands of roses in the* GIRLS' *hands,
suddenly flaring up*]:   But see!

Who ordered that these roses should be plucked?

FIRST GIRL: What, do you not remember? Could it be
Another than –

PENTHESILEA: Than who?

HIGH PRIESTESS: – The victory,
The long-desired, we were to celebrate!
Was this not the command of your own lips?

PENTHESILEA: Curses upon this foolish raw impatience!
Curses, while still the bloody tumult rages,
Upon the thought of orgies such as these!
Curses upon desires that in the breasts
Of Mars' chaste daughters, like a pack unleashed
Of baying hounds will drown the trumpet's tongue
Of brass and all the crying of their masters!
The victory, is it then won, that with
The scorn of hell my triumph is prepared?
Out of my sight! [*She destroys the garlands.*]

FIRST GIRL: O mistress! What is this?

SECOND GIRL [*picking up the roses*]:
The spring, for miles around, will give no more
To deck the festival –

PENTHESILEA: O that the spring
Withered! O that the star on which we breathe
Lay broken, like these roses, on the ground!
O that I could tear up the firmament
And all the planets like these wreaths of flowers!
– O Aphrodite!

HIGH PRIESTESS: O unhappy wretch!

FIRST PRIESTESS: She is destroyed!

SECOND PRIESTESS: Her soul is given up,
A victim to the Furies in this rage.

A PRIESTESS [*on the hill*]:
The son of Peleus, maidens, I implore you –
See, he is but an arrow-shot away!

PROTHOE: Then on my knees I beg you – save yourself!

PENTHESILEA: Alas, my soul is weary unto death!
   [*She sits down.*]

PROTHOE: Horror, what would you do?

PENTHESILEA: Flee if you will.

PROTHOE: But you – ?

MEROE: You stay – ?

PROTHOE: You will – ?

PENTHESILEA: I will stay here.

PROTHOE: But you are crazed!

PENTHESILEA: You hear me. Let me be.
  I cannot stand. Am I to break my bones?

PROTHOE: Most wretched lady! And the Peleid,
  An arrow-shot, you hear it –

PENTHESILEA: Let him come.
  Let him set steel-shod foot, I do not care,
  Upon this neck. And why then should two cheeks
  That bloom like these be longer set apart
  From earth and filth from which they once were
      born?
  With horses let him drag me headlong home,
  And let this body, full of youth and life,
  Be cast upon the open field in shame,
  Like carrion, as a breakfast for his dogs,
  Or for the loathsome birds, let it be offered,
  Dust, if he cannot see I am a woman.

PROTHOE: O queen!

PENTHESILEA [*tearing off her necklaces*]:
                Away, you hateful frippery!

PROTHOE: Eternal gods above! Is this the calm
  You promised me but now with your own lips?

PENTHESILEA: And you there, nodding on my head –
      accursed,
  More helpless you than arrows and red cheeks!
  – I curse the hand that for the fight today
  Adorned me, and the tongues of treachery
  That said it was for victory, as well.
  How with their mirrors they, the hypocrites,
  Stood round me left and right, and praised my limbs,
  Their godlike form, pressed into moulds of bronze.
  – The plague upon your wicked arts of hell!

GREEKS [*offstage*]: Onward, o Peleid! and be assured,

But few steps more, you have her, she is yours!
PRIESTESS [*on the hill*]: Diana! Queen! O, you are lost
 indeed,
 If you stay here!
PROTHOE: My sister heart! My life!
 You will not flee? not go?
  [PENTHESILEA *bursts into tears and leans against a tree.*]
PROTHOE [*suddenly moved, sitting down beside her*]:
        Do as you will.
 If then you cannot, will not – do not weep!
 I will stay with you. If it cannot be,
 It cannot, if it is not in your power,
 You cannot do it; may the gods forbid
 That I demand it of you! you maidens,
 Go, to the meadows of your home return;
 The queen and I, we will stay here.
HIGH PRIESTESS: What, you,
 Unhappy Prothoe, comfort her still?
MEROE: Not in her power to flee?
HIGH PRIESTESS: Not in her power,
 When nothing from without, no destiny,
 But her own heart –
PROTHOE: That is her destiny!
 You think that links of steel could not be broken,
 Is it not so? Yet she might break such bonds,
 But not the feeling in her that you mock.
 What rules within her only she may know,
 A mystery is every breast that feels.
 She strove to reach the highest joys of life,
 She touched, she grasped them; now her hand refuses
 To stretch out to another in their stead. –
 Come, now upon my breast let it be finished.
 – What is it? You are weeping?
PENTHESILEA: Ah, the pain –
PROTHOE: Where?
PENTHESILEA: Here.
PROTHOE: But can I fetch you – ?
PENTHESILEA: No, no, no.

PROTHOE: Be calm then; soon your fate will be accomplished.

HIGH PRIESTESS [*in a subdued voice*]:
O raving, both of you!

PROTHOE [*likewise*]: I beg you, still.

PENTHESILEA: If I should flee – I say, if it were so,
What should I do?

PROTHOE: To Pharsos you would go.
There you would find, for there I sent it on,
Your army gathered new that now is scattered,
There you would rest, and there attend your wounds,
And with the day's first light, if so you wished it,
Once more lead on the maidens into war.

PENTHESILEA: If it were possible! If I could do it!
The utmost that our human strength can do,
I did; yes, sought to do what could not be;
All that I had, I staked on this last throw;
The dice that spell my fate are cast, are cast;
And I must learn to read them – I have failed.

PROTHOE: No, no, my dearest heart! Do not believe it,
So poorly do not estimate your strength.
So lowly of that prize you will not think,
For which you strive, that you should be convinced
All that's deserving is already tried.
Is this poor string of pearls, of white and red,
That hung about your throat, of riches all
Your soul can summon up in sacrifice?
How much of which you do not think is still
In Pharsos for your cause to be attempted!
But now indeed – almost it is too late.

PENTHESILEA: If I made haste – ah no, it makes me mad!
Where stands the sun?

PROTHOE: There, straight above your head,
Before night falls you would be there already.
We would ally ourselves, the Greeks unknowing,
With the Dardanians, would reach in stealth
The bay where lie the Argive ships at anchor,
And in the night, upon a signal, up
They flare in flames, their camp we take by storm,

Their army, pressed from every side at once,
Is shattered, scattered, strewn about the land;
Pursued, attacked, then caught and crowned with wreaths
Is every head it pleased our eye to take.
O, happy should I be if I could see it!
I would not rest, beside you I would fight,
Not fear the heat of day, nor ever tire,
Though I must wear and fret my every limb,
Until my dearest sister's wish was granted,
And at her feet the son of Peleus, conquered,
At last sank down, reward of all our toil.

PENTHESILEA [*who during this speech has kept her gaze fixed
on the sun*]: That I on wings wide-spread and quivering
Might cleave the air!

PROTHOE: What's that?

MEROE: What is she saying?

PROTHOE: What do you see, princess?

MEROE: Where do you fix – ?

PROTHOE: Beloved, speak!

PENTHESILEA: Too high, I know, too high –
In ever-distant rings of fire he plays
About my bosom filled with strange desires.

PROTHOE: Who is it, my beloved queen?

PENTHESILEA: Good, good.
– Where must I go? [*She summons her strength and stands up.*]

MEROE: So you will be resolved?

PROTHOE: So, then, you will arise? Then, my princess,
Let it be like a giant, and do not falter,
Though you must bear the very weight of hell!
O stand, stand firm as does the vaulted arch,
Because its blocks all seek to fall asunder!
Hold up your head, the keystone, to withstand
The lightnings of the gods, and bid them strike!
And let them split you to the ground in two,
But never tremble more within yourself
While one breath still remains to hold the stones
Like mortar in your youthful breast together!
Come now, give me your hand.

PENTHESILEA: This way, or that?

PROTHOE: The rocky cliff, the safer, you may climb,
Or choose the gentler valley at your feet.
Which way will you decide?

PENTHESILEA: The cliff above!
There I will be the nearer to him. Follow!

PROTHOE: To whom, my queen?

PENTHESILEA: Your arms, my dearest maids.

PROTHOE: As soon as you have climbed that further hill
You are in safety.

MEROE: Come away!

PENTHESILEA [*suddenly stopping on a bridge*]: But hear!
Before I go, one task remains to me.

PROTHOE: Remains to you?

MEROE: A task?

PROTHOE: Unhappy queen!

PENTHESILEA: One thing remains, my friends, and it were
madness,
You must yourselves confess, if I had not
Attempted all that might yet bring success.

PROTHOE [*resentfully*]: O then I would that we were
swallowed up,
For now all hope is gone.

PENTHESILEA [*anxiously*]:   What is the matter?
What have I done to her, you maidens? Speak!

HIGH PRIESTESS: You think – ?

MEROE: Still in this very place you will – ?

PENTHESILEA: Do nothing, nothing, that should anger her.
I will roll Ida up on Ossa's summit,
And calmly set myself upon its peak.

HIGH PRIESTESS: Roll Ida up –

MEROE: Roll up on Ossa's summit?

PROTHOE [*turning away*]: O you Olympians, save her!

HIGH PRIESTESS: She is lost!

MEROE [*shyly*]: This task is one for giants alone, my queen!

PENTHESILEA: Why yes, it is; but should I yield to them?

MEROE: But should you yield – ?

PROTHOE: O gods!

HIGH PRIESTESS: But even if –

MEROE: But even if you might perform this task – ?

PROTHOE: But even then, what would you –

PENTHESILEA: Feeble creatures!
   Why, by his flaming golden hair I'd drag
   Him down to me –

PROTHOE: Who is it?

PENTHESILEA: Helios,
   When he so near above my head flies by!

   [*The* PRINCESSES *look at each other, speechless and horrified.*]

HIGH PRIESTESS: Seize her, take her away!

PENTHESILEA [*looking down into the river*]: But I am mad!
   There at my feet he lies! O take me now –

   [*She tries to jump into the river.* PROTHOE *and* MEROE *hold
   her back.*]

PROTHOE: O wretched queen!

MEROE: But now, lifeless she falls,
   See, like a crumpled garment in our hands.

PRIESTESS [*on the hill*]: Achilles will be here, princesses! All
   The band of maidens cannot keep him back!

AN AMAZON: Save her, you gods! From his effrontery
   Protect the queen of maidens!

HIGH PRIESTESS [*to* PRIESTESSES]: Come! Away!
   Not in the battle's tumult is our place.

   [*Exeunt* HIGH PRIESTESS, PRIESTESSES *and* GIRLS.]

SCENE 10

   [*Enter a band of* AMAZONS *with bows in their hands.*]

FIRST AMAZON [*into the wings*]:
   Retreat! How can you dare –

SECOND: He will not hear us.

THIRD: Princesses, if we may not shoot at him,
   Then he will never check his mad advance!

SECOND: What shall we do? Speak, Prothoe!

PROTHOE [*busied with the* QUEEN]: Then loose
   Ten thousand arrows at him!

MEROE [*to their followers*]: Bring us water!

PROTHOE: But see you do not strike him to his death!

MEROE: I say bring water in a helmet!

ONE OF THE PRINCESSES: Here!
    [*She fills a helmet with water and brings it.*]

THIRD AMAZON [*to* PROTHOE]:
    We shall not. Do not fear!

FIRST: Here take your stand!
    His cheeks let them be seared, his locks be scorched,
    A fleeting kiss of death be his to taste!
    [*They prepare to shoot.*]

SCENE II

    [*Enter* ACHILLES *without armour or helmet, accompanied by
    a number of* GREEKS.]

ACHILLES: Well, maidens, what's the target for these
        arrows?
    But surely not this unprotected breast?
    Shall I then open too this silken tunic,
    That you may see my heart beat harmlessly?

FIRST AMAZON: Yes, tear it off!

SECOND: There is no need of that!

THIRD: The arrow there, just where he holds his hand!

FIRST: Now let him tear his heart, pinned like a leaf,
    Away in flight –

SEVERAL: Now strike him! Shoot!
    [*They shoot over his head.*]

ACHILLES: Stop, stop!
    You strike more surely with your eyes than these.
    By the Olympians, I do not jest,
    I feel that I am wounded deep within,
    And quite disarmed in every sense, I come
    To lay myself before your dainty feet.

FIFTH AMAZON [*struck by a spear from offstage*]:
    Merciful gods! [*Falls.*]

SIXTH [*likewise*]: Alas! [*Falls.*]

SEVENTH [*likewise*]:   O Artemis! [*Falls.*]

FIRST AMAZON: See how he raves!   }

MEROE: O most unhappy queen! }

SECOND AMAZON: {And says he is disarmed!
PROTHOE [*busied with the* QUEEN]: {She breathes no more!

THIRD AMAZON: While we are slaughtered by his men with
    spears!
MEROE: While all around our stricken maidens fall!
  What shall we do?

FIRST AMAZON: Bring the scythed chariot!
SECOND: Unleash the dogs to tear his flesh!
THIRD: With stones
  Thrown down from elephants let him be buried!

A PRINCESS [*suddenly leaving the* QUEEN]:
  Let it be so, then: I will try the shot.
  [*She takes her bow from her shoulder and bends it.*]

ACHILLES [*turning first to one* AMAZON, *then to another*]:
  I'll not believe it; sweet as silver bells
  Your voices to your harsh words give the lie.
  You there, with your blue eyes, are not the one
  To set the savage dogs on me, nor you,
  Who glory in your silken locks of hair.
  Why, if you were to speak the word in haste,
  And they let off the leash came howling on me,
  See, you would bar their way with your own bodies,
  And throw yourselves before them, all to save
  This manly heart that glows for you with love.

FIRST AMAZON: Foolhardy villain!
SECOND: Hear him, how he boasts!
FIRST: He thinks that we with flattery –
THIRD [*calling secretly to her*]:   Oterpe!
FIRST [*turning round*]:
  Ah, see – the greatest mistress of the bow!
  Still! Open up your ranks, you women!
FIFTH: Why?
FOURTH: Ask not, and you will see.
EIGHTH: Here, take the arrow!

THE PRINCESS [*fitting the arrow to her bow*]:
  I'll strike him so his thighs are pinned together.

ACHILLES [*to a* GREEK *standing beside him with drawn bow*]:
  Her, there!

THE PRINCESS: Olympian gods! [*Falls.*]
FIRST AMAZON: O fearful man!
SECOND: Herself she falls the victim!
THIRD: Gods eternal!
   And there, another band of Greeks draws near!

SCENE 12

   [*Enter from the other side of the stage* DIOMEDES *and the*
   AETOLIANS.]
DIOMEDES: Come, come, my brave Aetolians, this way,
   Upon them! [*He leads them over the bridge.*]
PROTHOE: Artemis, deliver us!
   Our hopes are at an end.
      [*With the help of some of the* AMAZONS, *she carries the*
      QUEEN *to the front of the stage.*]
THE AMAZONS [*in confusion*]: We are surrounded!
   We are cut off! We are their prisoners!
   Flee, save herself each one who can!
DIOMEDES [*to* PROTHOE]:   Surrender!
MEROE [*to the fleeing* AMAZONS]:
   What is this madness? Will you not stand firm?
   Look! Prothoe!
PROTHOE [*still with the* QUEEN]: Away, and follow them,
   And, if you can, restore our liberty.
      [*The* AMAZONS *scatter,* MEROE *follows them.*]
ACHILLES: Up now, where does she lift her head?
A GREEK: Look there!
ACHILLES: Ten crowns shall be my gift to Diomedes.
DIOMEDES: Again I say, surrender!
PROTHOE: To the victor
   I'll yield her, not to you! What do you want?
   The Peleid alone shall call her his!
DIOMEDES: Throw her aside!
AN AETOLIAN: Away!
ACHILLES [*pushing him back*]:   He will not breathe
   To leave this place, who would but touch the queen!
   She's mine! Away! What is your business here?

DIOMEDES: What, yours, is she? Why, by the Thunderer's
    locks,
  What reason can you give? And by what right?
ACHILLES: One reason on the right, one on the left. —
  Yield.
PROTHOE: Here. From your great heart I can fear nothing.
ACHILLES [*taking the* QUEEN *in his arms*]:
  No, nothing. —
  [*To* DIOMEDES] Go, and chase and beat the women;
  I shall remain a moment here behind.
  — Off! — For my sake. Do not dispute. With Hades
  I'd fight for her; should I not then with you?
    [*He lays her down by the roots of an oak-tree.*]
DIOMEDES: So let it be, then. Follow!
    [*Enter* ODYSSEUS *with the* GREEK ARMY, *from the same
    side as did* ACHILLES, *and crosses the stage.*]
ODYSSEUS: Hail, Achilles!
  Shall I send on your chariot and four?
ACHILLES [*bent over the* QUEEN]:
  No need for it. Let be.
ODYSSEUS: Good. As you will. —
  Follow! Before the women once more rally.
    [*Exeunt* ODYSSEUS *and* DIOMEDES *with the army, on the
    Amazons' side of the stage.*]

SCENE 13

ACHILLES [*opening the* QUEEN's *armour*]:
  She is alive no more.
PROTHOE: O might her eye
  Be closed for ever to this dreary light!
  I fear too surely that she will awake.
ACHILLES: Where did I strike her?
PROTHOE: From the blow she rallied,
  That tore her breast, and roused herself by force;
  With feeble step we led her to this place,
  And would have made attempt to climb this rock,
  But was it in her limbs, so torn with wounds,

Or in her injured soul, she felt such pain;
That you had conquered her, she could not bear;
Her foot gave way, and would not carry her,
And babbling madness from her bloodless lips,
She fell a second time into my arms.

ACHILLES: She quivered – did you see?

PROTHOE: You heavenly gods!
The cup is not yet emptied to the dregs?
O see, this queen of sorrows, see –

ACHILLES: She breathes.

PROTHOE: O son of Peleus, if you scorn not pity,
If any feeling stirs within your breast,
If you would spare her life, so quick to bruise,
And not let madness bind her in its fetters,
Then grant me one request, I beg.

ACHILLES: Speak promptly!

PROTHOE: Begone from here! Begone, o noble one,
Out of her sight retreat when she awakes!
Straightway remove the men that stand about you,
And not before the sun renews his course,
In distant mountain mists, let any man
Approach and greet her with the words of death:
You are Achilles' prisoner-of-war.

ACHILLES: She hates me, then?

PROTHOE: O do not ask, great heart!
If joyful on the hand of hope she now
Returns to life, then let the conqueror
Not be the first and joyless sight she sees.
How many things move in a woman's breast
That for the light of day were never meant.
If at the last her destiny decrees
That she your mournful prisoner must greet you,
Do not demand it sooner, I implore,
Than armed to face the truth her spirit stands.

ACHILLES: I would, this I must tell you, do to her
The same I did to Priam's haughty son.

PROTHOE: What, dreadful man!

ACHILLES: – Is she afraid of that?

PROTHOE: You would inflict that nameless horror on her?
　This fair young body here, o man of blood,
　Adorned with beauties like a child with flowers,
　Thus to be dragged in shame, and like a corpse –
ACHILLES: – Tell her I love her.
PROTHOE: 　　　　　　　　What? – What can this mean?
ACHILLES: Mean, by the gods! why, love, as men love
　　　　women;
　Chaste, but with aching heart; in innocence,
　But ever longing yet to take it from her.
　I want to take your mistress for my queen.
PROTHOE: Eternal gods, repeat these words again!
　You will – ?
ACHILLES: 　　May I now stay?
PROTHOE: 　　　　　　　　　O, let me kiss
　Your feet, o godly one! O now if you
　Were far away, now I would go to seek you,
　Yes, far beyond Atlantis, Peleid!
　But look: her eyes are opening –
ACHILLES: 　　　　　　　　She moves –
PROTHOE: Now is the moment! Fly, you men; and you,
　Quickly behind this oak-tree hide yourself.
ACHILLES: Away, my friends, retreat! [*Exeunt* GREEKS.]
PROTHOE [*to* ACHILLES, *as he goes behind the oak-tree*]:
　　　　　　　　　　　　Go further, further!
　And I beseech you, do not show yourself
　Until I call you. Will you promise this?
　I cannot answer for my mistress' soul.
ACHILLES: It shall be so.
PROTHOE: 　　　　　Now let us all observe!

SCENE 14

PROTHOE: Penthesilea! What is it you dream?
　In what far distant shining realm now dwells
　Your spirit, roaming with a restless step,
　As if its own home pleased it now no longer;
　While happy fortune, like a fair young prince,

Enters your bosom, and astonished there
To find such pleasant habitations empty,
Turns back again already, and to heaven
Will once more set its never-constant course?
Will you not bind this guest, o foolish one?
Come, let me raise you to my breast.

PENTHESILEA: Where am I?

PROTHOE: – Do you not recognise your sister's voice?
Do not this rock, this path and bridge, and all
This landscape in full blossom call you back?
Look at these maidens gathered here about you;
As if before the doors of a new world
They stand, and cry out: Welcome! as you enter.
You sigh. What troubles you?

PENTHESILEA: O Prothoe!
Ah, what a dream of horror I have dreamt –
How sweet it is, how gladly I would weep,
To wake and feel my poor tormented heart
Against this sister heart of yours is beating!
– It seemed to me that in the battle's heat
The son of Peleus struck me with his lance;
I crash amidst my brazen armour's ring,
The earth gives back the echo of my fall.
And while the army, terrified, retreats,
With all my limbs encumbered still I lie;
Then from his horse already he leaps down,
And with triumphant step approaches me –
And then he seizes me, who lie there fallen,
In his strong arms he lifts me from the ground;
I try to grasp this dagger and I cannot,
A prisoner I am; with mockery
And laughter I am taken to his tents.

PROTHOE: No, no, my dearest queen; to mock a captive
Is stranger to his great and noble soul.
If it had been the truth you dreamed, believe me,
A blissful moment there awaited you,
And in the very dust perhaps, in homage,
The son of gods had crawled before your feet.

PENTHESILEA: Might I be cursed, if I could bear this shame!
　　Might I be cursed, if ever I received
　　A man not fitly brought me by the sword.
PROTHOE: Be calm, my queen.
PENTHESILEA: 　　　　　　　Be calm, you say to me?
PROTHOE: Do you not rest upon my faithful bosom?
　　Whatever fate may yet decree for you,
　　We will endure it, you and I; be brave.
PENTHESILEA: I was as calm, my Prothoe, as the sea
　　Within the rocky bay; there was not one
　　Unquiet feeling stirred its waves in me.
　　That word: be calm! – now as a sudden wind
　　The ocean's open spaces, whips me up.
　　Why is it then that here we must be calm?
　　You stand so strange about me, so disturbed,
　　– And cast your looks, by the eternal gods,
　　Behind my back, as if there stood a monster,
　　With fearful threats upon its face, behind me.
　　– You hear, I only dreamt it, it is not –
　　– Or is it, then? Is it? Could it be true?
　　Where's Meroe? Speak! Megaris?
　　　　[*She looks round, and sees* ACHILLES.]
　　　　　　　　　　　　– O horror!
　　There he stands, there behind me, terrible!
　　Now this free hand of mine – [*She draws her dagger.*]
PROTHOE: 　　　　　　　Unhappy queen!
PENTHESILEA: O worthless wretch, now she would stay my
　　　　hand –
PROTHOE: Achilles, save her!
PENTHESILEA: 　　　　　　O, but she is mad!
　　He comes to set his foot upon my neck!
PROTHOE: His foot? You rave!
PENTHESILEA: 　　　　　　Away from me, I say!
PROTHOE: But will you look at him, or then be lost!
　　Does he not stand unarmed behind you there?
PENTHESILEA: What's that?
PROTHOE: 　　　　　　Why yes, and ready, if you ask,
　　To wear himself the garland of your fetters.

PENTHESILEA: No, say!

PROTHOE: Achilles! You must speak to her.

PENTHESILEA: He – and my prisoner?

PROTHOE: Why not? You see!

ACHILLES [*who has meanwhile come forward*]:
In every finer sense, o noble queen!
And I am willing, till my life shall end,
To flutter in the fetters of your eye.
[PENTHESILEA *covers her face with her hands.*]

PROTHOE: Now you have heard it, and from his own lips.
He, when you met, fell with you to the dust,
And while you senseless lay upon the ground,
He was disarmed – not so?

ACHILLES: I was disarmed,
And to your feet I was conducted here.
[*He drops on one knee before her.*]

PENTHESILEA [*after a short pause*]:
If it be so, then, youthful charm of life,
God with fresh roses in your cheeks, I greet you!
O now, my heart, send forth your streams of blood,
That here as if awaiting him have lain
Pent up in both the chambers of my breast.
Winged messengers of joy, springs of my youth,
Be on your way, run through my veins rejoicing,
And let your scarlet banner wave aloft
Upon the kingdoms of my cheeks, proclaiming:
The Nereid's son, the wondrous youth, is mine!
[*She stands up.*]

PROTHOE: O my beloved queen, be moderate!

PENTHESILEA [*striding forward*]:
Come all you maidens, crowned with victory,
You, Ares' daughters, come, from head to toe
Still covered in the dust of battlefields,
And let each one bring up the Argive youth
That she has conquered, lead him by the hand!
You girls, approach, with baskets filled with roses;
Where for so many brows shall I find garlands?
Out, fly across the fields, I say to you,

And draw the roses that the spring withholds
Out of the meadows for me with your breath!
Priestesses of Diana, to your office;
Your temple, glowing bright and charged with incense,
Fling open wide its doors to me with clangour,
As if I saw the gates of paradise!
First let the fatted ox in prime, short-horned,
Up to the altar steps be led; the knife,
Glittering, silent in the holy place,
Shall fell him that the arches shall resound.
You servants of the temple, nimbly then,
The blood, where are you? quickly stir yourselves,
With Persian unguents, hissing from the coals,
Let it be smoothly washed from panelled frieze!
And fluttering garments, be you all girt up,
Be filled, you golden goblets, to the brim,
You brazen trumpets speak, and horns resound,
Let jubilation with its melody
The firmament to its foundations shake!
O Prothoe! Help me rejoice and revel,
O think, my friend, my sister heart, imagine,
How I can make a feast more jubilant,
More godlike than Olympus ever saw!
The marriage-feast of brides that wooed in battle,
The proud Achaeans and the race of Mars!
O Meroe, where are you? Megaris?

PROTHOE [*with suppressed emotion*]:
Both joy and grief to you are perilous,
To madness both in equal measure lead.
You dream that you are in Themiscyra,
And when your over-heated fancy soars,
I feel I long to speak to you the word
That suddenly will pinion you again.
You are deceived: where are you? Look about!
Where are the people? Where are the priestesses?
Asteria, Meroe, Megaris, where are they?

PENTHESILEA [*leaning on her breast*]:
O Prothoe, let me be! Let this poor heart

Two moments in this stream of keen delight
Plunge like a dirtied child, and cleanse itself;
With every beat beneath its lapping waves
A blemish from my breast is washed away.
They flee from me, the cruel Eumenides,
I feel the nearness of the gods about me,
I would that straightway I might join their throng;
So ripe for death as now I never was.
But now, above all else: do you forgive me?

PROTHOE: O my dear mistress!

PENTHESILEA: Yes, I know, I know. –
Indeed, my own blood's better half is yours.
– They say that suffering can purge our spirit;
I, dearest one, I did not find it so;
It has embittered me and stirred in me
Unfathomed rage against both gods and men.
How strangely upon every face to me
The trace of joy was hateful where I saw it;
The child that played upon its mother's lap,
To me it seemed conspired against my pain,
How gladly everything that now surrounds me
I would see happy and content. Ah, friend!
Man can be great in suffering, a hero,
But in contented bliss he is a god!
– But now, about our business. Let the army
With speed make preparations for return;
As soon as they are rested, beasts and men,
The train with all the captives will depart,
And set its course towards our native meadows.
– Where is Lycaon?

PROTHOE: Who?

PENTHESILEA [*with tender reproachfulness*]:
                         How can you ask?
That handsome hero of Arcadia
You conquered with your sword. What keeps him from
     us?

PROTHOE [*confused*]: He – in the forest still remains, my
     queen,

Where all the other prisoners are waiting.
Permit that he, according to the law,
Shall not appear to me till we are home.
PENTHESILEA: Call him to me! – Within the forests still!
His place is here, here at my Prothoe's feet!
– I beg you, dearest one, let him be called;
You stand beside me like a frost in May
And nip the tender shoots of happiness.
PROTHOE [*aside*]: O most ill-fated! – Very well; begone,
And carry out the order of our queen.
[*She motions to one of the* AMAZONS, *who withdraws.*]
PENTHESILEA: Who now will fetch the maidens with their
roses?
[*She sees the roses on the ground.*]
Look! Blossoms, and so sweetly fragrant too,
Here in this place!
[*She puts her hand to her forehead*]
                What was that evil dream?
[*To* PROTHOE] Was the High Priestess of Diana here?
PROTHOE: I did not notice that she was, my queen.
PENTHESILEA: How should these roses come here, then?
PROTHOE: Look there!
The girls that robbed the meadows of their blossoms,
Left here a basket full of them behind.
Here is a chance I can indeed call happy.
See, shall I gather up these fragrant blooms,
And wind a garland for the Peleid?
[*She sits down by the oak-tree*]
PENTHESILEA: O dear and precious to me, how you move
me!
– So then. And these, here with a hundred leaves,
– Shall I? – Lycaon's wreath for you. O come.
[*She too gathers up some of the roses, and sits down beside*
PROTHOE.]
Music, you women, music! Make me calm.
I would be peaceful. Let us hear your song.
ONE OF THE MAIDENS: What would you hear?
ANOTHER: The victor's song?

PENTHESILEA: — The hymn.

THE MAIDEN: It shall be so. — Delusion! — Sing and play!

CHORUS OF MAIDENS [*with music*]:
Ares is fled!
See how his white chariot-team
Far off, steaming, to Orcus hurries down!
They open, the Eumenides, the terrible ones;
And now the gates again behind him close.

SOLO: Hymen, where art thou?
Kindle thy torch, and light us! light us!
Hymen! Where art thou?

CHORUS: Ares is fled! *etc.*

ACHILLES [*creeps silently up to* PROTHOE *during the singing*]:
Speak! Where will all this lead me? I would know!

PROTHOE: A moment's patience more, o noble soul,
I would entreat of you — then you shall see.
[*When the garlands are finished,* PENTHESILEA *exchanges hers with* PROTHOE; *they embrace and look together at the wreaths. The music stops. Re-enter the* AMAZON.]

PENTHESILEA: Has it been done?

THE AMAZON: Lycaon will appear,
The young Arcadian prince, immediately.

SCENE 15

PENTHESILEA: Come now, sweet son of Peleus and of
Thetis,
Come, lay yourself here at my feet. — Come closer!
Be bold! — You will not be afraid of me?
— Hateful, because I conquered, do you find me?
Speak! I, who laid you in the dust — you fear me?

ACHILLES [*at her feet*]: As flowers fear the sunshine.

PENTHESILEA: O well said!
Then you shall look upon me as your sun.
— O Artemis, my mistress, see, he has
A wound!

ACHILLES: A scratch here on my arm, no more.

PENTHESILEA: I beg you, Peleid, do not believe

That ever I have aimed to take your life.
True, gladly did I strike you with my arm;
But as you sank before me, know, this heart
Was envious of the dust that might receive you.
ACHILLES: If you do love me, do not speak of that.
You see it heals already.
PENTHESILEA: You forgive me?
ACHILLES: With all my heart.
PENTHESILEA: And now – now can you tell me,
What love must do, the child with rosy wings,
When he would bind the stubborn lion in chains?
ACHILLES: I think he has to stroke his bristly cheeks,
Then he'll be still.
PENTHESILEA: Why then, you will not stir,
More than a tender dove a maid has snared;
For all the feelings in this breast, o youth,
They are like hands, and see, they come to stroke you.
    [*She winds garlands round him.*]
ACHILLES: Who are you, wondrous woman?
PENTHESILEA: No, come here –
Be still, I say, and soon you will find out.
– Only a garland of these roses here
Over your head, and one about your neck,
Down to your arms, your hands, your feet, about
And up – your head again – and it is done.
– You breathe so deep?
ACHILLES: Fragrance of your sweet lips.
PENTHESILEA [*bending backwards*]:
It is the roses strewing forth their scent.
What more?
ACHILLES: But I would try them where they grow.
PENTHESILEA: When they are ripe, my love, then you
    shall pluck them.
    [*She puts another garland over his head and lets him go.*]
Now it is done. – O look, I beg you, see,
How roses with their melting glow become him!
How gleams his face like thunder dark among them!
The dawning day, in truth, my dearest friend,

When from the mountains Graces lead his step,
And dewdrops gleam like diamonds at his feet,
His gaze is not so soft and mild as this.
– But speak! Did you not think his eye did glitter?
Truly, to see him thus, would you not doubt
It could be he?

PROTHOE: Who, then?

PENTHESILEA: The Peleid!
– Speak! He that felled great Priam's greatest son
Before the walls of Ilium, – was it you?
Was it then really you, *you*, with these hands,
Drove wedges through his nimble feet, and dragged
Him round the city at your chariot-tail?
Say, speak! What moves you so? Are you that man?

ACHILLES: I am.

PENTHESILEA [*after a piercing glance at him*]:
He says he is.

PROTHOE: He is, my queen.
And you may know him by this ornament.

PENTHESILEA: By which?

PROTHOE: By this, it is the armour, see,
That Thetis once, his mother, sprung from gods,
Won from Hephaestus by her flattery.

PENTHESILEA: So, if it be, I greet you with this kiss;
Unruliest of mortals, you are mine!
To me you now belong, young god of war,
And when the people ask, you name them *me*.

ACHILLES: O you, who like the vision of a dream,
As if the realms of aether opened wide,
Stranger than strange, descend to me, who are you?
How shall I name your name when my own soul
Enraptured asks to whom it now belongs?

PENTHESILEA: When thus it asks you, name to it these
features,
Be they the name by which you think of me. –
But wait; here, you shall have this golden ring,
With every token for your safety's sake;
Show it, and you will find the way to me.

Yet rings are lost, and names may be forgotten;
If you forgot that name, that ring were lost,
Could you not find my image in yourself?
Your eyes tight shut, then do you see it still?

ACHILLES: I bear it diamond-graven in my heart.

PENTHESILEA: Then know I am the Queen of Amazons;
Mars as its ancestor my nation names,
Otrere was my great and noble mother,
And me the people call Penthesilea.

ACHILLES: Penthesilea.

PENTHESILEA: Yes, so I did say.

ACHILLES: My swan in death shall sing: Penthesilea.

PENTHESILEA: I give you liberty, and you may go
Amidst the maiden armies where you will.
For now it is another chain I think
To cast, as light as flowers, harder yet
Than bronze, about your heart and bind it fast.
But till it has been hammered link by link,
So finely wrought within love's glowing forge
That neither time nor chance can ever break it,
You shall, as duty asks, return to me,
To me, sweet friend, you hear, for it is I
Shall tend your every need and every wish.
Now tell me, will you do it?

ACHILLES: As a foal
Seeks out its fragrant manger's sustenance.

PENTHESILEA: Good. I shall trust you to. And now
    straightway
We must make homeward to Themiscyra;
Till we are there, my train shall all be yours.
You shall be given canopies of purple,
You shall not lack for slaves to do your bidding
And to attend your every kingly wish.
Yet since upon the march, you understand,
So many cares will keep me, you must stay
Together with the other prisoners;
Not till Themiscyra, o son of Thetis,
Can I with all my heart be bound to you.

ACHILLES: It shall be as you say.

PENTHESILEA [*to* PROTHOE]:   But tell me now,
  Where is your young Arcadian?

PROTHOE: My queen –

PENTHESILEA: So gladly, dearest Prothoe, would I see
  Him crowned here by your hand.

PROTHOE: O, he will come –
  This garland shall not fail to crown his head.

PENTHESILEA [*starting up*]:
  But now – so many matters call on me,
  So let me go.

ACHILLES: What?

PENTHESILEA: Let me rise, my friend.

ACHILLES: You flee? You go? You leave me here behind?
  Before my longing breast may learn from you
  The key to all these wonders, o my love?

PENTHESILEA: Friend – in Themiscyra.

ACHILLES: Here, here, my queen!

PENTHESILEA: Friend, in Themiscyra, Themiscyra!
  Now let me go!

PROTHOE [*agitated, holding her back*]:
                My queen! What would you do?

PENTHESILEA [*puzzled*]:
  I must review the armies – This is strange! –
  And speak with Meroe and with Megaris –
  Why, by the Styx, I cannot stay to talk!

PROTHOE: The armies still pursue the Greeks in flight;
  Meroe leads them; let these cares be hers;
  You still need rest. – When once the enemy
  Has drawn back all his men across Scamander,
  Here you shall see them, your victorious forces.

PENTHESILEA: Here, in this very field? – Is this the
       truth?

PROTHOE: The truth. You may rely on it.

PENTHESILEA [*to* ACHILLES]:   Be brief, then.

ACHILLES: How can it be that you, you wondrous woman,
  Leading a warlike army, like Athene,
  Fall unprovoked as from the clouds upon

Our battle with the Trojan forces here?
What is it drives you, armed from head to toe,
Like Furies with this rage we cannot fathom,
To hurl yourself against the Grecian peoples;
You, who in beauty only and in calm
Need show yourself, so lovely, for the race
Of men entire to crawl before your feet?

PENTHESILEA: Ah, son of Thetis! No, it is not granted
To me, this art, this gentler art of woman!
Not at the feast, like daughters of your country,
When, keenly vying in their joyful sport,
The noble youths of all the land are seen,
May I pick out my bridegroom at my will;
Nor set a flower thus, or thus, to take
His eye, or draw him with a modest glance;
Nor tell him, when at last the morning breaks
Amidst the echoing glades of nightingales,
Leaning upon his breast, that it is he.
Upon the bloody field of war must I
Seek out the youth my heart would make its own,
And capture with an arm encased in bronze
The man this gentle bosom shall receive.

ACHILLES: And where and when did you receive this law,
Unwomanly, – forgive – unnatural,
To other nations of the world unknown?

PENTHESILEA: Far off, and from the holiest of urns,
O youth, and from the lofty peaks of time,
The unapproachable, for ever veiled
By heaven in its clouds of mystery.
The word of our first mothers laid it down;
We hear it, son of Thetis, and are silent,
As you obey the words of your first fathers.

ACHILLES: Speak plainer.

PENTHESILEA: Very well! Then hear my story.
Where now the Amazonian nation rules,
There lived before, obedient to the gods,
A Scythian people, warlike, proud and free,
And equal to all others in the world.

For centuries this people named its own
The fruitful orchards of the Caucasus;
When Vexoris, the Ethiopian king,
Swept through the foothills, swiftly threw the men,
Allied in battle, down before his ranks,
Filled all the valleys, slew old men and boys,
Each one of them his flashing swords could find;
That whole illustrious nation met its end.
The victors settled, like barbarians,
In our own huts with impudence, and fed
Themselves upon the fruit of our rich fields,
And, that our cup of shame might overflow,
They forced from us the favours due to love;
They tore the women from their husbands' graves
And dragged them in to share their shameful beds.

ACHILLES: A fate of devastation, o my queen,
It was that gave your state of women birth!

PENTHESILEA: But what is not to be endured, we shake
Its weight with fearful struggle from our shoulders;
Only a lesser suffering we bear.
Many long nights in silent secrecy
The women lay in Ares' temple, wore
The steps with weeping and with prayers for rescue;
The beds that had been so dishonoured filled
With daggers, ground and polished like the lightning,
Cast in the hearth-fire's flame from ornaments,
From brooches, rings and chains; only the wedding
Of Vexoris the Ethiopian king
With Tanaïs the queen they were awaiting,
To kiss with them each guest upon his breast.
And when the wedding-feast at last had come,
The queen struck him with hers, clean to his heart;
So not the shameful one, but Mars she wed,
And all the race of murderers, from daggers,
In that one night knew the caress of death.

ACHILLES: Why, what a deed was this, in truth, for women!

PENTHESILEA: And now these words in council were
proclaimed:

Free as the wind on open fallow field
Are women who could do this mighty deed,
And shall no longer serve the race of men!
Let there be now a nation, fully fledged,
A state of women, where from this day on
Imperious voice of man shall not be heard;
To make its laws itself, as it is fitting,
Obey itself, and be its own defence;
And Tanaïs shall be proclaimed its queen.
The man who once sets eye upon this state
Shall close his eye that day for ever more;
And if by any chance a boy be born,
Son to those tyrants, let him be sent down
Straightway to Orcus, to his savage fathers.
At once the people crowded Ares' temple,
Eager to crown the mighty Tanaïs
Protectress of the state these words proclaimed.
As at the ceremony's height she rose,
To mount the altar steps and grasp the bow,
The mighty, golden bow of Scythian kings
The high priestess in splendid raiment held,
A voice was heard, there in the temple, crying:
'The mockery of men it will provoke,
This state, no more, and to the first assault
Of warlike neighbours surely will succumb;
For never will the strength to wield the bow
Be found in woman's arm; her full ripe breasts
Will hinder what must be a task for men.'
The queen stood silent, waiting for a moment,
To see how words like these might be received;
But as she saw the stir of cowardice,
Tore off her own right breast, and gave the women
Who were to wield the bow the name they bear: –
– And fell in faint before the words were uttered –
The Amazons, that is, the Breastless Ones! –
And then the crown was set upon her head.
ACHILLES: Why, by great Zeus, she had no need of
        breasts!

Surely she could have ruled a race of men;
With all my soul I kneel to her in homage.

PENTHESILEA: Upon this deed was silence, Peleid.
And nothing but the bow was heard, that sang
As from the pale and icy deathlike hands
Of the high priestess, down the steps it dropped,
The royal bow of gold, and in its fall
Three times gave echo from the marble floor,
That boomed like sounded bells, and laid itself,
Silent as death at last, before her feet. –

ACHILLES: – I hope that in this commonwealth of women,
You do not follow her example.

PENTHESILEA: Why, –
It is not done – with such a zeal as hers.

ACHILLES [in astonishment]:
What? Then you do? – It cannot be!

PENTHESILEA: What is it?

ACHILLES: So then, this monstrous tale, it is the truth?
And all these creatures in their loveliness
About you here, the flower of their sex,
Each perfect, like an altar every one
Adorned to kneel before with vows of love,
Are mutilated? Vile, inhuman deed!

PENTHESILEA: What, were you ignorant of that?

ACHILLES [pressing his face to her breast]:   My queen!
The seat of tender feelings, youthful, warm,
For such an idle, barbarous –

PENTHESILEA: Be calm.
These all were saved; they fled, here to the left,
Where now they dwell the nearer to the heart;
I hope you will not find I lack for any.

ACHILLES: Indeed, a waking dream by morning's light
Would seem to me more truthful than this moment.
– Go on.

PENTHESILEA: What do you mean?

ACHILLES: How will this end?
This commonwealth of women, in its pride
Founded without the help of men, without

    Men's aid how does it propagate itself?
    What, does Deucalion, from time to time,
    Throw you head-first one of his earthen clods?
PENTHESILEA: Whenever, after yearly calculation,
    The queen decides the state must have restored
    What death has taken from her, then she bids
    The fairest women from –
    [*She stops, and looks at him.*]
                         You smile?
ACHILLES: Who? I?
PENTHESILEA: I thought you smiled, my love.
ACHILLES: Why, at your beauty.
    Forgive me, it distracted me – I thought –
    Perhaps you climbed down from the moon to me?
    [*Pause.*]
PENTHESILEA: Whenever, after yearly calculation,
    The queen decides, what death has taken from her
    The state must have restored, she bids the fairest
    Of women from all corners of the realm
    Come to Themiscyra, and in the temple
    Of Artemis she prays that they may know
    The blessing of Mars' seed within their wombs.
    This festival, in gentle quiet, is called
    The festival of maiden buds; we wait
    Until the snows have melted and the spring
    Has set his kiss upon the breast of nature.
    At this request, Diana's great priestess
    Presents herself to Mars within his temple,
    And there prostrate upon the altar lays
    Before the god our state's wise mother's wish.
    Then will the god – if he will hear her prayer;
    For often he refuses it, the mountains
    Amidst their snow in food are not too rich –
    The god will show us then, through his priestess,
    A people, chaste and noble, to appear
    To us instead of him and take his place.
    The name and country of this people spoken,
    Rejoicing spreads through city and through land.

As brides of Mars they are received, the maidens
Are given weapons from their mothers' hands,
Arrows and daggers; and upon their limbs,
Attended all around by joyful hands,
Is swiftly laid their wedding-dress of bronze.
The day of glad departure is announced,
And when the trumpets softly sound, they leap,
The maidens, whispering, upon their horses,
And with a silent tread, in secrecy,
They make their way through shining forest nights
Far off to reach the chosen nation's camp.
When we are there, we rest before his gates,
Two days to be refreshed, both troops and horses;
Then like the fiery hurricane we fall
Swiftly upon the forest groves of men,
And sweep the ripest of the ones that fall,
Like seeds that fly when treetops bend and crack,
Away into the meadows of our homeland.
There in Diana's temple we attend them,
Through holy festivals of which I know
Only the name: the festival of roses –
And which on pain of death no one may see
Beyond the company of brides themselves –
Until the seed in us has blossomed forth;
Then give them presents, every one, like kings,
And at the festival of ripeness, send
Them home on chariots splendidly adorned.
This festival is not a day of joy,
O son of Thetis; many tears are seen,
And many a heart is seized with dark despair,
And cannot see how mighty Tanaïs
For that first word she spoke deserves our praise.
– What is it that you dream?

ACHILLES: I?

PENTHESILEA: You.

ACHILLES [*distracted*]:   My love,
More than I can explain to you in words.
– And am I thus to be sent home as well?

388

PENTHESILEA: I do not know, o do not ask –
ACHILLES: Why, strange!
[*He pauses, deep in thought*]
– But one thing more you will explain to me.
PENTHESILEA: Gladly, my friend. Be bold.
ACHILLES: I cannot grasp
That you should fix your hot pursuit on *me*.
It seemed as if you knew me.
PENTHESILEA: So I did.
ACHILLES: How then?
PENTHESILEA: You will not smile? It is so foolish.
ACHILLES [*smiling*]: Like you I say: I do not know.
PENTHESILEA: Then you
Shall hear it. – See, I had already known
The happy festival of roses three
And twenty times, and always from afar,
Where from the oaken grove the temple rears,
The joyous sound had come to me; when Ares,
Upon Otrere's death, who was my mother,
Took me to be his chosen bride. For we
Princesses of the nation's royal house
May never join the maidens' festival
Upon our own desires; but when the god
Requires us, he will call us worthily,
And through the lips of his most high priestess.
My mother lay, still pale at death's approach,
Within my arms, when solemnly there came
The call of Mars to me within the palace,
That summoned me to rise and go to Troy,
To meet him there and bring him home in garlands.
It happened that no nation ever named
To take his place could more delight the brides
Than this, the Greeks that were embattled there.
So all around were glad rejoicings heard,
In all the market-places noble songs
Praising the deeds of heroes in this war;
Of Paris' apple and the rape of Helen,
The Atrides that led their men in arms,

The quarrel, and the burning of the ships,
And of Patroclus' death, and with what splendour
Of vengeful triumph you had honoured him;
And every mighty scene of all this time. –
Dissolved in tears, lost in my grief, I heard
Only the half of what the messenger,
The hour Otrere died, had brought to me;
O let me stay with you, I cried, my mother,
Your noble rank employ this one last time,
And bid these women go, and leave us here. –
But she, great queen, who long had wished to see
Me leave her for the battlefields – for when
She died, our throne was heirless, to attract
The eyes of some ambitious neighbour state –
She said: 'No, go, my dearest child! Mars calls you!
It is the Peleid your wreath shall crown;
Then be a mother, proud and glad as I –'
– And softly pressed my hand – and died and left me.

PROTHOE: And so she named his name to you, Otrere?

PENTHESILEA: She named him, Prothoe, as well a mother
In confidence before her daughter may.

ACHILLES: But wherefore? Why? What law is there
            forbids it?

PENTHESILEA: It is not fit that one of Ares' daughters
Should choose her own opponent; she must take
Whichever one the god in battle brings her;
Good fortune to her though, if in her zeal
She shows herself before the noblest foes.
– Not so, my Prothoe?

PROTHOE: It is.

ACHILLES: So – ?

PENTHESILEA: Weeping
I lay throughout a long and grievous month,
At my dear mother's grave; I did not even
Take up the crown that empty lay beside it,
Until at last the oft-repeated cry
Of the impatient people all around
My palace, ready for the battlefield,

Swept me by force upon the throne. I came,
Heavy with grief and with unwilling heart,
To Ares' temple; in my hands there lay
The sounding bow of Amazonian queens;
To me it seemed my mother soared about me,
And nothing was more holy, as I held it,
Than to fulfil that wish with which she died.
And after I had strewn her tomb with flowers,
The sweetest and most fragrant, I set off
To lead the army of the Amazons
To Ilium – and it was not so much Mars,
The mighty god whose voice had summoned me,
No, but Otrere's ghost I sought to please.

ACHILLES: Your sadness at her death lamed fleetingly
The strength that is the pride of your young breast.

PENTHESILEA: I loved her.

ACHILLES: And what then?

PENTHESILEA: As I approached
Scamander's banks, and all the valleys round
Were echoing with the battles fought for Troy,
My pain was healed, and in my soul I felt
A joy to know the noble face of war.
I thought: if now I were to see them all,
The greatest days that history can number,
Repeated for me here, if all the band
Of heroes whom the poets celebrate
Descended to me from the stars, I should
Not find a better man to wear my wreath
Of roses than the one my mother chose:
The tender, savage, sweet and fearful one
That laid great Hector low! O Peleid!
My thought in every hour I was awake,
My every dream was you! The world entire
Lay spread before me like a tapestry;
In every stitch and square I saw displayed
A deed of yours, so great for all to see,
And in my heart, as pure and white as silk,
With blazing tints I branded them each one.

Now I could see you as you cut him down,
Before Troy's gates, the Priamid in flight;
As all afire with victory and triumph
You turned away your face, while he must drag
His bleeding head upon the naked earth;
As Priam came beseeching to your tent –
And o, I wept hot tears to think of it,
That there must yet be feeling, pitiless one,
To stir within your bosom, marble-hard.

ACHILLES: My dearest queen!

PENTHESILEA: But what then must I feel,
O friend, when you yourself at last I saw!
When in Scamander's valley you appeared,
Surrounded by the heroes of your nation,
Day-star amidst the paler stars of night!
It could not have been otherwise if he
Himself had come with his white chariot-team,
Driving in thunder from Olympus' heights,
Ares, the god of war, to greet his bride!
Dazzled I stood, when you escaped from me,
By such an apparition – as at night
When lightning strikes before a wanderer,
The gates of bright Elysium with din
Fly open for a spirit, and are closed.
In that same moment, Peleid, I guessed
From whence this feeling surged into my breast:
The god of love had found his mark in me.
But soon I was resolved on this twin course,
That I would win you, or that I would die;
And now the sweeter of them is accomplished.
– Why do you look – ?
    [*A noise of weapons is heard in the distance.*]

PROTHOE [*secretively*]:   Son of the gods! I beg you,
You must reveal the truth to her at once.

PENTHESILEA [*starting up*]:
The Greeks are coming, women! Up!

ACHILLES [*holding her back*]   Be calm!
They are your prisoners, my gracious queen.

PENTHESILEA: Prisoners?

PROTHOE [*secretively to* ACHILLES]:
                                    By the Styx, it is Ulysses!
  Your men, hard pressed by Meroe, give way!

ACHILLES [*muttering to himself*]:
  Would they were fixed in solid rock!

PENTHESILEA: What is it?

ACHILLES [*with forced gaiety*]:
  Why, you shall bear the earth's own god for me!
  Prometheus shall arise from where he sits,
  Proclaiming to the races of the world:
  See, this is man, this was how I would have him!
  But I'll not follow to Themiscyra,
  But rather you, to fairest Phthia, me;
  For when my people's war is ended, there
  Shall I lead you rejoicing, and shall set you, –
  What bliss is mine! – upon my fathers' throne.
    [*The noise continues.*]

PENTHESILEA: But what – ? I do not understand –

THE WOMEN [*in agitation*]:   O gods!

PROTHOE: O Peleid, will you –

PENTHESILEA: What is it, then?

ACHILLES: Nothing at all, do not be frightened, queen;
  Time presses, you will see, when now you hear
  What was the fate the gods for you decreed.
  Indeed by love's decision I am yours,
  And I shall bear his chains eternally;
  But by the luck of arms you fell to me,
  Before my feet in splendour you sank down,
  When in the field we met; not I to you.

PENTHESILEA [*drawing herself up*]:
  O horror!

ACHILLES: No, I beg you, my beloved!
  Not Zeus himself can alter what has happened.
  Master yourself, stand like a rock, and hear
  This messenger, who, if I do not err,
  Comes here with some unwelcome news for me.
  But you, you understand, he brings you nothing;

Your destiny is done, and sealed for ever;
You are my prisoner; a hound of hell
Would guard you not more savagely than I.

PENTHESILEA: I am your prisoner?

PROTHOE: The truth, my queen!

PENTHESILEA: Eternal powers above, on you I call!

SCENE 16

[*Enter a* GREEK CAPTAIN, *and* ACHILLES' MEN *with his armour*.]

ACHILLES: What is it, then?

CAPTAIN: Withdraw, o son of Peleus!
The luck of battle, ever-fickle, calls
The Amazons once more to victory;
Towards this very spot in strength they charge,
The battle-cry they shout: Penthesilea!

ACHILLES [*stands up and throws off the garlands*]:
My weapons, here, my horses, bring them up!
My chariot! My wheels shall break their bones.

PENTHESILEA [*with quivering lip*]:
No, see him, terrible! Is this the same – ?

ACHILLES [*furiously*]: Are they still far from here?

CAPTAIN: Here, in the valley,
Already you may see their golden crescent.

ACHILLES [*buckling on his armour*]:
Take her away!

A GREEK: Where?

ACHILLES: To the Grecian camp,
A moment, and I will be with you there.

GREEK [*to* PENTHESILEA]:
Come then, get up.

PROTHOE: My queen, alas, my queen!

PENTHESILEA: And not one thunderbolt, Zeus, will you
send me!

SCENE 17

[*Enter* ODYSSEUS *and* DIOMEDES *with the army.*]

DIOMEDES [*crossing the stage with his men*]:
  Away, Dolopian hero, from this place!
  The only way that's open to you still,
  The women even now are cutting off.
  Away! [*Exeunt.*]

ODYSSEUS: Come, take this queen away, you Greeks.

ACHILLES [*to the* CAPTAIN]:
  Alexis! Do this service for me. Help her.

GREEK [*to the* CAPTAIN] : She does not move.

ACHILLES [*to the* GREEKS *attending him*]:
                              Bring me my shield! My spear!
    [*Crying out, as the* QUEEN *resists*]
  Penthesilea!

PENTHESILEA: O great Thetis' son!
  You will not follow to Themiscyra?
  You will not come with me into that temple,
  That rears amidst the crowns of distant oaks?
  Come, I have not yet told you everything –

ACHILLES [*now fully armed, steps before her and holds out his
  hand*]: To Phthia, queen!

PENTHESILEA: O – to Themiscyra!
  O friend, I tell you, to Themiscyra!
  Where Dian's temple rears amidst the oaks!
  Though Phthia were the dwelling of the blest,
  Yet, o my friend, yet to Themiscyra,
  Where Dian's temple rears among the trees!

ACHILLES [*lifting her up*]:
  You must forgive me then, my dearest queen,
  But you shall have your temple; I will build it.

SCENE 18

    [*Enter* MEROE *and* ASTERIA *with the* AMAZON ARMY.]

MEROE: Kill him, the dog!

ACHILLES [*letting go of the* QUEEN *and turning*]:
                              Is it the storm they ride?
AMAZONS [*pressing in between* PENTHESILEA *and* ACHILLES]:
  Rescue the queen!
ACHILLES: By this right hand, I say!
  [*He attempts to drag her away with him.*]
PENTHESILEA [*pulling him back towards her*]:
  You will not come? You will not?
ODYSSEUS: Fool, away!
  This is no place to stay and wrangle. Come!
  [*He drags* ACHILLES *off with him. Exeunt all* GREEKS.]

SCENE 19

  [*Enter the* HIGH PRIESTESS *and her* PRIESTESSES.]
THE AMAZONS: Triumph and victory! The queen is saved!
PENTHESILEA [*after a pause*]:
  Curses for ever on this shameful triumph!
  Curses on every tongue that celebrates it,
  The air be cursed that carries on this news!
  Was I, by every noble rule of war,
  Not his by conquest and the luck of battle?
  When man does battle not with wolves and tigers,
  But with his own kind, can there be a law
  In such a war, I ask, by which a captive,
  Who has surrendered to his enemy,
  May be released from his victorious bonds?
  – O Peleid!
AMAZONS: You gods, what do I hear?
MEROE: Priestess most reverend of Artemis,
  Come nearer, here, I beg you –
ASTERIA: She is angry,
  Because we freed her from the shame of bondage!
HIGH PRIESTESS [*coming forward from the crowd of women*]:
  Why then, my queen, it was a worthy crown,
  This shameful word of insult, I confess,
  To set at last upon your deeds this day.

It was not just that you, ignoring custom,
Sought out your own opponent in the field,
Not just that you, instead of conquering,
Yourself lay in the dust, not just that you
In payment for it garland him with roses;
Your loyal people are to feel your anger,
Who break your fetters, for you turn away,
And summon back your conqueror to you.
So be it, noble child of Tanaïs;
I beg then – it was error, nothing more –
That you forgive us for our hasty deed.
The blood that it has cost I now regret,
The prisoners that we gave up for you,
With all my heart I would we had them still.
Free, in the people's name, I now pronounce you;
And you may go wherever you desire.
Run after him, with fluttering of skirts
That fettered you, and let him weld the crack
Together where we split your chains in two;
It is indeed the sacred rule of war!
But we would ask permission of our queen
To give up now this war, and make our way
Homewards again, back to Themiscyra;
For we at least, we cannot *beg* the Greeks
Escaping there, to wait for us and stand,
Nor bring them down, beseeching them like you,
To crawl before us, victor's wreath in hand.
  [*Pause.*]

PENTHESILEA [*hesitating*]:
Prothoe!
PROTHOE: Sister heart!
PENTHESILEA: Will you stay with me?
PROTHOE: To death, you know it – But, my queen, you
   tremble?
PENTHESILEA: No, nothing, nothing. I will soon be calm.
PROTHOE: Great was this suffering. Be great to meet it.
PENTHESILEA: All lost?
PROTHOE: My queen?

PENTHESILEA: The noble youths we captured?
   And by my fault?
PROTHOE: Be comforted. You will
   Return them to us in another war.
PENTHESILEA: O never more!
PROTHOE: My queen?
PENTHESILEA: O never more!
   In night eternal I will hide myself!

SCENE 20

    [*Enter a* HERALD.]
MEROE: A herald comes, my queen!
ASTERIA: What do you want?
PENTHESILEA [*with a flicker of joy*]:
   From Peleus' son! – Ah, now what shall I hear?
   O Prothoe, bid him go!
PROTHOE: What is your message?
HERALD: My queen! Achilles sends me here to you,
   The son of Peleus and of reed-crowned Thetis,
   And through my lips would speak these words to you:
   Since it is your desire to lead him back
   A captive to the meadows of your homeland,
   However his desire, contrariwise,
   To his own native meadows you to lead;
   He challenges you one last time to meet
   In battle, life or death, and let the sword,
   The brazen tongue of destiny, decide,
   Before the faces of the gods in justice,
   Who is the worthier, you or he, which one,
   By their divine decision, there to lick
   The dust before the feet of his opponent.
   Have you a mind to venture on this contest?
PENTHESILEA [*momentarily turning pale*]:
   O wait until the lightning loose your tongue,
   Accursed messenger, to speak again!
   For I would just as gladly hear a block

Of stone in noisy avalanche crash down
The precipice with countless fathoms' fall.
[*To* PROTHOE] You must repeat it word for word to me.

PROTHOE [*trembling*]: The son of Peleus sent him, I believe,
To challenge you to fight him once again;
Refuse him quickly now, and tell him no.

PENTHESILEA: It cannot be.

PROTHOE: It cannot be, my queen?

PENTHESILEA: The son of Peleus sends to me his
challenge?

PROTHOE: Am I to tell him no, bid him be gone?

PENTHESILEA: The son of Peleus sends to me his
challenge?

PROTHOE: To battle, yes, my mistress, as I said.

PENTHESILEA: He knows I am too weak to fight with him;
And sends his challenge, Prothoe, to battle?
This faithful bosom will not move his heart
Until his spears have torn it with their points?
All that I whispered to him, did his ear
But hear as sounds of empty melody?
The temple in the trees – he does not care?
My hands have wreathed an image carved in stone?

PROTHOE: Forget him, for he knows no feeling.

PENTHESILEA [*ardently*]: So,
This was the strength I needed to resist him;
Now he shall crawl and lick the dust, and if
The Lapiths and the giants were his protectors!

PROTHOE: My dearest queen –

MEROE: But will you not consider –

PENTHESILEA [*interrupting them*]:
You shall have *every* captive back again!

HERALD: In battle, then –

PENTHESILEA: I will present myself;
Before the face of all the gods – I call
The Furies too to witness – let him strike me!
[*Thunder.*]

HIGH PRIESTESS: O if my words provoked, Penthesilea,
I beg you, let my grief –

PENTHESILEA [*suppressing her tears*]: No, holy one!
  It shall not be you spoke to me in vain.
MEROE: Most noble priestess, it is you must sway her.
HIGH PRIESTESS: Do you not hear his anger, queen?
PENTHESILEA: I call him
  With all his thunderbolts upon my head!
FIRST AMAZON COLONEL [*in agitation*]:
  Princesses, this –
SECOND COLONEL: Impossible!
THIRD COLONEL: We cannot!
PENTHESILEA [*quivering with frenzy*]:
  Come here, Ananke, mistress of the dogs!
FIRST COLONEL: But we are scattered, weakened –
SECOND COLONEL: We are tired –
PENTHESILEA: You, Tyrrhoe, the elephants!
PROTHOE: My queen!
  Would you with dogs, would you with elephants –
PENTHESILEA: You chariots glittering and armed with
      scythes
  To reap the harvest of the battlefield,
  Come, come in savage ranks to cut your swathes!
  And you who crush and grind this crop of men,
  That stalk and ear and seed are lost for ever,
  You, on your horses, gather here about me!
  And all the fearful pomp of war I summon,
  Destruction, terror, death, on you I call!
    [*She seizes the great bow, which one of the* AMAZONS *is
    holding. Enter* AMAZONS *with dogs on leash; later others
    with elephants, firebrands, scythed chariots, etc.*]
PROTHOE: Beloved of my soul, will you not hear me?
PENTHESILEA [*turning to the dogs*]:
  Up, Tigris, up, I need you! Up, Leaena!
  Up, you, Melampus with the shaggy mane!
  Up, Alke swift to catch the fox, up Sphinx,
  Alector who outruns the fleetest hind,
  Up, Oxus who tears down the savage boar,
  And you who do not fear the lion, Hyrcaon!
    [*Loud thunder.*]

PROTHOE: She is beside herself!

FIRST COLONEL: She is insane!

PENTHESILEA [*kneels, with every sign of madness, while the dogs set up a savage howling*]:

You, Ares, I invoke, you god of terror,
You, mighty founder of my royal house,
Ah! – down to me, your chariot of bronze;
Where cities with their walls and towers you shatter,
God of destruction, trampling down the people;
Ah! – down to me, your chariot of bronze:
That I may set my foot within it, seize
The reins and harness, hurtle through the fields,
And from the storm-clouds like the thunderbolt
Fall down upon this Greek and cleave his skull!
[*She stands up.*]

FIRST COLONEL: Princesses!

SECOND COLONEL: In her madness now restrain
her!

PROTHOE: My mighty queen, will you not hear me?

PENTHESILEA: Ho!
I must be sure my arrows find their mark!
[*She aims at* PROTHOE.]

PROTHOE [*falling to the ground*]:
O gods!

A PRIESTESS [*running behind the* QUEEN]:
Achilles calls!

ANOTHER PRIESTESS [*likewise*]:
The Peleid!

THIRD PRIESTESS: Here, here, behind you!

PENTHESILEA [*turning*]: Where?

FIRST PRIESTESS: Was it not he?

PENTHESILEA: No, here the Furies are not yet assembled.
– Follow, Ananke! Follow, all you others!
[*Exit* PENTHESILEA *followed by all the fighting forces, amidst violent thunder and lightning.*]

MEROE [*helping* PROTHOE *to her feet*]:
Horror!

ASTERIA: Away, be after her, you women!

HIGH PRIESTESS [*deathly pale*]:
  Olympians! What is this you have decreed?
  [*Exeunt all the remaining* AMAZONS.]

SCENE 21

  [*Enter* ACHILLES *and* DIOMEDES.]
ACHILLES: Hear, do this favour for me, Diomede,
  And tell that sour-faced moralist, Ulysses,
  I beg you, not a word of what I say;
  It makes me ill, I cannot bear to see
  That twitch of angry censure in his lip.
DIOMEDES: But have you sent the herald, Peleid?
  Can it be true?
ACHILLES: I'll tell you this, my friend:
  – But you, you understand, will make no answer;
  No, not a word! – This woman is a wonder;
  Half nymph and half a Fury – and she loves me;
  And I – in spite of every girl in Greece –
  By Hades! By the Styx! I love her too.
DIOMEDES: What!
ACHILLES: Yes. And yet a whim that's sacred to her
  Insists she beat me on the battlefield,
  Before she can embrace me with her love.
  And so I sent –
DIOMEDES: Madman!
ACHILLES: – He will not hear!
  Whatever it may be, in all the world,
  If he's not set his own two eyes upon it,
  Nor is there room for it within his brain.
DIOMEDES: But will you then – ? – no, tell me!
ACHILLES: Will I what?
  What is it is so fearful I would do?
DIOMEDES: But do you mean you only sent your challenge
  So that – ?
ACHILLES: By Cronos' son that shakes the clouds!
  I tell you she'll do nothing! Sooner would
  Her hand in combat ravage her own breast,

And when its life-blood runs, cry victory,
Than fall on me! – And only for a month
Am I to be her slave, to serve her will;
A month, or maybe two, no more; and *that*
Will not break down your Isthmus, where the sea
For centuries has gnawed away in vain!
Then I'll be free, she told me so herself,
As moorland stag; and if she'd come with me,
By Jupiter! my joy would be complete,
If I could set her on my fathers' throne.
　　[*Enter* ODYSSEUS.]

DIOMEDES: Ulysses, come, I beg you.

ODYSSEUS:　　　　　　　　　Peleid!
You have called out the queen to fight with you;
Do you intend, with all our men exhausted,
What has so often failed, again to venture?

DIOMEDES: No, no, my friend, no venture and no fighting;
He only wants to let her capture him.

ODYSSEUS: What?

ACHILLES [*flushing violently*]:
　　　　　　　　Do not let me see that face, I beg!

ODYSSEUS: He wants – ?

DIOMEDES:　　　　　　You hear, I say! To split her
　　　　helmet,
To rage and threaten like a gladiator,
To thunder on her shield until sparks fly,
And dumb and silent, like a vanquished man,
Lay himself down before her dainty feet.

ODYSSEUS: Has this man lost his wits, you son of Peleus?
And did you hear what he –

ACHILLES:　　　　　　　　I pray you, stop
That quiver in your upper lip, Odysseus!
I find it catching, by the gods, it spreads,
I feel the twitching down here in my fist.

ODYSSEUS [*furious*]: By Phlegethon the fiery! I will know
Whether my ears have heard amiss or rightly!
You, son of Tydeus, now, I pray, confirm
With solemn oath, and let me clearly hear

Your answers to the questions I shall ask you.
Will he, in truth, surrender to the queen?
DIOMEDES: In truth.
ODYSSEUS: Go with her to Themiscyra?
DIOMEDES: He will.
ODYSSEUS: And all our battles here, for Helen,
Before the gates of Ilium, the madman,
All that, just like a children's game, because
Some other trinket takes his eye, let drop?
DIOMEDES: By Zeus! I swear it.
ODYSSEUS [*folding his arms*]: Unbelievable.
ACHILLES: I hear he talks of Ilium's gates.
ODYSSEUS: What?
ACHILLES: What?
ODYSSEUS: I thought I heard you speak.
ACHILLES: I?
ODYSSEUS: You!
ACHILLES: I said:
I hear he talks of Ilium's gates.
ODYSSEUS: Indeed!
As well I might! I asked if all our battles
Before the gates of Ilium here, for Helen,
Had been forgotten like a waking dream?
ACHILLES [*drawing closer to him*]:
If Ilium's citadel, Laertiad,
Were swallowed up, you hear me, and a lake
With bluish waves flowed over where it stands;
If in the moonlight grey-clad fishermen
Hitched up their boats upon its weathervanes;
If pike held court in Priam's palace, rats
And otters lay in Helen's bed embraced:
I should not care; no more than I care now.
ODYSSEUS: By Styx, he is in earnest, son of Tydeus!
ACHILLES: By Styx! By the Lernaean swamp! By Hades!
By all the upper and the lower world,
And every other place; I am in earnest;
That temple of Diana I will see!
ODYSSEUS [*into* DIOMEDES' *ear*]:

404

Do all you can to keep him, Diomedes,
If you will be so good.

DIOMEDES: If I – indeed!
But you must be so good, and lend your arms.
     [*Enter the* HERALD.]

ACHILLES: Ha! Will she come? What news? Speak, will
       she come?

HERALD: Yes, son of Thetis, she is coming, now;
But bringing with her dogs and elephants,
And cavalry, a huge and savage troop;
I do not know, should this be single combat?

ACHILLES: Good. That she had to do. Come, follow me!
– By the eternal gods, o, she is cunning!
– You said with dogs?

HERALD: I did.

ACHILLES: And elephants?

HERALD: A terror to behold, o son of Peleus!
If it were to attack the Atrides
Themselves, encamped before Troy's citadel,
She could not arm herself with blacker horrors!

ACHILLES [*to himself*]:
They'll eat out of my hand, no doubt – Come, follow!
– O, they are tame as she! [*Exit with his men.*]

DIOMEDES: He is insane!

ODYSSEUS: Let him be bound and gagged – hear me, you
       Greeks!

DIOMEDES: The Amazons are drawing near – away!
     [*Exeunt all* GREEKS.]

SCENE 22

     [*Enter the* HIGH PRIESTESS, *pale-faced; other* PRIEST-
     ESSES *and* AMAZONS.]

HIGH PRIESTESS: Bring ropes, you women, here!

FIRST PRIESTESS: Most reverend!

HIGH PRIESTESS: Down to the ground with her! Let her
       be bound!

AN AMAZON: Is it the queen you mean?

HIGH PRIESTESS: But she is crazed!
  She is beyond restraint of human hands.
THE AMAZONS: Most holy mother! Why this furious rage?
HIGH PRIESTESS: Three maidens she has trampled in her
      frenzy,
  Whom we sent out to hold her back; on Meroe,
  Because on bended knees she barred her way,
  Imploring her by every name that's sweet,
  She set her pack of dogs to drive her off.
  As I from far approached her in her madness
  Straightway she bent, and tore with both her hands –
  Her look of rage and hatred turned upon me –
  A boulder from the ground – I had been lost,
  If I had not sought shelter in the crowd.
FIRST PRIESTESS: O terrible!
SECOND: O fearful, all you women.
HIGH PRIESTESS: Now she is raving, there among her
      dogs,
  With foam upon her lip, and calls them sisters,
  The howling pack, and like a very Maenad,
  With bowstring drawn she dances through the fields,
  Urging them on, with murder in their breath
  Surrounding her, to catch the noblest game
  That ever, so she says, was seen on earth.
THE AMAZONS: You gods of hell! What punishment is this!
HIGH PRIESTESS: So with your rope, daughters of Ares,
      swiftly,
  Where the ways cross prepare your snares for her,
  Hidden in brushwood, laid before her feet;
  And when her foot is caught in them, then leap
  And seize her like a dog with madness stricken;
  Then we may tie her up and take her home,
  To see if there is hope of saving her.
THE AMAZON ARMY [*offstage*]:
  Triumph and victory! Achilles falls!
  Captured the hero! See, the conqueror,
  With roses she will wreathe his vanquished brow!
    [*Pause.*]

HIGH PRIESTESS [*her voice stifled with joy*]:
  Do my ears hear aright?
PRIESTESSES *and* AMAZONS: You gods be praised!
HIGH PRIESTESS: Was this not sound of gladness and
      rejoicing?
FIRST PRIESTESS: The cry of victory, most holy one,
  More joy to me than any ever heard!
HIGH PRIESTESS: Who will bring news, you maidens?
SECOND PRIESTESS: Terpe! Quickly!
  Climb to the hill-top, tell us what you see!
AN AMAZON [*climbs the hill and cries out in horror*]:
  You fearful gods that rule the underworld,
  Bear witness: what is this that I must see?
HIGH PRIESTESS: What then – as if it were the Gorgon's
      head!
PRIESTESSES: What do you see? Speak! Say!
THE AMAZON: Penthesilea,
  She lies upon him with the savage dogs,
  She that was born of woman's womb – and tears
  Achilles' body, tears it limb from limb!
HIGH PRIESTESS: O horror! horror!
ALL: Terrible to see!
THE AMAZON: Here comes, with features pale as of a
      corpse,
  One who will speak this fearful riddle for us.
  [*She climbs down from the hill.*]

SCENE 23

  [*Enter* MEROE.]
MEROE: Most holy priestesses of Artemis,
  And Ares' virgin daughters, hear my words:
  I am the African Medusa, I,
  And where you stand shall turn you into stone.
HIGH PRIESTESS: Creature of horror, speak your news!
MEROE: You know
  How she set out to meet the youth she loves,

She who for ever shall be nameless now –
And with her youthful senses in confusion
Arming the ardent wish to make him hers
With every terror weapons can provide.
By howling dogs and elephants surrounded,
With bow in hand, we saw her drawing near.
When civil war that rages in the state,
A loathsome figure, dripping blood about him,
Approaches terrible with giant stride,
Swinging his torch to sear the flowering cities,
He is a sight less wild and fierce than she.
Achilles, so they tell us in the army,
Had only challenged her that he might let
Her freely beat him, foolish youth, in battle;
For he, he too – how mighty are the gods! –
He loved her, for her youth had moved his heart;
To Dian's temple he would follow her;
Now he draws near in sweet anticipation,
And leaves his friends behind him as he comes.
But when she thunders down in rage upon him,
Armed with such terrors, he who but for show
Has taken up a spear, so unsuspecting,
He halts, and turns his slender neck, and listens,
And flees in horror, halts, and flees again;
Like a young roebuck when in rocky heights
He hears the roaring of the savage lion.
He cries: Odysseus! – with an anxious note,
And fearful looks around, cries: Son of Tydeus!
And tries to flee, and find his friends again;
And stops – already he has been cut off –
And holds his hands up, ducks and hides himself
Beneath a pine-tree, o unhappy wretch!
That droops its dark and heavy branches down.
Meanwhile the queen is drawing closer still,
The pack of dogs behind her, looking out
Over the rocks and forests like a huntsman;
And as he parts the branches, and would throw
Himself upon the ground before her feet,

– His antlers give away the stag! she cries,
And straightway with the strength of madness draws
The bow, that in a kiss its two ends meet,
And raises up the bow and aims and shoots,
And drives her arrow through his throat; he falls;
Hoarsely the cry of victory is raised.
Yet still he lives, unhappiest of mortals,
The arrow far protruding from his neck,
Lifts himself up with fearful gasps, and stumbles,
And rises up again and tries to flee;
But she: Set on! cries, Tigris! on, Leaena!
On, Sphinx! Melampus! Dirke! On, Lycaon!
And rushes – rushes on him, o Diana!
She-dog herself, the savage pack entire,
And tears him, tears him by his helmet, down;
One fastens on his breast, one on his throat,
The ground gives back the echo of his fall!
He, struggling in the purple streams of blood,
Touches her tender cheek, and calls to her:
Penthesilea! O my bride, is this
The festival of roses that you promised?
But she – the lioness had heard his cry,
That gnawed with hunger seeks about for prey,
Howling amidst the barren wastes of snow;
She tears the armour from his body, sinks
Her teeth and locks them in his milk-white breast,
She and the dogs, in savagery vying;
Oxus and Sphinx upon the right their teeth,
She on the left clamps hers; when I appeared,
The blood was dripping from her mouth and hands.
        [*Pause of silent horror.*]
If you have heard me, women, speak to me,
And let me hear from you some sign of life.
        [*Pause.*]
FIRST PRIESTESS [*weeping upon the breast of the* SECOND]
    So skilled in every craft of womanhood!
    Such pure delight when she would dance or sing!
    So full of wisdom, grace and dignity!

HIGH PRIESTESS: O this is not Otrere's child! The
　　Gorgon
　Gave birth to her within the palace walls!
FIRST PRIESTESS [*continuing*]:
　She was the daughter of the nightingale
　That dwells about the temple of Diana.
　Rocked in the oak-tree's lofty crown she sat
　And sent her trill, and sent her fluting trill
　Through silent night, to touch the wanderer
　Far off, and stir strange feeling in his breast.
　The snake with dappled back she would not tread,
　That spread its coils beneath her gentle feet;
　The arrow that had pierced the wild boar's breast,
　She called it back; his eye that glazed in death
　Had power to draw her melted with regret
　Upon her knees beside him to the ground!
　　[*Pause.*]
MEROE: She stands there dumb, and fearful to behold,
　Beside his corpse, the pack go sniffing round,
　And gazes, as upon an empty page,
　The bow in victor's style upon her shoulder,
　Into the void of space, and speaks no word.
　With creeping flesh we come to her, and ask
　What she has done? No word. Whether she knows us?
　No word. If she will come with us? No word.
　A horror seized me, and I fled to you.

SCENE 24

　[*Enter* PENTHESILEA, *with the body of* ACHILLES *covered
　with a red cloth;* PROTHOE, *and others.*]
FIRST AMAZON: Look, look, you women! There, she is
　　approaching,
　A wreath of nettles on her head – o horror!
　Entwined with barren twigs of bitter thorn,
　Instead of laurel, following the corpse,
　Hideous, proudly shouldering the bow,
　As if he were her hated enemy!

SECOND PRIESTESS: O see, these hands – !

FIRST PRIESTESS: O women, turn away!

PROTHOE [*falling upon the* HIGH PRIESTESS's *bosom*]:
O holy mother!

HIGH PRIESTESS [*with horror*]: Artemis, I call you:
I am not guilty of this loathsome deed!

FIRST AMAZON: She comes and stands before the high
priestess.

SECOND: She motions, see!

HIGH PRIESTESS: Away from me, you horror!
You citizen of hell! Away, I say!
Take, take this veil, and hide her from my sight.
[*She tears off her veil and throws it in the* QUEEN's *face*.]

FIRST AMAZON: O death in life, she takes no notice of it!

SECOND: She motions still –

THIRD: She motions yet again –

FIRST: Still motions to the feet of the priestess!

SECOND: See, see!

HIGH PRIESTESS: What do you want? Away, I say!
Go to the ravens, shade! Away, and rot!
The peace of life your look will kill for me.

FIRST AMAZON: Ha, that was what she wanted –

SECOND: Now she's still.

FIRST: The Peleid, yes, that was it, before
The feet of Artemis' priestess should lie.

THIRD: Why at the feet of Artemis' priestess?

FOURTH: What does she think to do?

HIGH PRIESTESS: What does this mean?
This corpse? I will not have it! Let it be
Buried by mountains, inaccessible,
And with it the remembrance of this deed!
Did I, you – what to call you, no more human? –
Did I command this fearful murder from you?
If soft reproaches from the mouth of love
Can drive you to such deed of horror, let
The Furies come to teach us gentleness!

FIRST AMAZON: And still she sets her gaze upon the
priestess.

SECOND: Straight in her face –

THIRD: Unflinching, firmly fixed,
  As if she sought to pierce her through and through.

HIGH PRIESTESS: Go, Prothoe, go, I implore you, go,
  I cannot bear her sight, take her away.

PROTHOE [*weeping*]: O grief!

HIGH PRIESTESS: Be resolute!

PROTHOE: The deed that she
  Has done is too appalling; let me be.

HIGH PRIESTESS: Be strong. – She had a fair and lovely
        mother. –
  – Go, offer her your help and lead her on.

PROTHOE: I will not set my eyes on her again!

SECOND AMAZON: See how she looks upon the slender
        arrow!

FIRST: Turns it this way and that –

THIRD: Measures its length!

FIRST PRIESTESS: The arrow, so it seems, that struck him
        down.

FIRST AMAZON: It is!

SECOND: See how she wipes it clean of blood!
  See how she dries each single stain away!

THIRD: What must she think?

SECOND: And look, the feathered flight,
  See how she dries it, combs it into curls,
  So neatly! Everything as it should be.
  O see!

THIRD: Is it her custom so to do?

FIRST: To do this for herself?

FIRST PRIESTESS: Her bow and arrows,
  These she has always cleaned with her own hand.

SECOND PRIESTESS: O, sacred in her eyes, it must be
        said –

SECOND AMAZON: But now she takes the quiver from her
        shoulder,
  And puts the arrow back in rightful place.

THIRD: Now she has finished –

SECOND: Now it is accomplished –

FIRST PRIESTESS: Now once again she looks out on the
    world!
SEVERAL WOMEN: O grievous sight! O desolate indeed
  As sandy wastes with never blade of grass!
  A garden ravaged by the lava-stream,
  Boiled in the bowels of earth and vomited
  To smother every flower of its bosom,
  Still is more fair to look on than this face.
    [PENTHESILEA *shudders violently, and drops her bow*.]
HIGH PRIESTESS: Creature of horror!
PROTHOE [*frightened*]:   Now what must we see?
FIRST AMAZON: The bow, the mighty, tumbled from her
    hand!
SECOND: See how it drops –
FOURTH: Rings out, and sways, and falls –
SECOND: And once more quivers on the ground –
THIRD: And dies,
  Even as it was born to Tanaïs.
    [*Pause.*]
HIGH PRIESTESS [*suddenly turning to* PENTHESILEA]:
  My noble mistress, will you pardon me?
  The goddess, Artemis, again is pleased;
  You have done satisfaction for her anger.
  The founder of the commonwealth of women,
  The mighty Tanaïs, I now confess,
  Wielded the bow not worthier than you.
FIRST AMAZON: She speaks no word.
SECOND: Her eye –
THIRD: She lifts her finger,
  All bloodstained, why, what will she – See, o see!
SECOND: O sight to tear the heart more sharp than knives!
FIRST: She wipes a tear away.
HIGH PRIESTESS [*sinking back on* PROTHOE'*s bosom*]:
         O Artemis!
  O, such a tear!
FIRST PRIESTESS: A tear, most holy one,
  That softly makes its way into the heart,
  Sets ringing all the stormy bells of feeling,

And cries out: Grief and pain! so that the race
That quickly hears such promptings rushes out
Of streaming eyes, and gathered to an ocean
Weeps for the ruin of her noble soul.

HIGH PRIESTESS: Now then indeed, if Prothoe will not
  help her,
Here she must perish in her hour of need.

PROTHOE [*her features expressing the most violent struggle, approaches her and then speaks, her voice still broken by tears*]:
Will you not sit and be consoled, my queen?
Will you not rest upon my faithful bosom?
Much you have fought, upon this fearful day,
And suffered much – from so much suffering
Will you not rest upon my faithful bosom?

[PENTHESILEA *looks round as if for a chair.*]

A seat for her! You see that she desires it.

[*The* AMAZONS *roll up a stone.* PENTHESILEA, *helped by* PROTHOE, *sits down on it.* PROTHOE *then sits down herself.*]

You know me, sister heart?

[PENTHESILEA *looks at her; her face clears slightly.*]

                              Your Prothoe,
Who loves you still so tenderly.

[PENTHESILEA *gently strokes her cheek.*]

                                    O you
To whom my heart bows down on bended knee,
You touch me so! [*Kisses the* QUEEN's *hand.*]
                        You must be very tired?
Ah, how you show what work it is you do!
But – victory is not so cleanly won,
And every trade leaves trace upon its master.
Yet would it not be good to wash yourself,
Your hands and face? Shall I have water sent?
– My dearest queen!

[PENTHESILEA *looks at herself, and nods.*]

                        Yes, it is what she wishes.

[PROTHOE *motions to the* AMAZONS, *who go to fetch water.*]

– You will be glad of it, it will refresh you,

And gently, laid upon a cooling carpet,
You will be rested from this hard day's work.
FIRST PRIESTESS: But when you sprinkle her, o have a
    care,
She will remember.
HIGH PRIESTESS: Certainly, I hope.
PROTHOE: You hope so, holy priestess? So I fear.
HIGH PRIESTESS [*appearing to reflect*]:
  But why then? – Only that we dare not do it,
  Or else the body of Achilles should –
    [PENTHESILEA *looks furiously at the* HIGH PRIESTESS.]
PROTHOE: Stop, stop!
HIGH PRIESTESS: No, no, my queen, no, it is nothing,
  You shall have everything just as it is.
PROTHOE: Take off your victor's wreath, your thorny
    crown,
We all have seen you were the conqueror.
And let me free your throat as well – So, there!
But look, a wound – and deep, I see! Poor queen!
Why then, it was no easy task you had –
But now for that your triumph is the greater!
– O Artemis!
    [TWO AMAZONS *bring a large, shallow marble basin with*
    water.]
                Here set the basin down.
Now shall I pour some water on your head?
And will you not be frightened? – Why, what is it?
    [PENTHESILEA *drops down from her seat on her knees in*
    front of the basin, and pours water over her head.]
There! That was brave of you indeed, my queen!
Does it not do you good?
PENTHESILEA [*looking round*]: O Prothoe!
    [*She pours more water over herself.*]
MEROE [*joyfully*]: She speaks!
HIGH PRIESTESS: The gods be thanked!
PROTHOE: O, this is good!
MEROE: To life restored, to us!
PROTHOE: O, excellent!

Your head right under water now, my dearest!
There! And again! So! Like a young white swan!
MEROE: Lovely to look on!
FIRST PRIESTESS: How she hangs her head!
MEROE: And how she lets the water trickle down!
PROTHOE: Was this enough now?
PENTHESILEA: Ah, how wonderful!
PROTHOE: Then come with me, back to your chair again.
  – Now quickly give your veils to me, priestesses,
That I may dry these soft and clinging locks!
So, Phania, yours! Yours, Terpe! help me, sisters!
And let her head and neck be covered quite!
So, there! And now – upon your chair again!
  [*She covers the* QUEEN's *head, lifts her up onto the stone, and
  holds her tightly embraced.*]
PENTHESILEA: How strange!
PROTHOE: Are you not well?
PENTHESILEA [*lisping*]:   O, blissfully!
PROTHOE: My sister heart! Beloved! O my life!
PENTHESILEA: O tell me, am I in Elysium?
And you one of those nymphs for ever young,
Attending on our great and glorious queen,
When through the rustling of the oaken crowns
She softly sinks into her crystal cave?
These features, was it just for my delight
You took the features of my Prothoe?
PROTHOE: No, no, my dearest queen, it is not so.
No, it is I, your Prothoe, who holds
You in her arms, and what you see about you
Is still the fragile world, on which the gods
Will only deign to cast a distant glance.
PENTHESILEA: Yes, good. Yes, very good. It does not
    matter.
PROTHOE: What is it, mistress?
PENTHESILEA: I am satisfied.
PROTHOE: We cannot understand; explain, dear heart.
PENTHESILEA: That I still *am*, contents me. Let me rest.
  [*Pause.*]

MEROE: How strange!

HIGH PRIESTESS: How wondrously this thing now
  ends!

MEROE: If skilfully we could draw out from her – ?

PROTHOE: What was it then, that bred in you this fancy,
  That you descended to the realm of shades?

PENTHESILEA [*after a pause, in a kind of ecstasy*]:
  I am so happy, sister! More than happy!
  I feel that I am ripe for death, Diana!
  Indeed I do not know what happened here,
  But I could die this moment, and believe
  For certain that I conquered Peleus' son!

PROTHOE [*under her breath to the* HIGH PRIESTESS]:
  Take it away, the body, quick!

PENTHESILEA [*sitting up*]: O Prothoe!
  Who is it?

PROTHOE [*as the bearers hesitate*]:
  Are you mad? Away!

PENTHESILEA: Diana!
  Can it be true?

PROTHOE: Can what be true, beloved?
  – Here! Gather close together! [*She motions to the* PRIEST-
  ESSES *to stand in front of the body and hide it as it is lifted
  up*.]

PENTHESILEA [*holding her hands joyfully in front of her face*]:
  Holy gods!
  I am not bold enough to look around.

PROTHOE: What would you do, my queen? What are you
  thinking?

PENTHESILEA [*looking round*]:
  O love, you tease me!

PROTHOE: No, by Jupiter,
  The world's eternal god!

PENTHESILEA [*with mounting impatience*]: You holy women,
  I beg you, part your ranks!

HIGH PRIESTESS [*pressing in with the others*]:
  Beloved queen!

PENTHESILEA [*standing up*]:

Diana! O, why should I not? Diana!
Yes, once before he stood behind my back!

MEROE: See, see! How horror seizes her!

PENTHESILEA [*to the* AMAZONS *carrying the body*]:

Stop there! –

What are you carrying? Stand! I will see.

[*She pushes the women aside until she comes to the body.*]

PROTHOE: My queen, I beg you, seek to know no more!

PENTHESILEA: Is it, you maidens? He?

ONE OF THE BEARERS [*as the body is put down*]:

Whom do you mean?

PENTHESILEA: I see that it is not impossible.
Why, I can wound a swallow's wing in flight,
So that the wing can yet be healed again;
The stag I lure with arrows to my park.
But it is treacherous, the archer's skill;
And if the gold of fortune waits our shot,
Deceitful gods will draw the bowstring for us.
– What, did I strike too close? Speak, is it he?

PROTHOE: O by the fearful powers of Olympus,
Ask not!

PENTHESILEA: Away from me! And though his wounds
Like Hades' jaws should gape before my face:
I will see him!

[*She lifts the cloth.*]

Which of you did this deed, you monstrous women?

PROTHOE: You ask us still?

PENTHESILEA: O, holy Artemis!
O, now your child can bear no more!

HIGH PRIESTESS: She falls upon the ground!

PROTHOE: Eternal gods!
Why did you pay no heed to my advice?
O it were better, luckless wretch, to wander,
With reason like the sun in dark eclipse,
Upon the earth for ever, ever, ever,
Than to have seen this day, of days most fearful!
– O dearest, will you hear me?

HIGH PRIESTESS: O my queen!

MEROE: Ten thousand hearts are here to share your pain!

HIGH PRIESTESS: Will you not rise?

PENTHESILEA: This rosy wreath of blood!
  This garland, here, of wounds about his head!
  Ah, how these buds with fragrance of the grave
  Go down to make their festival for worms!

PROTHOE [*tenderly*]: Yet it was love that garlanded him
    so?

MEROE: Ah, but too tightly!

PROTHOE: And with thorns of roses,
  So eager that this love should be for ever!

HIGH PRIESTESS: Be gone!

PENTHESILEA: But this you shall not keep from me:
  Who was it so presumed to be my rival?
  – I do not ask who slew him while he lived,
  And killed him; by our everlasting gods!
  Free as a bird he may depart from me.
  I ask who made the dead man dead to me;
  That you must answer for me, Prothoe.

PROTHOE: What do you mean, my mistress?

PENTHESILEA: Understand me.
  I do not seek to know who robbed his breast
  Of its Promethean spark. I do not seek,
  Because I do not seek; I will it so.
  I shall forgive him; he may take his flight.
  But who, o Prothoe, to commit this theft
  So basely scorned the open door, and broke
  Through every snow-white alabaster wall
  Into this temple; who so ravaged him,
  This youth, the living image of the gods,
  So fearfully that life and foul decay
  Will not dispute possession; who so tore him
  That pity will not weep for him, that love
  Itself eternal, like a common whore
  Unfaithful still in death, must turn away;
  On him I vow to wreak revenge. Now speak!

PROTHOE [*to the* HIGH PRIESTESS]:
  O, what are we to tell her in her raving?

PENTHESILEA: Now, shall I hear the truth?

PROTHOE: O dearest queen,
If it will bring your sufferings relief,
Then take revenge on which of us you will;
Here we all stand and offer up ourselves.

PENTHESILEA: Take care, or they will say that it was I.

HIGH PRIESTESS [*timidly*]: Who could it be, unhappy
wretch, if not –

PENTHESILEA: Princess of blackest hell in robes of light,
You dare – ?

HIGH PRIESTESS: I call Diana to my witness!
And let all those assembled here about you
Confirm my words! It was your arrow struck him;
And heaven! had it only been your arrow!
But as he sank to earth, you threw yourself,
In the confusion of your savage senses,
Upon him with the pack of dogs and plunged –
O no, my lips they tremble to pronounce
The thing you did. Ask not! Come, let us go.

PENTHESILEA: Then I must hear it from my Prothoe.

PROTHOE: O my beloved queen! You must not ask.

PENTHESILEA: What! I? I, – him, – you say – ? And with
the dogs – ?
I, with these dainty hands of mine, you say – ?
And this, my mouth, my lips that swell with love – ?
Ah, made for quite another task than this!
What, working busily together, they –
First mouth, and hand, and hand, and mouth again – ?

PROTHOE: My queen!

HIGH PRIESTESS: I cry Alas! upon your head.

PENTHESILEA: No, hear me, you will not make me believe
it.
And were it written in the night with lightnings,
And did I hear it in the thunder's voice,
Still I would cry to both of you: you lie!

MEROE: Firm as the mountains let this faith still stand,
It is not we will ever seek to shake it.

PENTHESILEA: – How was it he did not defend himself?

HIGH PRIESTESS: Unhappy wretch, he loved you! To
  surrender
 Was all he sought, and that was why he came!
 That was the reason why he challenged you!
 With peace and sweetness in his heart he neared you,
 To follow to the shrine of Artemis.
 But you –
PENTHESILEA: Why, there –
HIGH PRIESTESS: You struck him –
PENTHESILEA: I destroyed him.
PROTHOE: O dearest queen!
PENTHESILEA: Or was it otherwise?
MEROE: Creature of horror!
PENTHESILEA: Kissed him to death?
FIRST PRIESTESS: O heaven!
PENTHESILEA: No, – did not kiss him? Tore him, truly?
   Speak!
HIGH PRIESTESS: Alas! I cry upon you. Hide yourself!
 Let everlasting midnight cover you!
PENTHESILEA: It was in error, then. A kiss, a bite,
 They are so like; who loves with all his heart,
 May take the one and think he takes the other.
MEROE: Help her, eternal gods!
PROTHOE [seizing her]:   Away!
PENTHESILEA: No, no!
   [She struggles free, and kneels in front of the body.]
 You, wretchedest of mortals, will forgive me!
 By Artemis, I did but break my promise
 Because I do not mind my hasty lips;
 But now I tell you plainly how I meant it.
 My dearest, it was this, and nothing more. [She kisses him.]
HIGH PRIESTESS: Take her away!
MEROE: Why should she linger here?
PENTHESILEA: How often, clinging at her lover's neck,
 A woman says she loves him, o, so much
 That she could almost eat him up for love;
 But soon, if one would test her foolish word,
 Already she has had her fill of him.

See now, my dearest, this was not my way.
Look: at the time I clung about your neck,
I did what I had spoken, word for word;
No, I was not so mad as it might seem.

MEROE: O monstrous creature! What was this she spoke?

HIGH PRIESTESS: Seize her, carry her off!

PROTHOE: Come now, my queen!

PENTHESILEA [*allowing* PROTHOE *to lift her upright*]:
Yes. Here I am.

HIGH PRIESTESS: Then you will follow us?

PENTHESILEA: Not you! –
Go to Themiscyra, be happy there,
If it can be –
And above all, my Prothoe –
You all –
And – secretly, a word, let no one hear it:
Tanaïs' ashes, strew them to the winds!

PROTHOE: And you, my dearest sister heart?

PENTHESILEA: I?

PROTHOE: You!

PENTHESILEA: – Why, I will tell you, Prothoe,
I do abjure the law of Amazons,
And follow where this youth has gone.

PROTHOE: What do you mean, my queen?

HIGH PRIESTESS: O, most unhappy!

PROTHOE: You will – ?

HIGH PRIESTESS: You think – ?

PENTHESILEA: What then? But yes!

MEROE: O heaven!

PROTHOE: Then let me speak a word, my sister heart –
[*She tries to take her dagger away.*]

PENTHESILEA: What then? – What are you seeking at my
waist?
– Of course. Wait, now! I did not understand.
Here is the dagger.
[*She takes the dagger from her waist and gives it to* PROTHOE.]
And the arrows too?
[*She takes the quiver from her shoulder.*]

Here, I will empty all the quiverful!
　　[*She tips the arrows out in front of her.*]
Yet still I might be tempted –
　　[*She picks some of them up.*]
For this one – was it not? Or was it this?
Yes, this one! But it does not matter! Take them!
Here, take the arrows, all of them!
　　[*She gathers up the whole bundle of arrows again and puts them in*
　　PROTHOE's *hands.*]

PROTHOE: 　　　　　　　　　Give them to me.
PENTHESILEA: For now I shall descend into my breast,
　Deep as a mine, and dig there, cold as ore,
　A feeling that annihilates my soul.
　This ore I purify in sorrow's fire,
　Harden to steel; in venom plunge it then,
　In searing anguish temper through and through;
　Take it to lay on hope's eternal anvil,
　And grind and sharpen it to make a dagger;
　And to this dagger now present my heart:
　So! So! So! Once more still! – It is well.
　　[*She falls and dies.*]
PROTHOE [*supporting the* QUEEN]:
　She dies!
MEROE: 　　She follows him!
PROTHOE: 　　　　　　　And it is good.
　For here was not the place where she might stay.
　　[*She lays her on the ground.*]
HIGH PRIESTESS: O fragile is this human kind, you gods!
　How proudly she who now lies broken here
　But shortly blossomed on the peaks of life!
PROTHOE: She fell, because she bloomed too proud and
　　　　strong!
　The withered oak-tree stands the storm's full blast,
　The healthy he sends crashing to the ground,
　For he can seize upon its lofty crown.

MEDEA

Franz Grillparzer

A tragedy in five acts
1820

CHARACTERS

CREON, King of Corinth
CREUSA, his daughter
JASON
MEDEA
GORA, her nurse
A HERALD of the Amphictyonic Court
A FARMER
MEDEA'S CHILDREN
SERVANTS

Scene: Corinth.

ACT I

Before the walls of Corinth

[*On the left, in the middle distance, a tent. In the background the sea, part of the town stretching beside it on a tongue of land. It is early morning, before sunrise, still dark. In the right foreground stands a* SLAVE *in a hole in the ground, digging and shovelling up earth. On the other side* MEDEA, *before her a black chest with strange decorations in gold, into which she is putting a variety of magical instruments.*]

MEDEA: Speak, have you finished?

SLAVE: Soon, my mistress, soon.

[GORA *emerges from the tent and remains standing in the background.*]

MEDEA: The veil at first, the staff then of the goddess,
I shall have no more need of you, rest here.
The time of night and magic now is past,
And what will happen, be it good or evil,
Must happen by the open light of day.
This casket next: it holds a secret flame,
Devouring him that opens it unwary.
This other too, filled full of sudden death,
Begone you both from cheerful life's domain!
And many herbs, and stones of baleful power,
Where you were born I place you, in the earth.

[*She stands up.*]

So. Rest here now at peace for ever more!
But still there lacks the last and most important.

[*The* SLAVE, *who has meanwhile climbed up out of the hole and is standing behind* MEDEA, *waiting for her to finish, now as if to help reaches for something bundled up and fixed to a lance which is leaning against a tree behind* MEDEA; *the wrappings fall apart and the Golden Fleece, attached to the lance like a banner, is revealed, shining out radiantly.*]

427

SLAVE [*seizing the banner*]: Is this it, here?

MEDEA: No, stop! Do not unveil it!
Let me look once again upon you, fatal gift!
You witness of my nation's last decline,
Stained with my father's and my brother's blood,
Monument of Medea's guilt and shame!
  [*She steps on the lance-shaft, breaking it in two.*]
Thus with my foot I break you, send you down
To night from whose dark womb you rose so grim.
  [*She lays the broken banner in the chest with the other things, and closes the lid.*]

GORA [*coming forward*]: What are you doing here?

MEDEA: You see.

GORA: You'll bury
The tokens of a service that protected you
And will do still?

MEDEA: Protected, do you say?
It gives no more protection than it gave,
And so I bury them. I am protected.

GORA: What, by your husband's love?

MEDEA [*to the* SLAVE]: Have you not finished?

SLAVE: Yes, mistress!

MEDEA: Come then!
  [*She takes the chest by one handle, the* SLAVE *takes the other, and they carry it to the hole.*]

GORA: O what occupation
For this, a prince's noble princely daughter!

MEDEA: Why, if you think it hard, do you not help me?

GORA: I am Jason's woman, not yours;
When was it known that one slave served another?

MEDEA [*to the* SLAVE]: Now lower it and throw the earth
    upon it!
  [*The* SLAVE *lowers the chest into the hole and shovels earth over it.* MEDEA *kneels beside him.*]

GORA [*in the foreground*]: O let me die, you gods of my own
    land,
That I no more must see what now I see!
But first cast down your vengeful thunderbolt

Upon the traitor who has served us so!
First let me see him die, and then kill me.

MEDEA: It's done. Now stamp the ground and firm it
    down,
And go! I know that you will keep my secret,
You are a Colchian, and I can trust you. [*Exit* SLAVE.]

GORA [*calling after him, angrily and scornfully*]:
Don't let your master know, there will be trouble!
So, have you finished?

MEDEA [*going to her*]:   Yes. Now I am calm.

GORA: The Fleece as well you buried?

MEDEA: That as well.

GORA: You did not leave it back in Iolcus with
Your husband's uncle?

MEDEA: You have seen it here.

GORA: You kept it then and you have buried it
And so it is over and done with!
Let the past be blown away,
No future, there is only present.
There was no Colchis and there are no gods,
Your father never lived, your brother did not die,
You think of it no more – it never was!
Then think as well you are not wretched, think
Your husband loved you, faithless as he is;
Perhaps it will come true!

MEDEA: Gora!

GORA: What then?
You think I will be silent?
The guilty should be silent, and not I!
If you persuaded me to leave my home
And be a slave to your defiant lover,
Where I with fetters on my own free arms
Must sigh long nights away in bitter grief,
And every morning by the sun renewed
Curse my grey hair, the days of my old age;
A laughing-stock, a butt for all men's scorn,
Suffering want of everything but pain,
Then you must hear me when I choose to speak.

MEDEA: Say then!

GORA: What I foresaw has come to pass.
Scarcely a month ago the sea threw up,
Resentfully, seducer and seduced.
Already you are fled by men with loathing,
To all the Colchian woman is a horror,
A terror she who speaks with powers of darkness,
If you but show yourself men hide in fear
And curse you. May their curse fall on themselves!
Your husband too for both your sakes they hate,
The consort of the Colchian princess.
His uncle closed the door before his face,
And when that uncle died, men know not how,
The city of his fathers banished him.
He has no house, no home, no resting-place;
What do you plan to do?

MEDEA: I am his wife.

GORA: And so, what will you do?

MEDEA: I'll follow him
Through pain and death.

GORA: Through pain and death indeed!
Aietes' daughter begging at the door!

MEDEA: Let us entreat the gods for simple hearts,
More easily to bear a simple lot!

GORA [*laughing grimly*]: Ha! And your husband?

MEDEA: Day is breaking. Come.

GORA: Do you evade me? You will not escape me!
The only speck of light in all my grief
Is that I see, by our example see
That there are gods, and debts must all be paid.
Bewail your luck and I will comfort you,
But you must not mistake it, and deny
That justice is pronounced on us above,
Denying pain, that is your punishment.
Ills must be plain to see, if we would cure them!
Your husband, tell me! Is he still the same?

MEDEA: Who else?

GORA: O do not play with words!

Is he the same who took your heart by storm,
Who battled through a hundred swords to reach you,
The same who on that long and fearful journey
Defeated her resistance, that would die
And in her sorrow sent all food away,
Winning her all too quickly with his ardour?
Is he the same? You tremble, then? Yes, tremble!
He fears your sight, he shuns you, flees you, hates you,
And as you did your own, he will betray you.
Bury them, bury them, tokens of your deed!
The deed you cannot bury!

MEDEA: Silence!

GORA: No!

MEDEA: Silence, I say! What are these frenzied ravings?
What comes let us await and see, not summon.
So everything that once has been, is still
And ever present? If the moment is
The cradle of a future, why not then
Grave of a past? What happened, should not happen,
And I repent it, bitterer than you know;
But must I then myself destroy myself?
Let us be clear, and with the world at one!
To other lands, where other nations dwell,
An angry god has led us; here we find
What in our homeland we called right is wrong,
And what permitted, here pursued with hate;
So let us alter too our speech and ways
And if we may no more be what we will,
Then what we can, at least so let us be.
Whatever bound me to my fatherland,
Here I have sunk it deep within the earth;
The power that my mother left to me,
The knowledge of those secrets and their strength
I have returned to night that gave them birth,
And weak, a useless woman, seeking help,
I rush into my husband's open arms;
He shunned the Colchian woman, but his wife
He will receive, as it becomes a husband.

The day is breaking – with it life renewed!
What was, shall be no more; what is, remain!
But you, o earth, our ancient, gentle mother,
Keep safely what I have entrusted you.

    [*They go towards the tent. It opens, and* JASON *comes out with
    a* CORINTHIAN FARMER, *behind him a* SLAVE.]

JASON: You saw the king yourself?

FARMER: I did, my lord.

JASON: What did you say?

FARMER: That there was one to see him,
Well known to him, and sworn by vows of
      friendship,
That would not come into his presence, though,
With enemies and plots on every hand,
Until he promised peace to him, and safety.

JASON: His answer?

FARMER: He will come to you, my lord!
Poseidon's feast they celebrate out here,
With sacrifice upon the open sea-shore;
The king attends, his daughter coming with him,
And as he passes he will speak to you.

JASON: So, it is good. My thanks for this.

MEDEA [*going to them*]:   I greet you!

JASON: I you. [*To the* SLAVE] But you will go, the others
      too,
And break green twigs, as is the custom here
For those that come as suppliants to beg.
You must be quiet and peaceable. You hear?
Enough! [*Exeunt* FARMER *and* SLAVE.]

MEDEA: I find you busy?

JASON: Yes.

MEDEA: You give
Yourself no peace.

JASON: Unending flight, and peace?
I have no peace, or why then should I flee?

MEDEA: You did not sleep last night. I heard you go
And walk about alone and in the darkness.

JASON: I love the night, the daylight hurts my eyes.

MEDEA: And you sent messengers to see the king;
    Will he receive us?

JASON: That I wait to hear.

MEDEA: He is your friend.

JASON: He was.

MEDEA: He will agree.

JASON: A leprous company is to be shunned.
    You know that all the world avoids our sight,
    That even Pelias my uncle's death –
    False villain that an angry god destroyed –
    That people blame his death on me, your husband,
    The man returned from that enchanted land?
    Did you not know?

MEDEA: I knew.

JASON: Reason enough
    To wake and wander in the hours of night! –
    But what drove you to rise before the sun?
    What were you seeking in the darkness? – Why,
    Calling old friends from Colchis?

MEDEA: No.

JASON: Indeed not?

MEDEA: I tell you, no.

JASON: But let me tell you this,
    You would do well to leave such things alone!
    Do not brew potions, sleeping-draughts of herbs,
    Speak to the moon, no, nor disturb the dead.
    They hate that here, and I – I hate it too!
    We are not now in Colchis, but in Greece,
    It is not monsters that live here, but men!
    But yet I know that you'll not do it now,
    You promised it and you will keep your word.
    The crimson veil you wear upon your head
    Reminded me of scenes of long ago.
    Why do you not put on our country's dress?
    As I in Colchis was a Colchian,
    So you in Greece should be a Grecian woman.
    Why do you seek reminders of the past?
    We can remember it quite well enough.

[MEDEA *silently takes off her veil and gives it to* GORA.]

GORA [*half under her breath*]:
  And for his sake will you despise your country?

JASON [*seeing* GORA]: You here? Above all else I hate you,
      woman!
  When I behold those eyes, that brow, I see
  The coast of Colchis rising dim before me.
  Why do you foist yourself upon my wife?
  Be off!

GORA [*grumbling*]: And why?

JASON: Be off!

MEDEA: I beg you, go!

GORA [*dully*]: Are you my master? Have you paid for me?

JASON: My sword-hand itches. Go while there is time;
  So often I have longed to try your head,
  To find if it's as stubborn as it seems.

      [MEDEA *leads her off, resisting, and tries to soothe her.*]

JASON [*flinging himself on a grassy bank, and beating his breast*]:
  Burst from your walls, break out and reach the air!
  See where they lie, the towers and gates of Corinth,
  Stretched out as if to bask beside the sea,
  The cradle of my golden years of youth!
  They are the same, the same sun shines upon them,
  And only I another, changed within.
  You gods! why was my morning so serene,
  When you decreed for me so black an evening?
  Would it were night!

MEDEA [*bringing the* CHILDREN *out of the tent to* JASON]:
                      Here are two children
  To greet their father. – Come, give him your hand!
  Do you not hear? Your hand!

      [*The* CHILDREN *stand shyly aside.*]

JASON [*with hand outstretched towards them in a sorrowful gesture*]:
                      Is this the end?
  Father and husband to unruly savages!

MEDEA [*to one of the* CHILDREN]:
  Go to him!

BOY: Father, are you Greek?

434

JASON: And why?

BOY: Gora has told us you are Greek.

JASON: What of it?

BOY: She says the Greeks are cowards and deceivers.

JASON [*to* MEDEA]: You hear it?

MEDEA: Gora makes them so. Forgive him!
   [*She kneels down between the* CHILDREN *and whispers to each
   of them in turn.*]

JASON: Very well! [*Standing up.*]
                        There she kneels, that ill-starred woman,
And strains to bear her burden and my own.
   [*Pacing up and down.*]
The children: leave them now and come to me!

MEDEA: Go then, and do not quarrel. Do you hear?
   [*Exeunt* CHILDREN.]

JASON: O do not think me harsh and cruel, Medea!
I feel your grief, just as I feel my own.
How faithfully you push that heavy stone
That always rolling back upon us comes
To block each path and seal off each escape.
Was it *you* did it? was it *I*? It *happened*.
   [*He takes one of her hands, and with his other hand strokes her
   forehead.*]
You love me. Yes, I know you do, Medea;
Indeed, in your own way – and yet, you love me;
Not just this look, so many deeds have told me.
   [MEDEA *leans her forehead against his shoulder.*]
I know your head is heavy with much grief,
And faithful pity stirs within this breast.
So therefore let us carefully consider
How to escape what threatens us so near.
This city here is Corinth. Long ago,
When, but a half-grown youth, I had to flee
My uncle's furious rage, here in this country
The king, who once had vowed my fathers friendship,
Took me and kept me like his own dear son.
I dwelt with him for many years in safety.
Now –

MEDEA: You are silent?

JASON: Now that all the world
  Rejects me, persecutes me in blind rage,
  Now too I hope this king will be my friend;
  But one thing still I fear, not without reason.

MEDEA: What is it?

JASON: He will take *me* in, I know,
  The children too, because they are my children.
  But you –

MEDEA: If he will take the children in
  Since they are yours, then he will take me too.

JASON: Have you forgotten how it was at home,
  There at my uncle's, in my fatherland,
  When first I brought you back with me from Colchis?
  Forgotten all the scorn with which the Greek
  Looks down on the barbarian, on – you?
  Not all men know your nature as I do,
  Not all men have you for their children's mother,
  Not all men were in Colchis, as I was.

MEDEA: This bitter speech, what is the end of it?

JASON: The greatest of man's miseries is this:
  That he, whatever may befall in life,
  Is calm and self-possessed before it happens,
  Afterwards not. Let that not be with us.
  I go to see the king, maintain my rights
  And clear myself from their suspicions of us.
  But you with both the children must remain
  Far from the town in hiding, till –

MEDEA: Till when?

JASON: Till – What, you veil your face?

MEDEA: I know enough.

JASON: Why do you read so falsely what I say?

MEDEA: Let me have proof that I have read it falsely.
  Here comes the king. Speak as your heart commands you.

JASON: So we will stand the storm, until it breaks us.

[GORA *comes out of the tent with the* CHILDREN. MEDEA
goes and stands between the CHILDREN *and remains at first in
the distance, observing what happens. Enter* KING CREON *with*

CREUSA *his daughter, accompanied by boys and girls carrying sacrificial instruments.*]

KING: Where is the stranger? In my heart foreboding
 Tells me that it is he, cast out and banished –
 A guilty man perhaps – where is the stranger?

JASON: Here I am, and I bow my head before you;
 No stranger, though I am become estranged,
 Begging for help, a humble suppliant.
 Harried from house and home and driven out,
 I come to beg my friend for roof and shelter.

CREUSA: In truth, it is! See, father, it is Jason!
 [*Taking a step towards him*]

JASON [*taking her by the hand*]:
 Yes, it is I, as it is you, Creusa,
 The very same, radiant with gentle joy.
 O take me, lead me to the king your father
 Who stands so gravely gazing at me there
 And waits with his reply; I do not know
 If Jason earns his anger, or his fault.

CREUSA [*leading* JASON *by the hand towards her father*]:
 See, father, it is Jason!

KING: Greetings to you!

JASON: In your grave looks I read my proper place.
 I throw myself before you, grasp your knees
 And stretch my arm up to approach your face.
 Give what I ask, grant refuge and protection!

KING: Stand up!

JASON: No, not before –

KING: Stand up, I say! [JASON *rises.*]
 You come back from the Argonauts' campaign?

JASON: Scarcely a month ago this land received me.

KING: The goal of that campaign, you brought it with you?

JASON: Yes, for my uncle, him who bade me fetch it.

KING: Why have you fled the city of your fathers?

JASON: It drove me out; I am a helpless exile.

KING: The cause of banishment, though: what was that?

JASON: Infamous deeds whose guilt men said was mine.

KING: Rightly or wrongfully? This you must tell me.

JASON: Wrongfully, and I swear it by the gods!

KING [*quickly taking him by the hand and leading him forward*]:
  Your uncle died?

JASON: He died.

KING: How?

JASON: Not through me!
  As true as I am living, not through me!

KING: Yet rumour has it so, all through the country.

JASON: Then rumour lies, and all the country with it.

KING: One man would be believed against so many?

JASON: One man you know, against so many strangers.

KING: But how then did he fall, the king?

JASON: His children,
  His own blood raised their hands against his life.

KING: Terrible. Is this true?

JASON: The gods have seen it.

KING: Creusa comes; do not tell her of this,
  I gladly spare her from such grief and horror.
  [*Aloud*] It is enough for now. The other later;
  While still I can, I will believe your worth.

CREUSA [*joining them*]: You asked him, father? And it is
    not true?

KING: Do you but go to him, you need not fear.

CREUSA: You doubted him, you know. I never did,
  Here in my breast, here in my heart I felt it,
  They were not true, the things men said of him.
  He was so good; how could he do such evil?
  O, if you knew how they all spoke of you,
  So evil and so cruel! I wept that men
  Could be so wicked and so slanderous.
  Why, scarcely had you gone, the land resounded
  With tales of fearful, wild and savage deeds;
  In Colchis, so they said, you wrought such horrors –
  And in the end they found a wife for you,
  A fearful sorceress, that killed her father,
  Called – what was that barbarian name?

MEDEA [*coming forward with the* CHILDREN]: Medea.
  Here I am!

KING: Is it she?

JASON [*hollowly*]:   It is.

CREUSA [*clinging to her father*]: O horror!

MEDEA [*to* CREUSA]: But you are wrong; I did not kill my
      father;
  My brother died, but ask *him* if I did it?
      [*Pointing at* JASON]
  Of mixing potions, bringing death or healing,
  I have much knowledge, and of more besides;
  But I am not a monster nor a murderess.

CREUSA: O fearful! fearful!

KING: This, your wife?

JASON: My wife.

KING: Those children?

JASON: Are my sons.

KING: Unhappy wretch!

JASON: I am. Come here you children with your twigs,
  Offer them to the king and beg protection!
      [*Leading them up by the hand.*]
  My lord, you will not turn them from your presence!

BOY [*holding out his twig*]: There, take it!

KING [*putting his hands on their heads*]:   Poor young brood
      snatched from the nest!

CREUSA [*kneeling down to speak to the* CHILDREN]:
  Come here to me, unhappy, homeless orphans,
  How soon in life you must endure misfortune;
  So soon and o, so innocent as well.
  You are like her – you have your father's features.
      [*She kisses the younger.*]
  Stay here, I will be mother, sister to you!

MEDEA: Why do you call them orphans and unhappy?
  Here is their father, he that calls them his,
  And they will need no second mother while
  Medea lives. [*To the* CHILDREN] Come here to me!
      Come here!

CREUSA [*looking up towards her father*]:
  Are they to go?

KING: She is their mother.

CREUSA [*to the* CHILDREN]: Go then.

MEDEA: Why do you linger?

CREUSA [*to the* CHILDREN, *who have put their arms round her neck*]: Go, your mother calls you!

[*They leave her.*]

JASON: And what have you decided?

KING: I have said it.

JASON: You grant protection?

KING: Yes.

JASON: To me and mine?

KING: I granted it to *you*. Come, follow me.
First to the sacrifice, then to my house.

JASON [*turning to go, to* CREUSA]:
Will you give me your hand again, Creusa?

CREUSA: You cannot hold it as you used to do.

MEDEA: They go and leave me here alone. You children!
Come here to me, embrace me! Closer! Closer!

CREUSA [*turning back, speaking as if to herself*]:
One still is missing. Why does she not follow?
[*Coming back, but remaining at some distance from* MEDEA]
Are you not coming with us to our house?

MEDEA: An uninvited guest is turned away.

CREUSA: But no; my father offers warmth and shelter.

MEDEA: That was not how I heard the words you spoke.

CREUSA [*coming nearer*]:
I must have wounded you, I know. Forgive me!

MEDEA [*turning quickly towards her*]:
O sound so sweet! Who spoke that gentle word?
How often they have wounded me, how deeply,
But never did they ask if I was hurt!
I thank you, and if ever you like me must suffer,
Then may you know, as I have known from you,
A soft and gracious word, a gentle look.
[*She goes to take* CREUSA *by the hand,* CREUSA *draws shyly back.*]
Do not draw back! My hand will not bring plague.
For I was born like you the child of kings,
Like you, so did I once walk even paths,

440

Blindly put out my hand, take what was right.
For I like you was born the child of kings,
As you before me stand, fair, bright and radiant,
So did I once stand at my father's side,
His idol and the idol of my people.
O Colchis! o you country of my fathers!
They call you dark, to me you seem so bright!

CREUSA [*taking her hand*]: O grief!

MEDEA: So mild your look, so good and sweet,
No doubt you are so; yet beware, beware!
The way is slippery: one step – you fall!
Since in your fragile boat you glided down the stream,
Guiding your way by banks of branching flowers,
And gently rocking on the silver waves,
For that do you account yourself a sailor?
Beyond there roars the open sea,
And if you venture from familiar shores,
To far grey wastes the stream will sweep you on.
You look at me? You shudder now to see me?
There was a time when I myself had shuddered
To think of such a creature as I am!

[*She hides her face on* CREUSA's *shoulder.*]

CREUSA: She is not savage. Father, see, she weeps.

MEDEA: Because I am a stranger, from afar,
And not acquainted with this country's ways,
They scorn me and look down upon me all,
To them I am a fleeting, savage thing,
The lowest and the last of all mankind,
I who was first and greatest in my homeland.
I will do anything you ask of me,
But tell me what to do, do not be angry.
I see you are a gentle, modest nature,
Sure of yourself and with yourself at one;
A god denied to me that precious gift.
But I will learn, yes, learn so willingly.
You know what pleases him, what makes him glad,
O teach me, teach me how I can please Jason,
I will be grateful to you!

CREUSA: Father, see!

KING: Take her with you!

CREUSA: Come with me then, Medea!

MEDEA: Gladly I go wherever you will take me,
 Care for me, poor, forsaken as I am,
 And shield me from the glance of that man there!
 [*To the* KING] Yes, look at me, you will not frighten me,
 Although I see you planning nothing good.
 Your child is better than her father!

CREUSA: Come!
 He means you well! And come, you children too!
  [*Exeunt* CREUSA, MEDEA *and the* CHILDREN.]

KING: Well, did you hear?

JASON: I did.

KING: And she your wife?
 I had already heard the rumour of it,
 But I did not believe; and now I see,
 I can believe it even less! Your wife!

JASON: You only see the summit, not the climb;
 You cannot judge the one but by the other.
 In youthful vigour there I made my way
 Across strange seas to do the boldest deed
 Yet seen since there were men to live and think.
 All life and all the world I had to master,
 And there was nothing there but that bright Fleece
 That, through the night, a star in storm-clouds shone.
 None thought of our return, and just as if
 The moment when the prize was seized and won
 Should be our very last in life, we strove.
 And so we went, companions keen to fight,
 Exulting in the daring and the deed,
 By sea and land, by rocks and night and storm,
 With death before us and behind us death.
 What had seemed hideous, now seemed sweet and mild,
 For nature was more spiteful than the worst;
 Fighting with her and with the savage tribes
 The mildest man's soft heart grew hard as iron;
 The measure of all things was lost to us,

Each man must judge himself the things we saw.
What we had thought impossible, came true;
We saw the shores of Colchis, land of wonders,
O would that you had seen it in its mists!
There day is night and night is dread untold,
But those that live there, darker than the night.
There I found her who seems to you so fearful;
I tell you truly she was like a sunbeam
That through a chink can flood a prison cell.
Though here she may be dark, there she was light
Against the gloom of night all round about her.

KING: Never can wrong be right nor evil good.

JASON: It was a god who turned her heart to me;
She stood by me in many an hour of peril.
I saw emotion welling up within her,
But stubbornly she bridled it and checked it,
Only her actions, not a word betrayed it.
Then madness caught me too up in its whirl,
That she said nothing but provoked me more.
I fought with her embattled, and my love
Was like some new adventurous campaign.
I won her, with her father's curse upon her.
Now she was mine – whether I would or not.
Through her the wondrous Fleece came to my hand,
She led me down into that fearful cave
And there I seized it, snatched it from the dragon.
And when since then I look into her eye
The glittering serpent gazes out at me,
And I must shudder when I call her wife.
We sailed away. Her brother fell.

KING [*quickly*]:   Through her?

JASON: He fell by the gods' hand. Her grey-haired father,
Cursing on her, on me, our future, dug
Himself a grave with bloody fingernails
And died, they say, by his own frenzied rage.

KING: With evil signs your marriage was begun.

JASON: With worse did it continue in its course.

KING: What happened to your uncle? Tell me this.

JASON: Four years a god drew out our homeward journey,
By land and sea still driving us astray.
Cramped in the ship there, hourly side by side,
The sharpness of that horror rubbed away;
What had been, had been – She became my wife.

KING: And then in Iolcus, at your uncle's house?

JASON: Blurred now by time those memories of terror,
Myself half-savage, with my savage bride
I strode into the city of my fathers;
Remembering the people's loud rejoicing
When I set out, I hoped more joyful still
Would be my welcome, coming home a victor.
But silent were the streets through which I passed,
And all that met me stood aside in fear.
For what had happened in that gloomy land,
Increased with further horrors, rumour had
Implanted in my people's timid ear;
They fled my presence, and despised my wife.
Mine she was, it was me they scorned in her.
My wily uncle fed their enmity;
When I demanded my inheritance
That he had taken and withheld from me,
He ordered me to send my wife away,
A horror to him with her dark designs, he said,
Or else to quit his land, land of my fathers.

KING: But you – ?

JASON: But I? She was my wife,
She put her faith in me as her protector,
He that demanded was my enemy.
Had it been just, what he desired, I swear
I had not granted it; so much less this.
So I refused.

KING: And he?

JASON: He banished me.
That very day I should depart from Iolcus.
But I would not, and stayed.
Then suddenly the king falls ill. A whisper
Runs through the town, a rumour strange indeed!

Of how he sits before the palace altar,
Where they had hung with prayers the wondrous Fleece,
His eye fixed on it in a glassy stare.
Often he cried that he could see his brother,
My father he so spitefully had killed,
Quarrelling once about the Argo's voyage,
That he could see him, in the glittering gold
That he had bid me fetch for him, false man,
Out of that distant land, that I should perish.
When now such peril threatened the king's house,
His daughters came before me, begging that
Medea with her arts might save his life.
But I said No! Should I preserve the man
Who only planned for me and mine destruction?
They went, the maidens, weeping on their way,
I barred my door and thought no more of it.
And though they came imploring me again,
I did not change my mind, or change my No.
But when that night I laid myself to sleep,
I hear a shouting at my house's door;
Acastos comes, my wicked uncle's son,
And breaks in at my door with noisy mobs,
Crying I was the murderer of his father,
That in that very night had met his death.
Up I arose and tried to speak, but all
In vain, the people's shouting drowned my words,
And soon they took up stones, and war began.
So then I drew my sword, and fought my way.
Since then through Hellas' cities I have wandered,
To men a horror, to myself a torment,
And if you will not help me, lost for ever!

KING: I promised you and I will keep my word.
   But she –

JASON: Before you finish hear me out!
   You take us both, my lord, or you take neither!
   If she were gone, my life would spring anew,
   But I must guard what puts its trust in me.

KING: The magic arts she knows, they frighten me,

The power to harm can quickly breed the will.
No stranger she to guilt and wicked deeds.
JASON: If she will not be calm, then turn her out,
Then persecute her, kill her, me – us all.
But till that time give her the chance to see
If she can keep the company of men.
I beg by Zeus, protector of all strangers,
And by the right of hospitality
Demand it, that our fathers long ago
Set up for us in Iolcus and in Corinth,
Foreseeing in their wisdom what might be.
Grant me what I desire, lest you and yours
In like misfortune meet with like refusal.
KING: Against my judgement, I obey the gods.
She may remain. But let her once betray
That she falls back into her savage ways,
Then I will drive her from my city's gates
And give her up to those that seek for her.

But here where first I set my eyes on you
Let there be raised aloft a holy altar,
Sacred to Zeus, protector of all strangers,
And to your uncle Pelias' bloodied ghost.
There we in company will beg the gods
That they will bless your coming to my house,
And turn away what evils threaten us.
    And now come with me to my royal palace.

[*To his followers, who now draw near*]
But you will carry out what I commanded.
[*As they turn to go, the curtain falls.*]

ACT II

A hall in Creon's palace

[CREUSA *sitting,* MEDEA *on a low stool before her holding a lyre. She is wearing Greek costume.*]

CREUSA: Now take this string, the second, this one here!

MEDEA: Like this?

CREUSA: No, you must hold your fingers looser.

MEDEA: I cannot.

CREUSA: Yes, you can. But try in earnest!

MEDEA: I try in earnest, but I cannot.

[*She puts down the lyre and stands up.*]

My hand is only used to hold a spear
And to the rough and earnest tasks of hunting.

[*Holding her right hand close before her face*]

If only I could punish them, these fingers!

CREUSA: Why must you be like this? I was so pleased
To think of the surprise for him, for Jason,
To hear you sing your song!

MEDEA: Yes, you are right.
I had forgotten. Let me try again!
He will be pleased, you say, surely be pleased?

CREUSA: Of course! He sang it when he was a boy,
When he was living with us, in our house.
Each time I heard it, up I leapt with joy,
It always meant that he was coming home.

MEDEA: But now the song?

CREUSA: Come, listen to me then.
It is not long, nor very beautiful,
And yet it was so charmingly he sang it,
So proudly, obstinately, mocking almost.

O you gods,
You gods on high!
Anoint my head,

447

        Swell my breast,
        Over men
        To be victorious
        And over the dainty
        Maidens too!

MEDEA: Yes, they have granted him his wish.

CREUSA: What wish?

MEDEA: Why, what it says, the little song.

CREUSA: The song?

MEDEA: Over men to be victorious
    And over the dainty maidens too!

CREUSA: Why, do you know, I never thought of it!
    I only heard and sang it after him.

MEDEA: He stood there on the foreign coast of Colchis;
    The men he felled before him with his glance,
    And with that glance he threw a fiery brand
    Into the bosom of the wretch that fled him,
    Until the spark, long-stifled, caught and spread
    And peace and calm and happiness sank down
    Amidst the stifling smoke and crackling flames.
    He stood there glorious in his strength and beauty,
    A hero and a god, and lured, and lured,
    Till he had lured his victim to its doom;
    Threw it aside, and no one picked it up.

CREUSA: Are you his wife, and speak so evil of him?

MEDEA: You do not know him; I do, through and through.
    He, he alone exists in all the world,
    And nothing else but stuff for his own deeds.
    Selfish, yet for no end, but for its own sake,
    He plays with fortune, others' and his own.
    If it is fame that lures him, he will kill;
    If woman, then he goes and fetches one;
    What else he may destroy, why should he care?
    He does no wrong, but right is what he wills.
    You do not know him; I do, through and through,
    And when I think of all that I have seen,
    Then I could see him die and laugh at it.

CREUSA: Farewell!

MEDEA: You go?

CREUSA: Am I to hear you longer?
Gods! Does a wife speak of her husband thus?

MEDEA: According as he is; mine did such things!

CREUSA: I swear by heaven, if I had a husband,
So bad, so wicked as yours cannot be,
And children born to him and in his image,
Then I would love them, even if they killed me.

MEDEA: Such words sound well, but they are hard to
follow.

CREUSA: To follow easily would be less sweet.
But do what you think fitting, I will go.
First you inveigle me with gentle words
And ask me how it is you best can please him,
Now you break out in hatred and reviling.
Much that is evil I have seen in men,
The worst of all an unforgiving heart.
Good-bye, learn to be better.

MEDEA: You are angry?

CREUSA: Almost.

MEDEA: O do not you too give me up,
You must not leave me, be my shield and shelter!

CREUSA: Now you are mild, where you were full of hatred.

MEDEA: Of hatred for myself; for Jason love.

CREUSA: You love him?

MEDEA: Did I not, should I be here?

CREUSA: I try to understand it, but I cannot.
But if you love him I will be your friend,
And I will tell you ways I know for sure
To scatter all his stormy moods like clouds.
Come now. I saw this morning he was gloomy,
But sing your song to him and you will see
How soon he will be gay. Here is the lyre.
I shall not let you go until you know it. [*Sits down.*]
You do not come? You stand and hesitate?

MEDEA: I look at you and look at you again

And I can hardly see enough of you.
Sweet, good and beautiful in soul and body,
Your heart pure white and shining like your dress,
You float before me like a dove of peace,
With wings outstretched, above this life of ours,
Not soiling one bright feather in the mud
Where we must toil and struggle on our way.
Send down a beam of heavenly radiance
Into this wounded breast so torn with pain.
What grief and hatred and misfortune wrote,
O wipe it from my heart with loving hand
And set your own pure imprint in its place.
The strength that from my youth has been my pride
Has shown itself in all my struggles weak;
O teach me what it is makes weakness strong.
    [*She sits down on the stool at* CREUSA's *feet.*]
Here I will seek my refuge at your feet
And weep to you of what men did to me;
Will learn what I must do and leave undone.
Like your maidservant I will follow you,
Will hurry to the loom and sit and weave,
Do every task that in my land is scorned
And left for slaves and menials to perform,
But here fit for the mistress of the house;
Forgetting that my father king of Colchis,
Forgetting that my ancestors were gods,
Forgetting what has happened, what still threatens –
    [*Standing up and moving away*]
No, that can never be forgotten.

CREUSA [*following her*]:   What?
Whatever evils in the past have happened
Men will forget them, and the gods will too.

MEDEA [*on her shoulder*]:
You think so? If I only could believe it!
    [*Enter* JASON.]

CREUSA [*turning towards him*]:
Your husband comes. Look, Jason, we are friends!

JASON: I see.

MEDEA: My greetings. O, she is so good,
   She will be friend and teacher to Medea!
JASON: Good luck in the attempt!
CREUSA: Why then so grim?
   Here we shall spend our days in happiness,
   I will divide my loving cares between you,
   You and my father, you and she, Medea –
JASON: Medea!
MEDEA: What is your command, my husband?
JASON: The children. Have you seen to them?
MEDEA: Just now.
   They are so happy.
JASON: Go and look again.
MEDEA: But I was there just now.
JASON: Go, go and look!
MEDEA: If you desire.
JASON: I wish it.
MEDEA: I will go. [*Exit.*]
CREUSA: Why did you send her? They are well, you know
      it.
JASON: Ah! now I can be free, now I can breathe.
   The sight of her is like a stifling pain:
   I fight to hide it but it almost chokes me.
CREUSA: What must I hear? O you eternal gods!
   Such words she used, and now he speaks the same!
   Who told me wives and husbands loved each other?
JASON: O yes, indeed, when after fruitful youth
   The young man casts his glance upon a maid
   And sets her up as goddess of his longings.
   He looks to see if he can catch her eye
   And if he does, that is his happiness.
   He calls upon her father and her mother
   And pays his court, and they give their consent.
   There is a feast, and the relations come,
   And all the city shares in their rejoicing.
   Adorned with garlands and with fair bright flowers
   He leads his bride before the temple altar.
   Blushing and trembling in her modest veil

To think of what she yet desires, she comes;
Her father lays his hands upon her head
And blesses her and those that are to come.
Yes, those who court like that, they love each other.
It should have been my lot; it did not happen.
What have I done, just gods, that you from me
Have taken what you give the poorest man,
A haven from his toil, by his own hearth
And with his wife that knows his love and trust?

CREUSA: And so you did not woo as others do?
Her father did not raise his hand in blessing?

JASON: He raised his hand, but in it held a sword,
And gave us not his blessing but his curse.
But I, I paid him back and in good measure;
His son is dead, he himself dead and silent,
Only his curse lives on – or so it seems.

CREUSA: What changes these few years can bring about!
You were so gentle, now you are so rough.
Myself I am the selfsame that I was,
What then I wished for, still I wish it now,
What then seemed good to me, it seems so still,
What fit for blame, I still must blame today.
With you it seems not so.

JASON: That too, that too!
Misfortune's innermost misfortune is
That in its toils man rarely saves himself.
Here he must bend, there sway, himself be swayed,
What's right shifts here a hair's breadth, there a grain,
And when the course is finished, there he stands
A different man from him who first set out.
And what would soothe the loss of men's respect
Alone, his self-respect, that too is gone.
I have done nothing wicked in itself,
But willed so much, desired it, wished it, sought it,
Looked on in silence and let others do it.
I have not wanted evil, but set to
And never thought that evil would be bred.
And now I stand amidst its roaring floods

And cannot say it was not I who did it!
O youth, why can your days not last for ever?
Joyous in fancies, blissful in forgetting,
The moment striving's cradle and its grave.
How I would plunge into adventure's stream,
Parting the waves so boldly with my breast.
But when grave manhood enters in our life,
Illusions flee, and harsh reality
Comes creeping in and brooding on its cares.
The present then no longer is a tree
Beneath whose shade we rest, and pluck its fruits,
It is a grain of seed, impenetrable,
We bury it to see what future springs.
What will you do? Where will you live and be?
What will become of you? Your wife and child?
Such questions fall upon us and torment us. [*Sits down.*]

CREUSA: What need you have such cares, when you are
      cared for?

JASON: Cared for? O yes, just as you give the beggar
Before your door a basin of your leavings.
Can I be Jason and need others' care?
And put my feet beneath a stranger's table,
Go begging with my children for a stranger's pity?
My father was a prince, and so am I,
Who is there that will be compared with Jason?
And yet – [*Standing up*] I came along the noisy market
And through the spacious streets of this your city.
Do you remember how I strode their length
So boldly, when before the Argo sailed
I came to take a last farewell of you?
There tightly packed in waves they thronged my path,
Men, chariots and horses, gaily mingled.
Spectators on the roof-tops, on the towers,
They fought for places as it were for treasure.
The air resounded with the noise of cymbals
And with the noisy greetings of the crowd.
Tightly they thronged about the noble band,
Who richly clad, in armour gleaming bright,

The least of them a hero and a king,
Attended with respect their noble leader –
And I it was who led them, I their standard,
I whom the people greeted with their cries;
Now when I made my way through those same streets
Not one to look, to greet, to say a word.
Only when once I stopped and looked about me,
There came a man who said it was ill-mannered
To stand there in the way disturbing others.

CREUSA: You can rise up again, if so you will.

JASON: No, I am finished; I shall rise no more!

CREUSA: I know a way that's certain to succeed.

JASON: I know the way, but can you find it for me?
See to it that I never left my homeland,
That I stayed here in Corinth with your father,
That I have never seen the Fleece, nor Colchis,
Nor ever seen her who is now my wife.
See to it that she goes back to her cursed land,
Takes back the memory that she was ever here.
Then I can be a man again with men.

CREUSA: Is that the only way? I know another:
Simplicity of heart and tranquil mind.

JASON: Yes, gentle one, if you could teach me that!

CREUSA: The gods will grant it to all men that will.
You had it once, it can be yours again.

JASON: Do you still sometimes think of our young days?

CREUSA: I do remember, often, with delight.

JASON: How we were but one heart and but one soul.

CREUSA: I made you gentler, and you made me bold.
I put your helmet on my head – remember?

JASON: It was too big, you had to hold it up
With dainty hands above your golden locks.
Creusa, o, it was a time of joy.

CREUSA: And how my father was so pleased to see us,
Often in jest he called us bride and bridegroom.

JASON: It did not happen so.

CREUSA: As so much happens
Other than one had thought. But what of that?

We shall not just for that be less content!
    [MEDEA *returns*.]
MEDEA: The children are attended to.
JASON: Good, good.
    [*Continuing to* CREUSA]
The happy scenes of pleasures in our youth,
Where memories still cling by slender threads,
I visited each one when I returned,
And plunged and cooled my burning lips and breast
In bright-lit childhood's sweet refreshing fountain.
I saw the market, where I raced my chariot,
Drove on my flying horses to the goal,
Wrestled and fought with many an opponent,
While you stood looking on in fear and anger,
For my sake enemy to all my foes.
I saw the temple where we knelt besides,
The only place where we forgot each other,
And to the gods two pairs of lips sent up
Out of two breasts a sole and single heart.
CREUSA: And you remember all these things so well?
JASON: I draw from them a deep reviving draught.
MEDEA [*who has quietly gone over and picked up the lyre again*]:
    Jason, I know a song!
JASON: And then the tower!
You know the tower, by the sea-shore there,
Where you beside your father stood and wept
When I was boarding ship the second time.
I had no eye that day to see your tears,
For deeds were all my greedy heart desired.
A gust of wind sprang up, and tore your veil
Away towards the sea; I leapt and caught it
And carried it away for your remembrance.
CREUSA: Is it still with you?
JASON: Think, so many years
Have passed since then, and it is gone with them.
The wind blew it away.
MEDEA: I know a song.
JASON: You called to me that day, 'Farewell, my brother!'

CREUSA: Today I call, 'My brother, now I greet you!'

MEDEA: Jason, I know a song.

CREUSA: She knows a song
   That you once sang, listen and she will sing it.

JASON: O yes! Where was I, then? It sticks to me,
   A relic of my youth, and mocks at me,
   That sometimes I will idly dream and chatter
   Of things that are not and will never be.
   For as the youth dwells only in the future
   So the grown man dwells only in the past,
   But with the present no one cares to live.
   So there I was, a hero full of deeds,
   And had a loving wife and wealth and goods
   And somewhere for my children to be sleeping.
   [*To* MEDEA] What do you want?

CREUSA: To sing a song to you,
   That you when you were young would sing to us.

JASON: And *you* will sing it?

MEDEA: If I can.

JASON: Indeed.
   What, are you going with some childish song
   To give me back my youth with all its joys?
   Let be. No, we shall cling to one another,
   Because it happened so, as best we may.
   But let me hear no songs or suchlike things!

CREUSA: Will you not let her sing it? She has worked
   So hard to learn it; now –

JASON: Sing it then, sing!

CREUSA: The second string, do you remember?

MEDEA [*rubbing her forehead with her hand as if in pain*]:
                                      – Gone!

JASON: You see, I told you so, it will not do!
   Her hand is used to play a different tune.
   She lulled the dragon with her magic charms,
   And that was not much like your gentle song.

CREUSA [*prompting*]: O you gods,
                You gods on high –

MEDEA [*after her*]:   O you gods –

You gods on high, you just, imperious gods!
[*She drops the lyre and covers her weeping eyes with both hands.*]

CREUSA: She weeps. How can you be so harsh and
cruel?

JASON [*holding her back*]: Leave her. My child, you cannot
understand!
It is the gods' own hand that now she feels,
Here too it leaves its mark with bloody claw.
Do not presume upon the gods' own justice!
If you had seen her in the dragon's lair,
How with that rearing serpent she could vie,
Shoot double darts of poison with her tongue,
Flash death and hatred from her blazing eyes,
Your heart would then be steeled against her tears.
You take the lyre and sing the song yourself,
Banish the demon that is stifling me.
Perhaps you can; *she* cannot.

CREUSA: Willingly.
[*She goes to pick up the lyre.*]

MEDEA: Stop! [*She seizes* CREUSA's *hand and holds her back,
picking up the lyre herself with her other hand.*]

CREUSA: Willingly, if you will play it.

MEDEA: No!

JASON: Will you not give it up?

MEDEA: No!

JASON: Nor to me?

MEDEA: No!

JASON [*advancing on her and reaching for the lyre*]:
I will take it.

MEDEA [*without yielding, taking the lyre away from his reach*]:
Never!

JASON [*reaching after her hands with his*]: Give it!

MEDEA [*crushing it as she draws it away, so that it breaks noisily in
pieces*]: There!
Broken! [*Throwing it in front of* CREUSA]
Your lovely lyre is broken!

CREUSA [*starting back in horror*]: Dead!

MEDEA [*looking round quickly*]: Who? I live – I live!

[*She draws herself up and stands staring in front of her.
Trumpets offstage*]

JASON: Ha, what was that? You stand there in your
    triumph?

  I think that you will live to rue this moment!

    [*Trumpets again. Enter the* KING, *quickly.*]

JASON [*going to meet him*]: What is the meaning of this
    warlike sound?

KING: Unhappy wretch, you ask?

JASON: I ask, my lord!

KING: The blow of which I stood in dread has fallen.

  A herald stands before my palace gates,

  Sent from the Amphictyonies in judgement.

  He asks for you, and this your wife as well,

  Crying out banishment to all the skies!

JASON: Now this!

KING: It is so. Silence, here he is!

    [*The doors are opened. Enter a* HERALD *followed by two
    trumpeters, with other attendants behind.*]

HERALD: The gods send their protection on this house!

KING [*solemnly*]: Who are you and what is your errand here?

HERALD: I am a herald of the gods, sent by

  The Amphictyonies to give their judgement

  Spoken in Delphi's free and ancient city.

  With banishment I come and vows of vengeance

  Upon the guilty kinsmen of King Pelias,

  Who once was lord of Iolcus, now is dead.

KING: If you would seek the guilty, go and seek

  Among his children, in his house; not here!

HERALD: But I have found them here, and so I speak:

  Jason, accursed! Accursed, you and your wife!

  You are condemned of black and wicked arts

  By which the king your uncle strangely died.

JASON: You lie, for I know nothing of his death.

HERALD: Then ask this woman, she can tell you more.

JASON: What, did she do it?

HERALD: Not with her own hand,

  But by her arts of which you know full well,

Which you and she brought home from foreign lands.
For when the king fell ill – perhaps already doomed,
So strange were all the symptoms of his fever –
His daughters made their way to ask Medea
To heal him, cunning as she was in healing;
She gave her word, and went with them to him.

JASON: Stop! She did not! I would not let her go.
　　She stayed.

HERALD:　　The first time. But when once again,
Unknown to you, the maidens sought her aid,
She went with them, but claimed the Golden Fleece,
A horror, so she said, a sign of doom,
As her reward if she would surely save him.
The maidens promised it to her with joy.
She went in to the king where he lay sleeping,
And she pronounced her dark mysterious words.
The king sinks deeper, ever deeper into sleep.
To purge his poisoned blood, she bids them cut
Their father's veins, and that is done as well;
He breathes more smoothly as they bind him up,
His daughters feel with joy that he recovers.
Up rose Medea; went away, she said,
The daughters left him too, for he was sleeping.
A sudden cry is heard within his room;
The maidens rush to him – o, sight of horror!
There the old man lies writhing on the ground.
Burst are the bandages that bound his arms,
And in black torrents pouring forth his blood.
He lay before the altar, where the Fleece
Had hung; and that was gone. But *she* was seen,
The golden trophy thrown about her shoulders,
Striding in that same hour off through the night.

MEDEA [*in a hollow voice, to herself*]: It was my payment.
　　The old man's frenzy makes me shudder still!

HERALD: So that such fearful things shall be no more
To spread their poisoned breath throughout our land,
I do proclaim herewith the banishment
Of Jason the Thessalian, Aeson's son,

Party to crime, himself a criminal,
And drive him, as my sacred office bids me,
From Grecian soil, where gods have set their feet,
And send him out to wander and to flee,
With him his wife and those sprung from his bed.
His be no portion of his fathers' land,
In his ancestral gods no share be his,
No share, no rights in all the land of Greece!
    [*To the four points of the compass*]
Banished, Jason and Medea!
Jason and Medea, banished!
Banished!
Jason and Medea!
But any that protect or shelter him,
When he has gone three days and nights from here,
I promise death, if but a single man,
And war, in case a city or a king!
The sentence of the Amphictyonies
I do pronounce, according to the law,
That every man shall know, and look to it.
The gods send their protection on this house!
    [*He turns to go.*]
JASON: Why do you stand there still, you walls? Collapse,
And spare your king the task of killing me!
KING: Stay, herald, hear these words before you go!
    [*Turning to* JASON]
You think already I regret my promise?
If I believed you guilty, and you were my son,
Still I would give you up to those that seek you;
But you are not, and so I will protect you;
Stay here. And who will dare to touch the friend
Whose innocence is pledged by Creon's word –
Who dares to touch the son-in-law of Creon?
Yes, herald, son-in-law, my daughter's husband!
What long ago we once resolved upon,
In happier days, let it be carried out
Now when misfortune's angry waves surround him.
She shall be yours, you shall stay with your father,

This I shall tell the Amphictyonies;
And who will charge the man Creon acquits,
Acquits in giving him his daughter's hand?
Say this to them that sent you to my house;
And now the gods be with you as you go.

 [*Exit* HERALD.]

But her whom desert wastes have vomited,
A curse to you and all god-fearing men,
The authoress of horrors charged to you,
I banish from the confines of this land,
And death to her if morning finds her here.
Go from the virtuous city of my fathers,
Make pure again the air that you have poisoned!

MEDEA: So that was it? These words for me alone?
 But I have told you that I did not do it.

KING: Since he first saw you, you have done enough.
 Away, out of my house, out of my city.

MEDEA [*to* JASON]: And if I am to go, then follow me!
 You share the guilt, so share the punishment.
 Do you remember this? 'Neither shall die alone;
 Our flesh, our dwelling and our end be one!'
 That oath we swore before the face of death;
 Now keep it, come!

JASON: You dare to touch me?
 Away from me, you curse upon my days!
 Who robbed me of my life, my happiness,
 Who made me hate you straightway when I saw you,
 But foolishly call love the pain within!
 Back to the wilderness that gave you birth,
 Back to the savages where you belong!
 But first give back to me what you have taken:
 Give Jason back to me, vile criminal!

MEDEA: Do you want Jason back? Here! Take him! Here!
 But who will give Medea back to me?
 Did I seek you out in your native land?
 Did I seduce you from your father's side?
 Did I force love, yes, force my love upon you?
 Did I snatch you away from your own home,

Expose you to the mocking scorn of strangers,
And spur you on to crime and evil deeds?
You call me criminal? Alas! I am!
But what have been my crimes, and done for whom?
Let these pursue me with envenomed hate,
Banish me, kill me, for they have the right;
I am a loathsome thing to them, a horror,
And to myself a terror, an abyss.
Let all the world revile me, but not you!
Not you, those horrors' author and sole cause!
Do you remember how I clasped your knees
When you would have me steal that bloodstained fleece;
When I had rather gone and killed myself,
And you with cold imperious scorn cried: Take it!
Do you remember how I held my brother,
Broken and dying from your savage blow,
Until he tore himself from his own sister,
Fled from your spite, and in the waves sought death?
Do you remember? Come! Do not evade me,
Do not use *them* to shield yourself from me!

JASON [*advancing*]: I hate you, but I do not fear you!

MEDEA: Come then!

   [*In a subdued voice*]

Do you remember? – Do not look so scornful! –
How you, the day before your uncle's death,
The moment when his daughters went away,
Whom I dismissed despairing, at your word,
How you then came into my room to me
And looking with your eyes into my own –
As if some purpose, hiding shy within you,
Were looking in my soul to find its likeness –
And how you said: 'Would they had come to *me*
For medicine for their wicked father's illness;
For I would brew a potion he should drink
To cure himself for ever more, and me!'
Do you remember? Face me if you dare!

JASON: Why do you rave at me, creature of horror?
Make substance of the shadows of my dreams,

Hold up as mirror to my soul your own
And call my thoughts to take your part against me?
No, I know nothing, nothing of your doings,
From the beginning I have hated you
And cursed the day when first I saw your face.
Pity alone has kept me at your side.
But now I free myself from you for ever
And curse you, as the whole world curses you!

MEDEA: Not so, my wedded husband!

JASON: Go away!

MEDEA: When my grey-headed father threatened it,
  You promised not to leave me. Keep your word!

JASON: What you have done has forfeited that promise.

MEDEA: Husband I hate, come, come to me!

JASON: Away!

MEDEA: Into my arms, for so it was you willed it!

JASON: Back, I say! Look, my sword! And I will kill you
  If you'll not yield!

MEDEA [*nearer and nearer to him*]: Strike me, then! Strike me!

CREUSA [*to* JASON]:   Stop!
  Let her depart in peace, and do not harm her!

MEDEA: Are you here too? pure white and shining snake!
  O hiss and dart your tongue no more so sweetly!
  Now you have what you wanted: there – a husband!
  Was it for that, that with such flattery
  You wound your twisting coils about my neck?
  O if I had a dagger I would kill you,
  Yes, and your father too, that fair, just king!
  Was it for that you sang your songs so sweetly,
  Was it for that you gave me lyre and dress?
    [*Tearing off her cloak*]
  Away! Off with the gifts the traitress gave!
  [*To* JASON] Look! Just as I have torn this cloak in
    two
  And press one half against my bosom here
  And throw the other down before your feet,
  So too I tear my love, our bond, asunder.
  Whatever comes of it you must bear, you,

Who sinned against ill-fortune's sacred head.
Give me my children now and let me go!

KING: The children will stay here.

MEDEA: Not with their mother?

KING: Not with a criminal.

MEDEA [*to* JASON]:   You say that too?

JASON: I do.

MEDEA [*towards the door*]: Then hear me, children!

KING: Back, I say!

MEDEA: You bid me go alone, then? Very well!
But let me tell you this: before the sunset
You will give me my children. Now, enough!
But you, you hypocrite, who stand and look
Down upon me with show of purity,
I tell you you will wring those snow-white hands,
Envy Medea's lot beside your own.

JASON: You dare?

KING: Be gone!

MEDEA: Yes, but I shall return
And take what is my own, and bring what's yours by
    right.

KING: Why should we let her threaten to our faces?
If words will not, [*to his soldiers*] then let your lances
    speak!

MEDEA: Back there! Who is it dares to touch Medea?
Mark well the hour in which I leave you, king;
You never saw a worse, believe my words!
Make way! I go, and take my vengeance with me! [*Exit.*]

KING: Your punishment at least will follow you!
[*To* CREUSA] You shall not tremble, we will shield you
    from her!

CREUSA: I only ask if what we do is right;
For if it is, then who could do us harm?
    [*The curtain falls.*]

ACT III

The forecourt of Creon's palace

[*In the background the entrance to the* KING's *rooms, by the right-hand side wall a colonnade leading to* MEDEA's *house.* MEDEA *is standing in the foreground,* GORA *further upstage talking to a* SERVANT *of the king.*]

GORA: You, tell the king:
  Medea hears no messages a slave brings.
  If he has an errand to her,
  Let him come himself,
  Perhaps she will hear him. [*Exit* SERVANT; GORA *comes downstage.*] They thought you would go,
  Taming your hatred and revenge.
  The fools!
  Or will you then? Will you?
  I almost think you will,
  For you are no more Medea,
  The kingly child of Colchis' king no more,
  A wise mother's yet wiser daughter;
  Would you have borne, if you were, in patience
  So much, till now?

MEDEA: Do you hear, you gods? Borne, in patience!
  So much, till now!

GORA: I told you to flee
  When you wanted still to stay,
  Blinded and snared;
  When the blow had not yet fallen
  That I foresaw, pointed out to you, warning;
  But now I say: stay!
  They shall not laugh at the Colchian woman,
  Not mock at the blood of my kings,
  But give up the little ones,

465

Shoots of the royal oak they felled;
Or die and sink
Into terror and night!
Where are your instruments?
Or what have you decided?

MEDEA: Before all else I will have my children,
For the rest – we shall see.

GORA: Then you will go?

MEDEA: I cannot say.

GORA: They will laugh at you so!

MEDEA: Laugh at me? No!

GORA: What are you planning then?

MEDEA: I am trying so hard not to will, not to think.
On the silent abyss
Let the night brood.

GORA: And if you were to flee, where to?

MEDEA [*with anguish*]: Where? Where?

GORA: This land is no place for us,
The Greeks, they hate you and they will kill you.

MEDEA: They, kill me? *I* will kill them, *I*!

GORA: At home back in Colchis is danger too.

MEDEA: O Colchis! O Colchis! O land of my fathers!

GORA: Do you not know, have you not heard
That your father soon after had died
When you left Colchis, your brother fell?
Died? I think I heard it differently:
That grasping at his sorrow like a sword
Raging at himself, he took his own life.

MEDEA: Why do you make cause with my enemies
And kill me?

GORA: Now you see.
I told you, I warned you.
Flee the strangers, I told you,
But above all him that leads them,
The smooth-tongued dissembler, the traitor!

MEDEA: The smooth-tongued dissembler, the traitor! –
Did you say so?

GORA: Indeed I said it.

MEDEA: And I did not believe you?

GORA: Did not believe me, went into the snare
That tightens now about you.

MEDEA: Smooth-tongued dissembler! those were the words.
If you had said that, I should have recognized;
But you called him enemy and hateful and loathsome,
Yet he was handsome and friendly and I did not hate him!

GORA: Then you love him?

MEDEA: I? Him?
I hate him, I loathe him,
Like treachery, like falsehood,
Like what is most terrible, like myself!

GORA: Then punish him, strike him,
Avenge your father, your brother,
Our fatherland, our gods,
Our shame, me, yourself!

MEDEA: Before all else I will have my children,
For the rest – there is night.
What do you think? if there he went
In solemn marriage procession
With her I hate,
And from the palace gable to meet him
Flew Medea, crashed and dashed to pieces?

GORA: A fine revenge!

MEDEA: Or at the bridal chamber's door
She lay dead in her own blood,
With her the children, Jason's children, dead?

GORA: Your vengeance hurts yourself, and not him.

MEDEA: I wish that he loved me;
Then I could kill myself to torture him.
Or her? so false! so pure!

GORA: This is nearer the mark!

MEDEA: Quiet! quiet!
Back down where you came from, thought!
Back into silence, down into night! [*She draws her cloak
about her face.*]

GORA: All the others that went with him,
The Argonauts, on that wicked venture,

All of them with vengeance and punishment
The gods have stricken in recompense.
He only remains — and how long still?
Daily I hear, eagerly listening,
Drawing such nourishment, how they are fallen,
Fallen the shining sons of the Greeks,
Returned from Colchis, home from their robbery.
The women of Thrace tore Orpheus in pieces,
Hylas sank to a watery grave;
Theseus, Perithous made the descent
Down to Aïdes' gloomy dwelling,
To rob the mighty lord of the shades
Of his bright consort, Persephoneia:
But he caught them and holds them captive
In brazen fetters, in night everlasting.

MEDEA [*quickly unveiling her face*]:
Because they came there to steal a wife?
Good! Good! That was what *he* did, and more!

GORA: Heracles, who had forsaken his wife,
By another love tempted to stray,
She sent for her vengeance a garment of linen;
When he put it on, he sank to the ground
In torment and fear and pain of death,
For she had secretly dyed its threads
With vicious poison, speedy death.
He sank, and the forests of Oeta's crown
Saw him consumed, in the flames consumed.

MEDEA: And she had woven the garment herself
That killed him?

GORA: Herself!

MEDEA: Herself!

GORA: Meleager in all his rude strength
That conquered Calydon's boar,
Althaea killed, the mother her child.

MEDEA: What, did her husband leave her?

GORA: He killed her brother.

MEDEA: Her husband?

GORA: Her son!

MEDEA: And when she had done it, she died?

GORA: She lives!

MEDEA:　　　　　　Did it and lives! O horror!
This much I know and this much is clear to me:
I will not suffer wrong to go free.
But *what* is to happen, I cannot think of it!
He deserves everything, even the worst,
But – man is weak;
There should always be time to repent!

GORA: Repent? Ask him himself is he penitent,
For here he comes with hurrying step.

MEDEA: With him the king, my wicked enemy,
That lured him and led him astray.
I must go, I could not contain my hatred!
　　[*She goes quickly towards the house.*]
But if he, if Jason will speak to me,
Tell him to come to me in my room.
There I will speak to him, not out here,
By the side of that man, my enemy.
They are coming. Away! [*Exit.*]

GORA:　　　　　　　　And so she goes.
But I am to speak with the man
Who has ruined my child, brought it about
That I must lay my head upon foreign earth,
Must seek to hide the tears of my bitter grief,
So that strangers' lips do not laugh at them.
　　[*Enter the* KING *and* JASON.]

KING: Why does your mistress flee? That will not help her.

GORA: She fled, you say? She went. Because she hates you.

KING: You, call her out.

GORA:　　　　　　She will not come.

KING:　　　　　　　　　　　　She shall!

GORA: Go in yourself and tell her, if you dare.

KING: Where am I then, and *who*, that this wild woman
In all her savagery dares to spite me?
The maid the image of her mistress, both
The image of the foul dark land that spawned them.
Once more: let her be called!

GORA [*pointing at* JASON]: Him she will see;
    If he is brave enough, let him go in.

JASON: Go, shameless woman, my eternal hatred!
    And tell her to come out, that is so like you.

GORA: O would she were! Then you would not defy us.
    But she will see it yet; then woe to you!

JASON: I wish to speak to her!

GORA: Go in.

JASON: I will not!
    She must come out! and you, go in and tell her!

GORA: To see you two no longer, I will go;
    And I will tell her, but she will not come,
    Too bitterly she feels your injuries. [*Exit.*]

KING: She shall not stay a single day in Corinth.
    This woman but spoke plainly what she broods,
    Too dangerous by far such company!
    Your scruples too I hope are overcome.

JASON: Fulfil, my lord, your office as her judge.
    She can remain no longer at my side,
    So she must go; this sentence is a mild one.
    For truly, though my guilt is less than hers,
    My punishment is heavier to bear.
    She goes into the wilds where she was born,
    And like a foal whose harness is removed
    She gallops off defiant and untamed;
    But I must stay in silence and be calm,
    Burdened with men's contempt and mockery,
    And brooding over all the time that's past.

KING: Soon you will raise yourself again, believe my words.
    For like the bow, that in its swift release
    Speeds on the arrow flying to its mark,
    When once the weight upon its back is lifted,
    You will gain strength when she is far away.

JASON: Nothing I feel in me to justify such hopes.
    My name and reputation, they are gone,
    I am but Jason's shadow now, not he.

KING: The world, my son, will be more generous.
    The grown man's error is a weighty crime,

The young man's error is but a mistake
That's soon undone and put to rights again.
What you, a headstrong youth, did there in Colchis,
If now you prove a man, will be forgotten.

JASON: O if I could believe such words, what bliss!

KING: Only let *her* be gone, and you shall see.
Before the Amphictyonies I will
Defend your cause and plead your innocence,
And show that it was she alone, Medea,
Who did those things of which you stand accused,
That she the criminal, the limb of darkness.
The sentence will be lifted, and if not,
Then you will stand erect in all your might
And wave the golden banner in the air
That you brought home from lands beyond the world,
And in a stream will come the youth of Greece
To close their ranks about you and to fight
For you, now purified, raised up again,
Their paragon, the hero of the Fleece.
– You have it still?

JASON: The Fleece?

KING: Of course!

JASON: Not I!

KING: Medea took it from the house of Pelias.

JASON: Then she must have it.

KING: And must give it up;
It is the warrant of your future greatness.
I would yet see you great in strength and fame,
You, only son of him I called my friend!
King Creon is a man of wealth and power;
Gladly he shares it with his son-in-law.

JASON: What was my fathers', I myself will claim
From my false uncle's son that kept it from me.
I am not poor, if all may be restored.

KING: She that still thwarts us comes. Quickly have
done.

   [*Enter* MEDEA *with* GORA *from the house.*]

MEDEA: What do you want with me?

KING: My messengers
  You sent away with harsh and violent words,
  Demanding that you hear from my own lips
  What I command and what you are to do.
MEDEA: Speak, then.
KING: It is not new or strange to you.
  I but repeat the banishment already spoken
  And add that you shall go this very day.
MEDEA: And why this day?
KING: Your threats against my daughter,
  – Those against me are far beneath contempt –
  The savage manner which just now you showed,
  They tell me that your presence is a danger,
  And therefore I will have you gone today.
MEDEA: Give me my children and perhaps I'll go.
KING: You shall, for certain! But the children stay.
MEDEA: What, my own children? – But who is this man?
  With him there let me speak, with him, my husband!
KING [to JASON]: Do not!
MEDEA: I beg you!
JASON: Very well, I will,
  That you may see I do not fear your words.
  Leave us, my lord, and I will hear her speak.
KING: Against my will, for she is sly and cunning. [Exit.]
MEDEA: There, he is gone. No stranger now disturbs us,
  Now we are man and wife with none between us;
  We can speak freely as our hearts command.
  Tell me then what is in your mind.
JASON: You know.
MEDEA: I know what is your will, not what you think.
JASON: The first will be enough, for that decides.
MEDEA: I am to go, then?
JASON: Go!
MEDEA: Today?
JASON: Today!
MEDEA: That you can say and calmly stand before me
  And do not blush or drop your eyes for shame?
JASON: If I spoke otherwise, then I must blush.

MEDEA: Yes, that is well, speak always in such tones
  When you must make excuses before others;
  But when we are alone, stop this pretence!

JASON: My horror at your crimes you call pretence?
  The world condemns you and the gods condemn you,
  And to their judgement I must give you up,
  For truly it has not come undeserved!

MEDEA: Who is this pious man with whom I speak?
  Is it not Jason? Can he be so gentle?
  O gentle one, did you not come to Colchis
  And court with blood the daughter of its king?
  O gentle one, did you not kill my brother?
  What of my father, pious, gentle one?
  And did you not desert the wife you stole,
  O gentle one, so vile and infamous!

JASON: It is not meet that I should hear your insults,
  You know what you must do, and so farewell!

MEDEA: I do not know yet, stay until I do.
  Stay, and I will be calm. As calm as you are.
  So I am to be banished. What of you?
  I thought the herald spoke of you as well?

JASON: As soon as it is known that I am guiltless
  Of Pelias' death, the sentence will be lifted.

MEDEA: And you will live content from that day on?

JASON: I shall live quietly, as befits misfortune.

MEDEA: And I?

JASON: You bear the fate you fashioned for yourself.

MEDEA: I fashioned! And yourself are innocent?

JASON: I am!

MEDEA: You did not pray that he might die,
  Your uncle?

JASON: I did not contrive his death!

MEDEA: Did not tempt me, to see if I would do it?

JASON: In anger's heat we speak of many things
  That coldly reasoning we never do.

MEDEA: Once you accused yourself of this same crime,
  Now you have found a scapegoat for your guilt.

JASON: Thoughts do not suffer punishment, but deeds!

MEDEA [*quickly*]: I did not do it, though!

JASON: Who did?

MEDEA: Not I!

My husband, hear me first before you judge me.
As I stepped by the doorpost,
To fetch the Fleece,
The king lay there on his bed;
Then I heard screams; as I turn to look
I see the man spring up from his bed
Howling, writhing and rearing in pain.
Is it you, my brother, he screams,
Come to take vengeance, vengeance on me!
Once again I will kill you, once again!
And leaps to take hold of me,
In my hand the Fleece.
I trembled and cried aloud
To my own gods whom I know.
I held up the Fleece for a shield.
Then the grimace of madness contorts his features,
Howling he seizes the bands on his veins,
They burst, and in streams comes his blood pouring out;
And as I look about me, stiffened with horror,
There lies the king before my feet
Bathed in his own blood,
Cold and dead.

JASON: You tell me this, loathsome sorceress?
Take yourself off from me! Away!
My flesh it crawls. O that I ever saw you!

MEDEA: You cannot say you did not know. When first
You saw me, then you saw me at my work.
And yet you longed and set your heart on me.

JASON: I was a headstrong youth, a giddy fool.
What pleases boys a man will throw away.

MEDEA: O do not scold the golden age of youth!
The head is reckless, but the heart is good!
Better for me you were that young man still!
Come but a single step into that time,
When in the budding green of youth we found

Each other on the flowery banks of Phasis.
How open was your heart, how crystal clear,
Mine darker, closed in more upon itself.
But with your gentle light you conquered me
And brightly shone the darkness of my senses.
Then I was yours, and you were mine. O Jason!
So it is gone for you, that sweet, fair time,
So cares for house and home, for fame and glory
Have killed the blossoms on your tree of youth?
O see, in grief and anguish as I am,
I still think often of that time of spring,
And I can feel its warm breeze blowing still.
If then Medea was your love and pride,
How could she now become so vile and hateful?
You knew me and in spite of it you sought me,
You took me as I was, now keep me as I am!

JASON: You do not think of what has happened since that
    time.

MEDEA: Terrible things they are, I must admit it,
I have done evil by my father and my brother,
And I condemn myself for what I did.
Let me be punished, I will do my penance,
But you, you, Jason, shall not punish me!
For what I did, I did for love of you.
Come, let us flee, together flee, united
And go into a distant land!

JASON: And which?
Where to?

MEDEA: Where to?

JASON: You rave, and then you scold me
Because I do not rave with you. No more.
The gods have laid a curse upon our bond,
Since it began with bloody deeds of horror
And grew and sought its nourishment in crime.
Supposing that you did not kill the king,
Who else was there, who will believe it?

MEDEA: You!

JASON: And even if I should, what can I do?

So let us yield, and not defy our fate.
Let each take punishment in expiation,
You in your flight, because you cannot stay,
I staying here, though I would rather flee.

MEDEA: You have not picked the harder for yourself!

JASON: Is it so easy, then, to live a stranger,
Within a stranger's house, on strangers' pity?

MEDEA: Is this so hard, why do you not choose flight?

JASON: Where to, and how?

MEDEA: You had less scruple, once.
You came to Colchis, left the city of your fathers
And sailed to distant lands in search of idle fame.

JASON: I am no more the man I was, my strength is broken,
And in my breast the spark of courage dead.
That, I owe you. The thought of what is past
Weighs down like lead upon my timid soul,
I cannot raise my eyes, nor lift my heart.
The boy that was has since become a man,
No longer pleased with flowers, like a child,
He looks for fruit, reality and lasting.
I have my children and no place for them,
Inheritance for them I yet must win.
Is Jason's race to stand like dried-out heather
Beside the way for passers-by to tread?
If you have ever loved or honoured me,
Then show it as you give me back myself
And grant me rest in my own native soil!

MEDEA: And on your native soil a fine new marriage-bed?
Is it not so?

JASON: Why, what?

MEDEA: Did I not hear
Him call you kinsman, yes, and son-in-law?
Creusa lures you, that is why you stay;
Have I not caught you? No?

JASON: You never did
And do not now.

MEDEA: Is this your expiation?
And this is why Medea must be gone?

Was I not standing there beside you weeping,
While you went through your memories with her,
Stood sweetly lingering upon each step,
Carried away by echoes of the past?
But I will not be gone!

JASON: Still as unjust,
As harsh and wild as ever!

MEDEA: As unjust?
Then you would not have her to wife? Say no!

JASON: I seek a place to lay my head in rest,
What else may be I do not know.

MEDEA: I do,
And if a god will help, yet I will stop it.

JASON: If you will not speak calmly, then farewell. [*Going*]

MEDEA: Jason!

JASON [*turning round*]: What is it?

MEDEA: This moment is our last,
These words may be the last that we shall speak!

JASON: Then let us part, but not in hate or anger.

MEDEA: You lured me into love and now you flee me?

JASON: I must.

MEDEA: My father you have taken from me,
And now you take my husband?

JASON: I am forced.

MEDEA: My brother died through you, you robbed me of
        him,
And flee?

JASON: Blameless in flight as he was in his death.

MEDEA: I left my fatherland to follow you.

JASON: You followed where your own will led, not I.
Gladly I would have let you stay behind!

MEDEA: The world will curse me for the sake of you,
And for the sake of you I hate myself.
And you would leave me?

JASON: No, it is not I;
A higher verdict drives me from your side.
If you have lost contentment, what of mine?
Take in its place my wretchedness for yours!

MEDEA: Jason! [*She falls on her knees.*]

JASON: What more is there? What would you?

MEDEA [*standing up*]:   Nothing!

 It is the end! Forgive me, o my fathers,
 Forgive me, you proud gods of Colchis,
 That I could so abase myself and you.
 It was the last attempt; now I am yours!
  [JASON *turns to go.*]
 Jason!

JASON: Do not believe that I shall weaken!

MEDEA: I would not wish you to. Give me my children!

JASON: The children? I say never!

MEDEA: They are mine!

JASON: Their father's is the name that they will bear,
 And Jason's name is not a name for savages.
 Here I shall bring them up in decency.

MEDEA: To bear step-brothers' mocking? They are mine!

JASON: See that my pity does not turn to hatred!
 Be calm, for that alone can ease your lot.

MEDEA: Why then, it seems that I must plead with you.
 My husband! – No, for that you are no more –
 My love! – No, no, for that you never were –
 Man! – what, a man, to break your sacred word? –
 Jason! – pah, that's a name a traitor bears –
 What shall I say? Infamous! – gentle one!
 Give me my children, then I will be gone.

JASON: I cannot, do you hear, I cannot do it.

MEDEA: So harsh? You take the husband from his wife,
 And now refuse the mother too her children?

JASON: So that you may not say that I am cruel,
 One of the boys shall go away with you.

MEDEA: But one? but one?

JASON: Do not demand too much!
 This little almost sins against my duty.

MEDEA: Which, then?

JASON: The children, let them choose themselves,
 And which of them is willing, you shall take.

MEDEA: O generous, gentle one, a thousand thanks!

Indeed he lies who says you are a traitor.

[*Enter the* KING *with a* SERVANT.]

JASON: O come, my lord!

KING: So you have done with her?

JASON: She goes. One of the children I will give her.

[*To* SERVANT] You, hurry, go and bring the boys to us!

KING: What are you doing? Both of them must stay!

MEDEA: What I think little seems to you too much?
Beware the gods, o king all too severe!

KING: The gods severely judge a criminal.

MEDEA: They also see what drove him to his crime.

KING: A wicked heart drives on to wickedness.

MEDEA: What else can drive to evil, you think nothing?

KING: I judge myself severely, others too.

MEDEA: Punishing crimes, yourself you do commit them.

JASON: She shall not say that I have been too harsh,
Therefore I let her take one of the children,
His mother's comfort in distress and need.

[*Enter* CREUSA *with the* CHILDREN.]

CREUSA: You sent to fetch the children, I am told.
What do you want? Tell me what is to happen!
O see, they love me, only come this day,
As if we had been friends for many years.
My gentle words, to them so unfamiliar,
Won me their hearts, as their misfortune mine.

KING: One of the children is to go with her.

CREUSA: And leave us?

KING: So their father wishes it.

[*To* MEDEA, *who has stood brooding by herself*]
The children, they are here, now let them choose!

MEDEA: The children! Yes, my children! It is they!
All that remains to me upon this earth.
You gods, whatever evil thoughts were mine,
Forget them, give them back, both, both to me!
Then I will go, and praise you in your goodness,
Him I'll forgive and – no! not her! nor him!
Come to me, children, come! Why do you stand
And cling to her that is my enemy?

O if you knew what she has done to me
Then you would arm your gentle little hands,
Like clutching claws curl up your tender fingers,
And tear the bosom where you nestle now.
You lure my children from me? Let them go!

CREUSA: Unhappy woman, see, I do not hold them.

MEDEA: Not with your hand, you hold them like their
    father
Fast with your treacherous dissembling look.
You laugh? And yet I tell you you will weep!

CREUSA: Would the gods punished me, should I laugh now!

KING: Let us not hear these angry insults, woman,
What must be done, do calmly, or be gone!

MEDEA: You tell me rightly, o most righteous king,
Though not so generous, it seems, as righteous.
Or are you? Yes, why, maybe you are both.
Children, you see they send your mother on,
Far over land and sea, where, who can tell?
And yet these men, in generosity,
Your father and this good and righteous king,
They have permitted her, of her own children,
The mother, of her children, to take one –
One, do you hear, you gods on high? But one!
On her long journey for her company.
Which of you now believes he loves me most,
Come to me, for they will not let you both.
The other must remain here by his father
And stay with that false man and his false daughter!
You hear? Why do you hesitate?

KING: They will not!

MEDEA: You lie, you false, unrighteous king, you lie!
They will; but she, your daughter, lures them from me!
Do you not hear me? – Infamous, vile creatures!
Your mother's curse, the image of your father!

JASON: They will not!

MEDEA: Let that woman go away!
The children love me, am I not their mother?
But she is waving, luring them away.

CREUSA: I will be gone, though you suspect me falsely!

MEDEA: Now come to me! To me! You brood of vipers!
  [*She goes a few paces towards them; the* CHILDREN *run to* CREUSA.]
  They flee me! Flee!

KING: Now you must see, Medea,
  The children do not want you, so be gone!

MEDEA: The children do not want me? Not their mother?
  It cannot be, it is not true! –
  Aeson, my firstborn, my favourite,
  See how your mother calls you, come to her!
  I will not be rough and cruel any more,
  You shall be my darling, my only treasure –
  Hear me, your mother! Come!
  He turns away! He will not come!
  Ungrateful, image of his father!
  Like him in all his treacherous features,
  Hateful to me, like him!
  Stay here then, I do not know you! –
  But you my Absyrtus, son of pain,
  With the face of the brother I mourn for,
  Mild and gentle as he,
  See your mother lies here on her knees
  And implores you.
  Let her not beg you in vain!
  Come to me, my Absyrtus,
  Come to your mother!
  He hesitates! Nor you? –
  Who will give me a dagger?
  A dagger for me and them! [*She springs to her feet.*]

JASON: You have yourself to thank, your savage ways
  Have driven them from you to look for kindness,
  The children's verdict was the gods' own word!
  Go on your way, the children stay with me.

MEDEA: You children, listen!

JASON: See, they will not hear you!

MEDEA: My children!

KING [*to* CREUSA]:   Take them back into the house.

They shall not learn to hate the one that bore them.

[CREUSA *and the* CHILDREN *turn to go.*]

MEDEA: They flee! See, my own children flee before me!

KING [*to* JASON]: Come. To bewail necessity is fruitless.

    [*Exeunt.*]

MEDEA: My children! Children!

GORA [*coming forward*]:   Conquer yourself,

  Do not let your enemies see their victory!

MEDEA [*throwing herself on the ground*]:

  I am vanquished, trampled, destroyed,

  They flee me, flee!

GORA [*bending over her*]: Live!

MEDEA: Let me die!

  My children!

    [*The curtain falls.*]

ACT IV

Forecourt of Creon's palace, as in the previous act. Evening

[MEDEA *lies stretched out on the steps leading to her quarters.*
GORA *is standing in front of her.*]

GORA: Stand up, Medea, and speak!

  Why do you lie there, staring silently?

  Stand up and speak!

  What are we to do?

MEDEA: Children! Children!

GORA: We must be gone before night falls,

  Already it is evening.

  Up! Gird yourself for flight!

  They will come, they will kill us!

MEDEA: O my children!

GORA: Stand up, unhappy wretch,

  And do not kill me with your grief!

If you had followed me, listened to me,
We should be at home in Colchis.
Your kin would be living, all would be well.
Stand up! What use is weeping? Stand up!

MEDEA [*drawing herself half upright, still kneeling on the steps*]:
So I knelt, so I lay,
So I stretched out my hands,
Out to the children, and begged,
And implored: only one,
One alone of my children –
It had been death even to lose the second!
But not even the one! Neither came.
They fled and hid themselves on my enemy's bosom.
    [*Leaping to her feet*]
He though laughed at it, and *she*!

GORA: O the sorrow, the grief!

MEDEA: Do you call this recompense, you gods?
Loving I went with him, wife with man;
When my father died, was it *I* that killed him?
When my brother fell, did he fall by *my* hand?
I have mourned, in torment mourned for them both.
Burning were the tears I shed
As a sacrifice to water their grave.
Where there is no measure there is no recompense.

GORA: As you left your own, so they leave you!

MEDEA: Then I will strike them as the gods strike me!
Unpunished let no crime on earth remain,
Leave vengeance to me, gods! I will carry it out!

GORA: Think of your safety, of nothing else!

MEDEA: And what has suddenly made you so weak?
Then snorting with rage, and now so tender?

GORA: Leave me! When I saw the children flee
The arms of their mother that nourished them
I recognized the hand of the gods,
My heart was broken,
My courage no more.
I have nursed them, cared for them,
My joy, my happiness.

The only pure-blooded Colchians
On whom I could outpour
My love for my far-distant fatherland.
Long had you been a stranger to me;
In them I saw our Colchis again,
Your own father and your brother,
The house of my kings, and *you*,
As you were, not as you are.
I have cared for them, guarded them
Like the apple of my eye,
And now –

MEDEA: They repay you as ingratitude will.

GORA: Do not scold the children, they are good!

MEDEA: Good? And fled from their mother?
Good? They are Jason's children!
Like him in feature, in mind,
Like him, to share my hatred.
If I had them here, their lives held in my hand,
Here in the outstretched palm of my own hand,
And with a snap I could destroy
All that they are and were, all that they will be,
Like this! – Now they would be no more!

GORA: Woe to the mother that can hate her children!

MEDEA: What else is there? what else?
If they stay behind with their father,
With their shameful, faithless father,
What will be their lot?
There will be step-brothers,
Despising them, mocking them,
Them and their mother,
The savage from Colchis.
But they will either be serving as slaves,
Or else the bitterness gnawing their hearts
Will turn them sour, make them loathe themselves,
And if misfortune dogs the steps of crime,
Crime dogs more often yet misfortune's steps.
What is it then to live?
I would my father had put me to death

When I was still young,
Had not yet endured what I have,
Had not yet thought – what I do.

GORA: Why do you shudder? What are you thinking
of?

MEDEA: That I must go, so much is certain,
Less certain though what else is to happen.
If I think of the wrong that I have suffered
And of the crime they commit against me,
Then my heart is enflamed with revenge,
And most loathsome to me is what is nearest.
He loves the children, for he sees himself,
His idol, his own nature,
Mirrored at him in their features.
He shall not have them, he shall not!
But I do not want them, the hateful creatures!

GORA: Come in with me, what would you here?

MEDEA: Then empty all the house and desolate,
Destruction brooding in the ruined walls,
Nothing alive but memory and pain.

GORA: They will be here to drive us out. Come with
me!

MEDEA: The Argonauts, did you not say
That they all found dishonourable graves,
The punishment of crime and of betrayal?

GORA: They did so, and I doubt not Jason will.

MEDEA: He will, I tell you so, he will!
Hylas was swallowed by a watery tomb,
Theseus the gloomy king of shadows caught,
And she, what was her name, the Grecian woman
Who on her blood took her own blood's revenge?
What was her name?

GORA: I do not understand.

MEDEA: Althaea was her name.

GORA: That killed her son?

MEDEA: The very same! How did it happen? Tell me.

GORA: He struck her brother dead while they were hunting.

MEDEA: Only her brother, not her father too,

And did not leave her, did not spurn her, did not scorn
    her,
And yet she struck him to his death,
The fearful Meleager, her own son.
Althaea she was called – a Grecian woman!
And when he died?

GORA: The story tells no more.

MEDEA: No more? No, after death there is no more.

GORA: What use are words?

MEDEA: Do you still doubt the deed?
See! by the gods above, if he had given
Me both the children – No!
If I could take them, even if he gave them,
If I could love as much as now I hate them,
If there were something still in all the world
He had not poisoned for me, not destroyed;
Perhaps then I would go my way and leave
My vengeance to the gods; but no, not now!
They call me wicked, though I was not so,
But now I feel that wickedness can grow.
A horror slowly shapes itself within me,
I shudder – yet rejoice at it as well.
– When now it is accomplished, done –
[*Fearfully*] Gora!

GORA: What is it?

MEDEA: Come!

GORA: What then?

MEDEA: To me!
There they lie both together – and the bride –
Bleeding, dead. – He beside them tears his hair.
A horror, fearful to behold!

GORA: O gods!

MEDEA: Ha! ha! Are you afraid?
They are but vain and empty words I speak,
The will of old now misses its old strength.
Yes, if I were Medea still – I am no more!
O Jason! Why have you done this to me?
I took you in, I shielded you and loved you,

All that I had, I gave it up for you,
Why do you spurn me and abandon me?
Why do you drive my better spirits out
And fill my heart instead with thoughts of vengeance?
But thoughts of vengeance, not the strength to take it!
The power that from my mother I received,
From Hecate, grave Colchian princess,
Who vowed me to the service of dark gods,
I buried, for your sake I buried it,
Deep in the bosom of its mother earth.
The staff of black, the blood-red veil are gone
And helpless I stand here without them now;
A butt, no more a terror, to my foes!

GORA: Then do not speak of what you cannot do.

MEDEA: Well I remember where it is.
Out on the shore beside the rolling sea
It was, I coffined it and sank it down.
Two or three clods of earth – and it is mine!
But deep within my inmost soul I shudder
To think of it, and of the bloodstained Fleece.
I feel my father's and my brother's ghost
Are brooding there and will not let it go.
Do you remember? – On the ground he lay,
My grey-haired father, weeping for his son
And cursing me, his daughter. Jason though
Swung high aloft the Fleece in fearful triumph.
Then I swore vengeance, vengeance on the traitor
Who first killed those I love and now kills me.
O, if I had my instruments of blood,
Then I would do it; but I dare not fetch them.
For were I in that golden glow to see
My father's features gazing out upon me,
I should go mad, I know!

GORA: What will you do, then?

MEDEA: Let them come!
Let them kill me, now it is finished!
I will not go from here, but I will die,
Perhaps he will die too, choked with remorse.

GORA: Here comes the king, think now of your own
    safety!

MEDEA: Robbed of my power, what am I to do?
    If he will trample on me, let him come!
      [*Enter the* KING.]

KING: The evening gathers, and your time runs out.

MEDEA: I know.

KING: Are you prepared to go?

MEDEA: You mock me!
    What if I were not, must I then not go?

KING: I see you have good sense, and I am glad.
    By this you make your memory less bitter,
    And for your children wealth and goods assure;
    Well may they speak the name of her that bore them.

MEDEA: They may? Yes, if they will; is that your meaning?

KING: The care be mine that they may surely wish it.
    As coming heroes I shall bring them up,
    And one far day, who knows, may they not journey
    To Colchis and embrace their mother there,
    Grown old in years and of a calmer mind,
    With filial endearment to their breasts?

MEDEA: Alas!

KING: What is it?

MEDEA: Only a relapse,
    Forgetfulness of what has come to pass.
    Was it to tell me this that you came here
    Or is there something more you want from me?

KING: One other thing there was I had forgotten.
    Your husband carried wealth and treasure with him
    Fleeing from Iolcus when his uncle died.

MEDEA: He kept it in the house, go in and take it!

KING: And is that golden treasure there as well,
    The Fleece, the prize won by the Argonauts?
    Why do you turn away? Come, answer me!
    Is it there also?

MEDEA: No.

KING: Where is it, then?

MEDEA: I do not know.

KING: But you took it away
  From Pelias' house; the herald told us so.
MEDEA: He said it, so it must be true.
KING: Where is it?
MEDEA: I do not know.
KING: I will not be deceived!
MEDEA: Give it to me and you may take my life;
  But if I had it, you'd not threaten me!
KING: From Iolcus did you take the fleece?
MEDEA: I did.
KING: And now?
MEDEA: Have it no more.
KING: Who has?
MEDEA: The earth.
KING: What, do I understand you? So it was!
  [*To his followers*] Bring here what I commanded you. You
      know it!
  You think your double meanings will deceive me?
  The earth: I understand you all too well!
  Look straight into my eyes, and listen now!
  Upon the sea-shore, where you camped last night,
  When at my order men had gone to build
  An altar to the spirit of King Pelias,
  They found – do you turn pale? – there freshly buried
  A chest of black, with strange and unknown markings.
    [*The chest is brought.*]
  Look! Is it yours?
MEDEA [*rushing to it*]: Yes, it belongs to me!
KING: The Fleece?
MEDEA: Is in it!
KING: Give it up!
MEDEA: I shall!
KING: I almost feel regret I pitied you,
  Since you with cunning thought you would betray us.
MEDEA: Be sure you shall receive what's due to you.
  Once more I am Medea; gods, be thanked!
KING: Open, and give.
MEDEA: Not now.

KING: When else?

MEDEA: Quite soon;
Too soon!

KING: Then you will send it to Creusa.

MEDEA: Send to Creusa! – To Creusa! Yes!

KING: What else is in the chest?

MEDEA: Why, many things!

KING: Your property?

MEDEA: But I will give you some!

KING: I do not want your goods; keep what is yours!

MEDEA: But no! you will accept a modest gift.
Your daughter was so kind and good to me,
And she will be a mother to my children,
So gladly I would seek to win her love!
The Fleece draws you; will jewels perhaps please her?

KING: Do as you wish, but carefully consider.
Believe me that Creusa is your friend,
Just now she asked that we might send the children
For you to see once more before you go,
And say your last farewells for the long journey.
Because I thought you raving, I refused;
But as I see you calm, it shall be granted.

MEDEA: A thousand thanks, o kind and virtuous prince!

KING: Stay here and I will send the children to you. [*Exit.*]

MEDEA: He goes! He leaves me for his own destruction!
Infamous ones, did you not quake and shudder
Insolently to rob me of my last?
Yet thanks, for you have given me myself.
Open the chest, I say!

GORA: I cannot do it.

MEDEA: Of course; had I forgotten how I closed it?
The lock is guarded for me by my friends.
[*Turning to the chest*] Down what was up,
Up what was low,
Be opened, grave,
Your mysteries show!
[*The chest springs open.*]
The lid springs up. Now, powerless no more!

See, there they lie! The staff, the veil! Ah, mine!
  [*Taking them out*]
I take you up, my mother's legacy,
And strength flows through my heart and through my
    arm!
  [*Veiling herself*]
How soft, how warm! giving me life anew!
Now come, my enemies, united all
Against me, come! United you shall fall!

GORA: What glitters there beneath?

MEDEA: Yes, glitter, glitter!
  Soon blood will dull your gleam.
  See, here they are, the presents I shall give them.
  But you shall be the bearer of my gifts!

GORA: I?

MEDEA: You. Go to the daughter of the king,
  Speak to her gentle words of flattery,
  Give her Medea's greeting, and this casket.
    [*Taking the things out of the chest*]
  It holds a precious ointment for a bride,
  How she will sparkle when she opens it!
  Be careful though, and do not shake it!

GORA: Ah!
    [*She has taken the casket clumsily in her left hand. As she
    steadies it with her right hand the lid opens slightly, and a bright
    flame shoots out.*]

MEDEA: Did I not tell you that you must not shake it!
                Stay your threat,
                Flickering snake,
                Soon you may wake,
                Be patient yet!
  Now hold it and take care with it, I say!

GORA: A horror – I know it!

MEDEA: Do you begin to see it? Why, how clever!

GORA: And I must take it?

MEDEA: Yes! Obey me, slave!
  You dare to contradict? Silence! you shall, you must!
  Here in this golden bowl so finely dished

I set the casket, richly carved and glowing.
And over it I lay what lures them so,
The Fleece – [*Throwing it over the other things*]
      Go then, and carry out your task!
But over that again I wrap this cloth,
A mantle richly hemmed, fit for a king,
Mysterious to veil these mysteries.
Now go, and do as I commanded you;
Enemy sends this gift to enemy.
    [*Enter a* SLAVEWOMAN *with the* CHILDREN.]

SLAVEWOMAN: My lord the king commands me bring the
    children,
After an hour they must return again.

MEDEA: They will be there to see the bridal feast!
To your princess accompany this woman,
She is my messenger and bears my gifts.
But you, remember what I ordered you!
You shall not speak! I will it so! – Go with her!
    [*Exeunt* GORA *and* SLAVEWOMAN.]

MEDEA: It is begun, but not completed yet.
How free I feel, now that I know my will.
    [*The* CHILDREN, *hand in hand, make as if to follow the*
    SLAVEWOMAN.]
Where are you going?

BOY: In!

MEDEA: What do you want there?

BOY: Our father told us we must follow her.

MEDEA: But now your mother tells you you must stay. –
When I consider it is my own blood,
The child that I have born from my own womb,
That I have nourished here at my own breast,
That it is my own self rebels against me,
Anger within me stirs, and claws my heart,
And bloody thoughts rear up their fearful heads. –
But say, what has your mother done to you
That you should flee her and should turn to strangers?

BOY: You want to take us on the ship again,
So stifling and so giddy. We will stay.

Will we not, brother?

YOUNGER BOY: Yes!

MEDEA: You too, Absyrtus?
But it is better so. Come here to me!

BOY: I am afraid.

MEDEA: Come here!

BOY: You will not hurt me?

MEDEA: Why do you think I would? Have you deserved it?

BOY: You threw me to the ground one day because
I am like father, but he loves me for it.
I'll stay with him and with the gentle lady.

MEDEA: Yes, you shall go to her, your gentle lady! –
How like the traitor, o how like he is!
How like him when he speaks! But patience, patience!

YOUNGER BOY: I'm sleepy.

ELDER: Let us sleep, it is so late.

MEDEA: Yes, you shall sleep, and to your hearts' content.
Go over there, lie down upon the steps,
While I consider what I have to do. –
See how he leads his brother carefully,
Takes off his cloak and lets the younger have it,
Wrapping it round his shoulders for the warmth,
And now, their little arms in close embrace,
Lies down beside him there. – He was not wicked! –
Children!

BOY [*sitting up*]: What is it?

MEDEA: Nothing. Go to sleep.
What would I give if I could sleep like you!
   [*He lies down and goes to sleep.* MEDEA *sits down opposite them
   on a bench. It has gradually grown dark.*]
The night draws in again, the stars have risen,
And shed their soft and gentle light upon us.
They are the same today as yesterday,
As if all things were still the same today;
And yet there is a gulf between as deep
As lies between contentment and destruction.
So changeless nature, ever like itself,
So changeable we mortals and our fate!

If I recount the story of my life,
It is as if I heard another speak,
And interrupted: Friend, that cannot be!
She that you say is filled with thoughts of murder,
There in her fatherland you let her wander
Beneath the gentle light of these same stars,
As pure, as innocent of any guilt
As but a child upon its mother's breast?
Where is she going? To the poor man's hut –
It was his corn her father's huntsmen trampled –
She brings him gold, consoles him in his grief.
Why does she seek these woodland paths? She hurries
To meet her brother, waiting in the forest,
And now that she has found him, like twin stars
Radiant they go on their accustomed way.
Another comes, his brow is crowned with gold;
It is her father, king of all this land.
He lays his hand on her and on her brother
And blesses them, calls them his pride and joy.
Welcome to me, you fair and friendly shapes,
What, do you seek me in my loneliness?
Come closer to me, let me see your faces!
My brother whom I love, you smile at me?
How handsome, you my soul's own happiness.
Your father is severe, and yet he loves me,
Loves his dear daughter dearly too. Ha, dear!
    [*Springing to her feet*]
A lie! She will betray your greying head!
She did betray you, and herself,
You laid your curse on her.
'An outcast you shall ever be,
Like a beast of the desert,' – so you said,
'Shall know no friend and no place
To lay your head and rest.
But he for whose sake you betray me
Himself will be my avenger,
Will forsake you, cast you out,
Kill you!'

And see! your words are fulfilled;
See! I stand an outcast here,
Shunned by men like a beast of the desert,
Deserted by him for whose sake I deserted you,
Without a resting-place, alas *not* dead!
Thoughts of murder dark in my mind.
Do you enjoy your revenge?
Are you coming? – Children! children!
   [*She hurries across and shakes them.*]
Do you not hear me? Get up!
BOY [*waking*]: What is it?
MEDEA [*clinging to them*]: Put your arms around me here.
BOY: But I was fast asleep.
MEDEA: How could you sleep?
Because your mother watched by you, you thought?
Never worse enemy held you in his hand!
How could you go to sleep when I am near?
Go in, there in the house, there you may rest!
   [*The* CHILDREN *go into the colonnade.*]
So, they are gone! Now all is well again! –
And for their going, what is better, then?
Have I the less to flee, to flee this day,
Leaving them with my enemies behind me?
Their father, is he any less a traitor?
Will she the less be wed, his fine new bride?
Tomorrow when the sun is risen
I shall be alone,
The world an empty wilderness,
No children, no husband,
Wandering with bleeding feet
Wretched into exile. And where?
But here they will rejoice and laugh at me!
My children at a stranger's bosom
Strangers to me, far off for ever.
Can you bear that?
– But it is too late!
Too late to forgive!
Has she not now, Creusa, the dress

And the casket, the casket of flames?
– Listen! – Not yet! But soon they will echo
Through the king's palace, those shrieks of pain.
They will come, they will kill me!
Nor will they spare my children.
– Listen! A cry! And up flies the spark!
Now it is done!
No going back!
Let it be finished, all! Away!

[GORA *comes rushing out of the palace.*]

GORA: O dread! O horror!

MEDEA [*going to meet her*]: Is it done?

GORA: Ah! Creusa dead! The palace in flames!

MEDEA: Are you gone then, pure-white bride?
Would you still lure my children from me?
You lure them? you lure them?
Will you have them, even there?
Not to you, to the gods I will send them!

GORA: What have you done? They are coming!

MEDEA: Coming? Too late! [*She hurries off into the colonnade.*]

GORA: Alas! Even now, when I am old,
I had unknowing to serve such evil!
Vengeance was my own advice; but this!
But where are the children? I left them here!
Medea, where are you? You children, where?

[*She hurries into the colonnade. The palace in the background is
lit up by flames rising within it.*]

JASON [*offstage*]: Creusa! Creusa!

KING [*in the palace*]:   My daughter!

[*Enter* GORA, *rushing in from the colonnade and falling on her
knees in midstage, covering her face with her hands.*]

GORA: What was it I saw? O horror!

[*Enter* MEDEA *from the colonnade, a dagger in her left hand, her
right raised to command silence.*
The curtain falls.]

ACT V

Forecourt of Creon's palace

[*The palace in the background is burnt out and still smoking. The stage is filled with servants, busy at various tasks. Dawn.*]

[*Enter the* KING *dragging* GORA *from the palace. Several of* CREUSA'S SERVANT-GIRLS *follow them.*]

KING: Come out with you! Yes, it was you who brought
  The deadly present that destroyed my daughter!
  O daughter! O Creusa! O my child!
    [*To the servant girls*]
  It was she?

GORA: It was. Unknowing
  I brought death into your house.

KING: Unknowing?
  You'll not escape your punishment like that!

GORA: You think to frighten me with punishment?
  When I have seen with these my own two eyes
  The children lying dead in their own blood,
  Slaughtered by her who bore them,
  By her I nursed, Medea,
  Since then all horror seems a jest to me.

KING: Creusa! O my pure, my faithful child!
  Speak now, you monster, did your hand not shake
  To carry death into her presence? Say!

GORA: Your daughter does not worry me.
  She got what she deserved.
  Why did she seek to rob grief of its last?
  No, I am mourning for those two dear children,
  Whom I have seen dead by their mother's hand.
  I wish you all were buried side by side,
  The traitor too, that bears the name of Jason,
  And I were still in Colchis with my daughter

497

And her own children; would I'd never seen
You or your city; you deserve your fate.
KING: Wait; I will surely stop your insolence!
But is it certain that my child is dead?
So they all say, but none has seen for sure!
Could she not have escaped the fire?
The flames, are they so swift? No, stealthily,
Hesitantly they creep along the beams.
Who does not know it? Yet they say she's dead?
Just now she stood before me, like a flower,
And now she's dead? No, that cannot be true!
No, I shall always look, and look again,
And think, now she is coming – now – and now –
She must be here, so white and beautiful
As she steps down between the blackened ruins.
Who saw it happen? Who was there? Were you?
Speak then! O do not roll your eyes like that,
Kill me with words! Tell me she's dead!
GORA: She's dead.
KING: You saw it?
GORA: Saw it happen. Saw the flame
Leap from the golden casket, fly at her –
KING: Enough! No more! She saw! – Yes, she is dead!
Creusa! O my only child, my daughter!
When she was still a child, she burnt her finger
Once at an altar flame, and cried in pain.
I ran to her, I held her in my arms
And blew upon her burning hand to cool it.
She smiled, in spite of all her bitter tears
And gently sobbing murmured, 'It is nothing;
A little hurt, but stop it burning, burning!'
And now – [Turning to GORA]
                    If I should take my sword and run
You through a score of times – can that compare?
And she, that dreadful woman! Where is she?
She who has robbed me of my child!
                                            – I'll shake
The answer out of you with your life's breath

If you'll not tell me – where? Where has she gone?

GORA: I do not know, I do not want to know.

    To her destruction let her go alone.

    Well? Kill me, then! I do not want to live.

KING: We'll see; but first you shall confess to me.

JASON [*offstage*]: Where is she? Give her up to me! Medea!

    [*Enter* JASON *with drawn sword.*]

    They tell me they have caught her up! Where is she?

    You here? Where is your mistress?

GORA: Gone.

JASON: The children?

    They're with her?

GORA: No.

JASON: But then – they must be –

GORA: Dead!

    Yes, dead, you hypocrite and traitor, dead!

    She had to save them from the sight of you,

    And since there's nothing sacred here on earth

    For you, she took them from you to their graves.

    Yes, stand and stare at the dumb earth you may!

    They will not rise and answer, that sweet pair.

    For they are gone, and I am glad of it!

    No, not for their sakes – but for your despair,

    For that I'm glad! You hypocrite and traitor,

    Is it not all your doing? Yes, and yours,

    You faithless, double-dealing king, as well?

    Was it not you who set your treacherous nets

    About this noble creature, till despair

    And rage drove her at last to rend your snares

    And turn the glory of her kingly head

    To unaccustomed and unworthy work,

    To gore and murder. Yes, you wring your hands;

    But you may wring them for yourselves. You, king:

    Why should your daughter seek another's bed?

    And you, why did you steal her, if you did

    Not love her? If you did, why did you spurn her?

    Let others, yes, let me condemn her deed,

    But you have only reaped where you have sown.

No longer will you mock your Colchian slave.
– I do not want to live another day.
Two children dead, the third is hateful to me.
Take me away, and kill me if you will;
I know that I shall find a life beyond,
For I have seen that debts must all be paid.
    [*She is taken away. Pause.*]
CREON: If I did her injustice – by the gods,
  I swear that it was not my will! And now
To seek amongst those ruins for my child
And bury her, here in the peace of earth.
    [*To* JASON]
But you: be gone, I will not have you here;
I see I should not keep such company.
I wish that I had never seen your face,
Or welcomed you with hospitality.
My daughter you have taken from me. Go,
And let the voice of mourning still console me.
JASON: You cast me out?
KING: I say that you must go.
JASON: What shall I do?
KING: The gods may tell you that.
JASON: But who will guide my way? Who will support me?
See, I am wounded by the falling brands!
What, all are silent? None to be my escort?
So many followed me – and now alone?
Go then, my children's shades, go you before
And lead me to the grave that waits for me. [*Exit.*]
KING: Come then, to work; then everlasting mourning.
    [*Exeunt to the other side.*]

*A wild and lonely place
surrounded by forest and cliffs. In the foreground, a hut.*

[*Enter the* FARMER.]

FARMER: How beautiful the morning, gracious gods!
After the dreadful storms of that dark night
I see the sun in beauty rise again. [*He goes into the hut.*]
[*Enter* JASON, *staggering, leaning on his sword.*]

JASON: No, I can go no further. O, my head –
My blood is burning, and my tongue is parched.
Is no one there? Am I to rot alone?
Here is the hut where once I found a welcome,
When I a rich man and a father came
This way so full of new-awakened hopes!
[*He knocks.*]
Only a drink! Only a place to die!
[*The* FARMER *comes out.*]

FARMER: Who knocks? Who are you, stranger, tired to
death?

JASON: Only a drink of water! – I am Jason!
The hero of the Fleece! A prince! A king!
Jason the leader of the Argonauts!

FARMER: Are you that Jason? Then be off with you!
You shall not enter and pollute my house.
You that have killed the daughter of my king,
Expect no shelter from his loyal subject.
[*He goes into the hut and shuts the door.*]

JASON: He goes and leaves me lying by the wayside,
Here in the dust for all who pass to kick.
O death, I call you, take me to my children.
[*He collapses.*
MEDEA *steps out from behind a rock and stands before him,
wearing the Fleece like a cloak round her shoulders.*]

MEDEA: Jason!

JASON [*half sitting up*]: Who's there? Ah! Do I see aright?
Creature of horror, you again before me?
My sword, my sword!

[He tries to leap up, but collapses again.]

                         O gods! My strength is gone;
Broken and finished!

MEDEA: Stay! You shall not kill me.
My throat is for another's knife, not yours.

JASON: Where are my children?

MEDEA: They are mine.

JASON: Where are they?

MEDEA: Where they are better off than you or I.

JASON: Dead they are, dead!

MEDEA: You think that death's the worst;
But I know worse: exile and wretchedness.
If only you had not accounted life
Higher than it should ever be accounted,
Your life and mine would not now end like this.
And therefore we must bear it. They are spared.

JASON: You can say that so calmly?

MEDEA: Calmly! Calmly!
If only you could see into my heart –
You never could, you cannot even now –
Then you would see a raging flood of grief
That swallows up the ruins of my pain,
Rolls them in horror and in desolation,
And sweeps them on on its unending tide.
I do not grieve the children are no more,
I grieve because they *were*, and we still *are*.

JASON: O terrible!

MEDEA: And you must bear your lot,
You cannot say that it is undeserved.
As you now lie on the bare ground before me,
So once I lay in Colchis before you,
And begged you spare, but spare you never would!
You seized the future with unseeing greed,
Although I cried that it was death you took.
Now your proud will can have its dearest wish:
Death. Take it. I must go and leave you now;
For ever. Yes, this moment is the last,
The very last in all eternity,

That I shall ever speak to you, my husband.
Farewell. Now, after all remembered joys,
In all the suffering that now surrounds us,
To face all grief that future days may bring,
I say farewell to you, my husband.
It is a life of misery awaits you,
But yet, whatever comes, you must endure.
You were too weak to act; be strong to bear!
If you would die of grief, then think of me,
And let my greater sorrow comfort you,
For you have only left undone; I *did*.
Now I am going, carrying my load
Of monstrous suffering with me through the world.
If only I might kill myself; but no,
Medea shall not die by her own hand.
The life that I have led has made me worth
A better judge's verdict than Medea's.
I go to Delphi; there, at that same altar
That Phryxus once robbed of the Golden Fleece,
I shall return to that dark god his own,
And hang it up, unscathed by all the flames,
Undamaged even by the fearful blaze
That swallowed the Corinthian princess.
There I will show myself, and ask the priests
If they will take my head in sacrifice,
Or send me out into the desert ways,
To live, and suffer torment longer yet.
Look: here is what you fought for. Do you know
It still? It seemed to offer fame and fortune.
What is it men call fortune? Idle shadows!
What is it men call fame? An idle dream!
You foolish man! Your dreams were all of shadows.
Your dreams are over, but the night is long.
And now I go; farewell, my husband.
It was ill luck that we should find each other;
Now in ill luck we part. Farewell!

JASON: Alone! Deserted! O my children!

MEDEA: Bear it!

JASON: Lost! Lost!
MEDEA: Endure it!
JASON: Let me die!
MEDEA: Atone!
   Your eyes shall never see my face again.
     [*As she turns to go, the curtain falls.*]

MORE ABOUT PENGUINS

Penguinews, which appears every month, contains details of all the new books issued by Penguins as they are published. From time to time it is supplemented by *Penguins in Print*, which is a complete list of all books published by Penguins which are in print. (There are well over three thousand of these.)

A specimen copy of *Penguinews* will be sent to you free on request, and you can become a subscriber for the price of the postage – 4s. for a year's issues (including the complete lists). Just write to Dept EP, Penguin Books Ltd, Harmondsworth, Middlesex, enclosing a cheque or postal order, and your name will be added to the mailing list.

Some other books published by Penguins are described on the following pages.

Note: *Penguinews* and *Penguins in Print* are not available in the U.S.A. or Canada

PENGUIN CLASSICS

THE NIBELUNGENLIED

Translated by A. T. Hatto

Composed nearly eight hundred years ago by an unnamed poet, *The Nibelungenlied* is the principal literary expression of those heroic legends of which Richard Wagner made such free use in *The Ring*. This great German epic poem of murder and revenge recounts with peculiar strength and directness the progress of Siegfried's love for the peerless Kriemhild, the wedding of Gunther and Brunhild, the quarrel between the two queens, Hagen's treacherous murder of Siegfried, and Kriemhild's eventual revenge. A. T. Hatto's new translation transforms an old text into a story as readable and exciting as Homer's *Iliad*.

PENGUIN CLASSICS

NIETZSCHE
THUS SPOKE ZARATHUSTRA
Translated by R. J. Hollingdale

No modern philosopher has been more completely mis-
quoted and misrepresented than Friedrich Nietzsche
(1844–1900). His phrase, 'God is dead', his insistence that
the meaning of life is to be found in purely human terms,
and his doctrine of the Superman and the will to power
were all later seized upon and unrecognizably twisted by,
among others, Nazi intellectuals. This new translation of
Thus Spoke Zarathustra, a spiritual odyssey through the
modern world, is therefore of supreme value to us in
judging for ourselves a brilliantly original thinker who
has had a powerful influence upon such twentieth-century
writers as Shaw, Mann, Sartre, and Camus.

PENGUIN CLASSICS

GOETHE
FAUST

A two-volume translation by Philip Wayne

Goethe's activities as poet, statesman, theatre director, critic, and scientist show him to be a genius of amazing versatility. This quality is reflected in his *Faust*, which ranks with the achievements of Homer, Dante, and Shakespeare. The mood of the play shifts constantly, displaying in turn the poet's controlled energy, his wit, his irony, his compassion, and above all his gift for lyrical expression. *Faust*, which Goethe began in his youth and worked on during the greater part of his lifetime, takes for its theme the universal experience of the troubled human soul, but its spiritual values far transcend mere satanism and its consequences.

In Part One Goethe gives the world the famous human myth that embodied love and devilment and longing aspiration. In the second part he brings the constantly striving Faust through the utmost reaches of human speculation to a salvation evoking the most profound poetic compassion.

THE PENGUIN CLASSICS

The Most Recent Volumes